taking jana

It's her turn to drive.

RISSA BRAHM

NEED MORE OF RISSA BRAHM'S SERIES, PARADISE SOUTH—FOR FREE?

HEY THERE, LOVELY READERS O' ROMANCE!

Thanks so much for grabbing this hot & heartfelt story! For more on my Paradise South series and upcoming works, subscribe to my newsletter so you get all the news, plus exclusive goods like deleted scenes from the entire Paradise South series…**all for free!**

More details are in the **Author's Note** after the *Taking Jana* HEA. So enjoy your wild trip through the story and we'll meet up at the happy end! ~Rissa

ISBN 978-1-944557-06-5 (print)

ISBN 978-1-944557-07-2 (epub)

ISBN 978-1-944557-08-9 (mobi)

Published by: *108 degrees*™

Brahm, Rissa (2016-04-01)

Illustrated Romance Cover design by: Damonza

TAKING JANA (Paradise South series, Book 2)

TKA Distribution. Kindle Edition

For Linda.

CHAPTER 1

THE SHARP KICK to his seat might've been the last one he thought he could take.

A fight to the death. Antonio's hot Mexican blood coursed through his body and to his face, battling his calm, serene nature, and decades of martial arts and meditative training. His genetically predisposed fury threatened victory. Threatened to overtake him.

All from that one, hard kick.

It was all too reminiscent of the haunting kick to his ego—and heart—by his ex, Michelle. But it didn't matter who or what the source of the fire, he was so done swallowing his pride.

Because for ten long months now, Ms. Jocelyn Carlson, Antonio's highest paying limousine fare, had pushed him to his threshold with her relentless and chiding orders. She had all the class of a trailer park whore along with half of her billionaire ex-husband's wealth. It was a mean mix. Antonio had, up to then, taken it. He had become a slave to her every whim, every jolt, and every goddamn demand for far too long.

Well, almost every demand.

But damn the steady ten-fold fare. It wasn't goddamn worth it anymore.

Keep an even keel, Antonio. He pulled his earbuds out and chucked them onto the passenger seat. All the damn good they did. With his music on the highest volume, the backseat moaning still carried. He took a full breath then cleared his throat in warning while his finger remained where it was. On the button. Which allowed the upward motion of the center partition window to continue. He needed to drown out the noise, it was making him sick.

But then another shot to his seat rocked him forward toward his steering wheel.

A deep growl rumbled in his chest. This second kick, even more violent than the first, reverberated through Antonio's already screaming lower back. His jaw clenched and he stomped on the brake. Then he switched into the other lane, barely avoiding the tailgate of the truck in front of him.

But all the while—*fuck her!*—he kept his index finger heavy on that privacy window button. It continued its ascent, humming its smooth automatic buzz, almost blocking out her voice along with her heavy intermittent breathing, from the backseat. And within inches of Antonio's auditory freedom, the woman's moaning morphed into a follow-up to her kicking spree, a directive that met his ears like a slow-turning screwdriver.

"Tony, I swear, keep that fucking! Window! Down!" With that, she resumed her panting under her energetic and submissive male escort.

It wasn't even the demeaning mess she'd leave on his limo's leather upholstery that he'd spend an hour cleaning after dropping her at her condo on yet another late night, never earlier than one in the morning. What twisted his ego and stomped it flat into the dirt was the humiliation that he knew she intended for him. He sensed her purposeful luring, her pathetic attempts of enticing him every time she put on her backseat show. She'd challenge his eyes, daring them to peek in the rearview. Her rotating boy toys would narrate their sex play per her instruction, probably since Antonio would never give in, never glance up into his mirror, not even once, to see her bare body writhing and thrashing to match the sounds echoing in the backseat of his limousine. *His* limo. His business, his livelihood. His ticket home.

Since the very first time she'd ridden in his vehicle, she'd vehemently insisted that the center privacy window remained down. And until tonight, until now, he'd caved, let her have her way. But the countless scuff marks and upholstery rips and tears from her spiked heels would be no more. And her shrill and demeaning blitz of commands?

They'd end now.

He slowed, signaled, and pulled the car over.

Stopped at the side of the road, he lowered the privacy window all the way down, flush with the leather-clad partition. He pulled his seatbelt strap away from his slowly heaving chest. His anger filled his lungs, only kept in check by his mind, which focused solely on preparing the perfect words, as few as possible, to say to his tormenter.

He took in a slow and even final breath, while outside his window, the trickling truck traffic of the Newark, New Jersey industrial district zoomed by, as if moving past at a hundred and fifty miles an hour, but he knew they were all only going about the speed limit of forty-five. There were too many speed traps; he knew them well.

The glaring neon lights of the line of strip clubs, bail bondsmen, and pawn shops caught his eye as he turned his body to look directly at Ms. Jocelyn Carlson and her twenty-something playmate.

*

Jana Park ignored Ilana Simon as best she could. The other woman traipsed around the locker room naked, bragging to another newbie about some recent sex tape Ilana had made, set in one of her daddy's many limos.

"And it went, like *crazy* viral," Ilana said with a disgusting giggle.

God, Jana wished she couldn't hear the woman's monolog. It made her nauseated. Not the 'spreading her legs to the World Wide Web' part; what the hell did Jana care? And not the sex part, in a limo no less; no, that sounded, well, pretty fun. She knew she could use more of any type of sex, in any place at all, really. But her lifestyle didn't lend to any extra-curriculars. Her only focus now that she'd finally landed a spot on the Head Trauma Team was to snag the lead position.

But what made her ill was Ilana Simon's use of sex. It's how the woman had gotten her position there in the first place while Jana had sacrificed everything and worked her ass off to obtain her dream job. And to rise still to the highest ranks possible, she'd continue her hyper-focus, ready to eat, breathe, and hardly-ever-sleep her job for the foreseeable future.

Ilana Simon had skipped all that, and it more than racked Jana's nerves.

Stop dwelling, Jana, and get your things. She needed to get home, get a shower and a nap, and get back in eighteen hours.

*

Ilana, thankfully, had left the locker room, giving Jana a second's peace and quiet. She was about to pull her stuff from her locker when a text message pinged her phone. She took a quick glance.

Dane? The first contact in nearly a decade. *What the hell did he—*

"Jana, need you," Luly said from the doorway, interrupting Jana's confused wonder.

"Okay, Lu? What's up?"

"A father/daughter. Codes blue, pink." And her best friend vanished the very next instant.

Jana tossed her cell in her locker and hurried out. She'd read the text later. And go home later. Sleep later. *Priorities.*

*

Two rights and a left through the blinding white MMU emergency room maze, and she was in the thick of it, her blood pumping hard like she loved.

Her ears selectively caught the vital sounds and urgent directives being thrown about. "Spanish speaker over here," shouted the lead resident on duty at bed five.

Jana spun around toward the call, as she was as fluent in Spanish and Korean as she was in English. She'd saved dozens of lives by cutting the time it often took to find an interpreter. "On the way," she called, closing the gap from twenty feet away.

"Hey, I got it." Ilana Simon was already at the curtain.

Hell no. She might be good at fucking the chief resident, which had gotten the elitist bitch a spot in the ER in the first place—without merit and, in Jana's opinion, without much skill or an ounce of heart, to boot—but

Jana wasn't about to let Ilana muck up a code blue and pink. Not with the bullshit level-one Spanish she'd scrounged up from her year abroad, another tidbit the other woman boasted about. *Constantly.*

Fuck that. And fuck her.

Hell, if Jana's daddy had invested in her the same way Ilana's rich-ass father had in Ilana, Jana would be chief resident by now. But Jana's father hadn't. In fact, it had been the opposite. So here Jana was, shy of a year into her position, and this bitch waltzes in one month ago, all because she's not shy about spreading her legs.

"No Ilana." Jana controlled her voice and breathing, always in control, never emotional—a point of pride. "The nurse's station needs you, and the waiting room is packed. Go help take their load, please." Ilana puffed out her chest as she liked to do, rolled her heavily-lashed eyes, and reluctantly moved toward the nurse's station as Jana pushed through the curtain to bed number five.

Instead of looking at the victim on the gurney, Jana put her full attention to Tamara, her favorite charge nurse. She was always on it, always in high gear.

"The poor thing saw her leg and passed out. But I'm waiting for Dr. Pierce, anyway," Tamara said checking the drip line to the unconscious child. Seven years old, maybe eight. Her shinbone had a ninety-degree break in its mid-section, bulging through her blood-soaked pants, a death-red blotch spreading, growing, taking over the pale pink material of the girl's pants with each passing moment.

"Cut the pant leg while we—"

"Jana, curtain three please!" Luly called from a few beds away, a next-level urgency in her voice, rare for the mother of five. Nothing much fazed that woman, except for pending fatalities. Jana was sure it was too close to home for her friend; from the surfacing fear of her own kids lying before her, their life draining out by the second. For that reason, Luly'd been trying to get out of the ER and into a standard unit for months. Until then, she'd call on iron-hearted Jana to face the beast.

"Coming to three." Jana made her way down the long hallway. She was petite and most of the time her legs didn't move as fast as she wanted them to go. Her quickened steps made her feel like she was on a treadmill with too much time between points A and B, never enough ground covered, but certainly time enough for a thick knot to develop in her throat. She knew she was heading toward the father of the little girl she'd seen.

She pulled back the curtain to three. Luly turned to face Jana, her eyelids halved and solemn. Then Jana looked down at the man's chest. *Shit.* Jana approached the gurney and silently checked the chart: José Amarillo, father, thirty-five years old. *Only thirty-five, Jesus.*

The curtain rings rapidly clanked along the cubicle frame, startling Jana as Dr. Pierce charged in on high alert. But one glance at the man on the gurney, the doctor let go a loud sigh while Jana closed her eyes for a moment to settle her nerves. It didn't help. She actually felt a little queasy.

Why the hell was she letting this scene get to her? She'd seen worse only hours ago. But below her tough skin, she knew full well why. As the doctor glanced at the monitors, then at the patient, she felt a sinking in her chest. This was different. This was too close to home.

The doctor gave an imperceptible shake of his head to Jana, then he whispered, "I'll meet you at bed five."

Jana handed the chart to Luly as the patient's eyes opened, staring wide, squarely into Jana's, asking a billion wordless questions all at once.

She spoke to the barely lucid man in quick but clear Spanish. She knew there wasn't much time. She kept her voice steady, rhythmic, and he seemed to be listening to her explanation, to his prognosis, to her soft, summarizing close.

And as she spoke, she glanced at his wound through his opened shirt. An angel wing tat with the name "Ashley" in black cursive over his left pectoral; there was a 12-cm-long gash, as deep as it was long, through the bottom of the tattoo's wing feather. Dark blood oozed out and down his ripped torso.

Her heart ripped a little more from the sight. She swallowed back tears. It was the confirmation of his love, for his baby, for his Ashley. *Goddamnit.*

A deep guttural cough from the man interrupted Jana's thoughts and the threatening emotion she tried so hard to bank. The look in his eyes, *God*, a plea for air enough to speak. Then he found his voice.

"*Dondé esta m'iha? Ella esta bien? Ella esta bien!*" His desperate search for news of his daughter trailed off, replaced by the resounding beep of the monitor's flat line. It rang heavy in her ears as the trauma unit got small and quiet.

She called the time of death in her head, her pounding head. Jana's own pulse raced, counter to her seemingly slow-motion exterior. The energy, the stress of it all had to show up somewhere, and it was usually right up the center of her forehead.

The knowledge that this father was gone tightened her chest and closed her throat. And God, he'd loved his little girl. She felt it when he'd spoken his last words to her. It was raw and real love. And now it was all gone.

The Resident on duty, Dr. Bose, rushed in and called it out loud. "Time of death, 21:06."

Jana snapped her gloves off, trashed them, and moved back to bed number five to assist Dr. Pierce with the now fatherless girl, Ashley.

*

Jana read from the wristband, though she didn't need to. "Ashley, blink your eyes if you can hear me, Ashley."

Ashley squinted in an attempt to blink, dropping three large tears like cannon balls down her round, smooth cheeks.

"Good girl. My name is Jana, I'm a nurse. Sweetheart, you were in a car accident. You have one hurt leg that we're going to take care of now."

"Where's Daddy?" the seven-year-old blue-eyed angel whispered.

"Sweetie, he can't be here right now."

*

As it turned out, there was no mother to call. Jana Park took the child's hand while the team prepped Ashley's leg for amputation. As soon as they could get the form's sign-off from Child and Family Services or as soon as ten minutes passed, whichever came first, they'd get the child to the OR.

The child dozed for the minutes that felt like years before a CFS agent finally entered the ER. God, literally a minute before the ten-minute mark set by Dr. Pierce. Jana patted the child's hand.

"I want my dad here. Where is my daddy?"

Jana looked up at the doctor. Jesus Christ, this poor kid. She felt her jaw clench, but consciously willed its release, mustering all the calm and cathartic energy she could to infuse into the girl through her silent gaze.

"I'll get the sign-off," Dr. Henry Pierce told Jana while she kept constant eye contact with Ashley, not breaking it with so much as a blink.

Jana had been told what a natural she was, but she knew she had a special connection with children in particular. She began to hum something her grandfather had sung to her when she was small; a sweet Spanish lullaby. And Ashley stared as if hypnotized. Beyond the pumping pain meds and the child's large loss of blood from the metal shrapnel still embedded in her shin, the melody had a calming effect, or at least, Jana liked to think so.

Dr. Pierce came back a few moments later and whispered to Jana, "I got the signature. Go ahead and explain. We have"—his eyes glanced up at the wall clock—"half a minute."

Jana swallowed down the returning knot in her throat. This part was where Luly would have gotten sick. A child. A now fatherless, parentless child was about to lose a limb. But Jana, having no children of her own, felt this was no less heart crushing. It was that no one else in-unit had the balls to do it, or had the heart to do it right.

"Ashley, sweetheart, you have a really bad broken leg. And your daddy made us promise to get you one-hundred percent fixed, no matter what, because he loves you more than anything in the entire world. He can't be here right now, but a promise is a promise."

"I want my daddy."

"I know, sweetie. But only medical people are allowed in here right now. So, listen, Ashley, the cut in your leg is infected, and that bad infection can go through your body if we don't stop it now. Do you understand so far?"

"Yes," she whispered.

Jana took the girl's little hand in hers. "So we need to cut the part below your knee off and then replace it with a stronger leg, like a superhuman one."

The child's brows furrowed, eyes glazed and shifting as if unbelieving her ears.

"If we don't do this right now, the infection will spread. And we can't break our promise to your daddy."

The child closed her eyes. Large tears formed and then fell onto the wrinkled white sheets beneath her small body. An echo of pitter pat, pitter pat dictated Jana's own breath, hitching and waiting until the next teardrop approved a next inhale.

"Will it hurt?" the child asked through her little gasps.

Jana's teeth clenched, gnashing and gritting against each other as if that alone could help hold back her own threatening tear drops.

When the doctor nodded, Jana stood up, regaining her composure just like that. She smiled softly. "You'll be asleep, and when you wake up it will be sore for a time, but after that, no. It'll feel a little weird, but you will learn to walk and run again," she explained while the team set up anesthesia and got the gurney ready to head to surgery.

"Okay...I'll do it for Daddy, and he can help me learn how to use my new leg...because he is super...human...good at everyth...thing..." The child's hopeful voice trailed off, her eyelids falling as fast as Jana's heart, knowing the child would wake from surgery to a missing limb and a missing parent. Her father. Her everything.

*

Mouth gaping and silent for once, her heavily made-up eyes narrowed, Jocelyn Carlson sat facing Antonio when he turned around to face her. She was straddling her date mid-coitus, bare breasts displayed proudly, each topped by deep rose nipples, sharp, hard, like the sinstress's glare.

His glare met hers. "Please get dressed and get out of my limousine, or kindly refrain from placing your shoes or feet against my seats. And," he added, hyper-conscious of his mellow-yet-deadly sincere tone, "this privacy window stays up. Please choose now, before I continue driving." His voice had maintained that intended calm but was peppered with sharp darts of anger, almost out of his control. And it competed with nothing but the heavy panting from the man beneath Ms. Carlson and her exaggerating huffing from her flaring nostrils.

But it was his nostrils that burned, and his head too, as a wave of her perfume hit him and made him want to vomit. It was Michelle's scent, one and the same.

"I have never—"

"Choose," Antonio repeated, cutting her off while the pornographic scene filling his frame didn't faze him at all, but he was sure Jocelyn Carlson wished it did. She probably wanted his cock engorged and begging to get out, begging to get into her, begging to fill the insecure empty shell of a woman. But the exact opposite was the case. His entire body's blood flow was monopolized by his heated face and jackhammering heart pumping out his rage. The woman more than repulsed him. She was the epitome of pathetic, and made his manhood soft and his stomach sick.

The escort broke the silence. "I've lost it, babe—"

"Jason—"

"Rob. It's Rob."

"Whatever. Don't you move a goddamn limb, Rob."

"Yeah, I'm done." Her date pushed her off him, and Jocelyn Carlson landed on the seat with a creaky thud against the leather upholstery. She grumbled while reaching for her dress down around her ankles.

Her date slid forward to talk directly to Antonio. "Sorry man, you know, about all this. Can you just drop me at the closest titty bar? I know we're in the strip club district."

"You fucking little shit," the woman spat while Antonio turned back to his steering wheel and brought the partition up. He assumed she was talking to Rob, but it might as well have been meant for both of the men in the vehicle because who, after all, dared to buck Jocelyn Carlson?

Before shifting from park to drive, Antonio pressed the intercom button. "I'll drop you at a gentlemen's club, sir. And then, Ms. Carlson, I'll bring you back to your condo, unless you want to join your friend?"

"Go fuck yourself," she spewed. "Take me home."

A smirk formed on Antonio's mouth as he pulled back onto the main drag. He laughed in his head; a release greater than the largest orgasm was now flooding his entire being. A word came to mind: *Liberation*. Fucking freedom. He hadn't felt such a rush in as long as he could remember.

He stopped at a traffic light a block from the strip club called The Wet Spot. He knew the owner and owed him the business. He felt rage emanating from behind him, Jocelyn Carlson's crass and self-entitled aura seeping through the partition, under the seats, and through the micro spaces in the privacy window. He wished the witch would get out of the vehicle with her friend, but it almost didn't matter if she did. The oozing disdain from her royal highness met with the new, impenetrable shield Antonio felt surrounding him.

"Hey, man, I wanna tip you, but I don't have any smaller bills. Could you come in for a second, I'll break this hundred spot she gave me and—"

"No, man. It's fine. Go on in and enjoy. I appreciate the thought, though. Really."

He never stepped foot inside the clubs. He'd always hated the vibe and what the dancers lowered themselves to. The clubs made him feel gross. Even driving his first gigs in his hometown in Mexico, having to go into those places to wrangle up his clients to get them to the next destination, he'd always felt an urgent need for a sanitizing shower. He'd been nearly obsessive-compulsive about it. But it was always hours before he'd make it home, and that drove him insane. So he held firm to a blanket rule: never go inside.

His remaining passenger cleared her throat loudly, which, he'd learned from months of driving Jocelyn Carlson, was her most polite version of "fucking drive faster." He couldn't wait to be done with her and her special brand of degradation.

"Take me to my loft in the City instead." The woman's shrill directive came through the intercom.

Of course. Not to her luxury condo in Jersey City, a thirty-minute drive from Newark, but her Manhattan apartment, an hour plus away. Two hours round trip. Antonio reserved certain terms for only the most deserving people, and now she was officially one of them. *Fucking cunt!*

Fine, though. He'd do it. But he officially swore on his mother's grave that he would no longer sacrifice his dignity to meet his financial target, his "number" he called it. No, it didn't matter how much longer it took him, he'd get back to his home, his Puerto Vallarta, with his chest out and his head held high. Sky fucking high.

*

"I don't think I've ever heard or seen you cry, Jana Park. Like, ever."

Jana hid her face behind her locker door. She'd held it in check until the locker room. Then the dam had broken. But at least, when Ashley had woken up from the amputation, Jana was right where she'd been when the child had drifted off, wearing an expression of sheer strength and bravery.

"It's the lack of sleep between back-to-backs." Jana wiped her eyes but kept hidden still.

"Your schedule is all screwed up, girl. And I'm the one with the eight-month-old!" Luly laughed, coming up behind Jana and giving her a squeeze. "You need to take something and get some rest." Luly had been through four years of the grueling MMU nursing program with Jana.

Jana was the rock, and Luly was the soft green moss, the sweet motherly heart. Jana had kept Luly fighting through to graduation while Luly force-fed Jana home-cooked meals during their years of study sessions. Without Luly, Jana was sure she'd have starved or she'd have overdosed on preservatives from microwave meals. Jana hid it well, but she really loved Luly's affectionate nature. She needed nurturing, although she would never admit it out loud.

Luly squeezed her even tighter, and many beats passed. Jana patted her hand in thanks as a signal that she'd had enough, enough sentimentality. She definitely had her limits, and her limit was met.

Then Ilana walked in. "People die, lose limbs, shit happens, right Jana?" Ilana asked with icy shards in her tone as Luly let go of Jana. "Oh shit…

Jana! Did you get the message from your mother? She called like three times! Thanks for sending me to be your personal secretary, though."

Ignoring Ilana, not even willing to dignify the other woman's instigation with a response, she held back the question of what her mother had wanted. Instead, Jana dug through her locker, lifting her purse and coat sleeve to find her phone. Seven missed calls from her mother. And the text from her brother that she'd ignored five hours before for the incoming codes blue and pink. She studied the text, scrutinized it.

"What is it?" Luly asked.

"I've got to go." Jana felt dizzy, her mouth dried up, and her breathing turned shallow and strained. *Focus.* She yanked her things out of her locker and spun around to leave, shifting into high gear to face a new trauma that had just crashed into her world.

The trauma was in Fort Lee, New Jersey, where she was born and raised, more than an hour away in peak traffic. It was a coronary, a sixty-one-year-old male.

Her father.

*

Jana rushed out and Luly followed close behind her. Despite Jana's short stride, she moved like a bullet train through the corridors now. Luly ramped up to a jog to keep up, and through her panting, she peppered Jana with questions and supportive instructions. But Jana tuned her out. She needed to make out her mother's barely audible voicemail, which was in half frantic Korean, and part rushed Spanglish. But Jana got the gist of it.

Chang Park had been rushed to the Fort Lee Hospital after falling to the floor with chest pains at their family's Korean restaurant six hours ago. He'd had a heart attack. While she'd been caring for an innocent little girl who'd lost her father, Jana's own father had been undergoing a quadruple bypass.

A flood of icy fear rushed from her own chest to her head. She shouldn't feel bad. After all she'd done for them, for her parents. But damn it, family first. *Goddamn it, Jana!* Her *own* dad.

"I'll call you from the bus, Luly. And I need to call Nora too. Shit! Can you give her a heads up and that I'll reach out as soon as I can?"

"Of course, and no worries on that front. The woman loves you to death."

God, she hoped her boss loved her enough to keep her spot on the team open.

Okay, what else? Jana paused, her belongings held to her chest, unsure if she'd forgotten anything. She should stop at her place first because, God, how long would she be gone?

Then a voice from down the hall jolted her, ringing painfully in her ears. "I'll cover your shifts, Jana, if you need to be gone for a while!" Ilana crowed.

"Screw her. Don't worry about a thing, Jana. You take care of what you need to, and I'll handle *that* one. Call me—like, when-your-ass-hits-the-seat call me. I love you!" Luly's voice trailed as the automatic doors closed behind her. Jana flagged a cab, cutting off two other hailers without a thought.

"SoHo, 111 Sullivan then Port Authority. Fast."

Cab home, grab essentials, bus across to Jersey. Pray to the traffic gods.

"Nothin's gonna be fast right now, lady. Not on hump day. They say it's the most congested day of the—"

"Just, please!" *Breathe, Jana.* "Do what you have to, and drive."

Shit, should she have taken the subway? No, she needed not to think right now. She needed to zone. Point A to B. No decisions in between. She tossed a crisp twenty over the partition as the cab crept into the hardly-moving traffic. Maybe she'd switch to the uptown train from her place to the bus station. But she hated to be walking with her roller luggage.

Relax, Jana. You'll get there.

She'd be with her dad within an hour, two tops. By his side like she always had been, and always would be. Despite herself, she always would be. Her hand met her chilled cheek, tears streaming down and picking up the bum-rushing AC. First the little girl, then this. She tucked her chin, hiding her emotion from the rearview. God, she hated anyone seeing her cry.

CHAPTER 2

SHE HAD TO grab a few things and go. That one little piece of luggage at the very back of her closet would do. She parted her hanging clothes with shaky hands. There staring at her, held back by her right hand, was her black skirt-suit in plastic. *No, no.* She wouldn't prepare for that. She wouldn't need *that.*

Move it, Jana, let's go! She tossed the carry-on onto her bed and tore through the rest of her closet. Two pairs of shoes, four days of clothes, bras, panties, and then she moved to her bathroom counter for toiletries. She stuffed then zipped, and then looked around before stepping out the door. Sunglasses on the sideboard next to her keys. She threw them on to cover her red puffy eyes, even if it was midnight. *Anything else?* Her mind whirled. God willing she'd be back soon anyway. A week, tops. Her dad would be fine, and she'd be home again.

She locked up and left her SoHo rental piece of heaven to get to the uptown C train.

She hiked her purse strap high on her shoulder as her feet hit the pavement, and gave a corrective tug to her already disobedient piece-of-crap roller bag. At the corner where she needed to cross, she saw the electronic red hand signaling her to stop, but no cars were coming, the crosswalk beckoned, and time was wasting. She stepped out, her luggage thumped off the curb behind her, followed by the loud screech of tires.

*

Thankful to be only minutes from Jocelyn's place now, he drove through the Manhattan maze of dark city streets. Alleys and small parking lots hiccupped between the blocks of closed-down shops, hotels, and apartment condos. No people, no cars, no movement whatsoever except for the turning of the traffic lights through their cycles. He watched the street signs pass one after another, his eyes squinting and anxious for the final turn to deliver Jocelyn Carlson home.

Ah, Sullivan Street. He was almost giddy making the slow right onto her street when a blur of something caught his eye in his peripheral.

His foot slammed on the brake.

"Jesus fucking Christ!" Jocelyn Carlson screamed after thumping the back of his seat with what must have been her head. At least, this time, he knew the thump was unintentional.

His pulse racing, he threw it in park. The heartbeat in his ears didn't help drown out the continued backseat rant, so he looked over his shoulder and snapped, "Be. Quiet." He huffed. "I will be back in a second." And, miracle from above, his passenger shut her mouth.

Antonio jumped out and got to the front of his car where his almost-victim stood panting, no, fuming, palms down on his hood.

He adjusted his chauffeur's cap, swallowed hard, and cleared his throat. "Ma'am, are you okay? God, I am so, so sorry." He had been so eager to unload his passenger that he'd taken careless liberties on the less-traveled side streets. This was his consequence. And even though he'd had the right of way, he knew City pedestrians well enough. Thank God he didn't really hit her, but from her lack of response, he could safely say he'd scared the living shit out of her.

The petite woman stayed hovered over his hood, chest heaving, like she was catching her life-breath. Her stance looked as if she'd stopped the car herself, superhero style. And the fact that she wore sunglasses at midnight made the scene almost comical, but deadly serious at the same time. *Only in Manhattan.*

"Please, miss, tell me are you're o—"

"I'm fine," she huffed. "Just, for God's sake, be more careful!" She lifted her chin to catch a glimpse of his face, then flicked down at his plates as she backed away from the limo. "Jersey drivers," she said, adjusting her purse and little roller bag. Then she shook her head, glanced both ways, and ran across the street.

"Can I drive you anywhere?" he yelled after her, but she didn't look back.

"Can we get the hell out of here already!" His backseat fare shouted, bringing him back to reality.

*

After nearly being run over by a stretch limo, then practically groped on the subway, the lone lumpy bus seat was heaven. She inhaled deeply, counted to ten, then let it out, long and slow.

Okay. It would all be okay.

At least she got the front seat. Thank God for small favors. To avoid her inevitable motion sickness, looking straight out at the road ahead or sleeping were the only ways she could keep her queasiness in check. Meds didn't even work. But music helped. She rummaged through her purse for her earbuds and music player, but, damn it, she'd forgotten them at her place in her mad rush to get out of the City.

So she pulled out her phone for distraction instead. Reading her text messages was a bad idea, especially as her queasiness waxed with the bus driver's jerking response to the stop-and-go traffic, but she did it anyway. The ever-so-rare text from her brother. She took off her sunglasses to see her screen better. Ah yes, there were the words from Almighty Dane. And they made her stomach well with nausea. She shut the screen off the next second, then dug her thumbnail into her index finger as a quick anchoring remedy, a trick she'd taught her patients. For adults and kids alike, a small bit of self-inflicted pain to counteract a blood-drawing needle always did the trick. And beyond distraction, the self-infliction gave a slight sense of control, and right now, she'd take what she could get.

For the moment, she could put off calling her brother, but calling her mother, that chronic pain couldn't wait. She stopped pinching her finger and hit her mother's speed dial, trading one needle-like sensation for another.

*

Her mother's report was vague. Her father was now in the ICU post-op, and no one would say anything more. And Jin Park wouldn't ask anything more because Jin Park didn't like being out of her own comfort zone. Ever. Instead, she'd wait for Jana. Of course.

Jana got off with her mother quickly, having had enough before she'd even dialed her and then thought of Luly, a real mom and friend. She'd told Luly she'd call her, but couldn't bring herself to do it. Lu would force her into tears; her friend's sheer tenderness would turn on the spigot.

Instead, Jana did her best to zone out, even without her trusty music player. She entered into a virtual fog of emotional detachment, until the bus got to the dark and claustrophobic Lincoln Tunnel, crossing into Jersey.

She looked down again at her cell phone for a bit of light, a frame of reference. And again, the taunting urgent text from her long lost piece of shit brother—*Dad in hospital, can't be there. Go. 911.*

The longer she looked at the message, the more enraged, embittered, and sick to her stomach she got. A growl formed in her throat, but she held it back. She was surrounded by real life, other passengers with other problems, and the real outside world ahead of her too, reminding her how little and insignificant she was.

She glanced to her left. The woman across from her was nursing a tiny baby; it soothed her, the angelic infant's suckling, no wrongs in the world. She didn't want to poison the atmosphere for that little piece of bliss with her radiating hate toward far-off Dane.

But damn him. Her big brother, her protective older brother, who had taken her parents to the cleaners by gambling away their hard-earned money when he was supposed to be *earning* a college degree. Not only had he *not* graduated and not fulfilled the Asian-American male's dream their parents had held for their one son, but less important to her dad, Dane had stolen Jana's teen years, her college years, her innocence, her education, and her dream. Because when she'd applied junior year of high school to MMU and got in, her parents had had no funds for their daughter to go. They'd over-leveraged their home and their business. For Dane. Even if she'd gotten a scholarship, college was out. Her parents needed her.

And of course, she'd sacrifice her education to help at the family restaurant. Of course she would. There was no question.

So by day, at the sweet and innocent age of eighteen, it was high school AP classes for no reason at all at that point, then straight home to man the restaurant.

With a strong head for numbers, it took only weeks for Jana to realize that she'd have to work there for twenty years to dig her parents out of the hole her brother had dug. Forget earning enough for school, forget her future, and forget her girlhood dream of becoming a nurse, of helping people—other than her parents, that is. Forget about a life of her own. She was doomed to live in the hamster wheel.

A far off siren brought her back to her bus ride. She shifted her gaze from her phone to the view of the Hudson River out her side window, which mellowed her nerves for a moment until the rushing scene riled up her stomach. Eyes straight ahead again, her head swarmed with memories. The hundreds of bus rides along the Hudson she and Amber had taken, sharing earbuds, listening to chick bands telling them they were strong, fearless, invincible. Then they'd get to the club where they'd fearlessly strip off their clothes and their pride for wads of dirty, wrinkled dollar bills.

Amber had been her ticket out of the family's hole-in-the-wall Korean restaurant and into the club scene. She remembered the night Amber had come in to eat at Korean Soul—per her folks, the best authentic Korean food in northern Jersey. *Right.* Anyway, Amber, her high school's token "whore," the girl who *stripped*, paid her bill with large, crisp bills. As if possessed, Jana had to ask how could she make that kind of money? Sincere money. Exponential money.

Amber answered. And the very next night, Amber took Jana to meet the manager at The Wet Spot, an hour and a half south by bus. The rest was history—wadded, green, maddening history.

Glancing back down at her phone with disgust, she daydreamed of acquiring superpowers, powers of remote electrocution that she could send through the ether to her brother. Dane Park was three thousand miles away in California, "unable to get there."

Fuck him.

As she tapped her brother's number on her phone screen, she sent a mental apology to the peaceful nursing baby across the aisle.

*

He pulled up to her luxury apartment building, put the limo in park, got out, and went around the back to open her car door.

He pulled the door open and stood back to give her room to slip out. He was just glad to be ending his night and hoped he'd never have to see this woman again. Ten times the fare or not, he was officially done with her.

But no high heel hit the travertine drive. No movement at all, in fact. Only the sound of low, raspy humming…in waves.

"Ms. Carlson, we're here."

A crescendo of moaning was her reply.

Unbelievable. The level of drama with this woman. So being a billionaire was a pass to do whatever the hell she wanted? Goddamn her kind. It was not worth it. And it almost never had been.

Moving to peer into his back seat, he was somewhat prepared for what he'd find. After all, this crazy lady would have to top months of disgusting indiscretions in his limo, no doubt. He just wasn't prepared for what he'd do about it. His response would have to be well thought out, fast. He had a business to protect, and he couldn't afford a retribution lawsuit from a disgruntled, rejected, and bitter psycho like Jocelyn Carlson. *Bruja Rena!* She could bury him and all he'd worked for with a simple wave of her goddamn cursed high-flying broomstick.

His eyes met hers and he did well to ignore her hardened cherry nipples topping her creamy round breasts jostling up and down with her body's rhythmic rise and fall as she rode her own fingers. He wasn't blind.

But he was sick to his stomach. Kneeling there, facing him, she seemed ready to explode by the escalation of her moans. He glared at her, a continued streamline of control shooting from his eyes, meant to tell her all she needed to know, what he was, and who he was.

And also, who he wasn't.

He wasn't a male whore for sale, goddamn her. Not in her wildest fucking dreams.

"Please get your clothes on and leave my limo," he ordered, his tone low, unwavering. Then he took two steps back, the door still open.

But she only heaved harder, arching her back, her moans morphing into loud sporadic grunts as she seemed to be reaching her self-imposed climax.

The doorman of the residential skyscraper opened the lobby doors to allow an older couple their exit, and hearing the sounds coming from the back seat of the limo, rushed out toward Antonio, the man's eyes worried and questioning. The older couple only looked at one another and, seemingly offended beyond belief, scurried off down the sidewalk.

Glad for the witnesses, for his own liability and to help demonstrate the woman's insanity, Antonio acknowledged the doorman with a straight-lipped nod, a stoic surrendered expression for the record. The doorman stopped in his tracks between his golden-handled bank of doors and Antonio's limo as if he now understood who and what the source of the noise was inside the vehicle and assuredly wanted nothing to do with it.

Jocelyn Carlson's onslaught continued, and Antonio realized that he might very well have been the only man on Earth who gave this woman not even an iota of his attention, other than the standard professional service he provided to all his clients. And that apparently drove her mad.

As her hips thrust in his direction, faster and faster, she closed her eyes, maybe imagining him approaching her, reciprocating, fulfilling her delusional fantasy, but her frantic pumping received no reaction from Antonio. His eyes just kept her eyes locked in his sights, waiting for the melodramatic display to end and for her to remove herself from his limousine.

When she reached her release, her frenetic bucking rippled through her naked body. Then she folded over and kneeled back, only her face still looking up at Antonio. A glow came over her; a look of deep satisfaction spread across her heavily made-up face. It told him, clear as the moonlight reflected in the shining black enamel of the vehicle, that if he wouldn't indulge her, if he wouldn't give her what she wanted, then she would give it to herself, and he could damn well clean up her mess afterward.

But he met her look with a string of calm and calculated words. "If you're done now." He took another step back and swept his hand out to show her the way.

In a rage, she gave a performance fit for a spoiled princess. She pulled her dress up and over her bosom, snatched up her purse from the seat next to her, and stepped out.

"You have no clue—no fucking idea!—of what you're saying no to. I'll see you Saturday night. Ten PM sharp!" Then her harshness turned to fucked-up flirty, as she brushed his cheek with her still-moistened index finger and grabbed his chauffeur cap with her other hand. Popping it on her head with an air of flippant superiority, she winked at him and walked away.

He sighed over the loss of his cap, but relief filled his chest. "Ms. Carlson, you won't see me Saturday night. Or any other." He let silence fill the rest of his meaning. Nothing more was needed. He was done.

But the woman continued into the building, the doorman almost scared to look at the horrid creature. "Ten PM!" she shouted without looking back, giving only a dismissive wave over her shoulder.

Moving to close the car door, he noticed next to her puddle of pleasure another gift she'd left him. Her used black thong panties acting as a rubber band around a large wad of green bills, there just to mock him. She'd usually stuff and hide her discarded lace undergarments in his limo. This was the first he'd seen a more functional purpose for the nasty things.

He took the item in his right hand and tossed it to the doorman who caught it with sharp, one-handed reflexes above his shoulder.

"Keep it," Antonio called. "It's all yours."

He didn't need that woman's filthy money. He'd find another way. Any other way.

CHAPTER 3

THE RINGING STOPPED when a young child answered. "Dad! It's some lady named Jan or something!" A quick mental flash of Ashley, the child she had left at the ER, came and went, and a dull ache stayed in its stead.

Then a woman's voice replaced the girl's on the phone. "Jana?"

"Alexa. Hello." A heavy silence filled the connection.

"Um...so Dane is in the middle of something b—"

"It's fine, when is he getting out here?"

Jana's sister-in-law cleared her throat. "He...um...your mom is with your father right now. Have you spoken to her? If you haven't, she'll answer the hospital room phone, room 403. She's had trouble with her cell in the hosp—"

"I already spoke to her, Alexa. When will Dane be here?"

"Um, I'm, uh...not sure his schedule, he'll have to text or call you." Thicker silence.

"Thanks, Alexa, have him do that. Just...you have him do that." Her shaking fingertip pressed 'end.'

The baby across from Jana stayed asleep during the very short call. She guessed she was glad Alexa had answered and not Dane, for the baby's sake, at least.

But really, would she have had the balls to tell him what a fucker he was, to put his selfish ass in its place? She'd humped poles and grinded laps for almost a decade, but still she turned into a sheepish mess when it came to her father or brother. It was pathetic. Even without speaking to Dane in years, he had a power over her. She still cared about what he thought. But why?

She'd only been eighteen when he'd disowned her. So much for a big brother's protective nature. Still in high school, having never kissed a boy, let alone gotten undressed for one. It didn't matter. When Dane had found out through friends who'd ventured to the Newark clubs that she was dancing, he swore her off.

"A whore. My sister is a whore," he'd told her. Those words echoed in her head. But so did his ever-so-selfless promise to keep her "career" a secret from their parents. "For Mom and Dad's sake, for their pride, and for the health of their hearts," her brother had said. That was Dane, noble, honorable. And where was Dane now that their father's heart was actually sick and failing?

That righteous cocksucker. And how could Alexa be so damn blind?

Whatever. Nobody deserved to feel the blood-boiling hate that streamed through Jana's veins, and the more she thought about it, the higher her blood pressure got. And Dane just wasn't worth it.

She looked at the tiny baby in the mother's arms. A smile from the mother calmed Jana, lessening the disdain overtaking her, leaving her with the smallest hint of peace.

And when she looked to the front, the Fort Lee Bus Station was in view.

*

He was as white as the hospital sheets, the sterile walls, and the reflective floor tiles. Jana had seen her father fire-red angry. And she'd seen him golden proud, too—of his son or of his restaurant or of his board position on the Business Community's Charity Club. But Jana had never seen Chang Park so drained of color as he was now.

And the raw, flaming incision running up the middle of his chest made her entire body shiver.

Jana's eyes welled. She glanced swiftly from side to side as she wiped them dry to be sure she wasn't caught. *Be strong, for Christ's sakes. Jana, be strong.*

Her mother was asleep in the corner, her feet dangling inches above the floor in a chair that looked as comfortable as a bus stop bench.

And her father...how long had he been back from surgery? Jana picked up the chart at the end of the bed. Quadruple bypass, 17:00, only five hours ago. He probably hadn't been conscious yet. She read on. "My God." Her words escaped in a hush, the exhale of her prior gasp.

How had he made it all these years? Four coronary arteries had each been hovering at eighty percent blockage. She felt lightheaded and dizzy. She crumbled into the nearest chair which rolled along the smooth tile floor.

It hit the bed lightly.

Her father stirred. She spun the seat and then rolled the rest of the way to be face to face with her dad at the head of the bed. She put her hand on his.

"Dad, I got here as soon as I could, as soon as I found out."

"Yes, Ja-Na. I know," he whispered, his chapped lips formed a straight line, and with a stoic nod and a weak blink of his eyes he said, "You're at your job's mercy. It's okay...I'm sure you tried."

Amazing. Fucking unbelievable. No confusion or disorientation after the surgery, no questions concerning his physical state, fresh with transplanted arteries in his damn chest, but so ingrained in him was his dogma.

After flinching from what she should have expected from the old hard-ass, whom she couldn't help but love and try to please even still, Jana looked away from her father to regain her composure. She saw her mother's eyes were open then. And, as usual, her mother kept silent.

Jana returned her attention to her father, but he had already dozed off again.

Her mother feigned a smile, but her eyes were tired and maybe a bit helpless. She said in Korean, "He's been in and out like that for the last hour." Jin slowly stood up from the chair hidden in the corner of the icy hospital room and went to Jana.

Each of Jin's ashen hands held Jana's shoulders lightly while she placed a light kiss on her cheek. She whispered, "I tried so hard to reach you. And so did Dae Han, but you are here now, at least."

Yes, of course. The dutiful son tried. And her mother's use of her brother's Korean name almost made her laugh out loud. 'Greatness and Devotion.' What a complete crock of shit.

"Dane, Ma. He goes by Dane now. Remember, he tossed his Korean name to the curb like he did his family." She couldn't help herself. But she stopped there, her mother's eyes gauging Jana with an evil glower.

"Ja-Na, or *Jana*? Why you so hard on your brother when you do same with your Korean name? Not very nice."

Not…nice? Her heart pounded hot anger through her veins. And like she was going to correct everyone she met as to the correct pronunciation of her name? *Jesus.* "*Wrong syll-A-ble, buddy.*" No. But she upheld the most important aspects of her Asian culture—as a dutiful daughter always putting family first. And…where the hell was *Dane*?

It didn't matter. She didn't want to wake her father by ranting about all the hypocritical family crap slung at her, including how truly *not nice* her brother was to her, to her parents, so she stood up and led her mother out of the room.

The monitors' incessant noises, albeit familiar and usually even comforting to her, were far too disconcerting anyway being all wired up to her wilted, weakened, ghost of a father. She needed to tell her mother how serious things were with her dad. His diseased heart was the only important matter now, the Parks' highest priority.

*

In the gleaming white hallway outside the hospital room, her mother smiled like a porcelain doll at each nurse that walked past. God, her mother was clueless.

And it hit her. Jana could spell it all out for her mom, but her mother wouldn't have a fighting chance in hell of doing anything about her father's health. Knowing her father, and…well, knowing her mother, for that matter. *Dad doing what mom says? Yeah, right!*

God, between the assertive nature of Jana's maternal Korean grandmother and the Latino fire in Jana's maternal grandfather, she couldn't quite understand how Jin Park possessed so little spark of her own, no spark at all, actually. She played only the dutiful woman, the cooking, feeding, abiding woman. Maybe it was just the power of Jana's father and the countless years of losing the fight. But come to think of it, Jana hadn't ever heard her mother argue with her father, not even after bedtime as a child when sneaking from her room to watch more TV from the stairwell.

Arguments with Chang Park just didn't happen.

"Dad's heart, his health, is really poor, Ma. It's bad. He not only nearly died today, but seeing the surgery details, he's still in real danger. He'll have to drastically change his life—a new diet, no more cigarettes, no more stress, and lots more rest. That means no more restaurant, Mom. He's gotta be done with it."

"You so melodramatic, Ja-Na," her mother said.

Melodramatic? How could the woman be in such denial? God, how would her mother cope, or function at all even, without her father if he died? Because he still could die. The man was in no way out of the danger zone.

Jana wished she had a damn sibling who gave a shit, to be there to help her burn up the comfy-cozy insanity blanket her parents wrapped themselves in.

"Good evening, ladies. I'm Dr. Andrew Brighton."

Standing in front of Jana and Jin was a baby-faced cardiologist, so said the tag on his white coat. He looked not more than twenty-three. With his kind, bright blue-gray eyes through thick-rimmed glasses, he held out his hand in introduction. This one was far too young to have had more than two years, three tops, in the unit, but Jana was as open-minded as they came, so she decided to give him the benefit of the doubt. After all, her father had made it out of surgery okay.

"Jana, and this is my mother, Jin Park." She gave him a firm shake and made sure to include a warm smile. The man in front of her might very well be her only shot in bringing her parents down to reality.

"Sorry, but...can I take that in with me?" He smiled, gesturing to her father's medical chart in Jana's tight grasp.

"Oh, I'm sorry." She looked down at the chart and their awkward handshake lock. "I'm a BRN at MMU Hospital, Head Trauma Team. Just explaining to my mother how serious this all is."

"Ah, good. Good to have a family member who speaks the language. Your father could really use knowledgeable support by his side." He smiled at her, almost respectfully.

She didn't expect it, not of a resident, a young one at that. In her experience, they always had something to prove, and to speak to a nurse without condescension, she almost wondered what was wrong with him. There had to be an agenda. In fact, with people in general, wasn't there always? And in her experience, men especially always had some ulterior motive.

During her mental analysis of Dr. Brighton, she felt a nudge from her mother, not a subtle one either. She could feel her mother's vibe, her urgency, that a young doctor with no wedding ring was present. The only communication she ever got from her mother beyond "You hungry?" was "You dating?" But the nudge wouldn't do. Jin liked to go the extra mile when it had to do with a potential match.

"My daughter is single, all alone in Manhattan if you can believe it!"

For Christ's sakes, Ma. Jana could only smile apologetically to the doctor.

He smiled back and went to the door. "Very good. Well, again, it's nice to officially meet you, single Jana"—he winked—"and Mrs. Park. Shall we check on the patient?"

Her mother followed the doctor close behind and Jana next, trying to get her questions in before her father woke up, or she'd have no shot. "So a quadruple bypass with monitoring. Recovery time is what, five days? Ten?" Jana asked from behind her hovering mother.

"The surgery went well, so probably three days in the ICU, but then yes, five to ten more upstairs once he's in the clear. And then many weeks of solid bed rest at home. Six at least."

"And of course, the smoking must stop," Jana said with a volume unconsciously louder than her hallway whisper.

Chang Park's eyes opened.

Yes, she sure as hell wanted her parents to be called out in front of the young Dr. B. A male, a doctor, her ticket to getting through to them. The necessary piece.

"Hello, Mr. Park. I'm your cardiologist, Dr. Brighton. You probably feel—"

"Like hell," he grumbled. "And I need my smokes." He coughed then scowled.

"You'll feel soreness and pain, sir, for a—"

"I said I need my cigarettes. Jin? My smokes."

"Daddy, you came out of surgery. You've got to listen to Dr. Brighton."

Her father respected professional men. A sleazy lawyer, a dirty cop, a crooked stock broker—they'd still stand a better chance than a woman—even his loving daughter, a medical professional—when it came to advice meeting the ears of Chang Park. So, Dr. B., even with his too-youthful glow, would do. Well, he'd have to. Although, he'd become a fast enemy by denying her father his cancer sticks for sure. God, none of this would be easy.

Chang squinted at them all, then narrowed his eyes at his daughter. "My cigarettes. Help me up, Jin."

"Dad. You can't—" she started, but a light touch to her elbow by Dr. Brighton paused her wasted words.

"Mr. Park, it's vital that a complete lifestyle change is enforced. No smoking, no stress. A drastic change in diet. Or you won't live long at all. Not beyond a week or so, sir."

"And the restaurant has got to go, Dad," Jana blurted, unable to control herself. "It's a very large source of stress for my father. For both my parents."

"It isn't stressful; it's relaxing." Her father got his words out slowly, but they were laced with venom, no doubt.

"Either way, Mr. Park, it will be at least six weeks before you're relaxing anywhere other than in a bed," Dr. B. stated warmly.

"Dad, you can't be at the restaurant anymore. Period. You just can't," Jana asserted.

He took a deep, wheezing breath. "You and your mother will cover for a few weeks until I am better."

A surge shot up her spine. With that same familiar loss of air in her atmosphere as she had every time her father said anything non-negotiable. She was twenty-seven years old for God's sake. She had a career, despite Chang Park's definition. "Dad, of course, Mom and I will help at the restaurant. We'll find a real manager while a business broker can list it for sale and—"

"No. No manager. No broker, no sale," he whispered through his strained wheezing.

Despite the fact that other than her parents owning the building free and clear, thanks to Jana, the business had zero value. After Jana had dug them out from the debt incurred by Dane, the best the restaurant ever did was break even. It was Chang Park working a job…for free. His very own non-profit.

"Dad, be reasonable."

He slowly filled his lungs, wincing from the pain, and said, "I will be back in half the time this doctor says. Half. No one but family runs my place. The restaurant,"—he paused to cough while the doctor and Jana both glanced at the monitor's spike—"will be yours someday, and you can stop that bedpan slavery."

The bright-eyed doctor cleared his throat, obviously uncomfortable by the family dynamics and definitely concerned by his patient's increase in blood pressure. He bravely ventured a comment anyway. "I like your spirit, Mr. Park. You'll need it to move toward your new, healthier lifestyle. But to do that, I'll need you to understand how extremely serious your situation is." He moved closer to the patient, which apparently gave Jin direct access to Jana's arm.

"I need to talk to you outside while the doctor is with Daddy."

Her mother had the worst timing. She needed both her parents to hear, to wake up, and to be on board. How clueless they were as to the magnitude of her father's state, even though Jin knew it when she called her work and her cell phone and then her brother's. Why did the fact that Jana's father was out of surgery make Jin less worried about the man? The woman was back to oblivious now, almost more in denial than ever.

"Mom, we should all be here with Daddy and the doctor."

"It's really okay. I'll be back several times over the next couple of days," the doctor said, overhearing Jana.

Not part of the unspoken plan, Doc, but thanks. Jana grinned to be polite. *Fine.* "Daddy, I'll be back later tonight to relieve Mom. I'll get settled at the house and check in on the restaurant, okay?"

And she'd check the financials in the restaurant's back office, as well. She had to strengthen her case for selling the damn lead weight her father loved so much.

Chang nodded and returned his attention to the doctor, who was now only looking at Jana a little too conscientiously.

Jin pinched Jana's arm and whispered, "Smile!" in her ear.

Again, not subtle at all.

"It was nice meeting you, Dr. Brighton. Thank you for everything."

Then Jin pulled Jana outside the room as if an urgent wartime message had to be conveyed before the world came to an end.

*

Jana's mother was all nerves, and her anxiety was more than contagious.

"Mom, what is it? You're making *me* nervous, and I'm an ER nurse. Dad has already had a quadruple bypass today. How much worse could it be? Please relax and say what you have to say." And please make it something other than asking about the status of her food intake, and if she'd met a man to sweep her off her fucking feet like Chang Park had done for Jin. *Right.*

But there, outside the hospital room, her mother transformed into a different person, a person so serious, so strained by some infinite weight, a responsibility, maybe a heavily-toted secret, and so out of character, that Jana couldn't help smirking. And like the time she was caught smirking at her grandmother's funeral—just a coping mechanism—and she'd gotten slapped from then to her next birthday, she thought her mother might lift her hand and do it again, twenty years later.

But her mother didn't. Instead, Jin narrowed her eyes and spoke in hushed Korean. "Ja-Na Sun."

Nearly ten years ago was the last she'd heard her whole Korean name uttered by her mother, and it made Jana shudder.

"We, your father and me, you know, are so strong and healthy, always eating good Korean food. Well, you know, we don't really need or have health insurance."

"Don't be absurd, Ma. I got you and Daddy set up on a policy like three years ago, despite your ludicrous argument."

"Daddy canceled."

Jana's lungs deflated. And there was no next breath.

"He needed the money for something else, for the restaurant, and so many of Daddy's business club friends don't have insurance. So expensive, those monthly payments. Such a scam, they all say."

Right. A scam. It felt like the scam was on her because she knew very well what was coming. Her heart began to race.

Breathe!

But still, nothing.

Breathe damn it!

Through her nostrils, she inhaled. The sterile hospital air was thin, bleach-scented. Although she'd willed her lungs to work now, she couldn't fill them with a whole, satisfying breath. She needed to sit down. But no chair. Anywhere. So she leaned against the scuff-marked wall and stared at her mother.

"So now, here is the hospital bill statement or whatever they call it"—her mother pulled out a folded mess from her purse—"and we need you to take care of it because there isn't enough, you know, in our bank to pay with." Then Jin looked down at her purse. At least she knew to look away, not daring to meet Jana's eyes. Because Jana didn't know if her death stare would actually kill her mother, and worse, she didn't know if she wanted it to.

But it wasn't her mother's fault. It was her father. Chang Park and his coronary had pushed Jin against the metaphorical wall. Just like when Jana had run to them, screaming with excitement with her Manhattan Metro University acceptance letter in hand a decade ago. Her mother was the one to break the news: "Ja-Na Sun, there is no money." And the woman looked away in the same guilt-stricken way.

"The billing lady assigned to us wants to speak to someone about the ambulance and the rest of the expenses to come. She didn't understand me, with my accent."

Of course, her accent, after forty fucking years in the US. "What did she not understand you saying, Mom? That your eldest child, the god-blessed son, is a selfish, broke asshole, so your 'pathetic, unmarried nurse' of a daughter will come to the rescue? Again!"

Jin shot Jana a look that was equal to slapping her clear across the face. Hard. Again, Jana was shocked her mother didn't actually raise her hand and do it, first the smirk, then this? And they both knew Jana wouldn't have had the balls to ever speak that way to her father. Why then was it passable to disrespect her mother?

Jana had no answer for that. Damn it, she should really speak this way to both of them, to finally turn off the spigot of her ever-flowing support and the full financial coverage of her fully grown fucking parents. And goddamn her siphon of a brother.

Jana shook her head as her eyes darted to the gleaming white floor. *Remember, Mom is under his thumb, Jana.* How could she even put this on Jin? If Jin ran things, if her mother was in a different marriage, a different life, and if her mother was more like Jana's iron-fisted grandmother, Jin might have stopped Chang's absolutely ludicrous decision to cancel their health insurance, and they'd have their own resources to cover this mess. And maybe even have life insurance and other contingency plans.

So, just how much was the burden they lovingly heaped on her shoulders? She dreaded opening the folded mangle of a bill, but her fumbling fingers opened it anyway.

First page, "ambulance," sans health insurance, "twelve hundred dollars". She swallowed back a ball of tightly-wound fear as she flipped to the next page because she knew. She knew what was coming, being in the damn medical field. She wished to God she didn't though.

Line item, "quadruple bypass." Her eyes followed across the page, and her knees got weak. Her head throbbed. *One hundred and fifty-two thousand.* She stood there with the paper rattling in her cold trembling hands. Still seven to ten more days to go in the hospital. Then the follow-ups, drugs, physical therapy, home care, and all the rest.

All Jana felt was nausea. A panic attack would have been welcome at that point, or mild hysteria, even. But no, nothing. Any and all emotion including the hope and joy she'd accumulated over the last year of living her dream, her nursing position at one of the most prestigious hospitals the world over, all vacated her being that instant, leaving a cold robotic numbness.

Jana lifted her eyes and looked up at her mother. Then like a zombie, she kissed her mother's cheek and left the small cowering woman outside her father's hospital room, as Jana dutifully made her way toward the business office to discuss her father's financial situation—now Jana's situation.

And it all begins again.

CHAPTER 4

S HE TIPPED THE cab driver well, despite her new completely fucked situation. He'd driven well enough, but most of all, he'd stayed quiet. Noiselessness was what she needed, vitally. Anything else would have been the tipping point. In her fragile, icy state, she thought for sure she'd shatter into pieces. She laughed as the green bills left her hand and slid into those of the bearded driver. What was the difference anymore between twenty dollars and twenty thousand? Or two hundred grand even?

At one time, while selling her soul, dancing on top of her obliterated moral compass, the cash she'd have lying around, all stuffed in shoeboxes and tucked under her mattress, was too much to count. And as she inserted her key to unlock the glass door of the Park family's walk-up, her overactive mind heard her mother telling her to "smile" at the doctor. Why not say, "Land him, Jana!" She cringed at the thought. Being with a man for his money wasn't something she was capable of. Her mother could keep her fantasies because that's all her mother had. And as for her mother's reality, Jin Park could keep that too. If Jana wanted to be a trophy on a leash, she'd have snagged one of her doting club regulars years ago.

No, she'd be deeply connected and enthralled and in total symbiosis with whomever her future partner would be. A long time away, though, not until she cleaned up her parents' new mess. Because she couldn't burden anyone else with this load; she had her pride and she had a conscience. Even if her parents so obviously did not.

But, she'd admit at her lowest points, like now, it was tempting to just connect with a man who had resources. But she also remembered the day-time talk shows she'd zoned out to for the years she worked nights, disbelieving the women who had strategized marrying rich. The thought made her ill, especially knowing that the husbands those women manipulated around the chessboard to hit their wallets, well, those men had been coming to her for lap dances every week. She'd have none of that. No marriage of convenience, no money contract. She'd rather stay alone than ever, ever buy in.

The musty stairwell smell was familiar enough, but the hint of seafood and pickled cabbage in the air was what hit home. She watched the top of the stairs get closer, her purse threatening to fall off her sagging shoulder and her roller bag thumping up each mocking step, each *thud* making her flinch as the throbbing in her head marched to the beat.

Jana got to the top, got the house door open, and fell into the cluttered apartment with a surrender and a disdain that matched the energy of her ER on a night of a massive city train wreck.

Tossing her purse and dropping the roller bag where she stood, she moved her limp body to the brown plaid couch, the one she'd known as a child, the very same. She'd offered to replace the repulsive thing a billion times over, but her father would have none of it. He'd take what will no doubt be hundreds of thousands from her now—actually, again!—but not a new couch.

Her hands went up to her pounding head, fingers massaging her temples. Not helpful, not a dent of relief. Exhale.

Sleep? Eat? Neither was even thinkable.

Action. She had to do something. She had to attack.

She grabbed her purse and headed back down the stairs fumbling through the clanking ring of unmarked keys as she went. God, how many times had she told them to label the keys? Taking no care on the steps, she stumbled but caught herself on the rickety banister. Her heart pounded through the scare until her fingers found the jagged silver key by memory. She caught her breath and put the key into the side door at the bottom of the stairwell.

*

The chairs were up on the larger round tops, but the two-tops lining the walls were still dirty, chairs only pushed in by the assumedly rushed closing kitchen crew, unmonitored since ten hours ago, so why would he or she or they give a shit, right? The floor had definitely not been swept, but again, who, if not her father, would be there to say—or yell in her father's case—a thing about it. There was a makeshift closed sign hanging on the front door, but she'd definitely need to give her and her mother at least two days' leeway. She pulled the paper down, grabbed a pen from her bag and hand wrote, 'Until further notice, due to Family Emergency.'

She walked back through the kitchen, which reeked because, in addition to the floors, the damn garbage had been skipped. She decided then that she'd find the papers she needed to run preliminary numbers and get the hell out of there, out of the entire building for that matter. The option to sleep in her childhood bedroom upstairs was out too, since the ventilation from the kitchen was building-wide. And Jana's old bedroom had the benefit of being directly above the kitchen, closest to the stench.

She got to the back office door and before even messing with the keys, she pulled out a small container of menthol vapor balm from her purse. A nurse comes prepared with the minimum essentials. She dabbed some under her nose to be able to function in there for even a few minutes.

Not having been in the back office too often when she was younger, she had no immediate recollection of the key, so she tried the rest of the bunch. The eleventh key clicked.

Just the sight of the closet-sized hole of an office with all the stacks and samples and catalogs and broken knobs and parts made her crumble to the grease-slicked floor and sob. She gasped between every few outpours, but covered her mouth with her shirt as a pseudo-filter, knowing the poisonous sewage-like air of the thirty-year-old commercial kitchen was killing her slowly with each and every intake.

After all the years she'd worked to escape the potential of becoming her parents in that restaurant, and then the fight to save them, then her escape from the strip club scene...after all that, now she was being stuffed back into a dark black hopeless box, one she didn't think she'd ever have the strength to climb out of in the first place.

Three years in at The Wet Spot, Newark, then four more at the Manhattan sister club during her nursing school stint. God, she'd been gyrating eye-candy by night, at the mercy of horrid, horny men and boys, while by day, a nursing student, busting ass on organic chemistry and pharmacology when she should have been sleeping. Why hadn't she drowned her nursing dream in the Hudson years ago? She could have kept dancing at The Wet Spot for Christ's sake, eventually worn down enough to take an offer from one of her many creepy regulars, as a mistress or hell, as a dutiful wife. Why not dive right into a loveless, fuck-filled marriage of comfort and ease? And when her tits started to sag, she'd be traded in for a younger, tighter version of the shell of a woman she'd once been, but she'd still have the ease and comfort, right? She'd even have it better than her mother by this time.

God, why had she put herself through any of the upward struggles? She'd gotten into her dream school, then for a taste of the energy surge at one of the best hospitals in the entire fucking world, to have her family take it away from her, snatch it the fuck away. Again!

The floor safe, covered with dust, dented at the top edge, stared at her. She laughed out loud through her salty, pathetic tears. The undoubtedly empty safe, except for maybe twenty dollars of coin rolls, doubled as a printer stand and a "refrigerator" magnet door, with vendors' phone numbers haphazardly stuck onto its rust-splotched surface.

God, she'd probably need to help her mother replenish the coins tomorrow. Because Ilana back at MMU Hospital had probably already snagged her week's shifts. And because why wouldn't a skilled, trained nurse need to go to a Fort Lee, New Jersey bank to get twenty bucks of dime and quarter rolls for an already dead restaurant? And the joke of the century: She'd have to come up with ten-thousand percent more than that for her father's hospital bills.

She pushed herself up off the floor. Her tears had slowed. The odor of the place was making her gag while the mint balm made her upper lip tingle and not much else. She dusted off her backside, wiped her face, and fully entered the dingy broom closet of an office. The huge CRT monitor took up most of the damn space, dangerously weighing down the warped, albeit thick, piece of plywood mounted to the entire length of the wall, acting as a desk. Under the 'desk' was the decade-old computer tower, which, to her surprise, powered up when she pressed the greasy little 'on' button. Why was she even thinking her parents had kept any information updated on the damn thing? They'd told her up front they wouldn't use it when she'd bought it for them before moving closer to campus. She'd gotten them a brand-new tower and LCD monitor to make their lives easier. Where the hell the thin panel monitor was, though, she couldn't imagine. They'd probably given it to Cousin Daniel, their acting accountant, as payment for some tax prep.

While the computer booted, she saved time and her soon-to-explode stomach, by rummaging through the twelve-inch pile of papers next to the kitchen equipment catalogs her father had no business thumbing through.

She was looking for the most recent tax returns that her spineless cousin, Daniel Kwon, prepared for them every year. And every year that asshole would conveniently forget to tell her parents they needed to quit, that the state of their business' financials was abysmal. But Daniel's folks were doing great in the carpet and flooring business, and the passive aggression was clear to no one but Jana.

Nothing in the pile, so she threw open the file cabinet drawer as her guts started to really turn. Wow, alphabetized? That was an unforeseen second surprise. Categorized by what? 'All-Food Service.' Okay, by vendor name then. 'Blue Tickets.' Okay, so, no, by topic. She prayed 'CPA' would be in the 'C' section because there was no 'Accountant' under 'A.' Her father had always bragged about Cousin Daniel becoming a 'Certified Public Accountant.' Yes, the title was his thing. But in C, there was no 'CPA' file, but before she closed the drawer to move her search to the lower M-Z drawer, her eye caught something. Laughing her ass off, but choking on the putrid air at the same time, she found a file labeled 'Cousin Daniel.' C for Cousin. *Of course.*

It was a thick file and—hallelujah—it had the current year's return all the way through five years back. She yanked the folder, slammed the self-locking office door, and sprinted out of the kitchen, out of the restaurant, taking a deep and only slightly less disgusting breath in the stairwell. It wasn't nearly satisfying or clearing enough. She opened the exterior door and stuck her head out for the fresher, albeit hotter, summer air.

Yeah, the oxygen was way better outside, so she ran up to get her roller bag while balancing the file under her arm, then back down, escaping, letting the door slam shut behind her. She'd call a cab and sleep at the hospital, standing up if she had to, but she wasn't about to reenter that stench.

*

She locked the door behind her and leaned against the brick wall of the building. She called the cab that had dropped her off. Who knew cabbies carried their own business cards these days? She wouldn't know since subways were her sole means of getting anywhere she didn't walk to in the City.

The cab dispatch lady said it would be a ten-minute wait, which was plenty of time for Jana to review the folder tucked under her arm.

Having done years of tax returns for Charlene, Amber, and a few of the other girls at the clubs, and, of course, her own, she felt confident when she let the file fall open in her hands. The Tax Form 1040 for that year was on top. Just what she'd thought, hardly breaking even. It was worse when she considered the fact that her father under compensated himself to minimize payroll taxes. So much for them counting on Social Security in three years. *Jesus.*

With her clothing already tainted by having even stepped into that kitchen, she crouched down to sit on the filth-strewn sidewalk. She pulled a pen from her purse for her fidgety fingers to jot down notes and numbers as she thumbed through more of the documents. By the time the cab came to take her back to the hospital, she'd figured that the restaurant wouldn't last more than a month without her father standing in it morning to night.

She then added the accruing medical bills and took into account that she'd be making *zero* money while missing work for the foreseeable weeks while her father was in the hospital. Then he'd be brought home, and he'd assumedly need expert care that they couldn't afford. Would they need her to do it then? Probably, except for her father's extreme lack of trust in her; she was a hospital piss-pan maid and nothing more. Yeah, she definitely had to hire someone, an experienced homecare professional, a real hard-ass. Add another seven or eight grand to the pit.

She knew the coverage available to the uninsured at her hospital was difficult to acquire, and Jersey was even worse. Even Medicaid was out of reach for her folks because their current tax returns showed just over the maximum allowed to even qualify. They were in the gap, and although they'd be eligible a year from now when the restaurant was dead and gone, this year, now, she was just, well, extremely fucking screwed.

She remembered her savings account, which had approximately thirty grand in it, savings for an eventual down payment on a brownstone in Brooklyn. *Reset that clock.*

And with her few empty credit cards, maybe twenty thousand available on them, she'd take out cash advances.

She couldn't ask her parents' extended family; it would ruin their reputation, more important to Chang Park than his daughter's life, she was certain.

She laughed out loud when she realized that she'd completely skipped her brother as a source of help. She had taught herself on a deep, subconscious level that Dane was an empty, cold-hearted stone, not worth skipping across a murky, scum-covered retention pond.

Fuck. Just, *fuck!*

She swallowed hard, then looked down at her phone. Her finger slid across the screen three times, swiping through names and numbers from her past until she found Eddie's number, her old manager at The Wet Spot.

She'd blurred her lines before for her family. Now, it seemed, she'd have to blur them again.

CHAPTER 5

W HEN THE OPERATOR'S recording said that Eddie's number had been disconnected, she ended the connection and tried again. She got the same automated message, though. Eddie was the go-to guy for the entire Tri-state area; he'd had thousands of contacts in the strip club industry. His number was disconnected? How strange.

She looked at her phone in thought, then browsed through more contacts until she got to her next lead. Never too late at night to call Amber, and so she hit her number as the cab pulled up.

*

Amber sounded great on the phone, even though it *was* too late to call her, as she was apparently no longer dancing. She was, in fact, being a new mom, hushing a rudely awakened baby, thanks to Jana's pre-dawn call.

"Oh God, I'm so sorry, Amber. Go back to sleep, I can call another time."

"Don't you *dare* hang up, Jana Park. It was feeding time in a few minutes anyway, love. How are you?"

Jana's heart warmed. Her sweet friend with what sounded to be a newborn? And the little thing's crying didn't seem to fluster the new mom at all. Jana smiled. Amber hadn't always had that ability, to be calm and controlled in the face of chaos, and neither had Jana. It was Charlene who had taught them both the art of serenity, even and especially in front of the hundreds of hungry fantasizing faces at the club.

God she remembered in the very first week of Jana's life as "Winter," Jana had gotten out on that stage and had been slammed with queasiness. The queasy feeling like she got from her motion sickness, except that she wasn't moving, not a bit. In fact, she'd been paralyzed. Frozen stiff. When the jeering and booing started, her paralysis had turned to a quivering trepidation. God, she thought she'd pee right there on stage.

But Char had come to her rescue. "Dance like no one's watching," she'd ordered in a harsh whisper. Charlene had taught her to block out the noise, the catcalls, the club clientele's dirty, filthy looks, and intentions. And looking up at the bright blinding strobes, she began to dance like no one was watching.

And made a shit-load of money from it.

"God, it's good to hear your voice," Amber gushed.

"You too…you sound great. Like a happy little mama!"

"Yeah, I really am happy, Jana. I haven't danced in over a year now. Got pregnant by Dominic." The weekend bouncer at The Wet Spot, a decent guy, protective, with only a slightly dangerous jealous streak. "The club begged me to stay on, you know, the whole novel prego-dancer thing." When she was still dancing, they'd made Tandy stay on until late in her third trimester. It had made Jana sick to think about it. "But, of course, Dominic refused. And I've got my lines too, right?" Amber asked as if she wasn't entirely sure.

But Jana knew that Amber and Charlene had held to more stringent lines than most of the girls. So Amber screwed the steroidal head bouncer. She may have just wanted the out, and who could blame her? And there were far worse than Dominic. Far worse.

And as for Char, that was an entirely different story. Her lines had been crossed by force. And Jana shoved the surfacing thought back down deep into her mind's lock box, safe and far away.

"Man, you remember what Char did to me when she caught me in the back that time? Talk about lines." Amber had been inches from snorting her first line of coke when Charlene found her and pulled her away by the ponytail. Then she shoved her head in a shitty toilet bowl. Desperate measures, maybe, but with white snow being everywhere in the club—front and back of the house, in the parking lot, and being sold out the back door—Char did what she had to. Jana and Amber were like little sisters to her, she'd said.

And the trio were the only girls in the club who walked the straight and narrow. Their mantra: "Never high, never fucked, get in and get out with the bucks." Completely cheesy, but they needed the levity, and, more importantly, they always needed the reminder because some of the shit that went down in the club was crazy enough to send someone over the edge, seeking the great high, white escape. But they'd stayed clean, and that's how they'd made such bank, the highest grossing dancers in the place.

"Feels like a lifetime ago, doesn't it?"

"For sure. And Jana, that's so amazing for you, getting the nursing thing done! I hate that you need to jump back into dancing again. But you can get in and get out, a few months tops, right?"

"One month. One month is all I think I can take. I gotta get back to my ER, to my Trauma Team. If they even hold my position that long. Yeah, I'll make the rest of the debt up over a few years' time, juggling credit cards. Hold off on buying a place. But yeah, one month is definitely all I can do." Jana was telling herself as much as she was telling Amber.

"You still in the same shape, hun?" Amber asked, slightly distracted with the baby, who was now cooing into the phone.

"Despite the lack of sleep and the little time I take to eat, I look fit. And I do my yoga and crunches each morning, so yeah, I'm good." She wasn't as worried about her body as she was about her emotional state and, more than that, her ability to swallow her pride again.

"Good, you'll need it, sweetie. The young ones are coming in even younger now…it's totally insane! Fresh, young pussy overrides all, right?" Amber laughed while the baby hummed. The sweet rolling noise swelled and fell as Amber must have been bouncing the child in her arms.

Jana jolted forward suddenly, jarring in contrast to the mesmerizing baby sound at her ear. The cabbie had slammed his brakes for some asshole who'd cut them off. "Shit!" Jana directed at the cab driver.

"You okay?" Amber asked.

"Yeah, no, I'm fine. Jersey drivers."

"Don't I know it…so, hey, you remember Char called the young new-bies the 'tight twats'?" Amber laughed into the phone.

"Yeah, sure." Jana smiled softly, solemnly. Yeah, she remembered. God, she hadn't understood anything, let alone what tight twats or a virgin vagina *actually* meant to men until Char awakened her to the fucking real world. Jana had always been petite, young and sweet looking. Innocent. And after hearing Char's 'The great virgin dream of men' theory, it all became crystal clear to her, how men saw her. As a tight-twat virgin. But one that was up on stage spreading it for them. Oh Lord, the dream in living color. All the way through her dancing career, Jana made tons of cash working the young virgin girl angle. Charlene had even helped her dress the part in schoolgirl uniforms to the nth degree. It paid the bills, but still to this day it made her sick to walk by a parochial school during dismissal. How sick and twisted the whole thing had been. Still was.

"Well, anyway, if you're still toned, you have nothing to worry about, even the tightest cunts still get coked-out or out of shape in no time at the club. You'll be golden, as always," Amber said with a hint of obvious envy. "You're a gorgeous Latino-Asian mutt!" Amber blurted.

Jana laughed. She had a healthy-sized ass but didn't have the full and curvy voluptuous thing going on up top. She was on the small side of a B cup.

Char had damn near made a marketing plan for her at her start. Jana fulfilled two very specific niche markets in the club scene: the Lush Latino, with the full-fledged backside, lips, and lashes; and the Exotic Asian fantasy, with the eyes and high cheekbones, small, tight frame, and long, lustrous hair. How crazy, to view one's attributes as marketable. But it was business, it was money.

"Oh, and forget about the pole, girl…no one can touch you there!" Amber added. "I'm still jealous of your 'Open-V' and your damn 'Helicopter.' And, oh God, your 'Caterpillar' drove them insane! None of the girls do much more than a climb anymore."

Jana had had a unique and unknown advantage at the start of her dance career. She'd been a gymnast since age six and had competed all the way up through high school until senior year, in fact, when dancing took over her schedule.

"Jesus, I actually miss the pole. I almost joined one of those new pole fitness clubs, but it was too close of an association, you know?"

"Yeah, totally." Then the baby started crying for something. "She's hungry for boob, one second, doll," Amber said, then whispered sweetly to the baby to hush and eat.

Jana caught herself imagining herself in Amber's place. Or being the woman on the bus, with nothing else in the world mattering but that tiny, innocent being at her breast. A small ache surfaced in her chest until Amber's voice brought her focus back.

"Okay, sorry. Anyway, J, I wish I could make a call for you, just to get you started quicker, especially if Eddie isn't answering his cell. Which is totally weird. But Dominic burned the bridge with Eddie and the Demontes when I got knocked up, and he wouldn't even let me step on property now, let alone call, even if I did know anyone there anymore. But hell, go there; see if Eddie is still there. That boy'd do anything for you."

"Yeah, I'll do that."

"Just, you know, keep in touch. Tell me how it goes. And so I know you're safe."

Jana caught the underlying worry, because when Char had left for Vegas, they both wished they could've prevented what had happened. But Jana knew they couldn't have. It was out of anyone's hands. Jana had even spoken to Char the day before. One day before.

"Of course. I'll text you my status after I go down there tomorrow night. Listen, Amber, it was so good hearing your voice. God…you sound like an amazing mama," she said as a tiny pang of something Jana realized was envy rose up again in her chest. But thank God she had no innocent soul dependent on her now. Because she had her parents to deal with right now, and she could hardly handle them and their debts.

So, all she could do was to pray that in this lifetime her parents would learn to stand on their own two feet and finally release her so she could live her own life. Her own dreams.

"Good hearing your voice too, love. We're out in Morristown now. Come and visit us if you can. I'd die to see you, and you can meet Charlie—"

"You named her—"

"—Yeah. Charlene, Charlie for short."

"I love it, Amber." Jana choked on her breath, holding back the sudden grief she had worked too hard to hide for the entire phone call. There had been no funeral, no closure, and as the years passed, Jana thought it best to keep it buried. What was the point of hashing out that shit? "Oh, hey Amber, gotta go, just pulled up to the hospital."

"Yeah, sure, okay. Just, stay in touch, love. Please, stay in touch."

Jana pressed 'end' on her screen and looked out at the road in front of her, the cab still several minutes from the hospital.

She gathered her hair back into a ponytail, pulling it tight enough to reset her state of mind with a bit of brain-clearing pain. Her trick again—hurt for hurt—this time not for motion sickness but to balance out every-thing else, topped by thoughts of Char. She divided her hair in two, gave each side one more good yank, the hair band now snug against her skull. She brought her arms down to her lap, and only then noticed a new tiny bruise on her forearm that hadn't been there hours before, at least not when she was holding her father's hand at the hospital. She must've done it subconsciously. God, she really needed to find some earbuds.

CHAPTER 6

WATCHING MANHATTAN'S LIT up skyline across the river from the window while the cab weaved through the barren streets of Fort Lee, Jana went over her plan in her head.

She'd relieve her mother, send her home to sleep, then after a three-hour power nap in that horrible hospital room armchair, she'd deal with her father. Her mother would come back and she'd get down to Newark and hope that Eddie was still running The Wet Spot.

Because Eddie was her ticket. Beyond Amber and Charlene, Eddie had been key to her ability to make the money she had because he made the schedule. And Eddie had definitely favored Jana. He'd never been shy about crushing on her from day one, but besides and despite that, he kept her on as many rotations as she wanted, even though she didn't reciprocate Eddie's advances. While most men in the industry would have cut her off immediately for denying them, he put her, and kept her, on the rotation more consistently than any other dancer. She didn't delude herself; Eddie wasn't selfless by any means. The bumps in pay he got from Jana being on the schedule were motivation enough. The men she drew into the club made his cover-count skyrocket. And her regulars booked the back rooms as if their money grew like grass in the suburbs.

She hadn't seen or spoken to Eddie since she transferred to The Manhattan Sweet Spot. He and his pocket were pissed. And Charlene had been leaving too, heading out to Vegas for bigger things; he'd lost two top earners in a single month.

But that was the business, and everyone knew nothing was forever in the club scene.

At that time, she'd been dancing for two plus years, and had figured out that beyond catching her folks up financially, she could actually fund nursing school too. She had reapplied to MMU not expecting to get in. But for a second time, she had. And The Sweet Spot was only a few blocks from campus.

But the real perk, compared to Newark's club scene, was the exponential money to be had in the City. Even though, at the start, she'd been low on the totem pole—far fewer peak shifts and no private room demand—she'd still made twice as much money as she had in Newark. And once she acquired her own following at The Sweet Spot, well, astronomical history. She had never imagined having so much cash before, every last dollar of which would all go to cover the remainder of her folks' debt and all of her college tuition. And for the next four years, she worked all night, hit class and studied by day, and grabbed some sleep and food somewhere in between. That's how she got out of the clubs and obtained her ER spot.

But here she was again, the Newark club on her brain. Chills shimmied up her spine.

Just focus, Jana.

Okay, so the money would be less, but she, logistically speaking, couldn't afford to get to the City from Fort Lee every day, not with the traffic. And if anyone from her ER saw her on stage, well, that was just unthinkable. She calculated that as long as she got full shifts and lap dance priority in Newark, in four weeks' time, she could rake in thirty to forty grand, and that was based on figures from years ago. It was always safer to be conservative. From Thursday through Saturday, she'd have no problem pulling in two grand a night. Then, if she worked three weekday nights, she'd add another three to her weekly pot. Nine thousand a week. Yeah, thirty-two in the month would make a dent, combined with her savings and credit card advances. Oh, and she could try to sublet her apartment in SoHo while crashing at her folks' place here…*ugh*. Still, she could do this. She could stop this new boulder her parents had hurled at her from steamrolling their lives and her life along with it.

Finding the financial solution in her mind was only a dopamine rush for an instant, though, as her hand went up to her shirt collar, holding it closed, and closer to her skin from the thought of baring her body again to those men and their starving eyes.

The cabbie cleared his throat, bringing Jana out of her zone. The cab sat idle in the hospital portico for who knows how long. The driver's narrowed eyes glared at her in the rearview, showing his obvious readiness to move on with his shift, back to his own never-ending rat race, even though the meter was still ticking up every second she sat there.

She too had to get on with things. She stared at the bright white light shining through the hospital's automatic doors, which were opening and closing rhythmically, again and again, because the cabbie had pulled up too close to the damn sensor.

She began to gather her things as the driver's expression in the rearview willed her to move her ass.

Look, asshole, it's not like you aren't charging me for sitting here.

Being rushed to do something she resented and detested—and by this piece of shit!—made her jaw clench and her stomach cramp. She wanted to send Driver Dredge in to her parents, into the hospital, in to pay the damn hospital bill that was mounting every second, and then send him down to Newark after that to get naked and gyrate for an audience of horny assholes!

She took a few deep breaths, shot him back a look in his little mirror, and tossed a wad of crumpled ones over the divider. *For interrupting me and my procrastinating.*

She got out of the cab, and instead of helping with her bags, the driver only sat and straightened out the crumpled bills. Walking through the automatic doors, she glared over her shoulder one last time, only to catch the dickhead gawking at her ass through his passenger side window. She cringed while chills shot up her arms.

Get used to it, Jana. And fast.

She sighed long and hard, then continued on, weary and spent, dragging her baggage behind her.

CHAPTER 7

ER FATHER WAS asleep and her mother was glowering at her from her awkward fetal position in that armchair in the corner of the icy room. Jin had put on so much weight over the years, her fire hydrant stature made the chair look more uncomfortable than it probably was.

"Go home, Ma," Jana commanded in a hush.

Jin pushed herself out of the armchair's clutches and put up no argument.

"I sent the cab away because the driver wasn't nice. Ask the registration desk to call you another one."

Jin nodded, red-eyed and drained, but not too exhausted to mention before leaving, "The doctor asked about you, Jana. You should meet with him for a date."

"A date, huh? Ma, how about I meet with him about Daddy, here in this hospital room? Go home and sleep. And don't worry about the restaurant. I added 'until further notice' to the hanging 'Closed' sign, so you don't have to open for a few days, at least." Hoping in the end, she could still convince them to close permanently.

"Oh no, Jana, Daddy will never have that. I need to open every day. Every day! He made me promise."

"Jesus, Mom. You can promise all you want, but you can't function without him there, and from the looks of the place tonight, you can't count on the staff either. They don't give a damn. *I* wouldn't eat there in its current state." And she grew up eating the food cooked in that kitchen, never spotless-eat-off-the-floor of kitchens, but she'd never gotten sick. Now, though, *Jesus*. She wouldn't send Ilana Simon to eat at the place.

"Jana, you don't understand…we can't make our customers mad. They count on us."

"The numbers say that not too many people do count on you, Ma. And one or a dozen patrons, you don't want anyone to get sick, do you? The place needs some serious attention," Jana offered, wanting to shout at both her parents for how oblivious they were about their health code violations, their staff, and of course, their own finances! But she reeled herself in an instant later, seeing the hurt in her mother's eyes. "Look, your husband had a heart attack and open-heart surgery. Your customers will more than understand. It would even make them think bad of you if you didn't close for a few days."

"You can open the restaurant for me in the morning. After you get a few hours' sleep," Jin said too loudly; her father moaned and shifted, but didn't wake completely.

"Ma, the shop is closed today. You're sleeping, then coming back here to sit with Dad. I have a meeting tonight I have to go to."

"A meeting?" As if to say that a meeting of Jana's during this horrible tragedy was unimportant and maybe even inappropriate, while the woman was insisting that Jana open the damn sinkhole of a restaurant?

"Yes, Ma, unless *you* would like to find a mere two hundred thousand to *almost* cover this." Jana swept her arm out to show Jin the equipment-filled hospital room. "Isn't that what you asked me to handle last night? Because I am sure you didn't even think to ask Dane, right? Not for financial or even moral support?"

Jin shook her head, embarrassed maybe, or ashamed? Disgusted even? Or maybe just defensive? Both her parents still touted for her brother, even after everything he did to them, to her. "Dane and Alexa are having another baby. He can't be here. And they need the money for when the child arrives. You don't have children, Jana, so you couldn't understand."

Wow. When she thought her parents could not shock her further. Her brother was broke with another kid on the way? And that was her problem how? In the very few flings she'd had over the years, she'd used birth control. Had they heard of it?

But that wasn't her business. Apparently, what was her business, and her problem still and always, were her parents' problems, and they always all rested solely on her.

Maybe it was because she was the childless spinster who had all the time in the world to spin a few hundred grand out of thin air. The insanity; that was what hurt most. That her mother was completely serious, with not an ounce of awareness as to the sickness of her comment, of her mindset.

"Mom, you're exhausted. Go home. Rest." She attempted to sprinkle her words with sugary sweetness, but they turned out to be a powdery poison instead. Whatever. She needed the woman out of her face.

Jin picked up her purse in a slight huff and left, thankfully, without another word.

Jana folded herself into the chair her mother had made warm for her, and despite the ridiculousness of the hard arms and seat of the damn thing, and the maddening thoughts overrunning her blood-boiling mind, she fell asleep.

*

Antonio had told dispatch to ignore all of Jocelyn Carlson's future requests. And he'd deleted all of her lengthy and abusive voicemails from his company cell, too. *Pathetic.*

Now he had to prepare for a high-ticket replacement, or replacements. It would more than likely take a few better paying clients to make up for the loss of his one, but he had no choice. He wouldn't be able to live with himself if he crawled back to that depraved lunatic and her obscene displays, her oozing, deplorable melodrama.

Making the phone call to Jake Demonte would be somewhat easier to stomach than letting that wealthy, gold-digging whore back in his back seat.

Before Antonio had left his seaside town on the Pacific Coast of Mexico, he'd had a great cooperative arrangement with Jake Demonte. The man owned the largest gentlemen's club in Vallarta until, rumor had it, competing drug cartels had pressured him out for allowing one source over another to supply his club's patrons and dancers. It became too much of a hassle, and Jake owned a chain of other clubs that he could fall back on anyway in Florida, Jersey, and New York.

Antonio had made out well promoting and bringing new clientele to Jake's Vallarta club at the time. The kickbacks from Jake had actually funded Antonio's travel to New York.

But more than a good business co-op, Jake made it clear that he felt he owed Antonio. "You need anything when you're up there, Tone, anything at all, you call. You hear me? I still haven't forgotten what you did for my kid," he'd told Antonio before he'd left. Jake was referring to the time Antonio had pulled his son out of the way of a dumb-ass drunk in the club parking lot some ten years back. Antonio had been in the right place at the right time was all; anyone would've done the same.

But still, he did as Jake told him and didn't hesitate to call. He hadn't really had a choice after he was laid off by the Manhattan limo company, an inevitable next step after Michelle had slept with the owner of the damn outfit. Antonio had had nowhere else to turn. A proud Mexican man would never risk whatever vestige of pride that remained by calling on his family for help. His brother-in-law had already done enough by hooking him up with work papers and the New York connections.

Instead, he'd called Jake Demonte.

And when he had, the man hadn't hesitated to help him get out of the City and over to Jersey. Not only was Antonio's New Jersey limo license thanks to Jake's connections, but so was his access permit to the Newark International Airport and his first round of regular higher paying clients. The man also contributed to the down payment for his first owned limo and then financed everything else Antonio needed as his business grew. And Jake didn't gouge him with the interest rate on the loan, but he wasn't doing too badly for himself either. It was more or less a win-win, and Antonio knew it didn't have to be. Antonio needed Jake, not the other way around.

But Antonio, being the most prudent of the twelve Ruiz kids, knew to be careful and stopped asking for help for a good long while. Even though he knew Jake Demonte wasn't connected to any big-time Italian families, the bottom line was that the man had money and clout, which was all gotten by less than pristine means. He was just not a man Antonio wanted to get on the wrong side of.

And now, being in such close proximity to Jake's smallest club, The Wet Spot in industrial Newark, Antonio, ever-wary and a skeptic at heart, waited for Jake to call in favors as compensation. The credit for pulling his kid out of a car's path had to expire sometime, right? He'd worry and plan what he'd say. "Sorry, man, my trunk's too small for a dead body today." And he'd laughed it off each time.

Because Jake never did call for any other reason but to throw him Jake's own personal business when he had it. And Jake always paid him more than fairly. Antonio was very rarely surprised by people, but the strip club mogul had turned out to be an upstanding guy, one who happened to be in a super shady business.

And so now, after the sufficiently long hiatus on favor requests, he'd turn to Jake once again to help replace the money stream that was Jocelyn Carlson.

He took a deep breath then pressed Jake's personal cell number, really the only way to reach the man. It rang several times before the voicemail greeting came on, Jake's thick Jersey accent with the always-gruff tone: "Leave a message for Jake Demonte. Beep." The "*Beep*" was spoken. The message spelled out the man to a 'T,' Antonio thought.

"Hey, Jake, it's Antonio. Please call my cell when you get this. All is fine…just a quick question. Thanks." He didn't want to worry his financier. He didn't need Jake thinking the call was about him needing to miss a loan payment or anything like that. But he also didn't want to leave details that he wanted a lesser favor. More business.

Antonio looked down at his legal pad to add some figures, then he pinched the bridge of his nose. He was so damn close to his number, so close he could taste it. If only Jake would call back today and not next week or the week after that. Jake Demonte always came through, but *when* was often the question.

His cell rang, jolting Antonio out of his number-crunching zone.

"Tony, Jake Demonte. How you doin', son?"

Antonio put his pencil down and spun around in his desk chair to stare at his computer monitor with his target number as the screen's background. *Clear your mind.* "Jake, thanks for the quick call back. Good, I'm good, thanks. How are you? And the new club on the Island?"

"Behind fuckin' schedule, as construction always is. And with my kid on lead, Jesus Christ, don't get me started…he's a little blowhard wanting to fill my goddamn shoes after being out of school for only a few fucking months. And after I paid four years of college fucking tuition as high as my dick is long, what does he do?" The man paused for an answer to his rhetorical question.

But Antonio remained quiet.

"Well, I'll tell ya. He spends more of my money, for fuck's sake, that's what! On girls, coke, more girls! Says he's got a plan, an underground money river or some shit. Gonna get me and my clubs in trouble, Tone, that's what he's gonna do! Just unnecessary stress."

Antonio let Jake simmer a second. "God, Jake…sorry man. Dealing with family's gotta be tough."

"It is, it sure as fuck is. And I'll tell ya, I'll always be thankful to you pulling Johnnie to safety that time, Tone, but shit, maybe a nick here or there woulda done him some good. The ego on that kid, you know?" He snickered. "But on second thought, my ex woulda castrated me, so I guess I'm glad you didn't let him get a scratch."

"Yeah, man," Antonio said, laughing lightly and hoping like hell to end the discussion of the man's personal life as soon as humanly possible. The less he knew, the safer.

"But as for the new club, it'll come together. Just never as fast as you want."

"Sure, with anything, right?"

"With anything good, at least! So what's up, Tone? How can I help?"

"Well, I was calling to see if you needed me on anything major? I lost a big client, or more like, turned one away. I'm hoping to get my goal met, but I'm—"

"Still so damn focused. I never met someone as goal-oriented as you, Tone. Now if you'd just rub off on the kid. Damn his mother, spoilin' the shit outta 'im," the man mumbled, then came back on track. "Yeah, Tone, I'll see what I got. Absolutely. Maybe I can get my dad to swallow his damn pride, take some help. He's getting up there now, doctors and shit all the time. He shouldn't be behind a wheel, or behind a cane for that matter," the man said through his laughter. "Gimme some time, yeah?"

"God, Jake, thanks, man. I really appreciate it."

"Tone, listen, don't mention it. Will talk soon."

"Okay, Jake. Thanks again." And he ended the call.

He spun back around to his notepad. Based on the rate Jake had paid in past, he jotted some more figures. Maybe he'd get a few weekdays driving Jake's dad. That would fill the place of his lost nights with Jocelyn. And wouldn't cut into potential high-ticket money on a weekend night, especially with prom and wedding season here. That would be the way. It was no longer the three months he'd hoped for, but maybe six more months, and then he'd be done. Not bad. Definitely doable.

And then his cell rang again. That was quick, damn quick for Jake! He held his screen up to his glazed-over eyes after so much number crunching, and there on his screen was Michelle's image, with her bright eyes and wavy strawberry blonde hair, the photo he hadn't deleted, even though it'd been more than a damn year.

What the hell did she want?

CHAPTER 8

HIS SISTER CAME through the door, and the girls jumped up to greet her.

"I made enchiladas, still hot on the stove," Antonio called out to Celeste.

"Uh-oh," she cracked. His sister's authentic Mexican was nearly as amazing as their mother's had been, while Antonio's was less than stellar. "Thank you, brother! And thanks for picking up the girls again. God, the new manager keeps stopping me from leaving as I'm out the door. What would I do without you?" she said, freeing her hands of her groceries then kissing Antonio on the forehead.

He didn't want to start in on her again, but she'd left the topic wide open. "Why don't you rethink coming back with me then? Because, I don't know what you'll do without me either," he said in all seriousness. "You wouldn't have to work two jobs in Vallarta, or even one if you'd let anyone help you out—"

"Please, not again, Antonio." She shook her head at him, her eyes shifting to her three little girls. But the television was blaring, so he knew they couldn't hear a word. And he wasn't even close to being finished. "It wouldn't matter where in the world we were, I wouldn't take your money. Between you and Ray. And Isa...our baby sister, for Christ's sakes! I swear to God...I do have a shred of pride left."

"Fine, fine—no money. But in Vallarta, we'd all be there to help with the girls, at least. Your family, Celeste, is in Vallarta."

"I like it here. I want them to go to school here, and even, you know, get married here," she said as she began to put away the groceries.

Oh, so the girls were being geared to marry already, huh? They were only five, seven and nine! Talk about projecting, Jesus.

But for his logistical argument's sake, he steered away from anything to do with marriage, namely his sister's failed one. "You still want to stay here even though you're living in...this?"

She froze, hands full with boxes of crackers and cereal. "Hey, you watch it, Antonio José Ruiz. I've made a home out of 'this' and I won't have the girls hearing you say otherwise. When you have children, you'll understand."

He hadn't meant to insult her; he respected his older sister far too much, however stubborn she could be. And really, none of it was any of his business. He'd heard her undertone loud and clear. But it didn't mean he didn't have every reason to be concerned about her and the girls when he leaves because he really had thought she was coming back with him, and that she had only wanted the taste of America and nothing more.

"When Zack hooked us up with work visas and these contacts, we were just, you know, gonna make our money and head home. To where we belong...remember?"

"You may have thought that, but I had no idea what, or who, I'd find here, so I kept my mind open. And well...I like it here."

When Zack, Isa's husband, had offered his connections to any of Isabel's siblings for getting to and working in the US, Antonio had bitten. He'd, of course, wanted to crash through the financial ceiling he'd hit with his own limo business in Vallarta. A management position with a giant Manhattan operation would put him that much closer to his goal. But Antonio had always seen his move as a means to a financial end with a solid plan to return home.

Celeste had also jumped at the chance—for herself and for her girls. "The opportunity of a lifetime," she'd said. But she apparently meant the "lifetime" part more literally. The 'American Dream' and her chance at it had bitten her hard.

"'Liking' it here and 'thriving' here are two different things. And damn it, Celi, you're as stubborn as Mom was. I don't know why you won't accept even a little help?"

"I ask you for help all the time. You pick up the girls when I can't," she said, lifting her eyebrows at him. Then she continued to shove items in cupboards, murmuring and grumbling as she did.

"That's hardly help, Celi."

"It is, and that's all I want from you. You're my brother, not my goddamn husband. God, if I wanted to find a man, a father for the girls, I would."

Her words and tone were nonchalant, but he saw right through it. Hell, she'd been dressing as if she were on the hunt for a long while now, ever since Juan ran out on her. The asshole. What kind of man? The father of his nieces had left Celeste to raise three kids on her own, no financial support, no nothing. It was hard for Antonio to watch. His sister's struggle wrenched his heart.

"I'd worry about you and the girls here, Celeste." *With or without a man.* "Again, at least, in Vallarta, you'll have the family's support."

"You think I *need* a man, don't you? I can't survive without you or without Juan, right? Man's gotta bring the money, or there isn't any?"

"I didn't say that...Jesus! And that's not even the point." He shook his head at her. Her insecurities were leading to obvious defensiveness and goddamn idiotic statements. "The point is...you need a safety net...you have three little girls, Cel—"

"And those three little girls are mine. And they have a safety net...me! Money isn't everything, *hermano*! God, always with you...money, money, money!" She was now shoving groceries into the refrigerator in a frantic huff, unable to close the drawers and therefore, the door. "It's always your answer. But it doesn't solve anything. It always comes with strings, with a price, and I have my damn pride!" She paused, looked at her girls by the TV, obviously concerned that they'd heard her voice go as loud and shrill as it had.

"But if a man came along, taking money from him would be okay?"

She glared at him, a silent stare of death.

Damn it. He knew all too well what she had meant, making it on her own. Of course he knew, especially after reclaiming his pride from Jocelyn Carlson the other night. But there was also a time to ask for help like he had to do when he had been laid off two years ago from the Manhattan Limo operation, and now like he had to do to replace the lost revenue from Jocelyn Carlson. He'd had to tuck his tail and call in a favor.

"Sorry, Celi, but I want you to hear yourself. Remember what Juan did to you? I mean, I know you're strong and smart and an amazing mother and provider! But still, I worry, damn it. I worry. About the things out of your control, beyond money. Safety, security, health, yes?"

She shook her head, nostrils flared as she tried to regain composure. "You know what, Antonio, I worry about *you.* You've been obsessed, little brother. Your damn hyper-focus on your business, on the almighty dollar. Even putting off having a family? That worries *me.* I *have* kids! You're the one who's alone! Sorry, correction, you have your 'magic number' to keep you warm at night. Jesus, since you were six years old, nothing but your million-dollar mark! Only work, work, work…and never actually living! That's why Michelle went elsewhere—" She cut herself off, her face flushed immediately; she knew she'd crossed the line.

He glared daggers at his sister.

Who the hell was *she?* Juan had gone elsewhere, no sign, no word, leaving her with three kids. It'd been a totally different scenario with Michelle.

Michelle had known Antonio's dream. She had shared it, even. They had both wanted to keep nose to the grindstone until they were financially set, and then start their lives together, so she'd told him.

But, apparently, she'd lied. Michelle was slightly more zealous than he was, and obviously, a lot less loyal. She'd found a much quicker route to being *set.* Without Antonio, and with his boss, the well-off owner of NYC Limousine Service.

He shook the thought out of his head because, a few days ago, Michelle had called him. Wanting to talk. Needing to see him. Alone.

A surge of memories came to him when he'd answered her call. Hearing her voice sent chills through him in mixed sensations that threw him for a loop. But once the vibration settled in him, he knew the fact of the matter was that he'd loved her when they'd gotten married, and he couldn't help but love her still.

And if, maybe, hopefully, Michelle regretted what she'd done, saw the light, wanted him back, that fact would push him to consider the possibility of *them* again. Because his love for Michelle went well beyond his pride and far beyond himself.

And it fit. He'd seen in the paper a few weeks back that she wasn't with Gerald Simon, the prick had stayed with his wife, how lucky for Mrs. Simon. There was a picture of them arm in arm at some charity event. What a goddamn joke.

And, no, he wouldn't tell Celeste that he was meeting Michelle for dinner later that very night. He wouldn't and couldn't tell Celeste any of it because he wasn't prepared for the judgment in his older sister's eyes.

And he had to go meet Michelle or he'd regret losing this second chance for the rest of his life.

*

He regained his composure from Celeste's comment and focused on what the heart of the damn conversation had been—his supposed greed, was it?

"So, because I won't have kids the way Mom and Dad had kids, I'm a greedy bastard? You think it'd be way better to just pop 'em out without resources, no savings of any kind? And our parents didn't have just one or two of us with no proper home to raise us in. No, Celi, they had twelve. Twelve helpless dependents!"

"Hush! *Ay Dios Mio*, Antonio."

He lowered his volume as directed. "Don't you remember what it was like? God, a doctor's visit was called for only if there was blood out the ears."

"Don't be so dramatic."

He shook his head. It didn't matter. She could be in denial all she wanted. He knew. He remembered.

"I want to be secure first. That's my prerogative, and it's not selfish."

She paused in the kitchen and came over to the couch. "God, Antonio, I know you're anything but selfish. And…I didn't mean to bring her up. I really didn't."

He didn't say anything. What was there to say?

"Listen, I don't even know what we're fighting about, anyway. I admire your goal, and I admire your work ethic. Always have. And I know you're doing it for your future, your family's future. It's also okay that we, how do they say, agree to disagree? You know, with how we lead our own lives…yes?"

He still remained silent. He knew from his thirty-five years as Celeste's slightly younger brother to always let her have the last word. Any attempt at the alternative was pointless.

So he nodded as his phone vibrated in his pocket. He pulled it out to check whom the text was from.

A message from dispatch: *A certified package came in. From an NYC law firm.* His eyes kept on the text message for a reread. And another.

"Hey, you okay? Your left eye is squinting. You do that when you're pissed off about something."

"Yeah, no, I'm fine." He dismissed her analysis. "But I should get going." Because he didn't want his sister drilling him further, and he needed to calm his nerves in order to combat or surrender to the gut feeling making him nauseous and lightheaded at the same time.

Breathe.

"Okay." She stood up to give him a hug. "And hey," she said at his shoulder in her tighter than usual embrace, "whether we agree or not, you'll always be my pain-in-the-ass brother, from down the road or from another country, okay?" She released him from her hold and smiled warmly at him.

He smirked at her. Celeste was stubborn as hell, but she was family. Always family.

He put his phone back in his pocket. From the corner of his eye, he noticed his oldest niece practicing her kicks in front of the television.

"Tania, please back up from the TV. If you're not careful, you're gonna kick right through the darn thing."

Around his self-imposed and constant work schedule, being their uncle and their martial arts instructor was his joy, a peek into the future family he couldn't wait to have for himself. They were, in essence, his daughters by proxy, and he worried about the three little girls. Why wouldn't he? When he returned to Vallarta in what he hoped would be just a few months' time—knock on wood—his nieces wouldn't even have their *Tio* Antonio, their only male constant. Then Celeste would date some asshole that couldn't give a shit for them.

Antonio, don't think about it. They're not yours anyway.

"*Tio*, what is it? You look sad," Tania asked, coming toward him for a hug goodbye. Was his previous thought written all over his face? Kids were so damn smart. So intuitive.

It occurred to him then, what the hell was he rushing off for? To see what a Manhattan attorney had sent him? He was still trying to ignore his gut, which was telling him plenty about what the package contained. Or was he leaving then to get ready for dinner with Michelle? The woman hadn't treated him like goddamn family when she'd screwed his boss. And for how long really, he'd never know. Michelle wasn't the woman, the wife, the best friend, or partner he'd been so damn sure she was.

All while his family, his real family stared doe-eyed at him here and now. Celeste's girls, his nieces, were pure unconditional love. Michelle, on the other hand, maybe, probably, wasn't even worth a second glance, let alone a second thought.

He placed his cell and car keys on the side table next to the sofa. "*Vamos niñas,* shut the tube off, let's see those ax kicks...all of you...*ariba, ariba.*" He wrangled the other two girls up from the floor, pulled a pillow off the couch, and knelt down to their level. On cue, they lined up single file, even the five-year-old Laura knew the drill, mini-fists up in fighting position at her face. Their yells of "K'ya!" made his heart and chest swell. He winked and nodded at each of his nieces as they kicked up straight to the ceiling and down hard and strong through the pillow. Exactly the way he had taught them.

Yeah, he was in no hurry to leave them. No hurry at all.

Jana's mother didn't get to the hospital until 4:15 PM because, yes, she'd opened the restaurant, despite Jana's advice. What did it matter? Nothing would change. And Jana would have to hold her tongue about the finances of the restaurant for at least a few more days, waiting until her father stabilized. Let them play pretend until then.

And thinking about playing pretend, her father was, in fact, like a damn child. The force feedings of "healthy hospital slop" for breakfast and lunch were nothing compared to his behavior toward the staff. His rudeness toward the nurses was what really put her over the top. By the time her mother showed up, she had reached her limit. And her plan to attack her overwhelming dread about heading down to Newark had worked; Jana was motivated to be anywhere else in the world but in that hospital room, with the people who had given birth to her, even if the 'anywhere' was her old strip club.

CHAPTER 9

H E'D GROWN UP in a spiritual country, his superstitious, ritualistic, colorific Mexico.

So when his thumb bled from the thin paper cut given to him by the golden envelope, and then, at that exact same moment, his cell phone rang loudly from his pocket, he didn't wonder who it was, what the contents of the envelope were, or whether any of it was leaning toward good or bad news. He already knew. An hour before he was to meet with Michelle for dinner, alone, he already goddamn knew.

"Did you—"

"Open it? No, Michelle. Not yet." But again, did he really need to? The damn thing had already sliced him, maybe he should burn the fucking papers.

"I told the attorney not to send it. I was bringing it with me so I could explain, but his secretary..." she trailed off, probably knowing none of what she blathered mattered anymore.

So he stayed silent. She didn't deserve his words anyway, not to cushion her guilt, not to ease her conscience.

"He left his wife for me. I want to marry him, Antonio. And, well, we've put the inevitable off for far too long."

Inevitable? She'd been calling them "separated" for all this time. Why?

And how could he have let her infiltrate his already-cracked heart again? To think he'd even considered taking her back when he thought—hoped—she was meeting him to reconcile rather than to soften the blow of divorce papers. Either way, what the hell had he been thinking?

Those backstabbing cowards, Gerald-fucking-Simon and Michelle both. They deserved each other. They fucking deserved each other.

And thank God for small favors now. All the money in the world wouldn't have cushioned the blow if he and Michelle had already started their family and *then* Michelle chose to betray him. Slaughtering his heart *and* their kids'. Just, thank God.

"Antonio, please…"

"Goodbye, Michelle." He hung up and shut his phone off with his still-bleeding thumb. As if in slow motion, he pressed her out of his life. And the blood smear left on the home button was a perfect remnant of her, just goddamn perfect.

*

On her way to the bus station, Jana had the cab stop at a down-home mockery of a department store so she could buy and change into a cheap skirt suit. She grabbed a knock-off perfume at the register too. Hell, who needed a shower anyway? After all, she was diving back into the pit of despair; after one foot inside the club, she knew she'd want a full-on, high-pressure disinfecting shower.

God, this entire thing is awful.

*

Her bus ride down to the Newark club was a blur. Her defense mechanisms had kicked in, keeping her brain calm. And having her thumbnail stabbing into the pad of her index finger helped yet again. She stared straight ahead, content to be in the numb zone between the hospital and the club. Lingering in limbo, a respite, however short-lived.

Because it was when she caught the cab from the bus station to the club that her breathing quickened, and her palms got moist. Her finger no longer feeling any pain, she bit her bottom lip instead with such force that in only minutes, she tasted blood. In the pit that was her purse, not a single tissue. She caught sight of a tissue box in front of the driver's console.

"Excuse me? May I have a tissue please?" she asked looking in the rear-view at the orange-mustached driver, Ryan Duffy, or so read his badge hanging above the radio.

With an indiscreet eye roll toward the road ahead, he handed the box back to her. She took three, gave him a close-lipped thank you, and then dabbed her lip clean, glad she'd caught it before it had gotten on her white outfit. She balled up the tissue into one of the clean ones, and, finding no trash bag at her disposal, decided to place it in her purse rather than trouble Ryan Duffy again. And when she looked back up, straight ahead the sign for The Wet Spot filled her view. They were there.

She checked herself in the rearview mirror around Ryan's glares, and she quickly applied a thin coat of nude-colored gloss, smacked her lips, happy that the cut wasn't visible, and then she closed her eyes to reset her increasingly panicked nerves.

Jana did a final smooth over of her hair then outfit as they pulled into the parking lot of her old stomping ground. The slightly seductive, yet professional—for a strip club—polyester skirt suit was snug enough to show Eddie she was still in great shape.

"Well, Mr. Duffy, wish me luck…"

But he didn't. So she took the four-leaf clover hanging from his rearview as a sign of luck and then filled his upturned hand with his fare plus tip. Not the friendliest guy, but not a jerk like last night's cabbie. And anyway, she felt it was good karma to give Ryan Duffy his due since she was heading back into the industry where the dollar bill is king.

She got out of the cab as Jana Park, and headed for the club's main entrance as 'Winter Snow,' her long-abandoned stage name.

From the first tap of her high heels against the glossy black tile floor inside the club, a chill rose up her arms to her shoulders, then to the nape of her neck. Crossing her arms, sliding her hands over her goose bumps for warmth, she approached the bouncer. She shook her head, remembering how cold they kept it inside. "The lower the temperature, the harder the nipples," Eddie had told her once. "That's how the club's patrons like their sundaes, with rock hard cherries on top."

CHAPTER 10

"JOHNNIE, SORRY TO bother you, man, but this ex-dancer is here looking for Eddie…" Switched to a whisper, slightly muffled, like his hand was over the phone, "But she looks kinda professional-like. Selling something maybe? Like insurance or wine?" Then he raised his voice again. "You wanna see her? She says her name is Winter."

Winter? Johnnie froze. Then he turned to the surveillance monitor at the corner of his desk, clicked on camera one, the main door, and enlarged it to full screen.

He watched the screen, her luscious lips moving to answer his bouncer, Brandon, while he could hear her voice through Brandon's phone. Johnnie realized he'd never heard her speak all those years ago. Her tone was confident and almost melodic, a well-spoken goddess.

"Yeah, Winter Snow. Eddie knows me. I transferred to the club in the City about five years ago. Amber and Charlene were with me here for three years before that."

"She was at the—"

"I heard the answer, Brandon," Johnnie said, quickly straightening his desk of the piles of financials and blueprints and remnants of white powder, then toggled the surveillance monitor back to the thirty-two-camera view on the screen. He chugged the rest of his water and tossed a few mints into his mouth. "Have Erin bring her up."

He watched the screen as Winter made her way through each camera shot. The long, flowing black hair he remembered was pinned up in a messy bun, her firm yet voluptuous backside swayed in a little professional skirt, and her maintained physique made the outfit. Then her face; those cat eyes were to die for, not to mention her glossy lips, plump and lush. Picturing them around his cock got him steel hard in an instant.

And he remembered her lower lips too, fuck yes he did. Spread and pumping to the pounding beat on stage. And how she dominated the pole, like no other dancer could. And in his dreams, his hard cock was her pole, her luscious folds encompassing every last inch of his steel. Oh God, how her cunt still glistened in his fantasies, even after all these years, since his wet dream teens to now, as a full-grown and always hungry man.

He took his eyes off the cameras for a second to scan the office. A bit OCD, everything had to be sharp, straight, set. His wall, his shelves, the tech and wires, his filing cabinets, they were all as he needed them to be.

But what was that on the couch? *Shit!*

Johnnie took three huge steps toward the brown leather loveseat that was catty-cornered to his desk and pulled the start of something hot pink and lacy out from between the cushions; a thong left by who knows who as there were too many to count, all a blur really. He tossed the thong back behind the ancient sofa and sprang back to his desk chair. Shifting his body for a more natural and relaxed pose, he felt his piece lodged in his rear waistband. *Shit!* He pulled it out, quickly placed the small pistol in his desk drawer and re-tucked his shirt as the knock sounded on his office door.

"Yes, come on in." His feet were consciously planted on the floor. He tugged his black muscle tee down taut over the abs he'd worked his ass off for, and then placed both palms on the desk, ready to stand up for the woman of his fucking dreams.

"Hey, Johnnie," Erin purred sweetly through the partially opened door, hiding his guest behind her. "A visitor for Eddie."

Johnnie smiled his thanks as he rose, already hearing the usual underlying cattiness in Erin's raspy cigarette-riddled voice. It happened anytime a new girl came in, even if she wasn't competing for the same job. Even the scent of a chance for a semi-hot bartender like Erin to move up to the stage or a back room, and the unbelievable monetary increase that came along with it, brought the kitties' claws out.

The club girls' cutthroat and vindictive games came with the territory, he just never played into it. He didn't have time for that shit, not while his father had him overseeing the new club's construction on Long Island and running this place since Eddie had left. Or rather, since he had the douche ushered out for taking too big a piece of Johnnie's drug action, told his father to use him as his own personal bitch boy or something.

But Johnnie knew that at the new club and at this older club—hell, any and all strip joints for that matter, whether it was high-ticket vag or low-end pussy, Johnnie had learned from his father that all the club kitties were the same.

Except, that is, for Winter Snow. As far as Johnnie's years of observing went, Winter was worlds apart from the rest.

"Thanks, Erin," he said, wanting her to make her exit already so he could see his target in person, his gorgeous, unknowing guest.

CHAPTER 11

WINTER'S IMAGE HAD been branded into his memory. He'd been a fifteen-year-old volcano of hormones when he'd first set eyes on her. Picking up the weekend's revenues every Sunday with his dad at their chain of strip clubs had been an amazing, mind-blowing privilege. No. Not a privilege. A right. Repayment. Yeah, his absentee dad had owed him. Johnnie'd been raised by his mother while his father had spent Johnnie's entire childhood in Tampa, Miami, and Puerto Vallarta, the Demonte flagship clubs at the time. But when his father moved back up to Jersey to bring the family's northeastern venues up to par, that was when Johnnie not only got his father back, but he got a magical, eye-popping, and much-deserved key to heaven too.

And it didn't take Johnnie beyond the first visit to his dad's Newark club for him to discover what his type was, his hot spot. Winter was it. And it wasn't just an Asian thing, no. Top to bottom and everything in between, it was a *Winter Snow* thing. She was unique. It was the way she moved, rode the poll, handled the screaming dicks at the stage's edge, and how she kept herself clean and pristine. No other girl had ever compared to her or what she did to him.

Erin turned on her heel to leave, almost knocking right into Winter, but she spun around again. "I almost forgot, do you need the bar levels from me? I can bring 'em up…after your visitor leaves," Erin said with one lifted brow.

"I'll come downstairs when I need them." An awkward silence followed. Johnnie's meaning: leave, now.

Erin shrugged and tightly circled Winter as she headed back downstairs. *Now kitty, play nice.*

Winter was finally left standing in his office doorway as incredibly sexy, sensual, and reserved as he remembered her. God, he could feel his hard-on throbbing to life again, within a moment of seeing her.

*

"Sorry to show up like this, but I was looking for Eddie? Eddie Cardell?"

She obviously didn't recognize Johnnie. He didn't blame her, but he had hoped.

Johnnie came out from around the desk to shake her hand in introduction, not caring if his erection bulged in his jeans. God, he hoped she saw how hard he was for her.

He took her hand in his while his left hand ushered her in with a delicate brush at her lower back. "You probably don't remember me," he said smiling evenly. "I'm Johnnie Demonte. My father, Jake, is the owner of—"

"Oh, wow," she said with her head cocked slightly. "You're not a teenage boy anymore...God, not at all." She laughed as her cheeks went from café latté to cherry red in a heartbeat.

Oh, yes, he liked that. He liked her...and the start of their first real conversation.

"So, you are running the show for your dad now?"

"I guess when Eddie left, my dad looked to me. With my MBA and the blood ties, he trusted I could handle things. I'm here *and* overseeing the build-out of a new club on the Island while my dad's doing some renovations at The Manhattan Sweet Spot."

He smiled proudly. God, it was unbelievable that she was there, in front of him, within arm's reach, and he was able to impress her, blow her mind. And God, would he ever blow her fucking mind.

"Busy man..."

"Yeah," Johnnie smiled, catching himself staring at her pout, wanting to take the mere two steps toward her and bite down. "I remember—oh, here. Please, sit down and make yourself comfortable. I remember you. You were a goddamn legend on this stage. And I even caught you at The Sweet Spot a time or two," he lied. He'd practically lived there after she'd transferred over. "It was so slammed, and they were all there for you. My father even remembers you for Christ's sakes. With four clubs and counting."

She smiled, her eyes down toward the floor. She was modest, fucking bashful almost. How he would pound that sweet shyness right out of her and make her scream for more. Yes, for him, she'd say and do sinful, dirty things. He would make that happen, no doubt in his mind.

Her voice woke him from his mental lusting. "You're sweet. I actually really needed that, being out of the scene for so long. I mean, I'm an ER nurse now. I can't believe I'm even here." He watched her eyes close softly as she paused her words. A heavy, jagged breath followed. Something was wrong. It was as if she was there against her will. Desperate. Of course, all the girls who come in were desperate to a point. But this was a professional woman back for more. What trouble was she in?

And how could he use that to his advantage?

"Hey, can I offer you a bottled water?" He sprang from her side to the mini-fridge by the sofa, not even waiting for a nod in response. He just had an urge to get her comfortable, nourished, taken care of. Maybe in lieu of ramming her senseless with pleasure beyond measure, this was all he could do while he waited for that opportunity. He'd have to be patient. Extremely subtle and patient.

"Here you are." Then he returned to his relaxed stance against the front of his desk. "If you don't mind me saying, you look a little upset. What can I do to help?"

She smiled a thank you then took a huge breath in. Then, on the out-breath, she said, "I came to see Eddie about getting on the schedule." Then she took a swig of the water he'd given her, her luscious mouth circling the rim of the bottle, distracting him for a second, but he quickly returned his full attention to her statement.

"Part-time?"

"No, full-time, every shift you can throw me, but especially the peak weekend nights, of course." She maintained eye contact with him now, as if getting over the initial hurdle had allowed her to move into an all-business mode. God, he liked this side of her, too.

"But your schedule must be crazy, being a hospital RN. How would you be able to juggle both?"

"I had to take leave at my position at the ER at Manhattan Metro. My father had a heart attack last night, up in Fort Lee." She stopped there and looked up at the ceiling as if she was holding back tears. And, from his take, maybe considering how much more she should tell him. God, he couldn't wait to have her in his bed, telling him everything there was to tell. He would give it two weeks tops before he had his fantasy fulfilled.

"God, I'm so sorry. And he's…recovering? Your dad?"

"Yes, he'll be home by late next week." She looked down at her hands. "Hopefully, that is. Hopefully, this will have scared him enough to change his habits, but in the meantime, I need to get a fast influx of cash for their bills. Long story, but I've gotta…." She paused there and swallowed back hard.

Oh Lord have mercy, his cock was raging for her.

She cleared her throat and continued, "I've gotta get back in the rotation for a month…six weeks tops."

Leaning on his desk, only inches from her seat, and inhaling her essence, a mix of exotic perfume he couldn't name, summer sweat, oh God help him, and a hint of some floral shampoo. He was taken.

His mind was whirling. Having her dance at his club, the club he now ran, was a dream come true and a nightmare at the same time.

The dream of her coming back into his club, being near her every night and in his office, his private office, was surreal. The opportunity to get her the way he wanted her, it overwhelmed his senses.

But the thought of her dancing there on his stage for other men and in the private rooms, her grinding their hard-ons, them always pushing for more, men other than him, he felt hot daggers of jealousy stabbing at him from within, even before he'd made her his. His skull was screaming from a new pressure headache, and he almost couldn't catch his breath.

He would have died to have her dance for him, though. But only ever for him.

He moved around to his desk chair in a flash, now sitting across from her, leaning into her over the tidy desk surface. He had a mind for this, formulating quick and dirty strategies to get to his ultimate wants and needs, a chess player with the wide angle and the patience to think it all through. He'd never admit that he ran the largest gambling ring his Ivy League campus had ever known, and he hadn't ever even needed the money. It was just fun for him. He was proud but smart enough not to brag his way into a hole.

He could tell she was desperate, but also, she obviously dreaded the thought of dancing again. She needed money, as they all did. But he would rather pull directly from his family's funds and give her whatever amount she needed than to know she was this close to him and stripping for the fuckers downstairs. And giving them lap dances. Fuck no!

He could easily afford any debt she might have. His father had all but given him the keys to the empire. But Johnnie sensed her pride. It was painted on her face like a diehard rooting for the underdog at the Super Bowl. So, no, he couldn't just offer her money straight out. He'd more than insult her that way. He could tell that she wouldn't be under any man's thumb, not consciously anyway. Even if he offered her a loan, she'd be skeptical.

Yeah, she had become a nurse, and she must have done well in nursing school to have landed a spot at that Manhattan ER while working at his family's city-based club full-time. No, she was a proud, strong, smart woman. Ambitious, too.

And she was not meant to be stripping.

She was meant to be on a throne, on a throne next to his, so help him.

*

He watched her eyes study the wall behind his desk, clad with his college degrees, his sports paraphernalia, and a few obligatory family photos.

She smiled and shook her head. "Groomed for this business, I see." She eyed the shot with him and his dad in front of the family's club in Puerto Vallarta on the Pacific Coast of Mexico. Sold a couple years back, much to his disappointment. He loved Vallarta. Pure paradise. Gorgeous pool of women from all over the world. But the Demontes didn't venture down there anymore, for safety reasons.

"Yeah, I was six or seven in that shot. My father's version of a family vacation for him and me. Three weeks every summer." He smirked. "I've definitely known the club scene all my life, despite my mother's best efforts. They divorced when I was five. My mom kept me pretty sheltered. She was hell-bent on my life being a hundred and eighty degrees from my father's."

"And here you are." She smiled and tilted her head in question, as if challenging him and flirting with him at the same time. *Yum.*

"Well, Eddie left my dad in a lurch. My mother is raging pissed but, you know, he's my dad. I'm not gonna leave him stranded."

She nodded like she genuinely understood. She searched his eyes for something, then said, "Eddie was a good manager, at least from the girls' perspective. I tried calling him, but his number is disconnected. Was he okay when he left?"

"Not really sure of the details," he lied and aimed to veer away from the subject, "but you know what, Dad was always too busy with the clubs to spend much time with me during my summer visits, so joining the business now, it's a second chance for us." Another lie. They hated each other, but money was a type of bond, right?

"I can imagine. And it's a man's dream come true, right? Strip club crown prince," she said, teasing and obviously testing him.

She had no idea that it was really when he saw *her* dance that he thought he'd died and gone to heaven. The others, they were old loose pussy that he had way too easy access to. But Winter was a refreshing kind of different. No, celestial-bodies different. And a lofty challenge to boot.

"Stopping in at each of his clubs when I was a teenager, yeah, I'm not going to lie, that was pretty awesome for any hormonal little shit, but now it's just the same old thing. For me, helping out now, Dad needing me and wanting me around, that's the high. And I get to see my father in action, you know? I think he's proud to have me with him, too." Johnnie paused, thinking about the times Jake had introduced him to some of the high-end clientele, to managers, and to some of the girls as, "My son." The feeling still sent chills up his spine. But he knew it was just surface bullshit. Most of the rest of the time Jake Demonte second-guessed him and berated the shit out of him. Bottom line, his father only cared about himself and, well, the club's bottom line.

So Johnnie had decided a while back to follow in his father's footsteps. And his bottom line had been to rake in the cash to buy pussy—a whole lot of pussy. But now, his eye was on Winter, and only Winter. She was his bottom line reanalyzed.

"And as for my mom, even though her worst fear was realized—*dun, dun, dunnn*—I'm still really close with her," he added for Winter's benefit. In truth, he hadn't seen or spoken to her in months. "God, I'm sorry. I'm rambling on and on, boring you to death probably," he ended, feeling his cheeks heat up. But he knew from the glint in her eyes that she was already becoming more relaxed, more comfortable. Per his plan, her mental checklist was being ticked off one item at a time: smart, educated, supportive of his family despite abandonment issues, and lastly, he cared about his mother.

"I thought you looked too young to remember me at all," she smiled, obviously fishing for his exact age.

"I'm twenty-four," he informed her. "I took a year off from school to do the obligatory Europe thing. I hated it, though. I was embarrassingly homesick," he lied again. He'd actually fucked his way around Italy twice before even calling his mother to tell her that he had landed on the continent alive in the first place.

"Europe, huh? Pretty lucky."

"I would have liked it better if I'd had someone to share the experience with, but that leads to another totally crappy topic. I've recently boycotted dating. My college girlfriend got really close with our econ professor behind my back. Again, too much information, sorry." He shook his head at himself. That last part was true. His econ professor, Dr. Madeline Sands, was a fine and fit cougar with a taste for young freshmen girls. And Janey, the freshman he'd been fucking, apparently needed a better grade, so she went about licking their professor's cunt good and clean. Then she introduced Johnnie for fun. He ended up taking them both together in her private office. Repeatedly.

"You're fine." Winter giggled. She was melting. Melting from the top down. "I'm sorry about your ex."

"You live and learn. I guess more than anything, I'm in sore need of someone to talk to." He smirked. Talking to the dancers at all was never high on his list of priorities. Talk was cheap. Action, well, he was addicted to action.

"We all need to vent," she said, then her eyes drifted down to her lap, confirmation to him that she kept her cards close to her chest. Her business was hers alone, and that suited him fine. For now.

"But here *you* are, your father sick and all, and you're sitting here sweetly listening to my dribble! You know, you always stood out to me as a real genuine sweetheart and too gorgeous to even hope to speak to. Even if my father had introduced me, I would've choked on my words." He smiled. "And I don't want to embarrass you, but"—he looked down at his hands then back up to her eyes—"the first time I saw you dance, you really took my breath away. You were in your own world; you danced for yourself. Untouchable."

He watched her eyes shift, unwilling to meet his, her cheeks redder now. And to keep from scaring her off, he added, "You know, not like the melodramatic aggression that most girls put out there on stage."

She raised her eyebrows. "Yeah, thank you. I'm verifiably horrible with compliments and attention. Ironic, I know." And she looked down at her purse again.

"Well, listen, Winter…" He looked down at his calendar. "For dancers…I have a full schedule for the next few months. It's because of the renovations happening at The Sweet Spot." He paused, noting her solemn look, more than disappointed, bordering on distraught even.

Now he would ride in on his horse. "But I have something else in mind for you. Not sure if you'd be interested, but I've been lacking something here, and I realize now what it is."

CHAPTER 12

S
HE WAS INTRIGUED by the man in front of her and by his
impending words before he even spoke them.

This clean-cut, baby-faced prep was playing gatekeeper for her reentry into the sultry underground she deplored. It was a little, well, a lot, too weird. At least in her years in the clubs, sleazebags were sleazebags. But Johnnie Demonte seemed different.

She watched his face, his innocent blue eyes searching hers. The subtle and sexy stubble above his soft red lips made her toes tingle. An immediate tinge of regret followed. Then those full lips of his parted as if ready for some idea, some proposal to fall out of them.

"You can consult. Build my team of girls. Hire and fire. But most importantly, train. No one worked the pole the way you did, and you're obviously as fit as you've ever been. You might be my secret weapon, Winter Snow. With you finding, filtering out, and working with the dancers, I bet we pull in numbers that blow the Manhattan club out of the water! And you'd get my Long Island girls prepped too."

Was he serious with this? Because he sounded serious. Passionate almost.

He sat across from her, his eyes drilling into hers, waiting while looking very pleased with himself. What was his motivation here? Eager to prove something to his father? Maybe, from the ambitious tone in his delivery. And she knew that fruitless desire all too well.

At the same time, she thought maybe he was just being kind. Could it be that he pulled this idea out of his ass to help her out? It was possible. Definitely possible, hearing his backstory. A fellow stranded soul.

And, yes, during their talk up to that point, he had been pretty bad about hiding his infatuation for her from years back. His body language said what his words had not. His nervous eagerness and his sweet, yet intensely sensual and searing looks.

But he'd also shown an unmistakable and honest concern for her, a sensitivity to her state of mind. Not that she hid her despair from being back in the sewer very well at all, but he seemed to give a shit. And hell, most owners or managers would have groped a tit to "make it all better" and moved on with their day.

And anyway, if nothing else, she had always been good at reading people. And she hadn't read this type of guy. Not in the clubs, for sure.

Then he comes up with this plan, this alternative for her? A potentially soul-freeing way to dig herself and her folks out of the new hole they had tossed her in, for dead, buck naked.

Johnnie had offered her a way, clothed and with her pride somewhat intact.

She wasn't blind. Again, she saw the raw desire in his eyes, still peering into hers. Even as she sat and thought. But it was different than the degrading, lust-filled hunger of the stage-side gawkers. It was more of an intimate fascination that filled Johnnie's gaze. And this pretty boy had access to the absolute hottest women in the Tri-state area because of his father, so she discerned that for Johnnie, getting into her pants wasn't the goal, at least not the main one.

If he wanted anything from her, it was obviously an ear to listen. And she didn't mind that. Actually, she had turned into such a bottled-up introvert, she kind of liked his outpouring about some pretty personal things she didn't ask to know about. She hadn't realized that she'd ever missed that aspect of a man's company. And really, she'd never had it before, never knew it was possible. And that she craved it was an even bigger surprise.

Johnnie was a few years younger than her and maybe worlds more innocent, but maybe not. She couldn't quite tell. But his sweet look and demeanor and his youth made her feel a rush of heat from deep within her core. Unwarranted. Completely against her code. God, was she craving…him?

No. It was hormones and emotions and stress and loneliness. That was all.

Because she had always been turned off by club guys, whether they were gawkers or staff, or management, especially Eddie. But, Jesus, the strip club king's own son? Him and his deep blue eyes, framed by thick, mile-long lashes that any dancer would die for. There, just staring at her.

Again, *no*! If it ever went there, she'd be stooping as low as Ilana in her ER for Christ's sake. Lower, in fact. Messing around with her employer in the industry she absolutely detested!

But now he was giving her an out, a real chance. Beyond the heat in her core, it was warming her goddamn heart. *Remember, Jana, this is not why you came here. Far fucking from it.*

Johnnie lightly cleared his throat, gently bringing her back. God, how long had she been in her own world? She blushed as he leaned forward in his desk chair. "I would compensate you well. If this idea works to reinvigorate this club's revenue stream and jumpstarts the new club in Merrick, well, hell…you'd more than deserve a healthy compensation package, but what do you feel is fair?"

Really? He was asking her? This really was too good to be true. Or was it?

"You look shocked," he said.

"I'm…yeah, a little taken aback. And…you know, my dad taught me that the one who names their price first always loses." She smirked.

But he kept his steady stare, silent and patient. And the corners of her mouth turned down because he was obviously going to make her name her price, no doubt.

So think, and do it fast.

*

She needed forty grand in combination with her credit cards and all, but really, at the end of the day, upward of two hundred thousand, if she were zooming out at the horrid nightmare. But she couldn't ask him for that much, for what she really needed.

I need time.

"I, uh, should probably think about it—the salary that is. But the position sounds…like something I could take on," she said, hiding her enthusiasm as best she could.

Because training, mentoring lost girls, lost like she'd been at eighteen, actually sounded okay, manageable. No, better than that. She could pay it forward…for Charlene.

Charlene's voice flooded her mind, her dear friend's firm words on her first night out on stage so many years ago.

Most veterans don't teach the newbies; they sabotage them. Jana knew she had been damn lucky. Char had saved her life a few times over, well beyond saving her ass on stage her first week. Char had been mother, sister, protector and true friend through to the end of their time at the Newark club before they'd parted ways—Jana to school and the club in the City, and Char to Vegas.

Johnnie's idea was much more than saving her from peeling down for the money she needed. Much, much more.

"I'm glad you like the idea. I might've suggested bartending, or even managing the place for me so I could expedite the new club's opening on the Island, but the same money wouldn't be there for you. And, selfishly"—he smirked—"I like the idea of working with you. Near you." He blushed and looked down at his hands.

She felt flushed herself and somewhat flattered. She changed the subject for both their sakes. "God, I don't think I could manage this place, anyway. In this business, a man is better at the helm," she said. She was smart. She knew the double standard all too well. And knowing was half the battle.

He nodded. "In most cases, but if there was a woman who could run this place, it'd be you," he said in a serious tone.

She appreciated the vote of confidence, but seriously?

"You've seen me dance, conquer a pole, sure. But I've never had to deal with the crap I know Eddie had to handle, and now you probably get to deal with on a daily."

Plus, at just over five feet tall, her stature didn't physically or psychologically lend itself to managing a venue like this. And another negative, she had a temper that could ignite a small propane plant. The club clientele alone could set her off if she had to deal with drunk, horny pricks 24/7, guys trying to push the limits with the girls. She'd get the place sued a few times over. As a nurse in Manhattan, she'd stood her ground during some pretty heavy ER clashes, but that was nothing in comparison to the shit she knew went down in a strip club.

"I saw you push your seven-inch spiked heel into the chest of a brute football player when he wouldn't let go of another girl on stage. You have balls. I've seen it firsthand." His eyebrows lifted as if to punctuate his point.

But his gaze didn't falter after that.

God, she swore he'd leap across the desk at her there and then, just by the look in his eyes. She grinned through the awkwardness, then he shook his head as if breaking a spell he was under. Her cheeks got hot. She should cut this off. Like, now.

*

Why could nothing be simple?

It is Jana. So simple. She just had to iron out the details and leave. Get in and get out. She could not, absolutely could not, let a male distraction enter her world right now.

"I really should get back to my father." *And catch up on sleep…in the hospital room armchair again.* Oh, that armchair. God, the thought of it made her back ache. No, she needed a bed. She'd try the house again, maybe her mother had aired out the place? God, she hoped so, since she'd apparently opened for business.

"Do you want to finish discussing salary another time then?"

Oh shit, right. "No, now is probably best, I don't have any time to waste." She pursed her lips, then sighed. "Do you really need me to name my figure? I just—"

"Fifty grand for a three-month contract plus a percentage of the increase in gross revenue. How does that sound?"

Fifty grand, clothes on…three months? That was more than the thirty to forty she'd pull stripping in one month. But three months away from her ER? Damn it, three months away from her Trauma Team? Forget about making lead, they wouldn't hold her current position that long, not a chance. She abhorred the mental picture of Ilana Simon in her place.

But fifty grand, without stripping?

Still no. That wouldn't cut it. She'd have to sink all her savings into the medical bills along with loading herself up with credit card debt. But with no job to go back to, and who knew how long to land a new ER spot? *Shit!* And she didn't want a new ER. Hers was the epitome, the premiere! A 4.0 GPA was only a quarter of the crazy she went through to land *that* ER!

Calm. Be calm. Her brain crunched quickly, but her nerves, the pressure, his stare, none of it helped. Okay, with nursing she got base eighty-five grand, a bump from her recent year anniversary. It would be another year before her next raise. But what did that matter? Because she'd...she'd... damn, now she'd lost her place in her head.

Shhhh. Start over. From a different stance this time.

Okay, so Johnnie had calculated before he'd said his number. She knew he had. He was smart, had business savvy, an Ivy League degree, and he was well traveled. Also, he wasn't the beggar here—she was. So if she stripped *elsewhere* for the three-month timeframe that he proposed, she'd earn a hundred and forty grand total, give or take. One-forty, three months, naked lap dances, lose ER job. *Fuck shit.* Versus thirty to forty in one month, naked, then eighty-five for the year from her ER position that she'd keep, but really, how would she live, eat? Even if she moved from Tribeca to, say, the Bronx, it wouldn't matter. Plus she'd be drowning in credit card debt while her savings would be sapped.

On the other hand, with one hundred and forty thousand for three months, and a prayer to God in heaven that she could puppeteer her boss, Dr. Nora Lance, to hold her spot so she could seamlessly resume her position at the hospital, on her team, and in her chosen life, she would be golden. One-forty, three months. That would get her out of this hell practically unscathed, financially speaking. Well, her savings would still be fucked, maybe credit card limits, too. But if she could keep her clothes on at that number, or close to it, then she'd make it out emotionally and psychologically. She'd be okay. Yeah, she could pull it off.

She shifted her eyes to Johnnie, who had a slight smirk on his mouth as if he liked watching her squirm. He was a flirt and an instigator, and he was forcing her to play his game.

Shit. His fifty to her one-forty. One-forty was based on stripping—clothes off. She didn't want to insult him. Okay, think. Fifty, and remember the commission. Maybe he really believed she'd make such a difference in the quality of the dancers and, therefore, the volume coming into the club that she'd rake in the cash with the commission aspect.

But then a separate doubt surfaced. Would she actually create that much of an increase in the club's revenue stream to make up the gap of what, ninety grand? Even at a five percent commission, she'd have to help bring the club's revenue up like $1.8 million. She really didn't know how much a club brought in, but the cover charge was twenty dollars per head, plus drinks and VIP add-ons. She figured she only needed…seventy thousand more covers? Seventy thousand more heads in the door in three months? *Jesus.*

Okay, so Johnnie was definitely pushing her against the wall. He was toying with her, and she was in no state right now.

"A hundred and fifty," she blurted, then covered her mouth, shocked at herself. But then she remembered her own calculations and sat up straighter. She had stripped for nearly eight years, damn it, and *he* didn't really know how badly she wanted to keep her clothes on. "Instead of consulting for the three months you're asking for, I could dance somewhere else and I'd make upwards of a hundred and forty. So, I figure—"

"Done." He smiled, standing up and coming around his desk. "But I'll throw in a bonus if you prep some of the higher-end girls to train more girls at our other clubs. My father will flip. This will be the game changer," he said, holding out his hand to her. But she could only stare at it.

Hold it. Okay, so, she was getting the best of both worlds, but it didn't seem like he was getting anything more out of her than the chance to impress his father? Maybe for a young rich guy who had it all, this was all he wanted.

Or maybe he was paying in now to call in a favor later. She'd seen it before.

Being under a sugar daddy's thumb was not going to happen to her. She knew that he, or rather his family, had the overwhelming cash to spare. What was the likelihood that he was helping her out while being careful not to insult her pride? Or was he really banking on her, depending on her to create the cash flow to more than pay her salary? In only three months? But what if the girls didn't respond to her? She was older now, an outsider at this point, and they could probably smell it from a mile away. The more desperate and insecure girls she'd known had always shown a jealousy-based passive-aggression toward women in general, but to a strong professional woman in a higher position specifically. They'd try to claw her eyes out, forget about listening to her.

Jana had an education behind her, a career now. They'd know.

The promise of more money lining their G-strings was her only hope, but it seemed like a hopeless *Catch-22*. They'd have to respect her first, then maybe they'd listen to her.

Shit! What was she getting herself into?

The sudden pressure she felt on her shoulders was crushing. And hell, did she just make a three-month commitment? What happened to one month? Or "six weeks tops"? How could she know if Nora would save her spot? What the fuck had she done? Did she already agree to this thing? Holy hell.

She was fighting back tears and nausea when her phone buzzed from inside her purse.

Oh God, thank you for this interruption.

She needed oxygen to reach her brain fast because she felt faint and insane and a few breaths away from keeling over.

She pulled from the depths of her being an obligatory smile when all she wanted to do was cry. "It might be the hospital, please excuse me."

She took her cell out and glanced at it. It was her brother. She stared. And pondered. The fucking nerve. *No, you know what?* She would bite the bullet. Again. Because, fuck *him*!

Her thumb hit decline on the phone, then she looked up at Johnnie Demonte. "When do I start?"

CHAPTER 13

S HE TOOK THE man's hand to shake on their new arrangement. He held it for a moment longer than she expected and then slowly let her hand slide out of his grasp.

"As soon as possible. I'll get you a separate phone so we can reach each other, and you won't have to carry the cell expense. And I'll get you a company credit card for gas."

"I don't actually have a vehicle. I don't drive, never learned, never needed to." She smiled, hardly embarrassed because most people who lived in NYC drove. And as for how she hadn't learned to drive before moving to Manhattan, growing up in the Jersey suburbs, well, she wouldn't go into it with Johnnie. She was already too flustered and busy ignoring her feelings about what the hell she was doing there to think about her father refusing to teach her to drive while he'd jumped to teach Dane. Her dad had even bought Dane a car, which her brother had wrecked after a month. But, no worries, the replacement car was nicer than the first.

"No car and you don't drive," he said, thinking out loud. "Hey, can you wait a quick minute for me?" He moved back around his desk to pull out his digital tablet. A minute later, he closed the cover of his device and came back around with his arm extended. "Come with me, Ms. Winter Snow—hey, what's your real name, now that we'll be working together and all?"

She wanted to keep with 'Winter,' but she had to tell him to do this deal. She had to just trust the guy. "Jana Park—Jana."

"Perfect. Come with me, Jana Park—Jana." He very naturally and confidently took her by the hand and led her out of the office. And her exhaustion, hypertension, and inner confusion let her surrender to his hand taking hold of hers. However unlike her, she was strangely relieved that he was taking the lead.

*

He stared at his phone, willing it to ring. *Jake, call with a bite, man. Please.*

Because now with the goddamn divorce papers mocking him from the tidy surface of his desk, he not only needed more driving time to distract him from that entire topic, but he needed that influx of cash to get him the hell out of here, back home to where he belonged. Back to Vallarta. Faster now.

And when his phone rang him out of his low, Jake's number showing on the screen, he hit accept after the first ring, not caring how anxious it made him seem.

"Hello, Jake?"

"Tone, hey. You okay, son?"

God, did he sound beyond anxious, did he sound desperate?

"Yeah, Jake, I'm good. Well, no. Michelle served me papers. Got me twisted up, I guess."

"Fuck man, sorry. I know how it goes, too. But good fuckin' riddance, that's what I say."

"Right, of course. For the best."

"Exactly. If it makes you feel any better, I gotchu, son. What you needed. It's not the gig for my father; you gotta deal with my piece o' crap son instead…but it's around the clock for three months. That what you had in mind?"

"Jake, man. Yeah, yes!" He was almost speechless. A three-month gig, seven days a week? Immediate numbers running through his head that would undoubtedly put him at his target. Actually, well over his target, and then he'd be done. Only three months more, and he'd finally return home to start his life in his piece of paradise: Puerto Vallarta.

"You there, Tone?"

"Yeah, Jake, I'm here, sorry. Just—I appreciate it. Really, man. It's just what I needed. Should I call Johnnie for the details?"

"Yeah, best do that. Gotta run here. But listen, don't let that little shit give you any lip. Oh, one second—yeah, this one, but bigger nipples—sorry, looking at signage. Oh, yeah, I picked the name of the new club: 'The Hot Spot.' You gotta stop in when I get it open next month."

Antonio smiled. Jake asked almost every time they spoke if he'd check out one or another of his clubs. But he of course never did. Jake may have thought Antonio was gay for all he knew, but it didn't matter a damn. They had a mutual respect running, so it seemed, and Antonio didn't feel obligated to enter one of Jake's pseudo-whorehouses to keep their rapport going.

"Good name, Jake, good name. And best of luck with the opening. So, I'll give Johnnie a shout, on the same cell number?"

"Yeah, same one, but actually go down to the club to talk to 'im now. He's waiting there for you—fuck, Janice, I said wait a goddamn minute!— sorry, son. It never ends. Will talk later."

"Okay, I'll talk to you soon. And thanks again, Jake." But Jake had already ended the call.

*

All the sacrifice, the hyper-focus on his business, and the extreme lack of focus on all else, had been for his future family. His true life-partner, whoever she may be, and their children would have all the security and resources that he'd never had. And they'd have it in his glorious home country of Mexico.

So what, he'd have to deal with Jake's prep-boy, a piece-of-shit son who used his daddy's money without warrant? That was nothing. He'd done a few jobs for Johnnie before, usually driving a hooker from the Avenue or a girl from one of "Daddy's" clubs to Johnnie's little Jersey-side fuck pad. But at least Johnnie was somewhat manageable, and his whores were respectful enough. The setup made him slightly ill, but he'd had worse with the months of Jocelyn Carlson, and it wasn't any of his business anyway.

He remembered his motto: "Keep your eyes on the road and drive." And as he headed toward the club to meet Johnnie Demonte, he repeated the words like a mantra.

*

How was this even possible? His fantasy woman was in his employ, in-hand, in his grasp. *Fuck yes.*

At the bottom of the stairwell, he slid his hand from hers and placed it at the small of her back, escorting her out of the club. He caught his bartender's narrowed glare and he gave her a satisfied grin in return. *Fuck her, that jealous bitch.* Winter, or Jana rather, was different. She wasn't just competition for Erin or any of the other girls there he'd slept with at the club. No, Jana was *the* one.

And he'd accomplished his goal; he'd let Jana come up with something she was comfortable with, on her terms. Or so she thought.

He opened the main door for Jana to leave in front of him, the sunlight a shock to his eyes, but it highlighted the curves of Jana's tiny, yet toned frame. When she saw the limo parked there in front of them, she turned to him with a disbelieving look, head cocked, one eye smaller than the other. Skeptical and fucking sexy as hell.

"Well…you'll be working with me every day, seven days a week to start. You'll need transportation. So, Tony here"—he motioned to the driver to come and open the car door for her—"will be at your service, door-to-door, to your house, to the hospital, to the club, or wherever else you need to go. My dad's known Tony forever; he's more than trustworthy," he reassured Jana in case she felt nervous for her safety.

And he knew Tony was trustworthy and loyal…to his father. His father spoke so damn well of the brown-nosing cunt that Johnnie wanted to throw up half the time over it. And the fact that Tony, the good fucking Samaritan, had pulled him out of the path of a drunk driver in the Vallarta club parking lot when Johnnie was like nine, didn't make Johnnie the least bit hesitant about using the guy as his beck-and-call boy. His father had made Johnnie promise not to tell his mother about the near car-crushing, but he'd never made a promise to lick Tony's asshole over it.

So now, with Tony and the sleek limo, Johnnie could more than impress Jana. It was perfect. It endeared her to him. Johnnie was easing her mind, and that would give her mind, and body, more room to think and focus on, well, Johnnie. "Tony, this is my new business consultant, Jana Park."

Johnnie looked at her as he made the introduction. The look of awe on her stunning face, assumedly over the full-service, no-holds-barred extravagance he'd lined up, made him hard. Rock-fucking-hard all over again.

"Nice to meet you, Ms. Park," Tony said with a polite and subdued nod.

"Jana. Jana is fine, please." She looked at Tony then turned to Johnnie. "Is this really necessary? I mean, I can just take the bus or a cab. Wouldn't a cab be less—"

"It's necessary, and it's already done." Johnnie displayed a close-lipped, non-negotiable smile, and ushered her into the back seat, then knelt down. "This is going to be a whirlwind for you, so I aim to make it as convenient, as doable as humanly possible. Let me do what I can, okay? You're probably doing everything for your family and nothing for yourself. And we have a pretty high goal set for the club, you and me, and such a small window of time to reach it. Just call these things, these amenities, an investment," he said as he handed her a small silver key.

"What's this now?" she asked, shaking her head.

"My family has a studio apartment five minutes from here. I only crash there when it's a slammed weekend and I'm too tired to get to my loft in the City."

She rolled her eyes at him.

"Really, it's all yours. The last time I was there was New Year's Eve, more than six months ago. Seriously, it's so you can save yourself some precious time, get some extra sleep, have some peace. I mean, with your father in the hospital, the financial strain, and our new project together…." He forced the key into her hand. "Tony knows the address."

"You know I won't use it, but thank you…for thinking of me." She smiled. "So…tomorrow, what time?"

"Let's have Tony bring you to me by five. We can have dinner, go over details and all. Then I'll introduce you to the girls if you feel the time is right, or if you'd rather observe and lurk to start, get your strategy formulated first. A busy Friday night will be great for that anyway."

"Lurking sounds like a perfect plan," she said, nodding with a slow blink of her spellbinding eyes. Then she grabbed a huge breath in. "Okay, dinner at five. And Johnnie, thank you. So much." She gave him a genuine smile, a bashful glow radiating from her eyes.

God, he could have attacked her then. Just tear her clothes off her fine little body and penetrate her ever-loving pussy. The driver being there made it all the more enticing. He was kinky that way. And he'd bet so was she, even if she didn't know it yet.

But, instead, he took her hand in his again, kissed it, and backed away so Tony could shut the door. As the door closed, he handed Tony the wad of bills he'd had in his pocket and then nodded goodbye through the tinted window at Jana as the limo pulled away.

CHAPTER 14

A KEY TO HIS nearby apartment? And Jesus, a limo? Aside from the horrible association from only two days ago, almost being killed by a limo, a Jersey limo nonetheless, Jana was completely uncomfortable with being provided any and all of this by Johnnie Demonte. Because, what did he really want in exchange?

Jana Park was totally unaccustomed to anyone taking care of her. Other than Luly, and that woman would have done more if it weren't for the many small people at home dependent on her. And Char was like that too. But, God, in her entire adult life, she'd never even had a man really dote on her, besides her regulars at the clubs. And that was, of course, different.

There were a few fleeting relationships through nursing school, but nothing ever lasted long enough to result in a caring, meaningful interaction. Her off-color night job—its schedule or its nature—usually got in the way before she'd even get to a point with the guy for him to really give a damn.

No one had made her swoon by any means, and none of them had really even tended to her basic needs, outside or inside the bedroom. In all honesty, the apathy was mutual. She'd always only had her nursing goal as her top priority. And, of course, her family.

Johnnie, though, he had it down, at least on the surface. All bases covered, from bottled water to a spare apartment if she needed it, not to mention the deal he just offered her—the one she'd accepted, which made her completely uneasy and unbelievably relieved at the same time.

And then this personal around-the-clock limo service? Raw guilt flooded her veins over it. She didn't deserve this. And even if she made financial miracles happen for the club by getting this tremendous influx of business, she'd never felt comfortable wasting money on such luxury. Even if the money wasn't hers to waste, that wasn't the point.

And the stretch limousine was definitely the utmost in luxury. She laughed to herself at the irony, realizing that although she'd almost been hit by one, she'd never actually ridden in a limo before. After all the offers that too many club patrons had extended her in past.

But there she sat, centered on the plush leather bench seat, with too much room to know what to do with. She looked straight ahead through the center partition so that the road ahead was within her field of vision, ready to keep her motion sickness in check. She'd just die if she got sick all over the fine leather interior. She'd absolutely die.

Tony, the driver, glanced up at her repeatedly through the small rectangular rearview mirror. Maybe he thought she sat there, smack in the middle of his back seat, on purpose, ready to chat. He looked nice enough, a clean-cut, seemingly professional and undeniably handsome man—a welcome change from the recent line of cab drivers she'd experienced over the last day and a half. But chatting with him or anyone for that matter was the last thing on her mind.

To keep her nausea at bay and her nerves from completely short-circuiting, she really only wanted, rather needed, to zero-in on the view ahead, his reflection not included, in silence. Not to be rude, but she was too tired. Too drained. Hopefully, he would intuit her exhaustion and understand.

Or maybe he didn't care about her etiquette at all. Maybe he was a gawker, catching a glimpse at a semi-pretty face? *Oh, and there they are again, those eyes. Takin' a peek, then back to the road.*

His eyes were gentle, kind.

God, she almost wished he was an asshole like her recent cabbies, offering no words, no smiles, no nothing. That might be way easier.

But he seemed nice. Mellow. Not an asshole, at least not on the surface.

Maybe deserving a word or two, at minimum. But she couldn't. She really was too beat to even utter a syllable. Because that would lead to words, then sentences, then potential backstory and explanation. And she couldn't muster the strength to explain anything to anyone, including to herself.

But after a minute of the limo's smooth, fluid course toward the highway, none of her mind's concerns mattered anyway. Her eyelids and her body began to sink as the inevitable wave of helpless exhaustion took over, and she began to drift off.

*

He had pulled up to the front of the club, and the crown prince Demonte had a girl pulled in tight to him, a small Asian beauty dressed in a slightly professional skirt suit—rare for arm candy of Johnnie Demonte's usual arm candy.

And after introductions, logistics, and a large wad of green bills was transferred to him, Antonio pulled out of the club's parking lot with his new contracted client.

He couldn't help but see her face in the rearview as he checked the truck behind him, a large semi following way too close. He pumped his brakes lightly and watched the truck back off a bit. God, she looked deep in thought, almost lost, and sapped, her heavily lashed lids half-fallen. Tired, high, or both maybe? But something else about her struck him, something more. Something he couldn't quite place.

"Where to, then?" he asked through the intercom, consequently startling her half to death, as told by her gasp and the stunned expression he glimpsed through the rearview. "Sorry if I scared you."

God, how stupid of me. He could've asked her through the open partition, which he'd left open because at first she seemed to want to talk or say something and he didn't want to be rude. Anyway, use of the intercom was a habit.

In a quiet and almost defeated tone, she gave him an address in Fort Lee and nothing more; hardly even cracking a polite smile. She only resumed her dazed look out his windshield. Hey, he'd take quiet over chatty any day.

The resonating silence motivated him to insert his earbuds, find his American eighties playlist, then heed his mantra: "Keep your eyes on the road and drive."

*

He figured he'd go up 95. It was the best route despite the rush hour traffic they'd be hitting right then. He didn't think she'd mind being stuck in the congestion, though. She had already fallen asleep.

As he moved through the stop-and-go, he looked in his rearview every few minutes at the tailgater behind him. And again he couldn't help but glance at her too. Especially now that she was asleep and he couldn't make her feel uncomfortable. Most passengers were opposite Jocelyn Carlson. Privacy was expected with the whole luxury package.

Jana Park. She was for sure Asian, but uniquely something else. He could tell by the shape of her eyes and her nose. In her lips and the curves of her body too, when he'd first seen her on Johnnie's arm. Whatever her ethnicity, she was definitely not hard to look at. And as for her demeanor, it didn't really matter to him, but he couldn't deny his curiosity. After all, he'd be driving the woman around day and night for three months. So far he couldn't make her out at all. Morose or exhausted or coming down from that possible high he suspected. Or just a snotty bitch? Just too early to gauge. And hey, what was the title, 'consultant,' code for? Johnnie's bullshit term for 'stripper' now? Or the new politically correct term industry-wide, maybe? Whatever the case and no matter her looks, her demeanor, or her purpose for living, she was connected to Johnnie Demonte and really, that was enough to know.

And as long as he was getting paid, and again, no one was throwing any demands at him in his limo, all would be fine. And in three months, he'd never see her again. Because he'd be going home.

CHAPTER 15

FORTY MINUTES LATER, he got to the address she'd given him, and he laughed to himself. Not only had she directed him to his favorite Korean restaurant in the northern part of the state, *Korean Soul*, but they were parked, well…in front of a restaurant nestled between a barbershop and a thrift store. There wasn't a single house in sight. She must've been worried about giving him her home address. He guessed he couldn't blame her, not these days. Maybe she already had a good sense about Johnnie Demonte. Either way, at least, she was cautious.

Her nap had morphed into a really deep sleep. She had fallen over on the seat, curled up like a baby. He had to wake her, but God, asleep there, she looked almost angelic. All the stress and the layer of something like grief she'd worn on her face when she'd gotten into the limo had all faded away.

Now he knew what was different about her, that thing he hadn't been able to place before. He could see an actual visible glow about her, soft and hardly perceptible. But he believed in energies. He used and manipulated such force fields in his martial arts, and she absolutely had an essence about her, especially radiant now as she wasn't awake to fight it. The woman damn-well glowed.

But Johnnie Demonte? What the hell was she doing with him? Or more like, what was he doing with her? Toying, manipulating, using—just pick the poison. And whichever it was, how soon would that little prick strip that radiance from this sleeping angel in his back seat?

None of your business, damn it. Eyes on the road, Antonio.

He sighed, then tried to wake his passenger. "Ms. Park? Ms. Jana Park?" He spoke through the partition. "Jana. We've arrived. We're here."

*

For seven plus years, she'd exposed her freshly shaven slit to hordes of lecherous men while three or four other girls slapped her ass or went at her tits like hungry kittens, but here she was, blushing from the awkward and somehow intimate wake up by Tony the Limo Driver? His gentle touch to her shoulder had sent warmth and chills through her all at once; the strange sensation still lingered as she sat up and wiped the drool from her chin. *Oh God, really?*

How badly she missed her solitary life; ER to home, home to ER, more or less alone. She so craved that again.

He stood outside the open door now, waiting to help her out of the limo.

"Traffic took its toll," he said, noticing her check the time on her phone, blurry-eyed. "You know, I can take you directly to your house. It's late and I'd prefer to bring you safely to your doorstep. I'm insured, bonded, and licensed. You don't need to worry about security matters on my end," he told her. His voice was thankfully mellow, matching the quiet of the night and the sleepy haze that still hung on her eyelids.

She rubbed her eyes and let out a light laugh, then shook her head. "No, no. I live upstairs. Above the restaurant. I wasn't worried about you having my address."

She grabbed her purse and slid out of the backseat. "I'm a New York City ER nurse. Not much scares me, least of all a chauffeur from the Jersey suburbs," she quipped, but her sarcasm even took her by surprise. She softened then, feeling badly. "Sorry. It's late and I'm just really tired. Thank you for getting me home. I don't know how this works. Do I call you when I need a lift next, or…?"

"Here you go." He reached into the compartment under his radio and handed her a business card. "During the day, I'll be waiting wherever you are, or I'll always only be twenty minutes away, at most, grabbing a bite or whatever. But either way, when I'm not parked where you are, just call my direct cell anytime, day or night. The Demontes have contracted me for three months solid. I'm all yours." His cheeks blushed immediately and his eyes shot to the ground with his last words.

She pretended not to notice as she took the card from his hand with a nod of thanks and shoved it directly into her purse. "Okay, well, can you come in the morning, like at six? I've got to get to the hospital, Fort Lee General. Then down to the club by five."

"Not a problem," he said as he moved back from her, reaching for his car door.

"Let me just…" she said as she rummaged through her purse in the dark.

"No tip, please. The Demontes have handled all costs." He gave her a mild smile, so professional, almost robot-like. He was a good-looking, well-built man, but with zero spark, no personality to speak of at all. She could tell this would be a long three months. But, again, she needed as little chatter and drama added to her pot as possible. Tony would work out fine.

She nodded her thanks again and headed toward the entry door of her parents' walk-up. The idea of sleeping in a real bed was drawing her in, but at the same time, she prayed to the heavens that the house stench was gone. But hell, she was so tired, a bed in a dumpster might be welcome at this point. Keeping low expectations when it had anything to do with her folks was a healthier route. Anyway, she'd undoubtedly catch some sleep, and would be as prepared as she could be for the next day, for more of her folks, the doctor, the bills, and then the club. Yeah, another day in paradise.

CHAPTER 16

I T WAS A rough night. Her mother may have opened the restaurant, but it didn't smell any better. Had the staff even cleaned it before customers came in? *God, I hope no customers came in.*

Either way, she'd been wrong. Her parents' place, or a dumpster, a paper mill, or a morgue; none of them were viable to sleep in, no matter how tired she'd been, and she should have known better. The queasiness in her stomach turned to retching her guts for an hour and a half in the middle of the night. The reek had crossed the line. She should've stayed in a hotel and spent the money, or in the damn hospital chair, and taken the paralyzing neck pain.

Anyway, she was showered and ready to go well before the sun rose, physically needing fresh air. Jana escaped the building with her life thirty-five minutes early. And strangely enough, the limo was already waiting for her.

Tony got out of the limo like a flash to open the car door for her. God, it was as if he'd sensed her coming down the stairs or something. It was slightly eerie, in fact. Hell, it was weird enough having the unnecessary limousine service in the first place.

"Good morning," he said, hardly looking at her, then he took her roller bag from her and loaded it into the trunk.

Again, all professionalism. But, really, this kind of dry, standoffish service-crap really made her squirm. She hated being waited on. She was a nurse, a service-oriented professional herself. She could stand a non-presence, a quiet shadow, but if this guy treated her like she was part of the elite upper crust, God, like Ilana-fucking-Simon, she'd go absolutely nuts. She'd be in this guy's presence every day for ninety days.

"Morning," she answered as she got into the stretch.

He nodded like in a damn movie, and she threw him a polite grin back. Oh, yeah, she'd definitely need a distraction, something to take her mind off of the awkward and sickening servitude-thing going on. She'd insist on sitting up front, but she didn't want him to think that was an invitation in the other direction, unnecessary small talk. God, if only she hadn't forgotten her earbuds and mp3 player; if she had those with her, she'd be set. And, come to think of it, earbuds would be ideal during time with her dad. She made a note in her phone as a reminder to track down a player, even a crappy one from the hospital gift shop.

Once on the road, she checked her phone for missed calls. No calls from family, a good sign. Nothing from work either. Luly had said she'd explain things to her boss, but now things had changed. Drastically. Now she'd be gone for three months.

Three. Fucking. Months!

She had to call Nora herself. She couldn't put that off. But God, she dreaded the call because she dreaded the response.

"So you're actually a nurse in Manhattan? Must be intense," Tony piped through the open partition.

Hmm. Okay. Maybe he felt the same need, to make things a bit more casual? But as she predicted, the alternative was the obligatory polite chatter, not a better option.

She shook her head to herself. A realization. There was no happy middle. She didn't want to be there plain and simple. She only wanted to be in her ER, so no matter what Tony the Driver did, too polite or too chatty, too gruff or too nice, he wasn't going to win. And she didn't want to take out her shit life on a stranger.

Damn it, she really needed those earbuds.

"Yes, intense is a good way to describe it," she answered as evenly as she could. Then she felt a kick in the gut as a surge of *intense* worry came over her—her ER, Nora, her shifts, Ilana taking them, Luly, Ashley the little legless girl, Ilana again. It all came rushing in. Her teeth gnashed out her nagging frustration.

"I…hospitals…clean. You're a brave…"

"What's that? Sorry…" Her mind's voice had muffled his words.

"Oh, I was saying about hospitals. Hate 'em. They're almost too clean, too sterile. But then, strip clubs, forget about it. Too filthy. I can't even step into one. I guess I'm a bit OCD. You're a brave soul in my book…across the board."

She swallowed, still attacked by her mental whirlwind, but she shoved the ball of anxiety down deep and continued. "Uh, I don't know about being brave, but, yeah, I love my job, I mean at my ER. But I'm on hiatus now. My father had a heart attack two days ago, here in Fort Lee." She kept it brief. She didn't feel the need to tell this guy her whole life story. Nor did she want to think about it. She'd have her parents staring her in the face in a matter of minutes.

"God, I'm really sorry," he said, seemingly sincere.

A minute of silence passed. She was glad for it. She looked again at her phone, checking that her volume was on high to be sure she wouldn't miss any calls.

"Your father's lucky to have a medical professional by his side, and putting your career on hold for him.…" He paused a beat, brows raised. "I can't say I see that too often." He smiled at her in the rearview as he prepared to make the turn into Fort Lee General.

It was true. Her parents were lucky to have her, not that they'd ever see it. But that didn't matter; they were her parents. Who else would they go to? She wasn't going to let her mind go there. No, Dane wouldn't ruin another goddamn day for her.

And wow, Tony's words really hit home. Maybe most people were like her brother, focusing only on good old number one while letting their family fend for their own pathetic selves.

The limo stopped, their chat was over. They'd arrived at the main entrance to the hospital. She was glad since his next question up would probably have been something along the lines of, "So, what does an ER nurse on medical leave have to do with The Wet Spot, Johnnie Demonte, and with strip club consulting?" She sighed. She really didn't have the answer if she had to give one in a sentence or less.

She gathered her things. "What time should I be out in order to get to the club by five?"

"Best to leave here by four, I'd say. Um, do you need your little luggage bag or would you prefer me to leave it in the trunk?"

"I'll take it with, thanks." She felt like a damn gypsy, but it was what it was. At least, she had a sufficient outfit to change into in the bag. And a hospital restroom was far cleaner than yesterday's department store and hands down better than her folk's place or the club.

Now on the curb, staring at the doors of the entrance, dread-fueled procrastination set in.

"First step's the hardest, huh?" Tony said through his driver's side window.

She turned to him and offered only a slight smile. He was right—again. Her heart pounded in her chest. She hated the idea of being in a room with her father for the entire day again, and the high probability that she'd get an updated hospital statement.

But she bucked up and moved her feet into the hospital lobby because her very lucky parents were waiting.

*

"Ask Jana. Chang, ask her," her mother nudged as Jana walked into the room.

In a not-so-quiet hush, Jana's father pulled her mom toward him. "She's not a doctor, Jin. She changes bedpans for Christ's sakes." Then he released the woman. "Just, goddamn it…wait for the doctor."

A close-lipped smile spread over Jana's face, and behind it, she held her tongue with her teeth and swallowed her already cracked and damaged pride. Let him sweat out whatever worry he had. Let 'em ask the doctor. Yeah. Definitely better that way.

Jana kissed her mother hello and goodbye, sending her home to rest. "I need to leave here at four, Ma, but from the looks of his vitals"—*and the sound of her father's ever-supportive words*—"Dad's getting back to his usual self. He could probably stand a night alone, even."

Her mother disagreed vehemently and said she'd be back "after her *brief* nap." *Ah, the subtle guilt trip.* Jana thought about making her mother another "Closed" sign there and then, one that read, "Should be Closed for Good." *For the health and safety of all.* But hell, if the woman wanted to run herself ragged, let her.

Once her mother left, she handed her father a book she'd brought him, *Catch 22* by Joseph Heller, ironically appropriate for her situation. It had been the easiest to reach on her parents' bookshelf, really.

A nod replaced a thank you from her father, and then silence followed. That awkward quiet was somehow louder than the beeping of the heart monitor.

"How are you feeling today, Dad?"

The rest of the day was reminiscent of his answer. "How do you think I'm feeling, Ja-Na? The food is putrid, the nurses are dumb, and my chest was pried open. I wish Dae Han was here to make sure I was in better hands."

Had he really said what she thought he'd said?

Yes. Yes, he fucking had.

"Well, Dane is not here, Dad." *As usual.*

And as usual, she was. Four o'clock couldn't come fast enough.

*

The only break in the torturous ten hours was when Dr. B. came in. He was very patient with her father despite her Dad's humiliating and horrid demeanor.

"Jana," Dr. B. said outside the room. "I think your dad could stand a few more days up here in the ICU before we move him to a standard room. Only taking precautions, nothing major to worry about."

Only the fact that the ICU costs were double that of the standard care unit, she knew.

"Are there developments I should know about, Doctor Brighton?"

"None that are of a medical nature per se. Your dad is very... strong-willed."

"Stubborn, you mean? He's a stubborn, chauvinistic, close-minded, grumpy old asshole," she finished for him. "Don't worry, it's not a secret. The man couldn't hide it if he were sedated." She smirked.

He smiled back, his gaze turning almost sympathetic. "Hey, would you like to sit in the café with me, take a break from...the patient." He laughed. "You look like you could use a coffee."

"Thanks, and yes, I could use time away from him and a watered down pick-me-up too."

They went to the crowded cafeteria and found a small round two-top by a window. "Anything else besides coffee for you?" he asked, shoving his glasses higher on the bridge of his nose.

"Thanks, no. I ate my father's sandwich a little while ago."

He brought back two black coffees and two pieces of pound cake. He patted the slight excess at his middle and laughed. "I need to keep my energy up." He winked. "I have rotations here, then I'm scheduled at my folks' private cardio practice until close. Eighteen hours is nothing, right? Because money talks, so say the parents. Med school loans to pay. Still, after ten years. But, God, I'm so tired. I'm surprised I'm able to talk and walk at this point," he laughed.

God, not necessarily what she wanted to hear from the surgeon who'd operated on her father's heart. But she gave a thankful smile back. She knew the reality of hospital shifts first hand.

He gently pushed one piece of pound cake her way, but she declined with a slight wave of her hand. Now more than ever, she had to stay fit. Dancing or not, the girls would need pole demos throughout training. A slice of pound cake wouldn't help her case at all.

"It looks great, but no thanks. Hey, other than the fine looking pound cake, I wonder how bad the rest of the cafeteria fare is here. Because I bet it isn't nearly as bad as what we've got at my hospital," she teased. But in reality, her hospital was state of the art down to its à la carte eateries and full-scale gourmet bistro. She was trying to bolster small town Fort Lee General, to be nice.

"Ah, that's why you're so thin and fit, and I'm so…not," he said, blushing a bit. His insecurity was kind of sweet, even refreshing.

She shook her head to brush off his concern. "No, no. I do eat. Total crap," she lied again, to make him feel better. "They run us nurses ragged. You're a doctor, you wouldn't know," she said with a giggle to close. Wait, was she flirting with him? Yes, she was. She was definitely flirting with her father's cardiologist. And she needed to stop before he misunderstood her. *Dear God.* She looked down at her coffee, black and hot, the way she liked it. But she sensed his searing stare on her forehead, and to break it, she got up from the table with a quick, "Excuse me for a second," to get a few creams and a fake sugar packet. Yeah, that would reset the vibe. Separation. Then, a do-over.

When she came back, she fixed her coffee and lifted her Styrofoam cup. "Here's to more hours in the day, better cafeteria food, and to healthy hearts."

"Cheers," Dr. B. said back. "To healthy hearts and maybe, I don't know…to future drinks?"

She smiled. So, her flirting had definitely gone too far. That was, at least, the nicest, least-sleazy pick-up attempt she'd ever experienced.

"Maybe more coffees, because I'm sure I'll need those over the next weeks here." She breathed out but then looked squarely at him. "But other than that, my focus has to be on my family."

He smiled and nodded. "No, of course. Who has the time anyway, right?"

CHAPTER 17

H E OPENED THE door for her, and as she slid into the backseat of the limo, he heard her let out a huge sigh.

Then Tony handed her a cup of coffee on a tray, complete with creamers and an assortment of sweeteners, a stir stick, and napkins.

She looked surprised. "Uh, thank you," she said, but only put the tray aside. "I actually just had a cup, and I'm already too jittery," she explained. "But really, thanks."

He reached for it back. "No problem. I knew your day would be a long one." He smiled, remembering his mother's time in the hospital. And she hadn't lasted more than a day. Those had been the longest hours, minutes, and seconds of his life.

Change of subject needed…for his own mind's sake. Breaking the ice should be easy. She was awake now, and more of the same light conversation from their morning ride couldn't hurt.

"How's your father?"

"An asshole."

Okay. Maybe not the lightest topic. He waited a beat. But she said nothing else on the matter.

"Do you need me to stop for you to grab dinner?"

"Thanks, but no. That's why I'm meeting Johnnie early. For dinner, before the club gets busy."

Dinner with Johnnie, *right.*

Light conversation might be out. That was fine. She didn't owe him her attention. He simply hoped to help lighten her mood. It couldn't be easy juggling it all.

But what about the 'consulting' title? Johnnie's words still nagged at his brain, cracking him up a bit and bothering him at the same time. Hell, he'd driven enough dancers to know they were brashly proud, almost in-your-face about what they did for a living, justifying it to anyone and their mother. Making ends meet by using their God-given assets was not something to hide, according to any he'd met.

"So…question, then I'll let you be," he said, smiling, trying to make eye contact in the rearview. "Johnnie called you his 'consultant.' Is that the new P.C. term for dancers these days?" he asked with a slight smile.

But his passenger only glared back at him, her head now cocked to the side. Palpable moments of harsh silence followed.

Then she spoke. "I'm *hiring* and *training* dancers for Johnnie—temporarily. But no, I am *not* a dancer." Her defensive tone sent chills up his spine. She then reached for her phone, ending the topic all at once.

So, she wasn't a dancer; she was a nurse and, temporarily, a 'hiring and training consultant' of dancers. *And none of it is any of my damn business.* He got it.

Her cell phone went up to her ear, so he started to put the privacy window up. A natural step after obviously offending her anyway.

"Please, keep it down," she said through the half-open partition. "I get carsick and need to see the road ahead."

At least, she'd asked nicely. He brought the center window back down. He could have uttered an apology then, but she was already on her call.

He had definitely and unintentionally ruffled her feathers with the stripper insinuation, and the entire interaction made her that much more intriguing.

*

A coffee from the driver—declined, but it was a nice gesture.

She really needed to focus, not get more wound up. She started preparing her mind for stepping into The Wet Spot again, to be called 'Winter' again, and being surrounded by catty strippers again, girls who she needed respect from, like, right away.

But then Tony started talking, giving her a slight eyebrow raise in the rearview. She smiled politely but continued with her thoughts, gathering up her courage, readying herself to see Johnnie again. But then her ears perked up.

Something about her being a 'consultant'—she knew that was coming— and that being the "new term" used for "stripper"? Oh, because she automatically had to *be* a stripper? And, it was any of his business? Fuck that, no she wasn't a stripper. In fact, she never had *been* a stripper. She'd *stripped*, but she'd never *become* a goddamn *stripper*.

And, who the fuck was this judgmental prick anyway? Johnnie said he was a trusted family contact? How goddamn unprofessional, though. He was downright offensive.

But what made it worse, he'd asked it almost innocently, like he didn't realize how screwed up the comment had been in the first place.

She'd shot back as brief an explanation as her self-control would allow, that she was *not* a "dancer"—she wouldn't even use the word stripper to this dickhead. Then she took out her phone because, fuck him. She'd make the calls she'd been putting off, a convenient escape before she tore this guy a new asshole.

And he could just mind his own damn business and drive.

*

Yes, she'd wanted him to be less servile, but insulting her was not what she'd had in mind. So as the phone rang through to Luly, she decided to simply ignore him for the duration; three months would be nothing. *Right*.

And she wouldn't even mention it or complain about it to Johnnie. Bitching about a gift was just low class. Anyway, dickheads were a dime a dozen. This was a good reminder, actually, of what she should expect and get used to over the next few months at the club, even if she wasn't going to be on stage, being in the club, she'd be unable to escape the general asshole-vibe of it all.

Luly's cell went to voicemail, so she selected the home number next. God, she wished she could have the privacy window up, but she'd get sick for sure. No, it was fine. She'd speak to her best friend in Spanish. She and Lu did it around Ilana all the time.

And then Tony, the judgmental prick disguised as Mr. Nice Guy, wouldn't be able to understand her. She knew from Eddie that the Demontes kept fellow Italians on the crew. Their most loyal guys were all named Eddie, Gino, or Tony.

And Jana needed to vent to Luly, to unload the weight. She'd tell her all about the club job and Johnnie, her father, the debt, her dick of a brother, and doormat of a mother, and she didn't want any of it being overheard and getting back to the club. It was no one's business but her own.

A thought entered her mind on the fifth ring… Lu would ask how long she'd be gone. Best to omit the truth on that point. She didn't want Luly to have to lie to their boss, and Jana wasn't prepared to tell Nora, or even admit to herself really, that she'd be out for three damn months. This charade was hers to shoulder. Luly didn't need to deal with that shit.

At last, Luly answered. "Hello, Jana?"

Jana almost broke down weeping when she heard her best friend's voice. But Tony's judgmental glances in the rearview reignited her raw anger, which helped combat the sappy emotional bullshit welling up in her chest.

But Luly had enough emotion for the both of them. The woman let it all out, blubbering with concern on the other end of the call. Luly pounded Jana with questions, like the usual mother hen that she is. And Jana fielded each and every one—in Spanish. She went over the past days' happenings, which made everything all the more real. And painful. But she got it all out. After she was done spewing, she actually felt somewhat better. But what felt truly cathartic was that Luly wanted to know. Luly truly gave a damn. Luly was there for her.

And was always watching Jana's back.

"But what's this guy's agenda, Jana? Consulting? It seems too good to be true, you know?"

"I know, Lu, but it's the only option I've got other than to outright dance. And I was ready to. I really was. But this guy offered an alternative, and it fits. Why should I question it? He's not like the owners and managers I've known, Lu. He's different. He's clean-cut, educated."

"Even worse, Jana. Sorry, I don't mean to get all negative, but make sure you aren't being taken advantage of. You have too huge a heart, and, well… just sayin', sweetie, to please be careful."

"Lu, I know. And I will be. Anyway, I had a fabulous reminder of the kind of pricks in and around the business with the damn limo driver only a minute ago—"

"Limo? What limo?"

"Johnnie insisted. He assigned a limo to get me to and from home, the hospital, the club, you know, to save time. For work…" She intentionally left out a detail, the key to the "family's apartment." The silence from Luly's end had already forced Jana to filter. "Anyway, Lu, it won't take me years this time; just weeks." Twelve weeks, God willing, no more than twelve. *Fuck me.*

*

She hung up with Luly after an emotionally draining fifteen minutes and now needed to know if she had time to make the dreaded call to her boss. But the scenery outside was unfamiliar. She had no idea how far they were from the club. So she was forced to ask up front, "How much longer?"

"Thirty minutes. There's a lot of traffic." Antonio answered politely and succinctly. That would work—short and sweet. Three months of short and sweet. Good.

She looked back at her phone. Thirty minutes…that was enough time to call Nora. But first, she'd check in with her mother quick, because really, she needed to be pushed up against the clock in order to hit her boss's speed dial button.

She pressed her mom's number.

In Korean, she told her mother that she'd be back to the hospital by dawn. She imagined it would be a late night, getting acquainted with the dancers and the current dynamics of the club. But she needed to sleep eventually, and she'd decided that instant that for efficiency's sake, she'd make the armchair her bed again. For now.

She'd also been in too much of a rush to tell her mother that she'd met with the doctor earlier. "Ma, you need to get Daddy on board with everything, get him to change his ways, his habits, his attitude, or he won't get better. They won't even move him out of the ICU until he comes around. And Ma, every day in the ICU is costing double. You following, Ma?"

Her mother didn't respond to her comment, maybe because she was too near her father to be candid. Instead, her mother made sure to comment on how tired she was from working the shop all day and was now on duty at the hospital. Jana ended the call with an endless sigh, which relieved nothing. Nothing at all.

And just so the tension in her gut could ratchet up a few notches, now it was time to call Dr. Nora Lance before reaching Newark. She had no other excuses.

*

She hit Nora's number. While it rang, she covered her mouth with her hand to try and muffle the upcoming call as her boss only spoke English. She swore she felt the driver's ears perk up, the nosy bastard.

Dr. Nora Lance answered on the eighth ring.

It killed Jana to explain to her boss that she'd be out for so long. But she shaped the details strategically. Little doses. "For no more than a month at this point," she said in a numb, robotic tone. Who was she kidding? She was spoon-feeding her boss outright lies. But she needed to test the waters, see if any strings could be pulled, and nail down official leave with a position hold. She knew chances weren't good, though. She'd only been at the MMU Hospital for a little over a year. But Dr. Nora Lance had voiced to her several times how vital Jana had been to the team. She'd pray Nora meant it and could make magic happen.

"You just take care of your family matters, Jana. Let me know if you need any support directly, if you need me to talk to any of his doctors. If they give my top RN any shit, I'll even come up there. You know I will!"

"I appreciate it, Nora! So much. The cardiologist seems pretty down-to-earth and experienced. But I will remember you offered. What I really want, though…just keep my position for me? That's what I can't handle losing." Jana's voice got shaky then, and there was no way Nora didn't hear it. So much for professionalism. But damn it, all her shifts and her training, her team, the patients, Ashley, her last charge, they all needed her there. And she needed them.

Her ER was her anchor, and her role there was her identity, her source of pride, her truest and best self. And here she was in a goddamn limo to the strip club she'd lost her metaphorical virginity to a decade ago.

"Jana, sweetie? You still with me?"

"Nora, sorry, yes. I'm right here."

"I was just saying that you have nothing to worry about. A month we can do. Not that it won't be damn hard without you! But your spot is saved—I'll have HR email you to that effect, no sweat. Now, if it were two or three months, I'd have a fight on my hands, but a month is really nothing. You take care of your family, and of yourself, Jana Park! Don't forget to take care of you!"

Chills sprinted up her spine. Holy hell, she was going to lose her position. She was for sure going to lose her fucking dream job!

Her goddamn parents were—again!—stripping her of her chance, her dream, her purpose, her life as a nurse in one of the most prestigious hospitals in the world.

Breathe, Jana. Breathe. And speak. She cleared her throat to find her voice. "Thank you, Nora, for being such a support," Jana said while wiping tears off her cheek she hadn't even realized were falling.

"Oh, sweetheart. Please don't cry. It will be okay. Your father will be fine, you'll be fine."

She'd be fine? Her sinking heart said otherwise. She had no words. Her new round of weeping was the only audible response possible.

"Hey now. Jana. Listen, you are always in control, twenty-four seven. You are brilliant at control in the ER. But you're not a nurse right now. You're a daughter. And it's okay to let it out."

Damn it, that wasn't it. She knew she had no control over her life or her fucking asshole family members. 'Jana the daughter,' 'Jana the dancer'—neither of them had ever had control. But 'Jana the nurse,' she'd had it all. And she needed to remain 'Jana, the nurse.' At her Manhattan ER, dammit! She needed that to be in-hand. Solid. "Please Nora, see what you can do about the longest leave of absence possible. Unpaid, of course! Just, I can't say what my folks will need and for how long, and I *cannot* lose my spot there. Please."

"Of course, Jana. I will talk to HR right away. Explain the situation. Of course."

"Oh God, thank you, Nora. And I'm sorry to be so emotional. Just thank you so much." She was embarrassed. She closed her hand more tightly around her mouth and the phone to block the road noise. "Oh Nora, let me let you go, the cardiologist just came into the room."

"Of course, go. Watch your email and I'll be in touch, sweetie."

*

She hit 'end' and readjusted her tear-blurred eyes to her surroundings, most immediately, a white, wispy tissue dangling in her face. She grabbed it from Tony's hand with a subtle huff. He could've pretended that he hadn't heard her crying. She looked up to the rearview as she wiped her face, his deep brown eyes set on the road. He at least knew not to make eye contact. But as she dabbed at her running nose, he glanced up, his eyes searching hers… those criticizing, crucifying eyes pretending to care. She didn't need his pity or his stupid tissues. He mocked her with his pseudo-innocence, his soft, almost empathetic look piercing through her.

She held his stare, though, and with her eyes and no words she told him all she wanted to say. *You're a chauffeur, asshole. Get the hell over yourself.*

CHAPTER 18

UP IN THE VIP rooms overlooking the stage below, Johnnie had prepared a table just short of candlelit. Tucked away in the farthest reaches of the loft level, easy red and pink indirect lighting set the mood. He was ready to subtly slay his fantasy girl.

When she walked in with her panther black hair falling down her back, spilling over her shoulders, he stood up, captivated, ready to greet her and devour her whole. God, he was glad she couldn't read his thoughts. They were incessant and out of control.

And he wouldn't even try to fight them.

The club's youngest dancer, Laynie, had brought Jana up to him. The girl stood and waited until Johnnie gave her a dismissive nod, then left them. Good little Laynie.

"I've actually never been up here," Jana told him as he kissed her on the cheek, her eyes taking it all in and maybe adjusting to the darkness.

"It was built just after you left. Here, please." He pulled out a chair for her. "So, you've been doing all right, with your father and all? And Tony is there when you need him?"

She cleared her throat then smiled. "Yes, yes. Thank you. Thanks for asking." She hung her purse on the back of her chair.

He could tell she was nervous and was controlling it as best she could. After sitting, her hands fidgeted on the table's surface. He'd put something lean and hard into her hands, into her body, just as soon as she felt comfortable with him. That was the plan. But for now, to calm her, Johnnie waved at the half-naked bleach-blonde server texting on her phone while holding up a wall. He cleared his throat and pointed at the top shelf behind the bar.

"I took the liberty of ordering appetizers and dinner for us. Hope you don't mind." This was how his old-style Italian grandfather had told him it was done. A real man. Despite the times, it displayed confidence, gentility, care, and of course, control.

"I've never…yeah, no, that's fine. Should I even ask what you chose, or did you intend it to be a surprise?" Her face brightened, seemingly liking surprises. Oh, would he surprise her up and down her tight, little cunt. And he'd enjoy the game of getting there very much.

"Surprise intended." He smiled as the waitress came over with tequila shots. "And here's to your first night back at the club, now as my consultant." He winked. "And to a successful business relationship." He lifted his glass.

Her glass tapped his as she tilted her head in brief thought, then tipped the glass back against her luscious, heart-shaped mouth. As she swallowed the drink down, he watched her throat ripple, then her shoulders shiver as the icy-hot liquid went down. Like his cock would go so far down that slender fucking throat of hers. He shivered at the thought. She giggled, probably thinking he'd been affected by the shot too.

"It's been a while since I've had a drink," he fibbed, placing his empty glass lightly on the table. Oh no, he definitely partied. Often and hard. But very different than other party-bound college-graduated guys, Johnnie Demonte didn't get stupid and sloppy when he drank or snorted. No, he was sophisticated. And he'd show her how sophisticated he was…in all ways.

He relished the thought of pleasing her in *all ways* while he watched and studied her, mesmerized at how she immediately softened, her lips slightly parted, maybe parched, thirsty for water, but he called for another round of shots instead. He watched her eyes as they scanned the club's bar, then down below them to the stage, watching the straggling girls work the pre-crowd and then only briefly meeting his eyes before darting back to their surroundings again.

Once the second shots were down, he could have flipped her open like a filthy magazine, thumbed through each and every page of her life, of her sex, of her juicy satin slit...but not yet. *Patience.*

Instead, he played all business. He'd make her trust his intentions, as there was no time or room for doubt. He explained his ideas, the roster of dancers he had now, things he had changed since Eddie's management, and the summary revenue he'd been pulling, and then the goal number he aimed to reach. She seemed awestruck, hanging on every sentence.

"So, what do you think?" he asked as their filet mignon entrees were served.

"They could use work for certain," she said.

"Oh, sorry, should I send them back? I had these cuts brought in special from—"

"God, no. I'm sorry...I meant the girls...the girls need work. The meal looks divine," she said, shaking her head and blushing perfectly.

He loved how he affected her, got rock-hard from it. "Good and yes. You have your work cut out for you. I can't wait to watch you train them into shape, though," he said with one eyebrow raised. Then he took his first bite of meat. He wasn't going to hide his attraction toward her. And he felt she wasn't hiding hers for him from the way her eyes drifted toward his, but would then shift away when he'd look to meet her gaze. *So sweet.* She was just so fucking sweet he could come.

"I, uh, need you to know, Johnnie," she said without touching her food, "that I really have to just keep focused, you know, on the project, and taking care of my family. Their financial matters are really overwhelming, only second to my dad's health, and I can't make him see the severity. It's like I'm the parent...or maybe I always have been." Her last words trailed, as if an afterthought.

"Of course. You must be incredibly bombarded. And I appreciate your focus, and there's nothing else that needs to be said, Jana. Really..."

"Are you sure? I kind of feel as though we have an unspoken...whatever—thing going on here. And, you know, I just can't act on that, especially being that you're my boss. But even if you weren't, I can't get distracted with—"

"I absolutely understand. Relationships require as much focus and attention as anything," he said, "if they're to ever actually work out." And the required focus or attention wasn't something he had ever really wanted to put in before…before now. "Friends. A relaxed friendship between colleagues can definitely be a positive outlet, yes?" He smiled, not hiding the glimmer in his eye. Oh, how he'd give her an outlet she'd never fucking forget.

Jana sighed, her shoulders loosened. "Friends sounds good."

*

She smiled, easing back into her chair, showing more of a change in her demeanor from his words than from the two shots of tequila.

His words had made her melt, and she'd see over the next weeks, as soon as she'd surrendered, that his actions would make her goddamn pour. Really, thank God she wasn't hearing his thoughts right now. But on the other hand, if only she could hear his perverse plans, see his mind's images of her gasping with shock and awe and bliss with the inevitable electricity he'd send shooting into her. He imagined the very sensation shoot up his steel hard shaft, and, God, he fucking wanted her. He could send the steaks crashing to the floor right then and lay her out on the table. Fuck her senseless. With everyone there watching. *Mmmmm.*

Compose yourself. He blew a slow stream of air through his nose and fought to find his voice. "You ready for dessert?" He lifted his eyebrows at the server who was back to texting. He shook his head, lifted his arm up in the air to wave at her, and the blonde rushed over with two bowls of strawberries and cream. "I figured a fruit something would be your pleasure. Your body is in phenomenal shape. I'm sure you eat and work for it. I keep the sugar intake down myself, but fresh fruit once a week isn't horrible." He smiled again. "After this, you wanna meet the girls? You met Laynie already."

"She's a sweetie. Reminds me of me then—on the shy side, but that became my biggest strength," she said, one side of her lip curling up, but a solemn expression wiped across her face as if remembering when she'd danced on stage like she'd wanted to be just about anywhere else. He could tell she'd hated it. But she had nothing to worry about now. He'd keep her off that stage and off their laps and all to his damn self. So help him.

"I actually remember one show you did to an old nineties alternative rock pick. It shocked me how slow it was, but you were mesmerizing, again, in your own world. The entire room was pin-drop quiet. You had them eating out of the palm of your hand."

She only smiled, and kept her gaze down, looking at her hands. Her fidgeting had resumed.

"Would you prefer to stay up here and watch, take notes? I actually have some things to take care of in my office. I'm going to be on the Island Monday through Friday, building inspectors all week long at the new club."

She looked confused and concerned all at once. He nipped her worry in the bud, though.

"But I'll have already introduced you to everyone tomorrow night in an official mandatory meeting. You'll be fine. I'll announce your position, hand you the torch so to speak, and you do what you want. Make training sessions mandatory before shifts all through the week? Whatever you feel is best, I'll back you up all the way." All the way, every way. Backways, frontways, sideways, and upside-down ways. *From now 'til fuckin' forever.*

She nodded. "Sounds fine...."

Maybe she wanted him there for support, or maybe to be near him like he wanted to be near her? But he did need to be onsite for the inspections in Merrick, but also, he *wanted* her to feel uncomfortable when he was gone, and pure contentment and satisfaction when he was with her. The association would expedite the timetable for him getting her. Having her.

"Oh, I'll be fine," she said as he watched her persona shift. She'd become what he imagined 'Jana the NYC ER nurse' to be like. "I'll call you if I have any questions, but it'll be better if 'Papa Bear' is gone, you know?" She smiled. "And I'll stay up here for now. Go do your office work. I'm good, really."

He nodded and inhaled her essence one last time before he pushed back his chair.

"Oh, would you send Laynie up on your way down? I want to get a feel for the place from a newbie's perspective."

She really would rock this place. He knew it, as he patted himself on the back for having thought up the grand plan. He'd get his cake and eat it too. Get to fuck the living daylights out of his forever fantasy girl, and take credit for the increase in revenue at the club. He couldn't wait to shove that shit in his dad's always-scowling face.

He leaned into her and whispered, "There she is...a perfect blend of timid and feisty. But obviously always *so* in control." He pushed his chair out, stood, then moved to leave, however reluctant he was to do so.

"Come say goodbye to me before you leave tonight, will you?"

"Sure...of course."

"Thank you for joining me for dinner."

"Thank you for having me."

Oh fuck, will I ever have you, Jana Park!

He smiled, placed a light kiss on her cheek as he might do to any associate, *not really*, and then couldn't help brushing his fingertips over her bare shoulder on his way by her. "A piece of lint," he whispered. Oh God, the electricity that shot through him from her skin blew the air out of his lungs.

He willed himself to walk, to go. But after he'd taken a whole five strides he had to look back at her, there at their table, hovering above everyone below. His royal highness.

CHAPTER 19

SHE MADE HER exit and was glad to breathe fresh air again. Well, industrial Newark fresh, that is.

She walked across the parking lot to the limo.

She smiled politely but made no eye contact with Tony the Driver as he held the car door open for her. Instead of the door slamming shut, though, she still sensed his presence. He was lingering. She turned her face toward the open door, wondering what the holdup was. She was damn tired and anxious to crash.

"I wanted to apologize for insulting you earlier. It was absolutely not my intention," Tony said in a calming baritone, countering the louder octaves she had bouncing around in her brain from inside the club. Even over the practically romantic dinner she'd had earlier in the night with Johnnie, they'd had to shout across the small table because of the reverberating bass resounding throughout the place.

She started to speak, to answer him, but he interrupted her by silently holding a small black device inches from her face. "It's an mp3 player. You're probably in real need of some peace and quiet, but maybe a musical distraction would do? It has playlists of every genre."

She stared at it. He kept his hand out for her to take it, and when she finally did, her nerves tightened and her breath hitched. She'd literally made a note to herself to—God, that was super strange and really just…nice of him.

Had she gotten him all wrong? From the tissue to wipe her tears, to the coffee he'd brought earlier, a thoughtful gesture to help her through her god-awful day with one hellish part extending into another. From putrid house to hospital to the dreaded strip club she abhorred. That she now consulted for. *Not stripped at, but consulted for.*

Shit.

Was that 'consultant' comment just him trying to make conversation? After all, the question wasn't baseless. He had been hired by Johnnie, a strip club owner, to drive her, a mysterious strip club 'consultant.' Had her brain spun his words into the biting judgment she'd expected to hear? Or believed herself, even?

And then what had she done? She'd basically spit in his face. So much for wanting to be treated like a regular person and not like a royal, elitist bitch. She'd ended up acting like one all on her own.

She fingered the small, sleek device and called up the courage to look at him and utter a thank you to start with, but he had already shut her car door and situated himself in his driver's seat. *Stealthy.*

*

He started the ignition and the limo rolled forward. "Where to for the evening?"

Oh right, where to? The hospital armchair's where to. *Ugh.*

God, if she didn't want to pay for a motel, maybe she should, at least, hire a maid service at her parents' place, and get the restaurant deep cleaned too. *To be ready for sale?* She could pray, right? Anyway, it might cost her a few hundred dollars, same as one week at a crappy motel. But the nastiness level was so high, especially with the restaurant operating—and the fight with her folks to close it had been a massive fail so far—she'd need to have it cleaned every week to make it habitable for her. And she had three months to go!

Well, for tonight, because she was again too tired to think on it or anything anymore, she'd have to surrender to her best option. "To the hospital, please."

She'd spoken with as soft a tone as she'd heard herself utter since being with her sweet little patient, Ashley. It threw her and made the fine hairs on the back of her neck stand on end. She inhaled deep to shake the chill, then leaned forward, both arms and elbows on the center divide. "Hey, um, thank you for this." She nodded at the music player in her hands.

"Don't mention it," he said, eyes focused on the freeway's merging traffic. Then he smiled up at the rearview mirror. She felt forgiven with that smile, and a kind empathy showed through his brightened eyes. A clean slate, then. She sighed with relief. *A clean slate.*

Before leaning back to settle in for the ride, she noticed a black gym bag on his front seat; a hairbrush and toiletries were just visible through the half-opened zipper. It never occurred to her that he probably lived in Newark or nearby it, on duty twenty-four seven, shuttling her all the way to Fort Lee. It was only day two, but he'd be expected to do that every day for three months?

And waiting for her wherever she was? Where the hell did he sleep? And shower? He smelled good, a subtle musk and aftershave thing going, so he showered somewhere. Right? *Yes, of course.* She wouldn't embarrass him by asking of course, but she felt even worse now, picturing him sleeping in his limo like she'd been sleeping in the armchair in her father's hospital room. Well, the limo would seem more comfortable than the chair, but still.

Maybe she was blowing things out of proportion, though. Maybe he had family in Fort Lee. She didn't have to feel bad if he had a place to stay or even a hotel room. "So, do you live in Newark?" She couldn't help asking.

"Close to the club, actually. Not the best neighborhood, but it's really close to work."

"Aren't you near work all the time—wherever you park your car?" She smiled then flushed. Was that rude? Yes, damn it, it was. *Nice insertion of foot into mouth, Jana.* Had she become a snobby bitch since becoming a Manhattan-ite? Or since getting on the Trauma Team? *Jesus, Jana, get over yourself.*

But Tony gave her a gracious smile and nodded. His muscular arm, noticeable even in his white cotton dress shirt, came up to adjust the rearview as if trying to see her a bit better. "The depot and dispatch, I meant.

Anyway, I'm close to everything, which is great. I can walk to the grocery store, the dry cleaners, the bank. And I love walking, a break from driving, you know?"

She did know, kind of. Not the driving part, per se, but she loved the City where she could walk most anywhere and only have to depend on her own two feet. "Yeah, I actually miss Manhattan a lot for that reason…well, for so many reasons."

He gave her a slight smile and sighed. "The City's too much hustle and bustle for me, personally. I felt swallowed up there. No space or time to breathe. It's a lot better for me here in the 'burbs, even with how much I work. I exercise more, I read more, I even volunteer a couple of days a week at the library. Yeah, I lost myself in Manhattan, and not in a good way. I guess I'm just not a city guy, not at all." His cell rang, interrupting his explanation. He slid a wireless earpiece on. "Excuse me for a second… Hey Celi."

She nodded and slid back. *Shit.* His talk of time for himself, and volunteering? While here he is stuck driving her ass around twenty-four-seven. Yes, he's probably getting paid well enough for the gig; but to be doing this seven days a week for three solid months? Sleeping away from his home, from his potential family?

Wait.

If she stayed at Johnnie's place in Newark then Tony could at least return to his own home every night. Johnnie said it wasn't ever used, and she'd have it to herself. And she'd be glad for a real bed in what was most assuredly cleaner and more sanitary than her folks' place.

And was it really necessary for her to be with her father every day at the hospital in Fort Lee? Her father didn't even want her there. And hell, her mom liked playing saint so much, she could keep doing the daily grind. Maybe it would force them to shut down the restaurant that much faster with the pressure and exhaustion of it all. Jana could go up every few days to check in on them. Meanwhile, she'd be pulling in the funds to afford her father's necessary care.

It was decided. Johnnie's apartment tomorrow night, no more armchair. She'd also give Tony off on Sunday. She'd arrange to take a cab up to Fort

Lee General without Tony or Johnnie even knowing, or she'd even consider giving herself a day off, a day off from the club and her parents and their bills. Yes. She deserved a day off too.

And Johnnie had said the studio was close to the club. It'd be cheap enough to cab there Sunday nights. Yeah, she would bring her clothes with her tomorrow and stay at the studio. She'd tell Tony after her stint at the club Saturday night. He'd probably feel relieved. After all, he'd given her a sense of relief with his kindness, his thoughtfulness, his brush-off of her rude reaction to him earlier in the day.

She pushed herself back from the partition and sank into the seat. The soft black leather creaked under her and molded to her body. She heard her own breath leave her as if her relief and comfort were so palpable she was separate from them. Maybe she'd found a small mobile sanctuary, a true gift between the two hells she'd be juggling. Tony the Driver and his fancy limousine could be the one piece of sanity she could count on over the next grueling months. Maybe?

*

Her mind quieted as the highway noises lulled her. She imagined a comfortable bed with crisp, clean sheets at Johnnie's apartment.

Shit, though. Johnnie's words and Luly's warning about him rang in her ears. Of course, she'd picked up on all of his sweetness and the hard-to-miss innuendos. Damn it, she felt regrettably drawn to him and could almost justify the release he'd provide. And, hell, she of all people deserved a good strong climax, a heavenly peak and then a soft, cushioned fall into sweet, freeing dreams.

But with Johnnie, her boss, the strip club crown prince, it just wasn't safe, not prudent. Not by a long shot.

But she'd be at his damn apartment! That was a mixed message if she'd ever heard one. What if he took it as a sign that she wanted him? What if there *were* strings attached?

No. She'd drawn her line, she'd been clear. Friends only. And he'd agreed to it.

Plus, he'd clearly said the apartment was for her alone. He'd promised no strings, and she believed him. She did.

But on the other hand, he was indeed a man. With natural inclinations, core controlling desires.

"*Be careful, Jana.*" Her guardian angels sang out in her head in unison.

Char had taught her well, and she knew Luly spoke from personal experience as a single mom, five kids later. She couldn't ignore the nagging question: Why was Johnnie making things so easy for her?

But it was too much to think about then. She was on overload as it was, and it wouldn't help to cycle through it in her head again, at least not anymore tonight.

She looked down at the little black mp3 player. She selected the 'New Age' playlist, put the earbuds in, and pressed shuffle. She let Johnnie and the club, and her family, and the bills just drift from her mind, and Jana drifted off to sleep in the backseat of Tony's luxury limo.

CHAPTER 20

ON SATURDAY NIGHT, Johnnie ushered in his new consultant, introducing Winter to the entire staff.

"This woman was the highest earner here at The Wet Spot for three years straight and then took the highest shares at our Manhattan club too," he said while she kept her head down, modest, calm, stoic even. But while his tiny-framed fantasy girl let the praise float right over her, she still had an extreme confidence about her, standing straight, chest out, almost like a ballerina.

"I'm really glad to be here," she said. He knew she was lying through her teeth. "And I'm going to show you all how to maximize your time at the club and make a hell of a lot more money. That's why we're all here, yes?"

The older dancers nodded or rolled their eyes while some of the younger girls smiled, or even lifted their eyebrows at each other, seemingly pumped at the thought of more action.

But when Roxy, the redhead he'd recently fucked, stormed out of the club with an evil eye targeted right at him, he knew others would definitely follow. That would be fine, though. Some of the vets there were dragging the entire club down anyway, something Johnnie had been telling his father for years. Jana would replace them and train them. He'd show his father the real possibilities the club held and that he had the balls to turn the key to those possibilities and open the lid on the place.

Jana didn't fluster a bit when Didi and Honor followed Roxy. Instead, she kept her poker face on and got right in there, bringing the girls up on stage, showing them how she worked the pole, and for fuck's sake, did she own that pole.

*

"You looked great up there," he said, handing her a water.

"Thanks. God, I didn't think you'd be watching." She blushed.

"Wanted to see their reactions. You think you can handle the cats while I'm out for the week?"

"Definitely. Not a problem. Laynie already gave me a good base last night with the who's who. According to her, the three who left were the biggest pains in the ass anyway. I'll train the rest of them in a rotation throughout this week, and based on performance and attitude"—she lifted her eyebrows in the direction of one of the older dancers sulking in the corner—"I will schedule who I want to keep and replace the rest next week."

"I love it." He motioned for her to follow him up to his office. As she did, Johnnie caught Laynie winking at Jana, but Jana replied with a simple headshake. Intuiting the silent communication to involve him fucking the living daylights out of Jana, he didn't care what the other girls thought. No, that was a lie. He fucking loved the thought of those catty cunts jealous of Jana. They damn well should be, whether he was sinking his cock deep, deep into her, or not...yet.

"I have a few things for you," he said, pulling out an older flip phone from his front pocket. "I want you to keep this with you. My number's already programmed in. And"—he led her further into his office, to his desk, while he pulled out his wallet from his back pocket—"I'm giving you an advance for the week since I won't be here."

"Whoa, Johnnie, that's really not—"

"You'll take it, please, and use it." He gave her the wad of cash and his best modest smile. "I know you're good for it, Jana. God, you're going to make magic here. Magic." He winked then leaned in to kiss her on the cheek, and she stepped back as quick as a timid mare.

"Thank you," she said, taking two more steps back. She shifted her stance, as if wondering what to do with herself, then remembering the green bundle in her hand, she shoved it into her purse and looked up at him like a deer in the headlights. Shocked and awed. *Perfect.*

"Last thing. I'd forgotten that I had tickets for a show on the Wednesday after next at Lincoln Center. They were for my ex and me," he fibbed some more, "and I'd hate to waste the second one. I was so ready to go on my own, be the 'strong bachelor with an empty seat beside him,' but I'm just not that brave." He smiled at her coyly. "Come with me…please. As a friend."

Her expression showed her apprehension.

"Hey, if there is anyone who deserves a distraction, a night out with a friend, it's definitely you," he said. "And it really would go to waste otherwise."

Her lips formed a close-lipped smile, a sigh lifted her shoulders then she nodded. "Sure. That'll be nice. And it's not a busy club night that I'd miss."

"Perfect," he said, liking how things were going his way at every turn. He gently spun her around toward the office door and began leading her out.

But she stopped and turned, her face only inches from his.

So close. So kissable.

"You are really great, Johnnie. Why *are* you so sweet to me?" she asked with her head tilted and her gorgeous brown eyes wide with skepticism. But she so wanted to trust him, he could tell.

"Look, I have a sweet spot for you, no secret there. But you work your ass off. I've seen that firsthand when you danced, and now you're a nurse? I know you're smart, educated, driven. I am drawn to you, what can I say? Bottom line, though…I respect you and I want to help, plain as that. Oh, and showing my father how much I can improve this place—we, I mean, we can improve this place—well, that's just cream."

She smiled. "Well, I appreciate everything, Johnnie. And I'll work for it. I think the club has a lot of potential. I'll do all I can." Then she turned toward the stairs and he followed her down, thinking how she sure as hell would work for it. He'd work her ass, riding it to the end of time. And she'd scream his name over and over again; ecstatic and trembling under his control all the way there.

CHAPTER 21

THEY GOT OUTSIDE to the parking lot, Tony waiting with the car door open for Jana.

He watched Jana give a quick and polite smile to the chauffeur but she hardly made eye contact. Johnnie's chest swelled. Because that fucking guy...of the girls he'd have Tony shuttle around, no matter the status of his female companions—low class or upper crust—they'd all eye Tony. Such the polite fucking gentlemen. And the man's physical stature didn't help Johnnie any, a head taller than him and broader in the shoulders too. Tony's strong, silent persona irked the fuck out of him, and he wished his father would find someone else, anyone else really, to chauffeur for their family. Someone who had a beer gut at least. But he guessed he shouldn't complain. Most people didn't have such an impressive bitch boy, after all.

Just then three dancers came out of the club and Johnnie watched as they ogled the high-class limo, Tony, and then Jana, or Winter to them. Then they whispered amongst themselves.

"Don't worry about them," Johnnie told Jana.

"Oh, I know. Remember, I was surrounded by it for nearly a third of my life. It doesn't matter what it is, a catty girl will catch it and rub it in your face. The difference now—I'm *really not* one of them." She grinned.

Damn straight she wasn't. *But wait.* Beyond the perks they saw Jana getting, his totally unsubtle attention toward her would have them wanting to scratch her eyes out. *And worse*, they'd shoot their filthy mouths off.

About him—to Jana. Because they *were* jealous little kitties. And although the thought of them all clamoring for him while Jana had already won him and his ever-loving cock was a total fucking turn on, he couldn't have them blowing his plan. Drawing him to be, well, who and what he really was. Jana wouldn't take her throne as top feline next to him if she didn't trust him.

"Listen. Don't take any shit from them. They'll be jealous of the special treatment." He referred to the limo with a tap of his hand on the top of the door as he slid by Tony and escorted her into the vehicle himself. "They'll try sabotage, lies, anything to rile you up, knock you down, or scare you off."

"I expect as much."

"They may even use me in their schemes, I've seen it before with head-liners we've gotten. Some of the older girls making up shit I've done or said," he said helping her into the car while Tony stood behind him, still hovering, ready to close the car door.

Goddamn this guy. Doing his job, yes, but right up in his fucking space. Johnnie knelt down in the doorway to get a modicum of privacy, right at the seat's edge, his hand an inch from her leg, and God, he could just squeeze her juicy thigh then yank it wide open for dessert. *Soon.* For now, he'd fin-ish speaking to his fantastic focal point without the lingering fucker behind him, right within earshot. *Focus.* "But like you said, you know their nature. If there's anyone who can handle them, it's you." He winked and patted her hand.

Tony cleared his throat.

Jesus fucking Christ! Yes, I know you're still there. "Give me a second, would you Jana?"

Johnnie felt his pulse in his neck jackhammering out his frustration. Couldn't the other man read the signs and vibes and neon fucking signs that he was working here? Obviously fucking not. Was the piece of shit in a rush or something? Whatever the prick's deal, he'd have to remind the douchebag who drew the lines here. And while he was at it, he'd make sure Tony knew good and well that this one, this catch, was more than off-limits. Being loyal to his dad didn't mean Tony was loyal to Johnnie. And Jana was out of this world. Even a righteous prick like Mr. Tony Perfection had to have noticed.

So he stood up, turned away from the open car door so Jana couldn't hear and brought the chauffeur a few steps away from the limo for a...pep talk.

*

God, he hated this guy. Could hardly muster manners, let alone say the man's name. Especially when he wasn't performing for a female audience, in this case, Jana, who was now officially out of earshot and busy with something in her purse.

He set to whisper. "Listen, man. I'll be out of town for the week. Take care of her like she's my goddamn sister, but know that she's anything but. In other words, watch out for her without laying your goddamn hands or eyes on her." He patted Tony's shoulder hard, drilling in his message while keeping friendly appearances for Jana if she happened to glance his way from inside the limo.

Tony replied with only a nod.

"Now, give us some motherfucking privacy. Please."

Tony and his goddamn professional poker face moved to attend to something at the front of the vehicle while Johnnie turned back toward Jana and knelt down in the doorway again to say goodbye.

"So, I'll see you next Friday night when I'm back from the Island. You need anything, call. Don't hesitate."

"I won't, thanks. I mean, I won't need anything, but if I do, I won't hesitate," she said then laughed. "Oh, I, uh, I'm going to start crashing at the studio if that's still okay. My folks' place is just—"

"Absolutely! That's why I gave you the keys. Free rein, honestly." God, he was good. He was so damn good.

*

Johnnie tapped on Tony's window. "Make sure she has everything she needs at the apartment." She saw Tony nod, and then they rolled out of the parking lot.

He looked up at the rearview to make eye contact. "There's a twenty-four-hour grocery on the way. Do you wanna stop to get some stuff?"

"Thanks. I should, but I'm just so tired," she said, but then remembered her original plan. She wanted to give him the full day off tomorrow. But she couldn't muster the energy to go grocery shopping tonight. Maybe tomorrow afternoon, and at least let him have the entire day until then to relax, and she'd let him completely off the hook next Sunday.

"Would you take me tomorrow afternoon to the store? I've decided to sleep in and not do anything. My parents will be fine for a day, you know?"

"Yeah, sure. You deserve a break," he said with his eyes still on the road.

Deserving? She wasn't feeling deserving. "So, listen…the other day, when you asked me, you know, about consulting, and I snapped at you…I think—"

"You owe me no explanation. At all. Really."

"No, I know," she said leaning closer to the partition. "I realized, you know, my defensiveness was just my disdain for the club scene. I'm so… raging pissed that I'm in it again at all. I danced for seven years to support my folks…and for school, and here I am. Déjà vu. But at least, this time, it's off stage, clothes on," she said, feeling heat rise to her cheeks. She closed her eyes to reset. "This consulting thing Johnnie put together, it's a huge deal, a real blessing. But anyway…I shouldn't have been rude to you. It wasn't cool."

"Please, no worries. And seriously, you have nothing to defend. God, your parents have got to know how blessed they are to have you, Jana."

She smirked and changed the subject to signify to Tony not only were her parents so the opposite of appreciative, but also, that he wouldn't even want to hear that pathetic saga—like, ever. "So, I'm kinda psyched about Johnnie's studio; cutting down the commute, increasing the sleep"—*in a bed, thank God*—"and hey, you can get to sleep in your own bed, right? Must be hard on you, out all the time. Your family must miss you," she said, noticing for the first time the wedding band on his left hand, now on the steering wheel as he made a right turn onto a side street.

He kept his eyes on the road; a hesitant silence broke their flow. "Yeah, well, my sister and her girls are all the family I've got close by. The rest are spread out all over."

"Oh, I just thought…you know, your wedding ring."

"No, I'm…not, you know. I uh, decided to get this a few years back.

Some clients, they have their bucket list item…with a chauffeur in a limo. It's easier for me to keep my professional lines and not hurt anyone's feelings…or lose a client." He laughed.

She smirked at him. "How many women hit on you from this back seat, I wonder?" she asked, full-on flirting.

He smirked right back at her. "It's not just women I'm proud to say," he said with a quick lift of his brows. "But we'll say…too many people to recount right now…because we've arrived." He smiled as if relieved to not have to go into it.

She looked out her window and saw a three-story brick walk up lined with young trees and sweet lampposts dotting the sidewalk in front of it. The building, the whole neighborhood, was a part of another world. She felt far from the Newark strip club district, but it was only like a six-minute drive away. *Crazy.*

"Some other time then. Say tomorrow?" She smiled. "Man, I'm sure we could swap stories that would *not* shock either of us, like, at all." She laughed.

"Yeah, if anyone could top my limo sagas, it would be you. Hell, between the club life and a metro ER, or rather a Manhattan ER! You might just beat my butt in a 'Most-shocking' competition," he said, his eyes smiling in the rearview.

"We'll see tomorrow, I guess. Okay, well, have a great night sleeping in your own bed." She smiled and slid out of the back. But he was already out and around to open her door. She nodded her thanks.

"Jana, I should come up, make sure you get in and that everything's working and you have everything you need…like Johnnie said."

"I'm really fine."

He narrowed an eye at her as if to say without words that he wasn't giving in. And she wouldn't fight it, she didn't want him to get in any trouble with Johnnie.

"Okay, let's go up then."

*

He followed her up at a safe distance, carrying her small roller bag for her.

The silence and his eyes potentially on her backside made her feel funny, self-conscious even. She was glad when they got to the second-floor landing.

At the apartment marked 2B, she searched for the key in her purse. She heard Tony breathing lightly behind her, but hardly audible over her damn panting. She hadn't realized what the climb up the stairs had done to her. And she thought she was fit. Tony wasn't winded or fazed in the slightest. Her hands were even jittery, and having finally found the key, now she couldn't get the key into the stupid hole.

"Here, let me." His hand brushed hers as he took the key, easily slid it in, and opened the door in an instant.

She looked up at him with a smile and took a step forward.

"Wait," he said, blocking her with his arm in order to check the place out first. So serious, bordering on protective, like her own security detail or something. He left her in the doorway, flipped on the light, and surveyed the small, some six-hundred-square-foot studio. "Looks okay, no gas smell, or—"

"A real bed!" She dropped her purse there on the floor and ran, throwing herself with absolute abandon onto the plush, crisp, and clean-sheeted mattress, the one from her very dreams. After she'd landed face down, she flipped over onto her back and stared up at the ceiling, feeling the cloud-like give of the bed, the most comforting sensation her body had experienced in…well, way too long. Not even her apartment's futon was this heavenly.

Tony cleared his throat.

Oh God. Her face got hot. She'd forgotten herself, or more, she'd forgotten her company. Rolling off the bed, she saw his gentle smirk.

"A few nights in a hospital armchair…." She grinned with a follow-up sigh as she moved toward the door to pick up her purse from the floor.

He grimaced with empathy. "I'll check the water and thermostat for you and be on my way."

"Thanks, Tony. Hey, would you drop the temperature to the lowest setting while you're at it?" It was hot and stuffy, probably because, like Johnnie had said, he hadn't been in there for forever. As soon as she heard the air conditioner respond, she sighed. This was heaven.

"So, tomorrow at three you said?" Tony asked, moving to the door. She could see the exhaustion on his face.

"Yes, please. Three o'clock."

"I'd feel more comfortable if you had my number readily available, in case. I gave you my business card."

"Yeah." She hunted through her pit of a purse and immediately decided she was too tired to rummage for it. "Please, can you type it in here for me?" She handed him the phone Johnnie had given her, also too drained to figure out the buttons of a new phone and too worn out to want to try.

He smiled as he took it from her; a small laugh escaped him as he typed, maybe because his fingers were too big for the small buttons on the anti-quated flip phone? "Poor old thing," he said of the device as he handed it back. "Funny how folks with money keep old crap, even though they can afford ten of the newest of the new." He snickered.

"Yeah, people are strange, for sure. I can't believe that only ten years ago this thing was the best. Now it's as good as a kid's toy." She'd actually given all of her old devices to Luly's kids to play with. They'd play ER with them, spouting out medical terms Jana had taught them. 'Code blue,' 'stat,' and, oh they just loved 'BM!' God, they cracked her up. She couldn't wait for her life to even out to have her own little one to hand stuff down to. And teach, and hold, and love. All just sweet dreams for now.

"So, I'm gonna, you know, go."

"Okay, yes. Thanks," she said moving behind him toward the door.

"No problem. And you're sure three o'clock? Won't you be hungry before then? I could bring you food or take you to the store earlier? Or a restaurant?"

"No, no. You need a break too. I'll find something. The neighborhood seems nice. There's probably a restaurant close by I can walk to, right?"

"Actually, yeah, there's a deli near the library, only three blocks down and two streets over."

"Perfect. And so, we'll swap stories tomorrow afternoon then."

"Right, tomorrow at three," he said, standing there for a beat, almost lin-gering, maybe with a hint of concern on his face? Seemingly unsure if she'd be all right there alone, like a guardian, a protector.

She smiled at him, nodding that she really was just fine.

He turned to leave. "Goodnight," he said as he closed the apartment door quietly behind him.

But his calm, overseeing presence hung there in the small studio apartment, and she felt lighter for it.

"Jana?" His deep voice startled her through the door.

"Yeah?"

"Lock the door."

"Right, thanks." She smiled as she turned the deadbolt. "Night."

She could hear his footsteps fading out as he moved down the hall.

He really was like a bodyguard. She hadn't known a man like him before, and she'd known a lot of men. *Remember, Jana, he's being paid to do a job.* Fine then, it was rare to find someone who took his job so seriously.

And talk about different. His make-believe wedding band struck her as curious and somewhat intriguing. What man—and a pretty damn attractive man at that—would try to turn away action for himself in his own limo? It was unheard of with the men she'd ever known. In her experience, men were wholly incapable of using their common sense before their cocks. But this man, Tony, actually wore a mock wedding ring to stave off sex? For professionalism's sake?

He had to be lying.

And if he wasn't lying, then what planet did this guy come from? Maybe he was gay. But no, he'd insinuated he'd turned down both women and men.

Too curious. God, there were just too many unexpected characters in her life right now, between her new boss and her chauffeur. God, *her* chauffeur?

She just needed sleep.

She looked down at the club cell phone in her hand, then slid it onto the kitchen counter. The phone skidded along like a pebble across a placid pond as she ran at the bed and dove onto it again.

She fell asleep in an instant. Makeup on. Clothes on. Lights on.

But her worries were finally shut off. At least for the night.

She woke up with a gasp…from a dream. She and a faceless man were driving down a winding scenic highway. It was sunny. She had her sunglasses on. And the companion had a cap on, yeah, a police officer's cap. The strangest thing was that her hands were on the steering wheel. *She* was driving—she hadn't been in the driver's seat of a vehicle in her entire life. And even though, ironically, the cop in the passenger's seat should've been stopping her from driving without a license, he was holding her hand, making her feel safe, secure. A sweet, gentle, comforting hand. A guiding and protective hand.

And, the dream still so fresh, she remembered the feeling of the wind rushing through the open windows. It had taken her breath away. And her favorite girl-angst rock band, *A.D.,* was on loud enough to compete with the torrent of fresh mountain air. Yes, mountains were the foreground and backdrop. Serene, royal green and purple-ridged mountains. And while driving through those mountains, she was in control. God, no motion sickness, even. Simply heart-pounding happiness. She was free.

Then she'd woken up. There hadn't been a cliff or a dead-end. Just her and her sweet and safe mystery cop driving far and free. The exhilaration lingered in her for a moment. Then it was gone. Because here she was, in her real life. No scenic mountain road. No, no. Just Newark-fucking-New Jersey.

She sighed and swallowed back a knot of disappointment. She got up, found a glass, downed two rounds of tap water, and then stripped off her pants, her shirt, and her bra under that. She scrounged for the light switch in the room, found it in the kitchen and flipped it off. Found the bed, crawled under the sheets, and fell back to sleep easily.

No more dreams. At least, none that she could remember when she woke up late the next morning.

CHAPTER 22

TONY SLEPT LIKE hell. Not the quiet, calm he was used to, especially being in his own bed as opposed to the all-too-familiar driver seat of his limo. But no matter where he slept, he always reached equilibrium. Just not last night. And carrying over to today, he couldn't pinpoint the unsettling feeling that nagged at him ever since leaving Jana at the studio apartment the night before. Not to over think it, he put it to sheer exhaustion and age creeping up on him.

He went to check his cell in case Jana had changed her mind about getting groceries, or for any dispatch alerts. But no missed calls. It occurred to him then that the restlessness he felt might have started when dispatch relayed the request from Jocelyn Carlson the night before, just after leaving Jana. That crazy woman wouldn't quit.

But, no, that wasn't it. Jocelyn Carlson's incessant car requests to dispatch annoyed him, but it also gave him a slight jolt of pleasure in denying her. He knew that maddened her endlessly and he liked it.

What the hell was it then…his unease? Cracking his knuckles, he bit his bottom lip in thought, replaying the night in his mind.

The ring. When Jana had noticed the ring, it had reminded him. Yes. It made him remember the four missed calls and two voicemails over the past few days from Michelle. Her voice oozed guilty-warmth, sweetly harping on and on about him needing to return the final papers. She couldn't wait to replace 'Ruiz' with 'Simon.'

Yes, that was definitely the nagging in his brain and in his gut.

He laughed out loud at the similarity between Jocelyn and Michelle. God, they both even wore the same poisonous perfume—each and every time Jocelyn had gotten into his limo, that damn *Giannia's Destino* burned his nostrils as it traveled up to his head where horrible memories of Michelle and Simon together would immediately surface, followed by a pounding headache for the rest of the damn night.

Damn you, Michelle. She had turned out to be two people in one. How had he been so blind? It haunted him. If he had just kept on course and not gotten distracted in the first place. But he'd been so sure Michelle was the one. They'd met at work, had the same balls-to-the-wall work ethic and lofty goals, and, he'd thought, a lofty love.

When he'd bumped into her leaving Simon's office, her forehead vein throbbing like it did only after she and Antonio made love.

At least, she didn't insult him by denying it.

But shit, she didn't even try to deny it! Beg for forgiveness! Nothing!

What a fucking cliché he'd become. And he couldn't just get over her, which was why he'd subconsciously let the "separation" drag out for so long.

But now, apparently, Michelle was officially ready to be done. *Divorce.* God, he could hear his mother rolling over in her grave. But it wasn't really religion or tradition that stopped him from signing those papers Michelle had broadsided him with. By Antonio not finalizing the divorce, he was making her wait, holding back what she wanted so badly. Pathetic, he knew. He was supposed to be so above such shit. It embarrassed him to admit it to himself.

So he pushed the topic way back, and just jostled his car keys in his hand, then began tossing them up and catching them coming down. Again and again. God, he didn't want to be home. He wanted to be out. Away. With Jana.

Whoa. What?

Yes, he wanted to be with Jana, listening to her, talking with her, glancing up at her in his rearview. Jana.

The memory of Jana diving onto that bed last night made him stir. Then wince…the bed of Johnnie Demonte.

It was a similar feeling he'd had with Michelle at the start. Innocent attraction, ever-growing intrigue, but with Jana, his contracted passenger and Johnnie Demonte's 'consultant,' it was different.

She'd been a stripper, and he had no respect for strippers. But had she *been* a stripper? She had *danced*, albeit naked, but she'd never *become* a stripper. That was obvious. And she'd done it for her family. Her situation may have been even more desperate than his had been growing up. Then she put herself through school and became a nurse. God, and now, when her family needed her again, she'd dropped everything? And she even found a slightly more reputable way to help her folks. She was something else entirely.

But he worried. He knew Johnnie and what he must really be trying to get out of her.

Damn it! That was it. Johnnie Demonte. Jana at his apartment. In his bed. Jana surrendering to his bed with such abandon. Then imagining Johnnie climbing into his bed after her, over her. Antonio's hands formed white-knuckled fists.

That was definitely it.

Because Michelle was just a lingering scab that he constantly picked at. Michelle wasn't the cause of this discomfort that had morphed into what was now a deep ache.

No, it was Jana, definitely Jana.

He stood up then. *Go for a run. Then to Tae Kwon Do. Shower. And three o'clock will come.*

CHAPTER 23

S
HE FELT LIKE she was walking through a movie studio, like she could saunter up to the flower-potted front porches and check behind the houses to see 2x4s holding up the facades.

Three blocks down she made the right. Not a soul in sight. Her stomach prayed that the deli Tony had mentioned would be open on a Sunday morning. It was eleven o'clock already, so chances were good. Then, if the place had Wi-Fi, oh man, she'd be set. For as little time as Johnnie spent in the studio, she wasn't entirely surprised it had no Internet or even a TV. The Demontes could for sure afford it, though. But like Tony had said last night, random things were a sticking point with wealthy people. After all, they didn't get or stay rich by tossing their cash out the window, did they?

But either way, at least, she was out in the fresh air and walking. She didn't know how much she'd needed that until her feet were on the pavement. Fresh air, movement, alone-time, oh, and that morning's shower had been all sorely needed.

The deli's neon sign came into view just as her club cell phone rang. She flipped it open, knowing it would be either Johnnie or Tony. She hoped it was Tony so that it'd be quick because the beginning of a low blood sugar headache was coming on.

It was Johnnie.

"Morning!"

"Hey, it's Johnnie."

"I know that…no one else has this number, right?" she said with a laugh in her tone. Except for Tony, but Johnnie's driver didn't count. "How are you?"

"Just got to Merrick and was thinking about you. Wanted to make sure the apartment had everything you needed."

Except for Wi-Fi. "Yes, thank you. Everything is so great. I haven't had a night's sleep like that in as long as I can remember. My place in the City is smaller, and the bed is harder, neither of which matter much 'cause I was hardly ever there with my ER hours," she said as her heart sank at the thought. God, Sunday mornings in her ER, buzzing and alive after the City's usual Saturday night party-scene slaughter. She just needed to get inside the deli to scope out a free Wi-Fi sign and check her email. That was more necessary than feeding herself.

But she couldn't rush Johnnie.

"Good, I'm so glad. Well listen, I wanted to get your dress size. I was so impulsive in asking you to join me for the show next Wednesday, I forgot that you'd probably not packed a gown in your rush over to Jersey for your dad! I mean, right?"

Oh God, he was right. What the hell would she wear? She didn't own anything appropriate for an off-Broadway matinee let alone an evening show at Lincoln Center. Nor did she have the money to buy a dress that even came close to par. Shit, she should have declined in the first place. She shouldn't be going out with her boss, the one who obviously has a thing for her. Hell, to be honest, she might have a tiny thing for him too.

"No, you know, I wanted to tell you, I really should decline, Johnnie, because my father will be close to—"

"You're coming with me in a new dress, Jana, and I won't take no."

Stunned, she knew he was trying to be sweet, but it was a little off-putting. She really didn't want to go. But she didn't want to insult him either. She was crashing at his apartment alone, and the job, the limo. He had been constantly kind, seemingly genuine.

"Size 2 petite, but—"

"I'll get the perfect gown for you. I can picture it already."

"Please don't spend too much—"

"I will spend what I like, and you can repay me by having dinner with me the day after our contract ends. And you will wear the gown I get you that night too. Deal?"

Dinner. Innocent enough. And it seemed like a confirmation that he respected her choice to keep their relationship casual while they worked together. Okay, this felt slightly better to her. "Deal. Empire waist is best for me if it's floor length," she hinted. "And *I'll* get the shoes. Just tell me what color and material," she asserted.

He laughed on the other end. "Fine. So, what are you doing now?"

"Heading for a bite to eat."

"Tony driving you?"

"Ah, no. Walking. Nice neighborhood, good weather…and I wanted some 'me' time, and a light walk hit the spot. Tony will be by later to take me to the grocery store, though. Then to work."

"Okay. Just be careful, you know, on your own. And remember, Tony was hired around the clock."

"No worries, Johnnie. He's at my disposal, and I insisted on being on my own this morning. He even wanted to come earlier and—"

"And what?" he spat then cleared his throat.

"Oh, just, you know, get me food, the groceries…" She felt his silence through the phone line. "He's doing his job, taking care of me like you asked him to."

"Okay, that's good."

"Johnnie, listen, my stomach is yelling at me to feed it."

"Oh, go, go. Sorry, let me know if the deli is any good. They opened not too long ago."

"Sure. I'll have a real Jersey sub for you." She giggled. "Talk to you later, and thanks, you know, in advance, for the dress."

"I can't wait to see you in it…okay, go, go, goodbye."

*

She walked into the deli and the most mouth-watering fresh baked bread scent wafted toward her. It was so intoxicating that the fact there was no Wi-Fi wasn't as immediately disappointing. She ate a twelve-inch sub loaded with the works. With the amount she'd be training, she felt entitled, and hell, at least, it wasn't pound cake.

After she'd finished, she went to the counter to ask where the closest Wi-Fi hotspot might be. "One street down, the library," the woman said, counting her till while swallowing down her own sandwich. "It has Wi-Fi. The only one in the area that's open on a Sunday. My daughter," she said as she pulled out her phone with one mustard-laden hand to show her a picture of a cute little girl in pigtails and a tutu, "takes dance. But they've got everything; art classes, chess, martial arts. You want it, they got it," the kind lady plugged with enthusiasm.

Jana pictured taking a daughter of her own to a class like ballet someday. Again, far, far off, though. If ever.

Jana dug deep for her smile. "And Wi-Fi on a Sunday to boot..."

"Exactly," the lady said with a nod then shoved her stack of cash back into the register. "I'm about to go and take a smoke break, sweetie. You need anything else before I do?"

"Oh, no. I'm set, thanks. Great lunch by the way." Jana waved as she headed out and turned right down the sidewalk toward the public library.

*

As she walked, she checked her personal cell to be sure there were no missed calls from her mother who she'd texted earlier to let her know she wouldn't be by until tomorrow. She half expected a ration of shit back, but no. Nothing. No communications from her ER's HR department, either. That made her nervous. She shoved her phone back into her bag with clenched teeth.

Relax. Nora had HR email, no doubt. *You'll see.*

She took a deep breath in, shook her hands out of the smothering anxiety, and she felt better. Present.

As the library came into view down the block, the breeze picked up, making her hair whip about, strands hitting her face. She tried to hold her thick mane back with her hands as best she could. She had to stop a few steps from the library entrance to tie it all back in a ponytail. Looking up, squinting at the sky in concentration as she glided her thick hair though the rubber band, she felt a presence approaching quickly and then passing her on her left, a tall, strong presence. Done with her hair, she turned toward the building, the stairs, and watched a regal, broad-shouldered man making his way gracefully up the steps. He was dressed in a white uniform, a black gym bag slung over his shoulder matching the black belt tied around his trim waist.

Even though the library was her intended destination, the strong, almost magnetic force of the man drew her up those stairs—it was like she was compelled to keep him in her sights. She entered the library, just close enough behind the man to watch him go through a set of double doors to the left of the librarian's desk. A "Free Wi-Fi" sign shouted to her on the wall ahead. She smiled to herself, *Wi-Fi, finally*. But first...

*

She walked straight past the desk and headed toward the double doors. She peered inside. About twenty children, young, maybe the oldest being eleven or twelve, all sitting cross-legged, lined a large blue mat. Except for four, who were balled up in a diagonal line in the center of the mat. They were all in white with a variety of solid color martial arts belts tied neatly around each tiny waist. They were silent, sweetly attentive.

A sudden and deep grunt from inside the room made Jana jump back. A man, *the* man, with his back to her so she couldn't see his face, flew past her eyes. Literally airborne with his top leg extended, foot flexed, he soared over the four small human bumps. He headed toward something on the far end of the room out of her field of vision. Then she heard a deafening crack.

The children clapped. Jana got closer to the door to see better. The man bowed to two adults who'd been holding the three thick boards he'd apparently broken for the demonstration. Then he turned.

Tony. Staring right at her. His head was notched to the side as a smile came across his face.

He walked in her direction, bowed again as he stepped off the mat, then headed to the door, coming out of the room to see her. God, she'd interrupted him, his time off, his class. *Damn it.* Her cheeks burned, her mouth dry.

"Hey, wow. Weird to see you here at the library. I would've thought you'd sleep in, hit the deli, but checking out a book on your free time?"

She smiled, then swallowed hard to find her voice. "Wi-Fi. I need to check email, waiting for an update from my ER. And wouldn't you know it, the Demonte apartment is sans data and TV."

He smirked. "They must not use the apartment for anything but...you know"—he cleared his throat—"sleep."

"Well, I can't believe what you did in there! You literally flew!"

"Yeah, flying down the highway got old fast." He smiled. "I've been practicing Tae Kwon Do since I was a kid. Now it saves my lower back, really keeps me limber." He twisted his torso for a half stretch then lifted his eyebrows. "And it keeps my spirits up. I love working with the kids. Hands down better than the immature adults I drive around in my backseat." He winked. "You being the exception, of course."

She smiled, not taking offense, sure that most of his other passengers were far worse behaved than she'd been yet. So, a sense of humor mixed with superhuman capabilities? Jesus, this guy.

"Well, saying I'm impressed would be an understatement. You know I'm Korean. Your belt shows seven degrees. You're a *Sabun*; I mean, wow!"

Now *he* blushed but stood a little taller still. She loved his balance of humility and his understated yet unshakable confidence. "Have you ever practiced?"

"No, no. My brother did, but I wasn't allowed. I watched a lot of martial arts on Korean TV, though." She half smiled, but then became aware of the twenty pairs of eyes turned toward the door, visible to her just over Antonio's broad shoulders. Her eyes lifted to let him know. "Sorry, you know, to have interrupted class. I just got curious. I'll let you get back to it."

"Do you wanna come in and watch? Meet the kids? My three nieces are in the class too." He seemed excited, like he had never had anyone, at least not any of his passengers—or clients were they called?—see him outside of his role as chauffeur. And a martial arts instructor, a Master *Dan*? The contrast floored her, although, it somehow fit. It actually really fit him—to a tee.

"Well, let me check my email, and then toward the end of class? So I don't totally disrupt your time with them."

"Okay. Sounds good. It'll be another twenty minutes. You'll wait?"

"Sure. Yes." She smiled as her eyes drifted from his defined collarbone down to the 'V' opening of his uniform, his chest wide, smooth and strong. Her eyes shot up to his face in an instant and her cheeks turned red from the unwarranted flood of heat rising up her body. *How mortifying.* Her feet were frozen in place, she couldn't even move away from the awkward face-to-face.

He grinned at her. "Okay then." He nodded then spun around to reenter the side room. "See you in a few."

She backed up and began to walk through the maze of wooden tables to find a seat. But the resonating warmth from being so close to Tony and the pounding in her chest made it hard for her to focus, to even pick a table. Tony the Driver was now Tony the Master, and he had made her dazed and confused like a silly schoolgirl.

*

She finally took a seat facing the classroom door and realized she'd forgotten to get the Wi-Fi code.

She shook her head to herself as she made her way back through the wooden maze to the librarian's desk. While waiting for the longhand version of the code, she pulled a few online college course brochures from the counter, thinking of the girls at the club and a flyer for open-call auditions for an off-Broadway show in the City. Laynie had mentioned theater was a forever dream of hers. Then she took the password from the woman behind the desk and went back to her seat.

Before her ass met the flattened chair cushion, one of her phones rang, jolting her up again. She scurried out of the building to avoid pissing off the readers dotting the large main room, as well as the currently narrow-eyed librarian.

Which phone? The smartphone screen was black, so she dropped it back in her purse and grabbed and flipped open the club cell. "Johnnie?"

"Who else would it be?" he said, no smile behind his voice.

Weird response. "Uh, no one. What's up? How are you?"

"Got the dress picked and found the perfect shoes to match, so give me your shoe size and—"

"Oh no, you don't. Johnnie, we had a deal. Don't spoil me any more than you already have, please."

"But they're seriously perfect. You can speak to the clerk. Here. She'll attest to it. Oh, what's that? You can't buy them separately anyway? She said I've got to get them, they're an item…"

She was glad he'd lightened his tone because at first he seemed bent out of shape. But whatever mood he was in, she really didn't want him spending more money on her. She'd already caved on the damn dress. "Johnnie, seriously, you need to let me cover the shoes. At least, take it out of this week's pay."

"*These* shoes, sweetheart, are the entire week's salary. Let me. I want to."

What the hell? Her father was in the damn hospital and she was not only going to an extravagant show in the City, but some man was spending big bucks on a dress and now shoes that, in combination, could feed a small village in Mexico for a week. She was about to be sick. She took a deep breath in and let it out before speaking.

"Johnnie. You are too sweet. Please don't buy the shoes. Chock it up to my pride. Please understand. Let me get my own."

Silence for a beat, then, "Okay. No problem, Jana. You and I really are cut from the same cloth. The dress is ink-black, like your hair. And the shoes you find will be fine, and you'll be radiant. No doubt."

She sighed in relief and swallowed hard. A strange vibe was building and she knew it was going to be difficult to undo. "Thank you, Johnnie. So much. And hey," she thought quickly, "my mother is waiting for my call. Let me talk to you later, okay?"

"Sure, of course, go. Talk to you tonight," he said with an almost manic quality to his voice. She put the phone away and wondered why they even had to talk later that night.

She went back inside slowly, the low vibration from the conversation with Johnnie contrasted so sharply with the frequency she'd been on before the call, after bumping into Tony. *Master Tony.*

She found a seat and shook it all off. Life could be really surreal and bizarre sometimes. *Sometimes?* Right.

Wi-Fi, email: focus. While she waited for her network options to pop up on her smartphone, she looked at the wall clock. Five more minutes until Tony's done with his class.

Her email inbox came up with the tap of her finger.

Zero new messages. Nothing from HR. Stark disappointment flooded her being. She clenched then unclenched her jaw. What to do?

She couldn't call Nora, not on a Sunday.

But she could email her.

She threw a quick email together along the lines of "checking in and following up," to indirectly ask *Will my position be held for me? For more than a month? If at all?*

Frustrated, she decided to save it as a draft for a minute. Never a good idea to shoot out an email when emotional. She could call Luly in the meantime, to see what her best friend knew. But after the fifth ring, she gave up. She was inside a library after all. And she didn't want to go back outside as it had started raining.

Screw it. She opened her drafts folder and without so much as rereading it, she sent the email to Nora. Then she stared at the clock. Waiting and breathing.

A ping sounded from her phone a few seconds later. "Message undeliverable." Her follow-up to Nora had bounced back. "Shit!" she said too loudly, somehow forgetting where she was among the book stacks and overheads. "Sorry," she whispered to the few people close by.

The wall clock showed it was time for her to meet a roomful of far too adorable kids. Totally uneasy, she stood up and headed to the double doors to be ready for Tony to come out of the classroom. But she could hardly unclench her teeth. Why had her email message bounced, and why had she not gotten an email from HR or Nora in the first place? Nora had said she'd get right on it, right? And her boss had undoubtedly felt and heard Jana's urgency.

And now she was an anxious wreck, her thumbnail about to dig into the tip of her index finger. But Tony, with his mellow and calm demeanor, had just bowed off the mat, turning her way now, waving her in.

Put your fake smile on, Jana.

Damn it, Nora, what the fuck is going on?

*

The class couldn't have finished fast enough. His heart rate never exceeded a walking pace when he practiced with the kids, but since seeing Jana, he'd been on fast-forward inside his chest, as if he'd run a marathon.

After he had released the kids with their final bows, he waved Jana into the room. He was glad, no thrilled that she'd stayed.

The kids, especially his nieces, were all enthralled with her. "Is this your girlfriend?" five different children asked, and he watched Jana's cheeks turn a new shade of red. It was hilarious to him, a rock-hard dancer-come-nurse who had shown and seen it all, blushing from the kids' onslaught. He swallowed back his laughter, though.

"No. Miss Jana is a friend of mine. And, a real hero. She is a New York City emergency room nurse; she saves lives every day." He winked at her, but all he could see in her eyes were welling tears. *Shit.*

As if on autopilot, he moved a step closer to her and put his arm around her, squeezing her shoulder, bringing her further into the room and infusing as much strength and comfort into her being as he could.

She gave the kids a brave smile and blinked her eyes dry the next instant. He felt her shoulders lift as she inhaled a mouthful of oxygen and he released his hold.

"Nice to meet all of you," she said, throwing him a slight nod, as if to say thanks and that she was okay.

"Please come and shake Miss Jana's hand in introduction everyone, thank her for her service, and tell her what you all want to be when *you* grow up."

"Yes, Master Antonio," they all shouted in unison.

Jana looked up at him wide-eyed. She was either surprised by the drill response, or by the use of his full name. Her expression was warm, glowing, like the first night in his limo, only, this time, she was awake.

She shifted her attention from him to the children, who had already formed a single-file line to meet and greet her. He felt a river of pride flow through him as each of his kids shook Jana's hand as he'd taught them, keeping full eye contact, proudly speaking their names, telling her their hopes and dreams.

He noticed how she listened and connected to each child. She was a real natural. And although she was the same height as some of his oldest students, she still exuded a tall, authoritative yet relatable air. The entire scene captivated him. Moved him.

"All right, students, please get your shoes on and go to your parents."

Again, "Yes, Master Antonio."

Jana didn't hide another smile in response to their obedient reply. To distract from his heated face, he waggled his eyebrows at her. She let out a giggle.

*

All the kids filed out except for his nieces, who waited by the classroom door chattering quietly amongst themselves, probably about their '*Tio* Antonio' talking to 'a girl.' Standing with Jana, unsure of what to do or say then, he noticed the bullets of rain hitting the roof.

"Pretty bad out there. Did you drive here?" he teased.

She smiled back and began to walk out of the room with him.

"So, I'll get you back to the apartment now. I just have to drop the girls off at my sister's first. I'll double back and bring you to the apartment right after that?"

She paused her stride. "This was supposed to be your free time until this afternoon," she said, obviously apologetic.

"Please, no worries. It was cool running into you. I, uh, actually had withdrawal…"

"Excuse me?" She tilted her head ever so slightly.

Heat reached his cheeks again. *What the hell, Antonio?* "Withdrawal… from driving you." He shifted then anchored his stance, trying to recover a modicum of pride. *Say something, dumbass.* "What I actually miss most is your height. Your head totally blocks my rear view, and what can I say, I love a challenge." He flashed a smile, and then cracked up.

She gave him a threatening glower in jest. "Are you commenting on my height, *Master Antonio?*"

"Yes, yes I am. But I regret it completely now. It's always the littlest foes to watch out for."

"That's right, and don't you dare forget it." Her expression, a spark of something deep and hot and strong—it threw him. And he couldn't rip his gaze from hers. She was so fiery. Electric pulses shot up his spine.

He focused his breath, his mind. *Control yourself.*

Clearing himself of jumbled sensations, he hunted for his voice, for words for the enthralling woman at his side. "I can't lie." He stepped an inch closer to her so his nieces wouldn't hear. "You are just really good company." *Lighten it up.* "Interesting company. Most of my passengers are, well, pretty dull. But you and all your cool and different moods and expressions, you keep me on my toes." He smirked and nudged her with his elbow.

And she gave a look back at him equal to a punch in the arm.

Warmth filled his chest. "I'm kidding, I'm kidding. Seriously, the last few days must have felt like a year for you."

"A little bit," she admitted.

"Well, I really do enjoy your company, and I could listen to you speak, with your multitudes of languages, or sing—"

"Excuse me, Master Antonio? The rain is getting worse I think. Shouldn't we be going?" his oldest niece asked with sincere worry on her little face.

"Your nieces call you *Master*, not Uncle?"

"In the *Do Jang*, all my students call the teacher Master." He wiggled his eyebrows again for her, then he turned to Tanya. "Yes, kiddo, let's get going."

"I'm ready too, *Master Antonio*," Jana said, head cocked, her tone absolutely flirty.

He gave her a slow-blinking eye-sigh, smiled, then took steps toward the door. "So, listen, I need to stop at my place to shower and change before picking you up again for the grocery run. The best store is literally next to my place, but it won't take me long at all. We'll still be on schedule, more or less."

"Well, I don't want you to go out of your way just because I happened into the library and interrupted your class–twice. I'll walk back; it's really fine. Rain won't melt me."

"No. You'll get sick. My grandmother told me so." He smiled.

"Well if the store is right next to your place, why don't we drop the girls off, and then I'll wait in the limo while you get changed, and then we can go to the store?"

"A perfect idea, but I wouldn't leave my worst enemy in a parked car in front of my house, not in my neighborhood. And you're someone I can stand, and, you being as attractive as you are, I'd for sure never see you again," he warned, then he caught her eyes shift to the floor. Bashful? From his comment about her looks? God, she was such an anomaly to him.

"Then I'll come up. Nothing can be worse than my folks' place. Not as horrendous smelling, at any rate. Days' old kimchi on crack-cocaine." Her brows lifted, her tone serious.

"Okay, since I couldn't argue with you anyway and I hate losing, giving in is less of an ego blow." He smiled. "It'll give us more time to get the groceries back to the studio before heading to the club."

"We're ready girls," he told his nieces who wanted nothing to do with him. They gave their full attention to Jana and fought over who got to hold her hands on the way to the limo. It was sweet, and Jana was sweet with them.

They went out the side entrance to the secure staff lot and ran to the stretch. They didn't get completely drenched while he fumbled with his keys to unlock the back door.

God, get it together, man.

The girls hopped in, squealing and chattering the whole time. Tanya scooted in to make extra room and patted the seat next to her for Jana to join them.

But Jana paused, getting both him and her more and more soaked by the second. She looked at him with a smile and stepped aside for him to close the door. "I'll sit shotgun with your Uncle Antonio," she said, and then hopped in the front passenger seat, slamming the door shut before he even knew what happened.

CHAPTER 24

"YOUR SISTER CELESTE is pretty awesome," Jana said after having had a quick chance to meet her when they dropped off his nieces.

"Thanks. I agree," he called from his bedroom.

"My best friend Luly is a single mom of five. It's crazy hard work, for sure. But Celeste seems to be doing a great job. Those are some super sweet girls," she said as she looked at family photos on the mantle of his tiny apartment.

He either had an army of siblings or he grew up with a slew of cousins because there were too many different kids to count in all the pictures. She turned around, about to ask him what the deal was when he appeared, his broad, strong chest at her eye level, inches from her face.

"Eleven. I have eleven brothers and sisters and twenty-five nieces and nephews. And always counting. They're all awesome, my vicarious kids, you know…until I have my own someday." He smiled but looked back at the photos quickly. "I'm this one." He leaned past her, his arm brushing her cheek as she turned to face the mantle again. "God, I was only like thirteen or so?"

She peered hard at the photo. Then looked back at him with a narrowed gaze. "Don't tell me you were one of those kids who totally skipped the awkward stage?" She looked again at the photo. "God, all the girls must've been chasing you, boy!"

"If they had, I didn't notice. I was already an entrepreneur by then, running my own big-time paper route," he said, laughing. "Or I was helping out at home."

"Huh. And is this cutie the youngest of the twelve?" She pointed at an infant in pink sitting on his lap.

"That's my littlest sister, Isabel. God, I can't believe how long ago that was. That I changed her diapers." He shook his head with nostalgia in his eyes. "It makes me feel so damn old. Anyway, Isabel happens to be my very favorite. Don't tell anyone, okay?" He winked.

She let out a snicker even as her heart sank in her chest.

*

Her look, big wide puppy dog eyes with a sheen of sadness, made him worry.

"What? What is it?"

"No, it's just, God, that's so sweet. You and your baby sister..." Then she officially looked as if she would cry right there on the spot.

"Jana?" He wanted to hold her, comfort her...something. But instead, he went with his gut and kept his distance.

She shook her head toward the floor. "Sorry, sorry. I'm being so stupid, so emotional, damn it."

He stayed silent but moved his hand to brush her elbow. "You wanna talk about it? Or no."

She swallowed then met his gaze. "I have one brother, and he's a real bastard, twelve bastards in one, really. And, Jesus, I've never even met his kid, with another one on the way supposedly. He left me stranded." She sighed then shifted her stance to hide her tears.

Her tears, they lit a fuse in him. He wanted to crush, pound, then rip apart the source of her tears. This prick, her brother. Whatever he'd done to her, he wanted him to pay.

But, damn it, Antonio, it's none of your goddamn business. Stay focused. And cue mantra.

*

He was so...concerned. She wasn't used to such genuine care. Especially from a man. Even Johnnie's focused attention toward her was obviously laced with undertones—well, strong undertones—of self-centered desire. But Tony, rather, Antonio, didn't seem to want anything from her. It was like he just wanted her to maybe…be okay?

Antonio. God his whole name fit him so well, so much better than Tony. It was a regal name. Strong. *Sensual.*

"God, I'm so sorry. I hope I didn't bring up bad memories for you—"

"No. Not at all. It's…awesome to see that love between siblings even exists." She didn't want to bitch about her brother. The thought of Dane made her angry enough, and she was having too nice a time. But she was too late. From the soft stare he directed at her, so many questions in his eyes, she'd already dampened the light mood of the day.

He stayed utterly silent.

"It's really okay. I won't bore you with the details. Some other time, yeah? Hey, how about that 'story shocker' competition we planned last night? Much more exciting than my family melodrama," she said then laughed, trying hard to recall the lighthearted mood from just minutes before. "Come on, let's go grocery shopping, and start the game. You can go first."

She stepped back from the mantle and moved to the front door. She turned to make sure he was following her lead in changing subject, mood, and setting but then she had to pause. Being out of such close proximity to him, she noticed the entire man as he stood in the center of his small front room. A third persona; magazine model? *Jesus.* Clad in faded blue jeans and a perfectly fitted cotton collared shirt, he halted her breath a moment. The shirt, a soft mint green, brought out the translucent hazel of his eyes that she hadn't noticed before. In fact, she'd sworn they were brown in color. A memory flash hit her, an image of his gaze in his rearview mirror from the last few days. She realized then that she hadn't taken a close enough look. But, God, now, those kind eyes, so clear in the natural light of the room, were looking directly at her and into her. How could she ever have thought those eyes held spite or judgment?

He cleared his throat, bringing them both out of the mutual spell they seemed to have fallen under. She felt her cheeks and ears get red hot, but, to her amusement, he was totally blushed, too. He nodded and gave her a surrendered smile as if acknowledging his auto response to her. To *them.*

He sighed. "Yeah, let's get the hell out of here."

*

Monday morning came fast.

"Good morning, *Antonio*." She grinned as he insisted on opening the front passenger side door for her. "You know," she said as she folded herself into the seat, "*Antonio* is much more fitting for you than *Tony*. I really do like it."

He liked it too, her saying his full name, his real name. Since yesterday's library run-in, then throughout their grocery errand, and to and from the club. He liked hearing it each and every time.

Other than his martial arts students and his late mother and sisters, everyone called him Tony or Tone, maybe saving a millisecond or two of their lives. Hell, not even Michelle had called him by his name; she'd called him 'Ant,' which had turned out to be a perfect foreshadowing for what she'd do to his heart, crushing it like an insignificant bug. *God, I should've known.*

And the way Jana, specifically, said his name…*dear God.* Since he'd given Jana the mp3 player, he'd found out that she had an amazing singing voice; she'd hum or sing quietly from the back seat, as if unconsciously. It was with that same musical quality that she said his name; it literally strummed melodically over her tongue. It soothed him. And he craved that soothing, like a caged beast waits for its calming song. Because although he portrayed calm and control on the outside, Antonio's inner makings were anything but. Simply being around Jana gave him a feeling of deep serenity that he'd only known at home, in Puerto Vallarta. Come to think of it, not ever as deeply as he felt in this woman's presence.

Don't even go there, Antonio. You cannot risk another Michelle-situation— you've been there, done that. He had to focus on getting home. And *only* getting. The hell. Home.

He gave her a slight smile, buckled up and started the ignition.

*

"I like riding shotgun much better," she said with a wide, playful grin.

Dear Jesus. She was only an arm's length from him now, and her effervescence alone was grabbing him by the throat and blocking air to his head. He could hardly think straight.

"You do, huh? It's official then?"

"Yeah. Pretty much. I mean, I don't think of you as a chauffeur, and I'm no prissy snob that needs serving, so why not? Anyway, I get way less woozy sitting up front. Plus, I can mess with the radio." She winked at him as her hand moved toward his radio.

He slapped her hand away playfully. "You think I let any female touch my controls," he said, a wide smile spreading across his face, but suddenly uncertain if she'd be offended by his half-intentional Freudian slip.

God, Antonio, what the hell are you doing? He searched her eyes then, hoping she didn't catch it. *Unlikely.*

She broke out laughing a beat later, and through her gasps found words. "I have no intention of touching your controls, buddy. At least, not with your pretend wedding ring on." Her laughter trailed off as she caught her breath.

He smirked at her. *Veer back to safe chatter, Antonio. And fast.*

He turned the "mock" ring with his thumb as he veered onto the highway, north to Fort Lee then he cleared his throat. "Anyway, a chauffeur's music selection, if you must know, is incredibly personal to him." He lifted his eyebrows at her to show his faux-seriousness and hit play on his CD player above the radio.

A soft chiming resonated within the space, then a sudden booming of... children's voices making silly animal sounds. Jana was so badly startled he watched her jump up in her seat, literally catching air.

He tried like hell to control his laughter so he could speak. He took a breath and smirked. "My nieces are the only females in the world who have ever gotten to choose what we listen to in *my* limo."

She lifted her brows at him, moved her slender arm to the radio knob to lower the volume a few notches, and then nodded her head as if defeated. "I get it, the girls have seniority, fair is fair. I dig animal noises anyway. Farm or forest, they're all game. I actually danced my best numbers to Old McDonald back in the day." She laughed, hearty and full, and it made his heart race. Her mood had become lighter than air and he couldn't help but catch the vibe.

Then she shifted her body in the seat to face him.

He could sense her mood shift.

"So, limo sex."

"Excuse me?"

"Limo sex. You've really never had sex in your own limo before?"

A personal question that lodged a knot of embarrassment combined with shock in his chest. The answer: Only with Michelle…on their wedding night. And it wasn't just sex.

"You know, I never have had sex in my limo, or any other limo for that matter."

It was true. Because he'd *made love* to Michelle in his limo. And although, he knew now, that it had been completely one-sided, to him, the intimate connection they'd shared in his limousine was more religious than attending church on Easter Sunday.

Lighten up, Antonio. Jesus. "Uh, what about you?" he asked, then chose his next words carefully. "I'm sure wealthy club regulars offered you a ride in their limos during your time dancing." He hadn't said "as a dancer," but, "dancing." And his take of her soft and thoughtful expression, she'd caught his purposeful distinction.

"Oh, they'd offered. But no. I kept to my rules. Dance, make money, and get out. Never once slept with an ogler, not even my highest paying ones. And no staff. I may have been the only one who kept that line," she said, shooting her glance downward, her hands fidgeting on her lap.

"You okay? Didn't mean to make you rehash—"

"No, I'm good. It was all so long ago, and…I asked you first." She paused, but he could see in his peripheral that she was looking at him as if wanting to say more.

"What is it?"

She took a sharp breath in. "Charlene. A long time veteran at the club and my mentor, I guess you could say. I had my lines, but she watched out for me, like a hawk really, so I kept to them. Because, you know, being so petite, I could assert all the rules I wanted, but if a bunch of drunken guys at a strip club wanted to…you know. Well, she saved my ass more than once when men wouldn't take no. But—" She froze and inhaled. Then held it.

He felt like saving her now, saving her from speaking about whatever it was. He hated the tension in her voice and the thick angst glazed over her face. But he also wouldn't dare interrupt her. Hell, he already knew from only a matter of days that she was stronger than steel. She'd continue if she wanted to, or she'd end the conversation altogether.

She let out a long breath. Then whispered, "No one was there to protect *her.* When I left Jersey for MMU and the Manhattan club, Charlene moved out to Vegas. Big dreams. Wanted to break into the real shows there. But it takes time to get a real gig outside of the club scene, and she needed to make ends meet. It was five guys. They used her up and tossed her out." She gulped down hard and shook her head, her eyes shut tight, as if to see, or maybe to escape, whatever nightmare was playing out in her mind. "I'd spoken to her the day before, and she was doing great, even had an audition for a several-year magic show stint at one of the bigger casinos."

"Jesus. I'm sorry, Jana." He got into the right lane, let off the gas a bit, and glanced over at her. "I'm really sorry." He placed his right hand over hers. He felt her warm silken skin, so soft. She let him keep it there, still as could be. When he needed his hand back on the wheel to get off at their exit, she let out a small sigh.

She cleared her throat. "I'm sorry. God, I'm such a downer. Guess I need to get as low as possible before having to see my folks." She half-smiled as she wiped her tears, now officially and undoubtedly the sad kind.

"I don't know you all that well, Jana, hardly at all, really. But without sounding condescending or anything, just with what I do know—your father's condition, working as much as you do, then, Jesus, losing your friend like that, and seeing whatever else you've seen in the clubs!—you're probably one of the strongest people I've ever met."

Then he drove on in silence.

Really, it was true. He'd once thought his mother had been the strongest person alive. Yesinia Ruiz had raised twelve kids, managed a husband and had held two jobs, but when she took her own life, he'd felt like the Earth had fallen out of its orbit around the Sun. Because he could no longer trust anything anymore, including the strength of the Sun's gravitational pull. Many years had passed before he began to believe in people again, in gravity again. And just as soon as he'd begun to trust his footing on this floating rock of a planet, he'd met Michelle.

But here and now, he was in awe of this woman sitting beside him. Jana Park was brave beyond his comprehension. Solidly grounded. A warrior. A warrior princess.

He pulled into the hospital drive as she clutched her purse close to her chest, getting ready to leave the limo and reenter Fort Lee General.

"Thanks for saying that, Antonio. God, I need every bit of courage every time I step into this place." She gave him an unconvincing smile. "Here's to another day in paradise, yes?" The somber and surrendered expression drawn on her face hurt his heart.

"I'll be here when you come out," he said to her before she shut her door. *I'll be here.*

*

She was totally drained after another horrid day with her father. She collapsed into the passenger seat and exhaled.

Antonio placed a bag containing a white box of hot food on her lap. "Best Korean food in North Jersey. I've been craving it ever since I dropped you at your house that first night. And even though your folks live upstairs from it, I wasn't sure if you've ever eaten there or had it in a while, since you said you've lived in the City for the last few years…but man, it's the best."

She couldn't contain her laughter. Crying, sobbing laughter. The takeout menu inside the bag had the *Korean Soul* logo she'd created more than a decade ago, and seeing it made her laugh harder still.

"What? Did you grow up on Korean food and now you despise it more than a needle in the eye? Or do you hate the place?"

She shook her head, unable to speak or breathe through her sputtering laughter. "Literally, I grew up on the food *and* I hate the place. It's my parents' place. My folks' restaurant. And with my mother running the show on her own…well, just tell me, did you already eat?"

"No, I was waiting for you." He smiled.

Thank God! Food poisoning Antonio by familial proxy would've made her feel terrible and would have possibly killed them both on the drive, the limo operator falling dead at the wheel then the limo careening off the highway.

But, wow that was sweet of him, getting dinner and waiting to eat with her. Too sweet, really. Warmth filled her chest.

"That's nuts. *Korean Soul* is your family's place?"

"Yup. My mother is insisting on keeping it running, but I'm praying that no one gets sick and sues them. Then I'd be doing this shit for the rest of my life! I'd kill myself, I swear," she said and took the boxes of food, opened the door, and moved to get out and throw them away. But when she looked at him to be sure he understood what she was doing, his face was solemn, a hint of what might have been anger tinted his eyes. "It's okay, we'll pick something else up on our way…and I'll pay."

His eyes pierced hers. "Please, don't ever joke about killing yourself." Then he turned to look straight ahead.

Whoa. A thick downpour of intensity drenched the air. "I'm sorry. Just a figure of speech."

He shook his head and blinked slowly. "Of course. Sorry to get all serious." He sighed and looked at her. "We can just…stop at a Mexican spot I know. They're good and fast."

Jana stared. She'd hit a nerve, or more like a deep wound, and felt horrible about it even though it was, of course, unintentional. She slowly climbed out of the limo to trash the food then came back in a second later. "Antonio, I didn't mean to—"

"No, my turn to tell you to just ignore *me*. You're fine. Really." He pulled out of the spot and headed out of the parking lot. Her phone rang before either of them could say anything else about it.

"Sorry, gotta take this. It's my best friend." Jana had texted Luly that morning with the bouncing email-saga.

He nodded as she answered Lu's call—in Spanish of course, wanting to speak as candidly as possible. And she had to take the call. Beside it being hard as hell reaching Luly in the first place, Jana needed to know what Lu may have found out about Nora, the department, her position.

"Lu, tell me everything!"

Luly assured Jana that her position was still being held...for now. Dr. Nora Lance had been transferred, and Dr. Roberts had replaced her with the chief resident from the geropsych unit, a chauvinist asshole named Dr. Grant.

"In two days' time? Over a weekend? And why didn't Nora even call me and tell me any of this? Isn't that strange? And is Grant planning any changes?"

"Not sure about Nora, maybe she's just swamped. It was literally Friday night that she got the news. And as for ER changes, none yet. Sounds like he'll be observing for the next few weeks. *Tranquilo*, Jana. I will keep you posted. It'll all work out."

So said Luly. Luly had a strange take on work, probably because she had a family to support. A job was a job, a hospital was a hospital, and money was money. Whatever paid the bills.

But for Jana, the MMU ER was the pinnacle; the level of care was unmatched, and her being a part of that team, well, it was reflective.

"But how are you? You doin' okay?" Luly asked, exuding a motherly tone, as always.

"Hanging in there. Everything's as you'd imagine. Well, except for my unexpected guardian angel, the limo driver."

"Guardian angel, huh? Thought he was a dickhead?"

"Well, I was wrong, maybe heard what I wanted to. But he turns out to be a really good guy. Unlike any man I've ever met."

"Not saying much for you, hun."

"I know, right? But he's…well, I guess I could call him a friend. Yeah, a man friend." *Hmm.*

"Hey, a friend with a cock might be really helpful for stress relief right now. Is he hot? 'Cause I know a chauffeur makes no money…but if he's nice to look at.…"

"Him not having money is more of a turn-on than anything these days," she said, thinking of Johnnie and the club and hell, her family and all the god-awful associations she had with money in general. "But yes, he's attractive." Who was she kidding? "Actually, he's really damn hot." She laughed while Luly catcalled in response.

"Girl, you deserve a little fun. Do your thing, Jana. Please! And hey, I can live vicariously through you. Have a fling for your beloved bestie, for Christ's sakes! Make it my birthday present."

"Lu, come on. Deserve it or no, I have no time or energy for a fun fling." Jana sighed. "Anyway, what I really need is for you to do everything humanly possible to make sure my position is held for me. It looks like I'm gonna be here for at least six weeks. Or possibly more. I can't handle losing all I've worked for, Luly."

"Don't worry about that, Jana. You're an amazing nurse, you can work anywhere.…"

"NO. No, I cannot, Luly. You know me and how hard I've—we've—worked to get into the rotation at MMU. THE Manhattan ER, Lu!"

"For all the raw life you've lived, Jana Park, you still think that shit matters? The name of the facility? The titles, the—"

"No, Lu, it's not that! The facility, the doctors, they are the best of the best! That's what matters."

"Beyond needing a livelihood, I thought we got into nursing to help people?"

A righteous punch to the gut from her best friend was not what she needed right now. Not after the several hellish days she'd had, with too many hellish weeks to come.

"Oh, Lu…sorry, I gotta go…got to the club and I'm late getting in." Jana hated conflict, she hated criticism, and she hated that the words Luly lovingly stabbed her with might have rung too true. Jana knew that Luly knew about her escapist coping mechanisms. She couldn't face this shit right now.

*

She ended the call feeling lousy, so she stared out the windshield as they tore down I-95, about thirty minutes away from the club. No traffic, although she wished there was. She needed more time to cool off.

"So…" Antonio broke the silence. "You think I'm attractive?" Antonio asked, his eyes focused hard on the road ahead.

"What kind of question is that?" She turned to him, shocked and laughing a little at the awkward remark. Then she got nervous. Was he teasing her? Yes, he had to be. She'd started to get his sense of humor yesterday during their grocery run. Yeah, he was messing with her. "I mean…uh, yeah, I guess you're an attractive person. Sure." Then she waited for the punch line.

"No, no…you said I was 'damn hot.' '*Esta rechulo.*' That's what you said."

Her breath got shallow. Cheeks burning. "You…heard? Understood?"

"I understood, yes." He cracked up. "That you think I'm *gooorgeous.*"

"Whoa, I didn't say that!" She got more frazzled.

And he only got more of a kick out of it, waggling his eyebrows at her and smirking.

"You were eavesdropping on my call?"

"Not really. I mean, it was easier to tune you out when you sat in the backseat, but now you're right next to me. And you have my mp3 player, so I can't even block you out with that." He laughed. "But anyway, you think I'm *seeeeexy.*"

She huffed and crossed her arms over her chest; he was enjoying himself a little too much.

"You're pouting."

"You're Spanish, not Italian?" she said, summarizing her understanding as she felt her cheeks get even hotter. Running through her memory, what else had she said to Luly on the call? *Crap!* Calls, plural! And on her last call to Lu, she'd called him a prick. Was that all? Oh God, she hoped that was all.

"I'm from Puerto Vallarta, Mexico, on the beautiful Pacific coast, where yes, Spanish is the native language," he teased.

Of course. How could she have been so stupid to assume he was Italian just because he worked for the Demontes?

"The question, though, is how do you speak Spanish so damn beautifully? You're Korean. And you speak Korean? God, you're trilingual, woman!"

She softened with the compliment. Any annoyance over the fact that he'd neglected to tell her that Spanish was his first language all but vanished. Now she just felt like a stupid, ignorant asshole. She sighed. "First off, sorry for calling you a prick...."

"You called me a prick?"

"Yeah, when you made the consultant-stripper comment."

"I must've successfully tuned you out then." He snickered, subtle dimples on his cheeks showing themselves as he messed with her further.

"Well, I don't think you're a prick anymore."

"I know. You think I'm *suuuper* fine!"

She punched him in the arm and gave him her death look as her cheeks flared up. Again. "Secondly, if I may continue..."

"Of course, *princessa.*"

She glared at him, then cleared her throat. "Thank you, sir. So...my maternal grandfather was Colombian. I was really close to him. My father would try to stop him from teaching me Spanish, but it motivated *mi abuelo* even more." She smiled, loving the memory of the family dynamic. Her grandfather had been the only source of positive male attention in her life. "Yeah, he wasn't about to let his daughter's asshole husband tell him to stop teaching *his* culture and language to *his* granddaughter. And, man, he went all out. Taught me the food, music, dance...even some *Cumbia* moves—"

"*Cumbia*, huh?" One side of his mouth lifted, a seductive glimmer in his eye to match the inherently-sensual national dance style of Columbia. Sensuality in dance and music never held the same stigma in South America as it did in the States.

"Yeah, *Cumbia*. And man did it ever help me get a step ahead in the clubs. For sure," she said with an assuredly proud glint in her eye. Then she immediately shucked the pride off for shame. "God, he'd roll over in his grave…"

"Hey, you danced because you had to, for your family."

"Yeah." She nodded, then shook her head and sighed. "Anyway, *mi abuelo…*" Just the image of her grandfather brought her comfort. "Well, he only spoke Spanish to me. It was like our own secret language; my father and brother hated it." She smiled. "He really was the greatest. And, oh man, his ceviche! He taught me the old family recipe. The best you could ever dream of!" She closed her eyes as she spoke, imagining that specific, delectable taste on her tongue.

"Whoa, whoa, hey now. *My mother* makes—made…" he paused, clearing his throat and quickly focused on the road to make a lane change, "made *the* most kick-ass ceviche. On. The. Planet. And *I* know *her* secret recipe," he said, turning to her, an unmistakable spark in his eyes.

She smiled and lifted a brow at him, her competitive nature surfacing. "We'll just see about that. We'll have a cook-off sometime." But as quickly as the words formed, so did the realization that it would never happen. She'd be too busy working, paying down her folks' snowballing debts, then God willing, she'd be back at her ER in Manhattan. So, ever being side-by-side in a kitchen with Antonio was just not likely.

And that made her feel a little sad. She enjoyed his company. He made her smile, let her breathe. Yeah, the thought sucked. With that downer in mind, she was ready to be back in her zone. "Hey, um, before we get there, I'm just gonna…." She held up her—his—earbuds and music player.

"Please, go ahead," he said. "Do your thing. I'll be sitting here, you know, driving. Me, smokin' hot modelesque man, driving along." He kept his eyes straight ahead as he said it, but didn't hide his perma-grin.

She pursed her lips at him, then allowed her mouth to curl into a coy smile. But then she looked away. Because she couldn't deny that of all the blushing embarrassment in her cheeks, there was an equal amount of heat flooding her core.

Eyes straight ahead, Jana. She had no choice but to keep her damn eyes on the road.

CHAPTER 25

H E'D BEEN DRIVING her to Johnnie's studio each night since last
Saturday. And he hated it. He hated thinking about Johnnie visiting
her, dropping in late at night. Antonio had brought one too many
girls there for that bastard over the years. Johnnie had been 'out of town'
before, but just to leave the club on slower nights so the prick could screw
around with hordes of whores at that very Demonte fuck pad.

Damn him. She was nothing like his cheap sluts. She was anything
but. Watching Johnnie speak to Jana made him ill. And the thought of him
touching her....

But why was it burning him so damn bad? She was a client, an acquain-
tance. Bordering on a friend. Albeit an attractive friend. Who spoke three
languages, including Spanish. *God, such beautiful Spanish.* Intelligent, funny,
endlessly hard-working, and giving. Jesus, for her family, she seemed to
only give.

And tremendously strong. Jana Park was a woman who knew how to
handle her shit. It didn't seem like she'd needed a man's help in past. So why
did he think she needed his help now? In his experience, women like her
took offense to a man overstepping. Besides, she'd probably dealt with far
worse than Johnnie Demonte.

No. Not necessarily the case at all.

Most pricks were obvious, true colors flashing like neon signs. Johnnie
Demonte was different. Manipulative. But Antonio had to consider, Jana

being as smart as he thought she was, that she knew this of Johnnie. Maybe, crazy as it might be, she wanted to be with someone like Johnnie. Maybe she was playing *him*? Yeah. Getting even with all fuckers like him by proxy.

He groaned, sick to his stomach. It almost didn't matter the reason for her being with him, or rather *potentially* being with him. If she *was* with him, she was too damn good, too pure, to be so. That slimy bastard.

He wished he could know so it would stop eating at him. But who the hell was he kidding? If the answer was 'yes,' that she was letting Johnnie—he couldn't even finish the thought—the confirmation that they were together would be too much torture.

Because what could he do if Johnnie Demonte was using her, manipulating her, playing the shining knight of her goddamn dreams? When in reality he was a sadistic, womanizing pimp. An Ivy League asshole with a BA for his puny fucking cock.

But it wasn't any of his business. None. Jana was a grown woman; a strong, independent, extraordinary woman who deserved the world—no, the universe. Not Johnnie-fucking-Demonte. Least of all Johnnie Demonte.

CHAPTER 26

IT WAS THURSDAY. She'd see Johnnie tomorrow night, and he'd want to see what progress she'd made. And she felt good about the changes and training at the club; she was even a little excited.

But really, she knew she was just tricking her own mind. This wasn't her life, her profession, her choice.

In actuality, the days had trudged by, and Jana felt like she was on a rusty old merry-go-round, the super hazardous hand-push kind on playgrounds from way back. Jana was stuck on one. Frozen, scared, and holding on for dear life in the center of the round steel disk. She was dizzy and only getting dizzier. The metaphoric "playground kids," the people in her current day-to-day, kept on pushing it around and around relentlessly. Harder and harder they'd push, faster and faster she spun; just out of control, out of her mind.

The one exception, though, was when she was in her mobile and temporary piece of paradise with Antonio at the wheel. He'd make her die laughing with his limo stories—she had quickly dropped out of the competition because her ER stories made her miss her real job too much, and her club stories made her hate her current one even more. He'd also tell her about his beloved Vallarta, and his huge family that had dwindled down to just his brother Ray, his sister Isabel, and Celeste and her girls in Jersey. She loved hearing about his siblings and their real, crazy, loving interactions. In general, the details of his life were a sweet distraction, a reprieve from her reality.

Then sometimes he'd remain perfectly silent. Giving her space, room to breathe, time to *be*. She thought it was a little crazy how in-tune he was to her needs, all unspoken, but he'd anticipate them just the same. It could've been that he was damn good at his job, super service-oriented. But, still, it was a little eerie. Not even Luly called her moods as well.

So for the entire week, from the hospital to the club, to the apartment and back again, round and round went the merry-go-round. Except when her new friend, her guardian angel, pulled up to take her away, if only for a short time, until the next insanity.

And of course, there were plenty of instances of insanity. She'd gotten not a single call or email update from her precious ER all week, and that drove her to the brink. And she'd made a small payment toward her father's hospital bill with the advance Johnnie had insisted on giving her, but that teeny drop in the bucket seemed to make the hospital all the more diligent, approaching her mother daily instead of phoning Jana. Now her mother was calling Jana upon each occurrence, gnawing on her ear like a rabid mutt on a bone, but slightly more needy. Oh, then after hours upon hours on the phone with four different credit card companies, Jana now had to wait 'til the following week for her cards' cash advances to hit her account so she could make a larger dent in the hospital bills. Then the billing people would lay off a bit, right? Unlikely. Round and round she spun.

Then, there were the girls at the club.

*

The dancers were super needy or full of attitude, one extreme or another. But she already knew that.

Today she got to the club a little early. She needed to pick through a pretty pathetic pile of resumes; many more of the existing girls had been weeded out because of the stringent training schedule she'd implemented. She also wanted to give the remaining girls some extra pole work before the Friday night peak, and, yes, to impress Johnnie. And she'd stay until midnight or later like she had every night this week. She needed to get this right. Make changes fast.

And God, the girls hated change. Again, something she already knew.

But they wanted their income to change! *She* needed their income to change; she needed the club's top line to change. Hell, the changes were only subtle tweaks to bring the atmosphere up: music choice, some costume guidelines, and of course, more elaborate pole work. But really, how much *class* could she possibly infuse into a club named The Wet Spot? In Newark-flippin'- New Jersey.

Anyway, it turned out to be a really good thing Johnnie was gone for the week. Even though she had gotten a virtual *carte blanche* from him with how she handled the training, the girls seeing that she didn't have to consult the owner with each of her desired changes made her authority that much more real.

The other reason; there was definitely less complexity with him out of town now that she was staying at his apartment. There was no gray area staring her in the face. No mixed messages and no opportunity for an awkward situation. That is, until he came back from Long Island.

Get back to work, Jana. She sighed as she looked down at the never-ending pile overtaking the small round two-top. Filtering through the half-completed applications and amateurish headshots, all with sugary-sweet vanity email addresses to match their chosen stage names, was downright depressing. And guilt-surging. She hated the idea of meeting these faces, these names, these hopeless souls. And worse, the thought of hiring them, roping them into the life. It felt too wrong.

No choice in it, though. She'd have to call down the list.

Or she could ask the existing girls to ask their friends.

Like Amber had wrangled her nearly a decade ago.

Shit, she hated this.

She looked up to give her eyes a rest from the pile, and from the situation. The place was dead, none of the girls were out on stage yet, but the bar had a few hardcore early birds already. She sighed, wanting to be anywhere else when she heard her name. Or rather, her stage name.

"Winter! God, is that you? Still givin' me the chills too. Damn," a man's voice came from behind her.

She put on a plastic grin and turned around in her seat. It was one of her very first regulars, a young attorney who had a really long last name and a really short first name, neither of which she could remember now. But she knew he helped pay for a hell of a lot of her parents' first debt and was one of the more respectful guys she'd ever danced for in her past life.

"Hey, wow. It's been years! How are you?" She couldn't cover for her lack of memory. She'd worked too hard to forget it all, as a matter of fact.

"It's Joe. Joe Papatheopoulos!"

"Of course, Joe!" He had aged over the years, deep etchings around the eyes, worry lines across his forehead, a dusting of gray at his sideburns. But he had the same kind eyes. If any regular had to recognize her, at least, it was one of the few benign ones.

"Wow! You look exactly the same, drop dead gorgeous. Amazing!"

"Thanks, Joe. Really good to see you," she said, her face starting to hurt from her too-large-for-life smile.

He waved to Erin, the bartender, for another drink. "And one for my old friend Winter here." He patted the stool next to him, signaling for her to join him.

"Oh, Joe, sorry. Nothing for me. I have to get back to my paperwork and then get the girls together—"

"Paperwork instead of pole work, huh? Moving up to management... good for you."

She wasn't going to explain. Not worth her breath. "Thanks, Joe. Yeah, taking on more responsibility these days."

He pulled out a card from his shirt pocket and came over to her. "Look, I don't believe in coincidences. You were legendary. Guys in my firm still talk about you. Take my card. Call me anytime you need any legal advice, whatever. For you or any of the girls," he said, then he lowered his voice to a whisper. "Employer stuff, domestic situations, even real estate and bankruptcy, we can help. And for you, Winter Snow, totally pro bono. After all, you made our entire damn decade!" He ended his monolog but continued to stare at her, as if musing over long-passed memories in his apparently inebriated head.

"God, thanks, Joe. Really," she said, relaxing her smile into a more genuine one. His offer was really nice. "And hey, enjoy your night, okay? The girls are training really hard on the pole, learning lots of new moves. See if you notice a difference, yeah?"

"Absolutely!" He winked and raised the glass Erin had set down for him. "Absolutely will do."

She held up the business card, nodded another thank you, and showed him that she was sliding it right into her purse.

She turned back in her chair to the pile of resumes and sighed.

*

"Hey, Laynie!" she called, spotting the girl heading back to the dressing room.

Laynie was Jana's favorite dancer, hands down. She was spunky and had a real talent for performing. Knew how to work the crowd. Jana thought she could go far, outside-the-club-scene far. And she was sure that no one had ever told Laynie that before. When she had given the beautiful young brunette the audition flyer she'd grabbed from the library, Laynie had lit up.

And it made Jana feel something other than numb. Maybe she could really make a difference to Laynie and to the other girls too? Get them trained, bolster them with confidence, teach them to work the system, save their money instead of shooting it into their veins or snorting it up their noses, and then get out and above this seedy, shitty no-type-of-life.

"Can you get all the girls together for me, sweetheart?"

Laynie nodded with a smile, snapped her thong at the hip with a wink, and headed to the back dressing room to do as she was asked.

It was an hour before the usual weekday crowd rolled in. They'd gotten used to coming in early, and the groans had even lessened. Because the alternative was bank-breaking. Jana wouldn't let them dance if they showed up even a minute late for training, which was only enforceable now, on the slower weekday nights. It was tomorrow and Saturday night that Jana had to worry about, with the drastic dip in dancers. *Shit.*

She sighed. Then stood up from her seat as the stage began to fill. "Afternoon, ladies. So, before we start"—she sighed again, then swallowed, feeling suddenly parched—"need to know if any of you have friends you think would want to come and—" But she halted her words there. What the hell was she doing? Recruiting more babies? Her gut twisted. Yes, her friend Amber had given her a path to solve her fucked-up family's money problems back in high school, and now she was back again for more, but most girls who got into the business weren't as directed, focused, as she was. Most washed straight down the drain.

"Sorry, never mind. Let's just stretch out, then get some pole work done." No, she'd work with the girls she had, and with the resumes…and if girls came in seeking a spot…but that's where it ended. The weekends hadn't been that slammed anyway, so said Laynie. They'd be fine. Except that if she'd been training them hard and right, they might get a big influx by word of mouth alone.

"Stretching, Winter? Really?" piped Sugar, rolling her crystal-green eyes without shame.

"Yes, Sugar…you've got to actually stretch and warm up before each shift. You wanna get hurt? Then what?" She was shocked. There was no fore-thought at all. "Listen, ladies. You have to be healthy and toned to do this kind of work," she went on, pointing to the pole. "To be great at it, to make the best money, you've got to physically train. You can all make astound-ing money here. There's more than enough green amongst these assholes," she pointed to the sea of empty stage-side seats, "to go around. But you've got to work for it. Be a cut above, and with how the other clubs in the area run things, it's not hard to do. It does mean eating healthy, working out, little to no alcohol, and no snow, no needles. None of it. Actually, starting now, today, if the no-drug rule up to this point went unenforced, it's being enforced now. If we even find any drugs on your person, you're out. And I don't care if you're the best of the best, even if you have a following. It doesn't matter. Any drugs, you're done. Everyone got it?"

She took the nods and mumbling as her answer.

And then she left them all there for several minutes.

She returned with a pile of papers.

"Take one and pass 'em. You can't dance here if you don't sign it. It reiterates what I said. No drugs. And there will be more rules to come. Don't like it, dance somewhere else."

Amidst the scoffing and whispers, she went up to the pole. She reached up, her muscles flexed and shifted as she maneuvered the pole with ease as she pulled herself into an Iron X. Laynie and a few others applauded as Jana's body maintained its perpendicular position to the pole, hovering in a parallel display of pure strength over the scuffed-up stage. Then her feet landed back on the stage floor. The whispers had stopped. She saw only wide eyes and gaping mouths. Even Sugar was silent.

"I made three times the money the other girls made in my time. The difference? I kept clean, and I kept focused. When I see you tomorrow before shift, I want everyone to be prepared to tell me their goals, I mean, their *life* goals."

"I can tell you *my* life goals now!" Sugar announced. "Feeding my baby daddy and our six mini-mouths. Got no other priorities but that right now," she said with her ultra-attitude stance, hip and chin jutting for emphasis.

Jana's hand swept wide, presenting the mostly empty club and its neon red accented darkness. "*This* can give *you* a whole lot more than the basics. Believe me. So if you're gonna be here putting it out there for these fuckers, I wanna show you how to really put it out there, and then bankroll a future for yourselves so that you don't have to put it out there a minute longer than necessary."

Sugar swiveled her gorgeous head of mile-high curls and spun around. The other girls either nodded or stared blankly.

No one ever tells them about a future. In fact, they're scared shitless into hoping to get through today.

"Let's get a new move in before the crowd comes," Jana said. She'd obviously talked enough for tonight.

*

She worked with them for an hour then let them go back and get ready while she went back to her table to collect her papers.

"You're pretty different," Laynie said as she came up behind her. "I mean, I've only worked here for a few months, but no one has ever set rules or asked about our goals or anything like that."

"Do you want to dance for these creeps forever?"

"God no. I want to get out of my dad's house, away from my brother and his friends"—she looked down—"and make something of myself." Jana realized with Laynie's words how too many girls had it far worse than Jana had ever had it. Jana's father had never lifted a hand to her. No, he acted as if she hadn't existed at all. And her brother, of course, saw her as a social pariah since his friends had seen her dance and called her out on it. But they'd never touched her. She would have stuck her spiked heels in their chests if they'd tried.

But this girl was obviously trapped; trapped at home and trapped at the club. "You can get out, Laynie. I did it; why the hell couldn't you?" Jana smiled at the pretty young thing. And Jana believed what she told her. Really. Char had told Jana the same thing. And Jana had gotten out.

Laynie tilted her head to the side as if sizing up Jana's sincerity or her sanity. The girl's eyes asked, "Who the fuck *really* gets out of this life?" Because although she was only eighteen, the girl in front of her seemed to know that most dancers usually, and easily, drown in this life. They'd get pushed into the strip club scene at the deep end of the pool to start with—sloppy money, hard drugs, and then lines were easily blurred, and soon there were no lines at all. The back rooms were often a short cry from hooking.

"We'll see," Laynie said, her tone sounding older than her years. "For now, just teach me how to make more cash," she said, back to being a teenager, smacking her pink bubble gum and linking arms with Jana. "I gotta bring home enough to replenish my dad's stash or I'll get a bruise that no cover-up can hide. No ogler's gonna wanna see a bruised up little bitch on stage, no matter how hard I work the pole."

"Sadly, love, they *would* wanna see it. Fucked up as it is, they absolutely would. But I wouldn't, and I'm the one who counts," Jana said, lowering her chin to be sure Laynie got her meaning. Jana knew it was best to stay out of these girls' personal lives, but she wouldn't goddamn hesitate to send the cops to Laynie's house if the girl was being hurt, and maybe then the sexual abuse Jana suspected—but who could prove—would end, too. God, this shit was too much, too sick, too painful.

She sighed watching Laynie hop up on stage, look down at Jana and wink. "See ya lata aligata."

"Have a great night," Jana said with a smile. Such a sweet kid.

Jana made her way to the upper bar, to her overseeing spot. Strobes and music shot on, a few girls joined Laynie on stage, and the waitresses loaded their trays with shots ready for the doors to open. Jana watched it all happen, while, thank God, she was far from it. Above it. So illusory, though, the superficial distance. It was more bearable for her, yes, but she was also more guilt-stricken too—being saved from the stares. And sitting pretty up in the balcony didn't abate the queasiness sparked by her ever-vibrant memory of stage dancing not too long ago. It didn't really block out the real-time, in-her-face foul nature of any of it.

She moistened her lips, having forgotten to grab herself some water, then she flipped open the club cell and dialed the number of the first girl in the resume stack. *Water can wait.* Getting more dancers in for the weekend could not.

CHAPTER 27

"HEY THERE, BEAUTIFUL," Johnnie whispered in her ear from behind.

He'd actually missed her. After only being in her vicinity for two nights the weekend before, he'd actually gone through withdrawals. He'd missed her scent, her smile, the quiet warmth in her voice. "Just so you know, I'm keeping the dress at my place in the City as a surprise. I'll bring you to my place before the show so it doesn't wrinkle on my drive over."

She smiled, blushed, and took in a gulp of air at the same time. "Thank you. Very much. I, uh, I can't wait to see it. But listen, I've been staying late with my dad every day. Do you think you could bring the dress with you? I can change at the club or at the apartment. The surprise is less of a thing than you having gotten it for me in the first place. And, of course, taking me to the show! I have never been to Lincoln Center!"

He searched her eyes, seeing the source of her discomfort was coming to his apartment in the City with him. He wouldn't push or it would all backfire. "Sure. Of course. I'll bring it to you at the studio. So anyway, how did your week go?"

"Fine. Good. The girls—"

"I meant, more importantly, how is your father?"

"Of course, right. So they finally moved him out of the ICU two days ago. He'll be under close watch, though, until next Friday. Then home." She gave him an attempt at a smile, but her wide, fear-filled eyes betrayed her.

"Don't you want your dad out of the hospital?"

"Honestly, it's almost safer for him to stay in. It's not cheaper…but it's safer. My mom is a pushover, and my father is a damn steamroller. I'm worried he'll be back to his old habits and get sick again. Or worse. Really what he needs is in-homecare, but…" She looked away. Definitely hiding her emotion, trying so hard to be strong, but she didn't have to do that with him. She could crumble, and he'd catch her. He'd sweep her up, take her home, and devour her.

But she stepped away from him and went to sit. Had she read his thoughts, his face? God, was he that transparent? His infatuation had been buried for years, and having her come knocking at his door in such desperation, he really couldn't expect his passion for her to stay completely in check.

But fucking put it in check, damn it! He needed to stay conscious of it to keep from scaring her away. It would take time to bring her around, organically, naturally. And he had three months. Plenty of time. But could his lusting-fucking-cock wait that long? Not a fucking chance.

Wednesday. Wednesday he'd get her alone, out of this context, this neon-lit tease-of-a-whorehouse that he ran. He'd make her know what she could have. With him.

"Listen, if he needs home care, I can take care of that for y—"

"Please don't. Don't even say it. I can't take your money, not without working for it. The advance was as far as my pride will let me go. God, you're too generous, Johnnie."

"Absolutely. No, I understand. Let's just see what happens then. Wait for him to be released from the hospital."

"Yes, right." She shifted in her chair and held her purse close to her, tight to her chest, her perfectly pert breasts.

He came around his desk and sat next to her in the other armchair. Time to change the subject. He smiled at her and said, "So, how did the training and hiring go?"

She angled her body toward him, relaxing into the new topic. "Good. Really good. The girls that are left are working hard. Some have even started choreographing combo routines."

"Terrific. How many left of the thirty?"

"Fourteen."

"Wow. So you've lined up a bunch more to vet?"

"Well, that's been a slower process, just haven't loved the choices in the pile."

"Just have the remaining girls bring in their friends." It wasn't hard. They all had slutty, sexy, hard-up losers they associated with. The only hurdle with that route was that the catty little bitches didn't always want to *help* bring in more competition. They'd love to work every shift. But then he'd be at their mercy. And what if one got hurt or drugged up and tripped out? The key to getting their little whore friends is to incentivize; free drinks or drugs, and they'll bring dozens of 'em.

God, had Jana been out of the business so long she didn't remember the ways of the industry? Because he couldn't run a busy weekend—that should get exponentially busier, fast—with only fourteen girls.

"What do you think?" he asked, getting no response from her.

But Jana only looked down, like she had some reservation. She kept silent.

"Or hey, you can steal a few girls from the competition; the entire avenue is fair game."

"Yeah, sure, I'll do that." She perked up. "And I do have a couple of girls coming in from the stack today, but I'll hit a few of the spots down the avenue on Sunday night."

"Best to get on it tonight in preparation for tomorrow night's volume. I've never run under twenty girls on a Saturday. Don't you remember how crazy it got last weekend? And it only stands to get busier after they see what you've done with them." He smiled, taking care to keep a soft tone and intentionally padding her ego.

But it worried him. Had she really planned to lead him into a weekend—busy, busier, or slow as hell—with only fourteen strippers on? He couldn't fill the stage and the lap dance demand with that. He should have checked in with her earlier in the week about the number of dancers. It was his own fault.

She nodded at him, her eyes slightly morose, but she gave him a subtle smile.

"Good. Let's grab our table in the mezzanine and watch from up there for a while before you head to the clubs down the way. I can't wait to see the changes in the girls we have left."

They walked down from his office and made a beeline to the upper loft. He got her talking about the week to lift her mood. She told him about the dancers who'd stayed and the push back they still gave, but that it was lightening up.

"If they get a bump in their money tonight, I guarantee they'll be kissing your ass tomorrow."

"We'll see about that. Between the training schedule and the new rules I had them sign off on—"

"What? Sign off? New rules for the club?"

"Yeah, a no-tolerance policy for drug possession—so far. As far as *use*, I know giving UIs is a whole legal issue, not something I could touch without talking to you first. But I do need them clean and healthy, punctual, and on it, you know? I need them to keep away from that shit."

He checked himself to be sure he was breathing evenly and shoved his hand into his front pocket to be sure his bag of coke was flat against his leg. She'd implemented what? He damn supplied and used with all the girls in the club.

"Yeah, of course. They need to be focused. I'm, uh, just not sure how well it can be enforced, you know? They're independent contractors, and we can't really legally or logistically check what's in their purses or bags each shift. Plus, they relax up there on stage when they're—"

"Johnnie, you know you can get in some serious shit if you look the other way. And for the girls, it's better for them. Staying clean…they stay healthy, they dance better, longer."

"Their health?" *Fuck their health!* But he caught himself. *Breathe.* "God, you're right, of course. And that's better for business." For his father's fucking business, that is. Not his underground coke ring, for fuck's sake. "I know it is. Like I know my investment in you was the best move I could've made."

She was facing him now, eyes searching him, for sincerity.

He put his hand on her shoulder. "You're right, Jana."

"Good, I'm so glad you see it the same way. And I had them all sign a statement, so you're covered, the club is covered, no worries." She'd had these W9s sign a statement? *Jesus Christ.* His dad would fucking flip if he found out. No records were kept on the strippers. None. Because no taxes were paid on them. Really, *none.* The girls did their own taxes and that was the industry's way. Only bouncers and bartenders were on the payroll. No fucking dancers! That's what was reported by the club. And that was all.

He took a deep breath and kept his smile plastered on his face, and he infused as much calm into his expression as he could muster. "Let's grab a seat, and we can talk more. The place is already filling up. That's awesome, right?" He ended on as light a note as he could to mask his worry for Jana's t-crossing and i-dotting frenzy in week one.

But as he followed her up the stairs, watching her firm ass cheeks wag and tease him with each step, he was immediately hypnotized. So goddamn fine, right in his face. He could pound the fuck out of her right then and there. He wanted to pull her down on his lap and he didn't care who saw, who watched. Actually, the more fantasizing assholes who watched him fuck her to heaven, the better. Because, fuck them, they couldn't have her. She was all his. Or would be.

And you know what? Fuck his father too. Fuck the right paperwork and the wrong rules. His family had so much money they didn't know what to do with it all. Now it was a matter of showing his father up, making that cocksucker see how he could bring in bigger cash, more than Jake Demonte, king of the clubs, ever could. So what if Johnnie's cocaine sales wouldn't be easy and flowing at The Wet Spot now? He'd hit the other clubs' dancers, which was even better, smarter.

Jana's way might really be the best way.

*

He pulled Jana's chair out then sat down across from her. "I trust you, Jana. I know your intentions and your methods are right, businesswise. It's just my father, and the industry in general…. There has only been one way of doing things, you know? I know you know. But I'm with you, though. I hired you, after all. I'm glad you've been making the changes you have been. Keep me posted, but I've got your back. I do."

She looked at him, head cocked to the side, grinning from ear to ear. "I know you have my back, Johnnie." She let out a giggle like she didn't have a clue what he was going on about.

God, had he shown no worry, expressed no issue with any of the shit she'd unloaded on him about club business? Had he really thought it all in his head and hid his frustration? Not a sign of it showed through?

Damn, he was good. Better than he thought.

"Good, just making sure. I know your father doesn't always have *your* back, so I wanted to make sure you know that I do." He smiled and took her hand in his. "I really do."

*

She'd never mentioned how her family treated her to Johnnie. She was super conscious of not discussing her parents, her brother, any of it, only the state of her dad's health. But maybe she had? Her mind had been all over the place, so who knows? She watched Johnnie head to the bar since the bartender and waitresses were obviously slammed, and she turned her attention to the girls on stage. Laynie and Didi were on the poles, and the guys were eating them up. She smiled and looked up at Johnnie as he returned with drinks.

"Should we? I'm supposed to head out to find more girls."

"Have one or two with me before you head out. I'm going to Merrick again for the week. It's nice to sit with you when I can."

Johnnie slammed a double and then another an instant later. He had turned absolutely pale when she mentioned the signed drug statements. She thought he'd be psyched that the girls wouldn't be putting the business in jeopardy and that they'd be more professional, dance better, and, well, bring in more money for the club. He'd tried to hide his sudden concern, but she could see right through it. Now, after his 'got your back' speech, she felt better, like he'd thought it out.

He was more similar to her than she'd thought. He seemed to be living under his father's shadow, just never good enough. She hardly agreed with her own father's ways but was torn by loyalty. Johnnie Demonte seemed to have the exact same issue, and now he was taking the risk, going with his gut, going with Jana.

She took one of the two shots, then excused herself, saying she had to use the restroom, but she only wanted to escape the second shot with him. Again, cleaner lines, although the liquid relaxation could have been helpful with her next task. She hated the idea of scouting for girls, let alone stealing them from other clubs. But she'd at least not be roping new ones into the business.

She made her way back to the table a few minutes later, and Johnnie was on the phone. He was speaking in a low voice, his eyes seemed defeated like he was being chastised, a boy in trouble. She stayed back, pretending to take a call herself, then walked away, downstairs, her escape from embarrassing him and from taking that second drink. She wanted to check on the girls anyway and then get out of there. The quicker she hit the other clubs, the quicker she'd be done for the night. The quicker she'd get to sleep.

Chastity, one of the oldest dancers to stay, came up to Jana with a name and number of a friend of hers who'd professionally danced and needed real money. "I've made more tonight than over the entire last month." And then she walked away.

Jana smiled at the passive thank you, then made eye contact with Laynie, who was upside down in an Inverted 'V' on the pole, stage left. The girl was glowing, green bills hanging from her G-string the whole way around her tight little waist.

Jana didn't feel the same kinetic energy flow she got when she saved a life in her ER, not by any means, but she did feel a small wave of something good rise up to her cheeks, that the training, that she, *was* making a difference.

She pulled out the phone Johnnie had given her and texted him that she'd see him tomorrow night, that she was heading out to scout for, and to steal, more girls.

CHAPTER 28

J ANA FELT GOOD Sunday morning. It had been a late night, so she
was definitely sleeping in.

She reviewed the weekend in her sleepy mind. The girls rocked it
on Friday night and were all well-funded for their efforts. And last night was
further proof positive. All the girls had left the club ecstatic and exhausted.
Gloriously, happily, wiped.

But with only fourteen girls split between the stage, the semi-private, and
private back rooms, she hoped the inflated results the girls were so pumped
about didn't backfire on her when she did find more dancers.

And the 'finding more dancers' fun, she learned, would take her more
time. Her efforts in scoping out the surrounding clubs didn't yield a lot. Jana
was only able to find three dancers worth stealing, and of them, only two
were willing to come over to The Wet Spot, but not until next Thursday.

She had to thank God for Antonio, the only reprieve between each of
the dives she had to venture into. Getting back into the limo to his calming
presence, which contrasted so sharply with the oozing sleaze of the clubs,
she'd felt soothed. And he'd have a cup of coffee for her, or a joke, a news
report, or an unimportant weather update at the ready. He made her smile.

She smiled thinking about those small, stupid gestures of his. Until the
club cell buzzed from the nightstand. She grabbed it fast, hating the jarring vibration.

"Hey…sleeping in?" Johnnie asked when the phone met her ear.

"Yeah, no. Just, yes. Really late night after you left. How are you?"

"Good. Really good. Fabulous weekend. I would have never thought it would be this quick. You're magic, woman. Simply magic."

She smiled with her eyes still shut, wishing sleep would stay, even as she talked to Johnnie for what she hoped would be a quick touch-base. "Awesome. Feels good. I'm really glad. For the club, the girls…"

"For you, Jana! My God. I'm gonna bring last week's balance and this week's pay to you on Wednesday, plus a sweet little bonus, just because."

Although in a haze, she calculated quickly in her head—*fifteen grand.* That would be a relief. With her bank account receiving the credit card advances on Wednesday or Thursday, she'd have the hospital administrator off her back for at least a few weeks she hoped. "Thank you, Johnnie. I appreciate it." Then there was silence. She so wanted to go back to her half-sleep.

"Are you in bed?"

"Yeah. I'm totally addicted to these sheets against my skin!" She rolled over and inhaled the fabric softener smell and laughed. "Why, are you?"

He responded with a low, quiet moan. "Yes. I am."

"Resting up for another long week?"

"Yes, another long one." A pause, then, "Jana? Do you have clothing on…? I mean, enough clothing? Do you need anything, like sleepwear? For me, in summertime, the heat leaves me wanting nothing on at all, you know?" A muffled laugh followed. Then breathing. Deep, heavy breathing.

She lifted her head off the mattress and placed it back onto the pillow, situating the phone more squarely at her ear. To hear better. To hear correctly. Because his breathing was definitely…thick, sultry. "I'm good with clothes. And the AC in the apartment helps. So, I'm really fine, Johnnie. Thank you, though."

A long low hum hit her ears, then morphed into words. "Good. Really good. Jana, do you like the apartment?"

Was he kidding her? Seriously.

Now, she'd *consensually* phone-fucked past boyfriends. Operative word, 'consensually.' And had done so enough times to know Johnnie needed her voice, her details, and her reaction. But she'd been clear with him, clear as

fucking crystal. "Sorry, Johnnie, it's the hospital, gotta go. Talk to you later."
And she hung up.

Jesus. If he would've asked. Not that she would have said yes, but who
knows? Because she sure as hell could've used the release too. Maybe her
line would have accommodated some innocent—and again, goddamn *con-
sensual!*—phone sex.

But now she was just skeeved out of her mind.

And hanging up by using a white lie? Asians believed in Karma, and
she was definitely brought up shoes-off-in-the-house, incense-burning Asian.
She'd also *never* use sickness as an excuse to get out of something, lest the real
thing come to light. That was karmic law. But she wasn't about to let him use
her like that. She felt gross, a little defiled even. And it really *could've* been
the hospital calling her about payment or a donation, not necessarily anything to do with her father's status.

She was now even gladder that Johnnie would be in Merrick again this
week so she wouldn't have to be around him so much. But shit, she'd see him
on Wednesday for the damn show. He'd be bringing a chunk of her pay with
him. So she had to go. No matter how badly she wanted to get out of it, she
had to. It would totally piss him off if she didn't because he had bought her
the dress. What the hell had she gotten herself into?

No, it wasn't anything as bad as Laynie probably had it, or God, Char
or so many of the other girls. But she was under this guy's thumb, and she
couldn't deny that she'd been warned.

Then her personal phone rang—the hospital.

Karma.

*

A shower. An ice cold shower. That's what he needed.

Antonio rolled out of bed and shook out the image of her from his head.
He felt guilty, fiendish, like she'd had enough men stealing her image for
their own sexual fantasies. But he'd gone to sleep thinking about her every
night for the last several nights and woke up the same way.

His thoughts, he justified, were different, though. She was singing in his visions, or speaking to him, telling him her thoughts and ideas. Stories. Sometimes in her lulling Spanish. God, that really got him. And sometimes just her giggle would fill his internal mental movie because he was the source of her laughter.

But he couldn't lie. Her sensual body, her being, her angelic silhouette, she was all there, there in his dreams. And, God, it was as if her form was sent from heaven to torment and torture him. And the more he tried to stay respectfully objective when looking at her stunning figure, the stronger the magnetic pull got, and the more he wanted to connect with her. A deep, locked-in connection.

But his dreams of Jana had at least replaced his nightmares of Michelle. He could only feel relief, an inner liberation from the hold his wife, God, soon-to-be ex-wife, had on him. With Jana taking over his dreams, the image of Michelle became fuzzy, blurry. It was better. He felt stronger.

The shower sputtered to a start, and he stepped under the water. Not having even turned on the hot, he had nothing to wait for. His hard-on was bordering on painful.

As soon as the water hit his chest and stomach, he blew out a stream of air with the shock. This would do it. This would cool him off, at least until noon.

He dropped his chin to his chest, letting the showerhead's icy daggers attack the top of his head and spill down his back. Shivers sprang from his shoulders, and he had to work to unclench his teeth.

He took the bar of soap and spun it around in his palms. Lather bubbled up through his fingers as he started humming a song from his playlist, one that Jana had been singing incessantly all week long, an older ballad by *ARBY*. It was officially stuck in his head. That might help his hard-on die down. Because without Jana's voice, only the words to go by, it actually made him think of Michelle, and she was a definite erection-killer.

Raise up. Or die.
Stand up. Just try.
You expect her to leave you, she will.
Don't just wait for it, you go first.

So just tear it up. Tear it out. Tear it down.
You be the one with the whip. Not in the ground.
And they're the ones begging for mercy.
They'll be lost and you'll be found.
Lost and found. Lost and found. You'll be found.
He slammed his fist on the wall. And then again.

If he'd just opened his goddamn eyes. Damn her. He pounded the tile a third time and immediately forced his mind's eye to replace Michelle with Jana. Jana's eyes, Jana's neck, and her body's curves. Then he imagined her voice.

Jaws clenched, feet anchored, biceps tightened, he thought of Jana. She was with him in his mind, right behind his tensed body. Her wet, slippery skin, radiating warmth; her nipples pressed against his back. Her hands held his hips and then slid around to his front and down, teasing his engorged length with her light, soft touch. He imagined her taking him in her slender hands while he took his rock hard cock in his right fist and stroked its pulsating length to its crown. Then he slid it back down, tight and hard. Her lips, he imagined, pecked light kisses on his back, down his spine, then back up to his shoulder blades. Her imagined breath gave him the chills and pushed him closer to the brink. His left arm rose up and slapped the wall and pressed forward, keeping him stable. He widened his stance, bracing himself. His fist glided along his thickness faster and faster. *Oh God, Jana.* His glutes tightened, his abs tensed, his shoulders held strong, supporting the quickness of his stroking arm, driving him closer and closer to release. *Jana.*

And when he went, the torrential groan that rumbled in his throat echoed in the small space of the shower and in his ears until he got to the very end of his intense orgasm. He still imagined Jana through to the aftershocks, exhaling hard with her name on his lips.

CHAPTER 29

H E ANSWERED HER call after many rings. His voice sounded raspy to her, spent. She had woken him. *Shit!*

"I'm so sorry, Antonio. Shit, I should've just called a cab—"

"Jana, what's wrong? Hell, it doesn't matter. I'm on my way."

"No, you'll miss your class."

"No arguments. You're at the apartment?"

"Yes. I'll wait out front."

Ten minutes later, Antonio pulled up, his dark hair a bit shaggy and wet, like he'd just jumped out of the shower, not even having time to drag a comb across his head.

"My mother called. Wouldn't say what happened. Just to come quick, and then she hung up. She won't answer her cell now. No one is picking up the hospital room phone either. And I'd rather just start heading up there while I wait through the never-ending cycle of the hospital's automated system, you know?"

"Buckle up. I'll be driving a little faster than normal." He pulled out and his tires screeched. "Don't worry…if we get pulled over, I have friends on the local force and in the state patrol. My students. We won't be delayed."

Antonio said not another word, completely focused on the road while Jana hung on hold through the various departments and levels to try and get any more information about her mother's call.

They were nearly to the hospital's exit when she finally got connected to the right unit. As she explained who she was to the operator, a text message flashed on her screen.

From her brother.

She put the call on speaker and looked at the text while waiting for another transfer.

Irresponsible much? Dad's being downgraded rms. for unpaid bill.

"Stop the car. Please. Just…pull over or get off the highway. Just stop the car, Antonio. Anywhere." Her breath was shallow. Her words pushed through clenched teeth. A freight train roared through her veins, to her chest, then her forehead, to the top of her skull.

"What? Is everything okay?"

"There is. No. Emergency." She exhaled the statement like a dragon decimating a village with one fiery flame.

"Your dad is—"

"Fine. He is the same. The big deal was him being moved into a room without a goddamn television." Her mother's cryptic phone call, the one that gave Jana a near-heart attack, was about the billing department 'needing' payment. Even though she'd been in daily contact with the hospital since last week when she couldn't take her mother as the middleman any longer.

And fucking boo hoo for her dad. No entertainment? Hell, maybe the lack of a TV would motivate him to get out of there, to get home. Maybe he'd get serious about his health, his life?

And then reporting to Dane? Again! The nerve of her mother, and the bloody gall of her bastard brother. He never even called her to check on things, let alone send a dime. Or better yet, how about coming out to check on their beloved dad? Fucking asshole! Even for a day? Oh no, the cost! Right.

She brought her attention back to the here and now. "Sorry, Antonio. Didn't mean to snap."

His eyebrows drew together while he shook his head. "No worries and don't be silly."

They drove for a few minutes, she didn't know where, and she didn't care. She knew they were no longer going north to Fort Lee, and that was all that mattered.

*

When her mind stopped reeling, her eyes came into focus on a road sign out her passenger side window. 'Welcome to Palisades State Park.' And the next thing she knew, they were stopped at a grassy expanse, a hill in front of them, blue sky beyond.

"Come," he told her, his eyes sweet and understanding, his voice comforting, yet solid. Antonio the Guardian. He was her glowing torch, lighting her way out of a dark, dismal hole.

She got out of the car, conscious enough to take her purse, but sensing the pureness of her surroundings, she felt almost silly doing so. They'd entered what seemed to be an unspoken safe-zone. Between the lush, pristine park setting and Antonio as her guide, she had not a question in her mind that she was as safe and secure as she'd ever been. But she slid her shoulder strap across her body even still. After five years in the City, she'd become an official New Yorker it seemed.

They walked along a quaint path winding through the bright green fresh-cut lawn, sporadic trees, park benches, small gazebos, and vacant playgrounds that dotted the way. Sunday, early morning, the place was practically all theirs. It was a bit too surreal.

*

Still not a word from Antonio since they'd left the car. She'd only just begun to breathe evenly. The volcano in her chest was simmering, but the molten lava circulating throughout her body was still dangerously hot, scorching right under the now cooling top crust.

She felt calm enough then to speak. They walked on as she told Antonio about her brother who'd abandoned her, robbed her and their parents of much more than money, and her burden, her obligation to her folks, that thankless lunacy. And the dilemma, the constant struggle to reach an unreachable standard in the eyes of her father.

Antonio listened, absorbed, and processed as she continued her dazed, robotic march and monolog while marching through the twisting, turning path.

When her rant was done, Antonio stopped her with a light touch of his hand on her elbow. "Jana," he said, shaking his head to go with narrowed eyes, and God, clamping jaws, shallow breath. "They don't, I repeat, they *do not*, deserve you."

Jana looked away from his drilling gaze. It didn't matter if they did *deserve* her or if they didn't. "It just is this way."

*

"Look," he said turning her body with gentle hands. "I wanted you to see this."

A memorial of the Twin Towers stood before her. Ghost-gray cement replicas, tall, plain, solid. Their mulch foundation base was formed in the shape of a heart.

Jana crumbled to the ground from where she stood. Staring, tears welling in her eyes.

Antonio joined her there on the ground, his presence a silent comfort, like the day outside the library when she felt him pass her by. And then her tears rolled down her cheeks so slowly and deliberately, she could almost count them as they fell.

How small her huge problems were, how insignificant, puny even. Her satirically selfish brother, her unsympathetic, ungrateful and needy mother and the heartless patriarch of her gene pool, Chang Park, none of them made the tiniest dent compared to the representation of tragic tyranny standing there in front of her face.

"You must think I'm pathetic."

"What are you talking about? How can you say that? God, you're anything but."

"I *have* a family *to* complain about. How many of those people don't have families anymore?" she asked rhetorically, pointing at the memorial. "My father is still alive. I'm sulking every day for the injustices of my brother, my parents, the financial crap, all while thousands no longer have dads, or brothers, mothers…futures."

"I didn't bring you here for you to feel guilty. No more guilt, Jana. This was to show you a mirror of your strength. You stand tall, as tall as these towers did originally and do again today. Despite everything trying to tear you down, you rebuild taller, stronger."

She let her purse drop on the ground, took a long deep breath and let her head surrender onto Antonio's shoulder. She exhaled. And let her thoughts go.

*

A long stretch of time went by until he gently touched her back, signaling for her to get up and to continue on with him. They continued their walk in complete and divine silence, entering tree cover, thick green leaves altering and shifting the yellow sunlight above. They reached an open clearing then, with tall jagged cliffs to one side and the great wide Hudson River ahead. She couldn't believe this existed. In all her life, from Fort Lee to her years dancing in Newark, then to Manhattan, she'd never imagined this piece of heaven existed, smack in the middle of the Bermuda Triangle that was her life. Not even her brief escapes to Central Park could compare.

"I'm married." He broke the silence as they approached the banks of the river. "Have been driving around with the divorce papers she served me a few weeks ago."

Jana looked at him. All her thoughts on her own mental bubbles of pain popped one by one as a new, larger one grew in her head. He was married? *Is married.* But divorce papers. Unsigned? Why? Was he still in love with her? Clobbering questions. Unanswered and overwhelming.

And what was her hitched breath all about? Why did Antonio's being married or not married or whatever he was matter to her?

Because it did. It mattered. Deep in her chest it somehow mattered a ton.

But she could only keep quiet. She turned down the volume in her head and listened for the answers to come.

He didn't say another word, though. He only reached for the ring on his left ring finger and twisted it.

The ring. His *real* wedding ring?

He twisted more, then yanked, finally pulling it off. He drew his right arm back with that gold band in hand, took a skip step ahead, and threw it. It flew so far into the Hudson River, she couldn't even spot where it landed and subsequently sank.

His chest was heaving, like he was out of breath, but, of course, he wasn't. It was just tumultuous emotion she was sure.

"Now I'm ready to sign the papers. Ready to be divorced. Ready to be done with her," he said as if in mid-thought. And for now, for her wringing heart, that was all she needed to hear.

He turned to Jana, smiling. He had a glow in his now golden eyes, a new color, a new shade she'd not yet seen. It must have been the rays breaking through the thin layer of clouds above. Diffused but clarifying light and with it, a sense of pure liberation radiated from him.

He plopped down on the grass, laid back, put his hands behind his head, and let out one loud, seemingly joyful breath.

She joined him, free-falling into the grass. With the tips of their elbows touching, she stared up at the sky full of those high-flying wisps thinking how any woman who'd won this man could ever think to let him go.

"I worked a lot."

Jesus Christ in Heaven. It was like he'd read her thoughts! Seriously?

"Well, I still work a lot." He spoke to her and to the sky above while chills, endless chills, continued up and down her, and in and out of her.

"But she said that's why she left, or rather, went *elsewhere*. Because I never focused on the most important thing—*her*. But the fact was, every minute I put into work was a minute closer to starting our life together, our family together. It was all for her!" He paused a beat then turned his head to look straight at Jana. "My goal was always to return to my home, to my

Vallarta, to start a family, but only after I was financially stable. Completely set. When Michelle and I got together and throughout our blip of a marriage, she was in love with the idea. She said so at least. She *seemed* wholly committed, my dream being her dream too. 'A slice of paradise with the man I love,' she'd said. Damn lies. All damn lies."

"Jesus, Antonio. I don't know what to say."

"It turns out, she was nothing but a gold digger. When my prick boss promised her all the bright shiny objects she could ask for, she took back her promise to me in an instant. We'd been married only seven months." He blew out a long breath and went on. "In the end, she accused me of marrying her for a green card. For a goddamn green card! My brother-in-law got me in at the Manhattan gig in the first place. All legit. How she thought I managed such a high position in such a large outfit without being legal, I don't know? And all I ever spoke of was getting back home. I never wanted a green card or citizenship. I don't know. I guess I overlooked a lot of her flaws throughout our relationship. My blindness—my fault."

Jana shook her head. And when her phone rang, definitely the club phone, as she knew the sound by now, she ignored Johnnie's call. She would have ignored all others too, even Nora's. She felt like she owed all her attention to the man lying next to her and not a single iota to anyone else.

But she couldn't think of anything to say to Antonio, and she somehow knew she didn't really need to. Instead, she began to hum. A song from his 'mellow yellow' playlist from the music player he'd loaned her, that first perfect gesture of kindness; at least, the first that she'd been aware enough to notice.

The melody brought her peace as the notes rattled in her throat and slipped from her lips. Then the lyrics came to her mind:

The phoenix, burning up in cleansing flame,
Just to rise from the ashes, life anew, breathe again.
The phoenix, incarnation of the sun,
Deepest in us, never doubt you are the one.
Never doubt you are the one. The phoenix.

"You should sing. I mean really sing. For people." He didn't hide the damp emotion in his eyes. She'd never known a man to be so raw and strong and completely unabashed. And she hardly even realized she'd been singing out loud and she blushed. Then she broke into a helpless smile. "Thank you. For bringing me here."

Before he could reply, her phone buzzed the moment away. Johnnie again.

CHAPTER 30

S HE KNEW JOHNNIE would keep calling if she didn't get it, and this moment with Antonio had come and gone, forever. She swallowed back her disappointment and apologized to Antonio with a look as the phone kept ringing from her purse.

He gave a gentle nod. "You need to take it."

So she answered it.

She prepared to keep her voice and mind level and even, despite her disgust at the crap Johnnie pulled only hours before. Despite it and because of it; he was still her boss. Wednesday's money was what mattered. Then there were only two more months after that. She had seven years in the game. Two more months was nothing.

"Hey there."

"Where are you?" Well, she could've been anywhere, doing anything, especially since the club didn't open doors for setup until 4 PM, so she couldn't imagine what business it was of his. At all.

Breathe, Jana. She sat up and crossed her legs. The wide river in her view made her mind clearer. She sensed Antonio had perked up, and she looked back at him. He was now propped up on his elbows. Protective radar. Then to Johnnie, she said, "I'm on my way to the hospital, why? Everything all right? At the club?"

"I thought when you had to hang up so quickly before, there was something wrong, you know, with your dad? Called a few minutes ago, too. What happened, you know, at the hospital?"

Okay, maybe he was concerned. And she had in all honesty forgotten her quick escape excuse. Her mother's cry-wolf tactic and the self-righteous dig by her brother had turned her brain to electrified gelatin. "Sorry, yeah, everything is fine. Just a false alarm that had me rushing up there until I found out it was a billing thing. I just about had a heart attack myself. I was so fuming pissed I had to stop and compose myself before seeing my family, you know?"

"Yes, of course. Well, I'm glad it wasn't anything serious. Can I do anything, come out to meet you?"

No! "No. I'm really okay, actually getting back on the road now towards the hospital. Thanks, though." She put the words out in quick secession, certain that she wanted Johnnie Demonte nowhere near the knotted ball of yarn her day had become, especially since he'd had a part to play in her day becoming such crap.

"You sure? If you need me, I can change stuff around here on the Island."

"No, Johnnie, you can't do that, and you shouldn't worry about me. I'll be fine, I'll be at the club tonight with the girls as usual. I'm meeting two girls I found from Piranha. Training, scheduling. Seriously, just do your thing." She had to keep things simple, and God, she was starting to sense, or rather, to know, that Johnnie was anything but simple. High maintenance was more like it.

She closed the crappy little flip phone and threw it back in her purse. Her body rolled back down to the soft grass, and she closed her eyes, trying to clear the disruption from the air.

Antonio's head fell back too. "Everything okay? With Johnnie?"

"Oh, yeah. Just...you know, he was concerned, about the 'hospital emergency.' He knew about the call from the hospital."

She looked at Antonio then, his lips pursed, his eyes narrowed as if he wanted to ask her something. Burning to ask her a question, his eyes almost quivering. But then he shook his head, turned his head back to resume his skyward gaze.

"No rain today," he said. The vanilla statement matched the vanilla mood that had been painted onto their canvas, covering up the vibrant strokes they'd shared only minutes before.

"Yup. All clear. Not a single cloud in sight."

*

Back on the thruway, he just kept quiet to let her think, to mentally prepare. She'd calmed down a lot, but had to still be boiling inside. Her loyalty to her family and the sacrifices she'd made were mind-blowing to him. He knew that sort of loyalty to family in Mexico. But he'd made an observation during his years in the States; there was something strange in the atmosphere, specifically in the great city of New York and its surrounding areas. The nameless something somehow stripped away that layer of noble dedication to blood before material gain.

And as far as he was concerned, Jana was a diamond in the rough. She was a precious gem they, her own family, continually tried to milk for all it was worth. But milking a stone would get them nothing. Nor would trying to crush it with their impotent scorn because, if they didn't know, a diamond is unbreakable.

Out of his peripheral vision he noticed her putting on mascara in the visor mirror and so he took extra care not to switch lanes suddenly or hit his brakes. Then she switched to lipstick. He never noticed her wearing any lip color, but he'd definitely noticed her lips. They were lush, almost heart-shaped. Each time she spoke to him, he found himself having to keep from staring at her mouth, that sweet bottom pout, whether smiling or singing or scrunched in thought. And when her tongue moistened her lips after sipping her coffee or pulling from a bottle of water—*Ay Dios Mio!*

He was glad when she closed up the tube, ending the torturous distraction. But then his eyes glanced at her, needing to see the final result. The barely-visible shimmering nude color on her lips became yet another facet of Jana he felt compelled to burn into his brain. Damn it, he was at her mercy.

Then, almost missing the exit, he turned on his right turn signal and quickly moved toward the Fort Lee off-ramp. He heard a small thud. She had dropped her lipstick. And he heard it roll backward as he continued up the wide turn off the exit ramp.

"You okay?"

She was leaning forward and down, reaching under the passenger seat, grunting through it as the seat belt fought her entire attempt. "Yeah, just"—she sat up then, treasure in hand—"got it." And when Antonio saw the white lace thong she was holding up in front of her face, he narrowed his eyes and winced.

"Jocelyn Carlson," he said, shaking his head in disgust.

"The ex-wife to the Wall Street mogul?"

"The one and only," he said, slowing to a stop at a traffic light. Then he took them from her with a handkerchief he'd pulled from the center console, flipped them over and found the usual *Tony's Mouth Here* written in red lipstick on the tiny strip of fabric that was the crotch of the used undergarment. "This is not the first pair. See...the wedding ring *was* for another reason, but it somehow backfired with this one. Jocelyn Carlson is clinically depraved."

"You've never...?"

"No, never. God." He cringed. "I told you, for professionalism alone," he said, scanning her disbelieving eyes. "Seriously, she sickens me. And *this* is my business"—he tapped his dashboard almost lovingly—"my livelihood. When I lost the corporate position in the City, I had to start from scratch. Driving, like I'd done back in Vallarta. And I rebuilt. I knew the money was here for the earning, yes, but it's in the form of horrendous women like Jocelyn Carlson. And those same women don't mind crushing people...like ants under their damn thousand-dollar spiked heels. She tried to get me to screw her then spin it around and screw me back. I'm not playing that game, or any game for that matter. Sick twisted shit."

"The grand game of life. Pretty much sucks all the way around the board." She grinned at him.

"Yeah, and at the end of the day, all you get are some nasty used souvenirs." He nodded to the panties. "But, at least, that's the last I'll see of Jocelyn Carlson. I finally refused to drive her anymore."

"So...you fired your richest client?"

"Yes. I was done being a doormat, you know? No amount of money is worth losing your pride over. Your identity. She just kicked my seat one too many times."

Jana gave him a questioning sidelong glance.

"Long story, but being done with her is how I had time for this gig. Luckily." He smiled at her, meaning so much more than the current context would allow. "And after this three-month contract, I'm done. Heading home. I will have reached my number."

"Your number?"

"I set a goal, a dollar figure, when I was six."

"When you were sick, with what?"

"No, six. Years old." He glanced from the road to her face. Her big brown eyes were melting caramel sweetness. "Yes, it was cute…but I was damn serious. And I'm really almost there."

"What's the number?"

"No one but Celeste knows it, and that's only because she strong-armed me. She was seven years old at the time, and inches taller than me." He snickered.

"So it's secret?"

"I can't jinx my goal by telling it!"

"Are you sure you're not Asian?" She laughed through her words. "Because we have a long list of superstitions, so many, in fact, we require separate schooling for them."

"Jesus, tell me about it! My Mexico is steeped in the stuff! Remind me to tell you the superstitious saga around my baby sister someday," he said, turning into the hospital. "But anyway, I'm close to the number and I can't wait to…well…get my life started." He smiled, liking the sound of his own words. *Get my life started.*

She smiled at him and nodded, like she was happy for him, except for a hint of a solemn reservation in her eyes. It vanished before he could place whatever it was that bothered her.

"Hey, where do you want these?" she asked as she took the panties in the handkerchief to free up his hand.

"Fold them up in the cloth and shove 'em in the glove compartment, please. I'll have dispatch deal with it. I'm sure they'll love that. And come to think of it, I wouldn't be surprised if more were hidden around the vehicle. I should probably go through the seat cracks too," he scoffed.

He pulled under the hospital's portico, right up to the automatic sliding doors, setting off the sensor. He watched her gather up her purse and her courage while the glass doors opened and closed, opened and closed. Jana stared at them as if those doors were waiting to eat her alive. She got the same look on her face each time he dropped her off, but this level of dread was palpable.

"Will you wait here for a little longer before going on errands or whatever?"

"I always do." He smiled. "I usually wait for an hour, cost-wise, but I actually won't leave at all today. I'll park it, and we can grab food together later, on the way back down to the club."

"Thank you," she said, with something more than relief floating on her voice. Her shoulders relaxed. And her two words somehow lightened his heart, maybe because he seemed to have lightened hers.

CHAPTER 31

"PLEASE, MOM," JANA said after pulling her out of the 'much lower quality' room. "You cannot call me with a '9-1-1' and no details, and then not answer my calls after that. And having Dane text me? Why are you even including him in our family's business at this point?" she demanded more than asked—Antonio's words about no longer being walked all over rang loud in her head. Why had she been allowing it for so long? "I'm here. I'm taking care of the bills. Not Dane. Never Dane, Mom. It's me doing it."

Then her mother's rant in harsh Korean began. "I'm at the restaurant morning until night, Ja-Na, then back here again. And you, we haven't seen you since—"

"Since yesterday, Ma. Since yesterday! Yes, today I was going to sleep in, because I took a job, separate from my actual career, and yes, it keeps me out late. But this other job will cover all the medical bills. Three months and I will have it near-done. Risking my career, yes, but I'm doing it. For you, and for Daddy!"

"You can help me at the restaurant, Ja-Na. *That's* what we need."

"Did you not hear me? Three months...completely paid down medical-debt. And maybe you're blind in addition to deaf...because you've obviously not looked at your own business's books, maybe ever," Jana shouted rhetorically, then took her mother's arm and pulled her inside her father's small, dank room. This was it. She was going to wake them both up from their clouded stupor. After all, her dad was more or less out of danger now, but post-surgery or not, he'd never be ready to hear what she'd had to say anyway, so there was no time like the goddamn present.

"Dad," she said in a quieter tone than she'd used outside with her mother, but jolting the dazed man just the same. "And Mom. I went through the books at the restaurant. In two weeks' time, you won't be able to stock the restaurant, let alone pay the staff. With or without Dad there, the place is a money suck. Cousin David knows it, but for some reason, he doesn't tell you. And with the state it's in, my God! Besides flushing money and time down the toilet, and both of your energy, the place is just unkempt. It's a lawsuit waiting to happen. And unless you guys seriously discuss—" A light rap on the door interrupted her long awaited and poignant final words. *Damn it.* "Yes?" Jana snapped at whoever wanted in.

"It's Sally from the business office." The one who'd made the decision to downgrade her dad's room. Jana could burn the woman alive with a glance for causing such unnecessary chaos, despite all of Jana's diligent communications and efforts to pay.

The woman must've felt the arctic chill of the room upon entering, with Jana's mother sitting with her mouth hanging open while her dad's eyes were scrunched closed, his hand at the bridge of his nose, and the permanent scowl on his face more pronounced than Jana had ever seen it.

"So sorry to interrupt...."

Of course she was. "What can we do for you?" Jana said with an appropriate tone of icy calm.

"Oh, yes, glad you made it here, Ms. Park. I left voice messages. Well, in addition to the need to handle the uninsured patient's bill more aggressively, we still have not gotten the patient's advanced directive or living will. We really shouldn't have moved him without having had those in the file, although we've asked for them repeatedly."

Jana looked at her mother, who shrugged her innocence. Well, who the hell else would they've asked for such papers? Her parents were children, just goddamn children.

"Yes, you're right Ms...."

"Buchard. Sally Buchard."

"You're absolutely right. My father, a post-op cardiac patient, should not have been moved to this basic room or even from the ICU to a standard room, without those documents on file. Would you maybe have thought to ask me for them since I'd been your contact on the billing? Instead of my mother, who's been completely overwhelmed, and is not a native English speaker?" But what was the point? The whole thing was an utter clusterfuck, and now she was taking out her rage on this Sally Buchard from the billing office. "Sorry. Sally, just never mind. I'll get you the papers you need right away and will handle the billing matter on Thursday like I'd told you last Friday when I met with you in-person at your desk. Will that work for you? Because, well, it's gonna have to."

"Um, yes, okay. Sounds fine," the woman stuttered as if she had a damn choice in the matter.

Jana would have fifteen thousand plus twenty to thirty-five grand by Thursday, and if Ms. Sally Secretary didn't like the nearly thirty percent pay down, they could take her parents' damn building, complete with decrepit restaurant and the putrid apartment above it.

As soon as Sally left the room, Jana returned her attention to her parents, who looked almost in awe, assumedly at how she'd handled the hell out of the prior episode. Irony happens. And usually, it happens too damn late to make any real difference.

"Where are the papers she needs? Where can I find them in the house?"

"Oh, Jana, I'll get them," her mother said.

"No. You won't. You haven't, and now I will. Where will I find them?"

Her mother narrowed her eyes and opened her mouth as if to argue.

But her father waved Jana over to him before her mom could utter a word. Her dad's breath was strained, but his general air had always been strong enough to squelch anything her mother had to say. "Top right of my suit closet. In one of the three or four cardboard file boxes." His voice had sounded raspy, withered. *Pathetic.*

She turned without another word and left the room.

When she got out of the wing, and past the reception area, she saw Antonio standing there, a warm smile lifted on his face.

"I didn't mean for you to wait inside for me."

"I, uh, was getting too hot in the car and didn't want to run the AC too much more… Fuel, you know," he said, obviously covering up his concern for her. And he could cover it up all he wanted. She appreciated his care just the same. She was glad to see him, her guardian angel.

Now he needed to help her sift through some files.

*

He drove to *Korean Soul* while Jana obviously tried to control her anger. Her nostrils flared and her fists clenched on her lap.

He still couldn't get over it, that her parents owned the joint. And although he'd always loved the food there, he'd never gotten the old man behind the counter to smile at him, not once. The irony. That he personally knew the man, the face, the glaring eyes, the very source of Jana's torment. And he hated the man for it. He hated what the man had put her through, what he continued to put her through.

"So if we get through the boxes and find the papers, say, within a half hour, we'll be back to the hospital by two-thirty, back on the road by a quarter to…"

"Jana, stop worrying about the time. If you're a little late to the club, so be it. Especially on a Sunday night. This is your family. The club will deal."

"Yeah, I can call down there, maybe have Didi and Laynie at least start—"

"You're worse than me, I swear." He laughed. He often worked until three in the morning. After cleaning out his vehicle, he would start his paperwork, billings, payroll. But the difference was, he had no one to tell him to go home, sleep, eat, live. Even though Celeste tried, he didn't listen. One reason he'd always run his own ship. "You need to take care of yourself and this family stuff first."

"My job, though. I can't take care of my family without this job."

"But it sounds or looks to me that Johnnie will bend over backward to help you…right?" It was his first attempt at fishing for the answers that were eating at him. What was Johnnie expecting from Jana, with all his attention, the apartment, full-time limo service? Jana, he had no doubt, would make an impact on the club's traffic—hell, he'd already noticed the influx of covers from last Saturday night over Friday just by sitting in the parking lot. But knowing Johnnie Demonte, there had to be more to it. Like, how on an early Sunday morning had that little shit already known she needed to get to the hospital? Had he been with her that morning? In bed? Goddamn it, how his stomach turned at the thought.

"He's paying me to do a job is all. The girls will be on time for training at four, and so should I. Oh shit, the new girls. I have the two girls from Piranha coming in to try out. If I don't build up the schedule, we won't be able to support next week's crowd."

"Hey Jana," he interrupted, touching her elbow lightly. "We're here at your folks' place."

Her nervous rant got swallowed up then by a long exhausted sigh. And by the time she'd unbuckled her seatbelt, Antonio was already out of the car.

"Come on there, speed demon." The next instant he was at her car door, ushering her out of the limo. "We've got some un-filing to do."

*

Antonio stood on a stepladder and pulled down the five musty, unlabeled boxes one at a time and placed them on the disgusting and ancient shag carpet in the tiny closet. She started dragging them out into the bigger space of her folks' bedroom. Then they got to work.

"Look for a folder or document with the headings health care directive, power of attorney, living will, anything like that. And sorry in advance. After seeing the filing system in the restaurant office, you might as well go through each and every paper. Their system is 'there is no system.'" She gave him a glib smile and tore into the box in front of her.

He carefully fingered through the box closest to him. His first find was a small, withered photo, and although it was probably not the right time, as they had no time, he pulled it out anyway.

"You are quite *la princesita* here," he said to Jana, who continued her intense search through her second box. "Jana, hey."

She looked up. He handed her the photo of a little girl, most obviously Jana, on the lap of a mustached man in a sombrero, most definitely her grandfather. She was dressed in a white puffed blouse and a thickly layered skirt, each layer a different vibrant color. It completely reminded him of his home. She had to have been four, maybe five years old. Pigtails and the same long lashes framing her golden eyes, as shapely and sharp as a kitten's.

"God, I remember that. He'd brought me some salsa music and the costume. We danced all day. My mother must've sneaked a picture," she said, musing over it for a second. Then she slid it into her purse and smiled her thanks as she went back to the boxes.

"Ahh, birth certificates. Might be on the right track here," she announced.

To keep with the ultra-serious tone she'd set, he hid his smile as he fingered through more photos of her and early school projects. Jana's roots, her backstory in crumpled paper form. God, she was a little strike of lightning as a girl. He looked up at Jana for an instant to match this version to the young one. Yeah, she still is. *Pure lightning.* Then he moved onto another box to keep with her furious pace. "Bank and financial here," he said. "Are you cool with me going through—"

"Yes, of course. I can guarantee there's nothing to know. They're flat broke."

He went through each paper, like she'd asked him to, but was getting distracted by her shifting and twisting body kneeling in front of him as she sifted through her own box, her delicate curves drawing his eyes away from the redundant documents. His ability to stay unaffected by her, with her magnetic beauty, was lessening with every passing day. Then there was their connection at the park, laying there beside each other in the grass and hell, all the days since the library, really. But to be honest, since the day she'd slid into his limo the first night, she'd captivated him.

And now his body was responding more often. Physical, electric charges bolted through him, and he had to hold himself in check with all his might. His advances were the last thing she needed right now.

Wait. The bank statements he'd been going through. A change in the dollar amounts. His eyes had picked up a difference just then and not a small one. There were average balances of two and three thousand dollars all the way back to the prior year, but he held in his hand a statement from thirteen months before with an *eighty-five thousand dollar* transaction. But it was leaving the account. He'd run through enough statements in his own business to know something was up, but before he said a word to Jana, he rifled back further, fourteen and fifteen months in the past. Sixteen months, then he got to a year and a half, when an eighty-seven thousand dollar deposit showed up entering the account. The line item was identified in the bank's detail as a HELOC: a Home Equity Line of Credit. He quickly went back to the eighty-five thousand dollar withdrawal and looked at the bank code: some numbers then 'wire transfer to Burbank, CA.' He remembered Jana telling him in the park that her brother was somewhere in California.

"I found the will. Here it is," she said, waving the one-page form in her hand. "So glad he's leaving everything to Dane," she laughed reading through it. "I'd rather have a damn heart attack myself than inherit this pit." She laughed. "So did you find anything besides my baby pictures?"

He couldn't decide. Show her this now? *Of course, show her.* What would ever prevent him from letting her see the unbelievable craziness that her parents' bank statements seemed to indicate?

But he knew in the deepest part of him why he was holding back his finding. Antonio couldn't bear to see her reaction. It would be another rip, or more like a gash, in her heart. God, he hated the thought of her in more pain, more never-ending despair caused by the ones who were supposed to love her most.

"No. Not the directive at least. But…here." He moved closer to her, and although it was stuffy in the house, and he'd maybe moved too close for her comfort, he felt he needed to be right there, ready to catch her when she crumbles from the shock.

She took the papers from him in her left hand while she hadn't yet pulled her attention away from the box she was on. "This is it! The health care directive." She pulled out the document and jumped up. "We got 'em. Would you mind putting these boxes back up, and then we can head out?"

"Sure, of course. But, Jana…" He stood up next to her, squared his body with hers, and put his hands on her shoulders to try to focus her attention.

"Why so serious?"

"Look at the statements I gave you, in your left hand."

Her eyes moved down to the papers while Antonio counted slowly in his head. When he got to seven, she was slowly sinking to her knees. At the nine count, he rejoined her on the moldy, ratty carpet that was cluttered with boxes.

CHAPTER 32

"CAN I RUN them in for you? Just tell me who to ask for."

She thought about the prospect of seeing her mother, who had to have known. She was Chang Park's goddamn puppet, after all, jumping and dancing with the pull of a string. Jana couldn't even look at the woman, let alone talk to her at that point. "Yes. Please...if you don't mind. Just ask for Sally Buchard."

Antonio was in and out in a few minutes, holding an envelope when he returned. "All set. Here are the originals. I had them make copies."

Thank God he'd thought of that. Where was her brain? Well, she knew. Her brain, her psyche, was reeling in an inferno of anger, and all she could think to do was drown it out with a numbing shot of alcohol. Not like her, but that's what she craved.

Time check: a solid hour before she had to be at the club. If she could just mellow out with a quick drink now, nothing a few mints wouldn't cover, she'd be fine and on time for the girls and training.

"Antonio, can we stop for a bite at that little pub before the highway?" She realized she hadn't really even eaten except for a yogurt before he'd picked her up at eleven-something that morning.

*

She matched him bite for bite on the burger and fries and ignored his lifted brows when she ordered a second beer.

He helped lighten her mood with some distracting stories about Jocelyn Carlson and her 'rotating johns' as he called them, and, with the liquid relaxants in her, she came back with a few of her own tales, mostly about high-powered attorneys and arrogant politicians getting caught in the private back rooms. The local papers had somehow gotten close-up shots to prove their indiscretions. "What people will do for money, with money, hell, on money!" She snorted then blushed a bit. Then she closed her eyes to anchor her whirling mind. She felt better, lighter. But dizzier. Her fingers massaged her temples before she slowly opened her eyelids again.

She threw back the end of her second beer as Antonio tapped his watchless wrist.

But as the alcohol had processed quickly through her small frame, she almost didn't care anymore about being on time. What the hell was the point? People don't change. They don't learn. Her parents didn't. Lending her bum of a brother more money or probably *giving* it! Just to throw it away. *Her* money, by the way. It was all her hard-earned, soul-despairing money.

They must've refinanced the house and restaurant, the very building she danced naked to pay down to zero. To zero for Christ's sake! Then she shook her tits and dry humped her way to a nursing degree. Now where was she?

In a fucking delusion was where. And now she thought she could make a difference to a bunch of lost girls. Because if she got to the club on time for training and taught them all about hard work, future planning, focus, and ambition, they'd get up and out and end up exactly the fuck where she was now: *nowhere.*

Antonio stood up, threw some green bills down and held out his hand for her. He was such a gentleman, so nice to her, but why? Everyone had a reason, an incentive. What was his agenda?

And then again, what the hell did she care what his motivation was for being so nice to her? He was thick and yummy, too delicious to ignore. Her core had quivered for him since the day he'd stood over her at the library, his plated bronzed chest showing through that crisp white robe.

She smiled when he offered her his hand as she scooted out of the booth. Then she took his hand, pulled herself up to stand, and held on to steady herself. Her legs felt like jelly. Without a next thought, she slid her free arm around his waist, getting definitive confirmation of the ever-defined torso she'd imaged too many times to exist under his shirt. What was she doing? Giving him a hug, maybe? A friendly, much-needed hug? But she couldn't answer her own question fast enough as she lifted to her toes, lifted her chin, her face, to meet his questioning hazel eyes.

And she kissed him. Her needy lips pressed against his soft sweet lips. Just lightly adjoined, but for a long moment. A lingering, alleviating, glorious moment.

Until he pulled away, stepping a full step backward.

And she could only blush hot red when she stumbled forward from his retreat, his chest saving her from falling flat on the bar's floor.

"Jana, are you alright?"

"Yes, damn it. I'm fine. Just fucking fine." And she grabbed her purse and huffed out of the pub.

CHAPTER 33

F UCK HIM...AND FUCK me!

Jana got into the back seat where she intended to stay. For good. She was mortified and angry at the rejection and at her life up to the rejection.

Fucking alcohol slowed her processes and her goddamn prudence! Her sound judgment!

She needed to be alone. To reflect and to decide what the hell she was doing and going to do about everything. Her lost pride and her out-of-left-field feelings or neediness, or whatever the hell that was back there. And, yes, what to do about her family and her absolutely fucked future. Yeah, the entire merry go round of *fucked*.

She looked back over her shoulder. He was coming to the car now. God, she wanted the divider up so goddamn bad. But of course, she couldn't have it without getting sick everywhere. So as he reached for his door handle she found her sunglasses, shoved them on, stuffed the earbuds in her ears—yes, his fucking earbuds, *ugh!*—and readied herself for complete separation. Church and state, client and goddamn chauffeur, her floundering soul and the never-ending ocean of shit her soul was drowning in.

*

She got to the club without a single word to Antonio and decided then that she'd not need him for the next few days. She wouldn't be going to visit her father, not until Thursday, after she got the money from Johnnie at the the-ater and from her bank. And she could take a cab to the club from the studio each night or goddamn walk.

She headed to the entrance of The Wet Spot and turned before going through the doors. Antonio rolled down his window on cue.

"No need to bring me back to the studio tonight. Actually, I won't need you until Thursday morning, 9:00 AM." She continued into the club.

*

Like a dagger to the chest, her words. And after the brutal silence for the entire drive down, add those sunglasses she hid behind with only her scowl visible to him in his rearview, she stunned his heart beat-less.

With her flip-of-the-switch attitude, an eerie, fearful feeling had drifted through him from the back seat, from her sudden ice-statue aura. It echoed in his chest. Stranger still, it was as if he'd seen it before, her frosty shield. It wasn't from any time he'd been shuttling her from place to next-dreaded-place. It wasn't inside his limo at all. It was as if he'd almost hurt her before, though they'd never met, or he'd remember. Jana Park, he was certain, he'd sure as hell remember. He was also sure that he'd never intentionally hurt this woman, this warrior princess who had graced his life. Not ever in a trillion years would he hurt her.

Yet—*Fuck!*—she was reeling in pain, and now wouldn't let him in to relieve it.

CHAPTER 34

I T HAD BEEN three sleepless nights since he'd seen her. In person that is. Her image kept flashing in his head, keeping him from sleep and from his usual focus. Because it wasn't the warm, sensual, vibrant woman he'd come to know and really fucking care for over the last several days—Jesus, only a little over a week! No, now, with those sunglasses she'd hidden behind and that icy scowl, she'd become an untouchable ice sculpture in his head and heart. Still, damn it, all he wanted to do was wrap her in his arms, in his warmth.

The entire situation screwed him up. Anxiety coursed through his veins while, at the same time, he'd zone out behind the wheel—traffic lights turned from red to green until blaring horns brought him back. Instead of conquering his usual pile of paperwork on his office desk, he'd pace and think and debate. Whether to call her or text her or drive over to the studio…or should he just wait it out? He was fidgety, even short-tempered, so noticed Celeste and the girls. And in contrast to last week when Celeste had described him as the "most alive" she'd ever seen him, it was definitely telling. Jana Park's absence shook him to the core.

Shook him, and now angered him, damn it.

How could she have written him off so easily? After the connection they'd made? She'd just given up on him. Forget about the undeniable spark between them, she'd abandoned their friendship.

And hell, he had to protect himself. Especially after Michelle. So he'd follow Jana's lead and throw in the towel too. He'd keep focused on getting home like he'd planned in the first place.

As if it's that easy, damn it.

Because there was more to it. And it was beyond the devastating effect of the shut-out, the silent treatment, the lack of Jana in his days and hours and minutes. Worst of all, his seeming rejection had made her feel more alone than she'd already felt. And he couldn't handle being a source of pain to her. Another source of pain.

Damn it! He hadn't meant to hurt or embarrass Jana—anything but.

God, a kiss from those lips would have been like finding an oasis after the longest, most arduous trek across the Sonoran. A kiss from her, he'd only dreamt about. But a kiss from her, a touch, a whisper, could not be stained or tainted by the emotional turmoil inflicted on her by her oblivious and vile family. And a kiss they'd share would not be gotten by pity either. If he ever had the chance of being with such a woman as Jana Park, it had to be complete and pure synergy, the two of them in a united moment, both aware, both choosing each other on total and conscious and absolute purpose.

And although he knew she thought he'd rejected her and was undoubtedly furious from her tornado of a day, he didn't see her getting over what happened between them at the bar. But she could get past it, then by association alone he guessed she'd think of this torturous time in her life every time she looked at him.

Who was he kidding anyway? They were heading toward different worlds. She wanted the City life, her esteemed ER. She'd only mentioned it a few hundred times in the week-plus that they'd known each other. Once she figured out what she'd do about her parents' finances, Jana would resume her big city life in Manhattan. And he'd rather die before being dropped into that maze again.

Really, their connection was nothing more than logistical desperation. Jana was being wrung out for money while he was finalizing a divorce and trying to get back home with his financial goal reached. Or hell, at this point, in one financial piece at all because he didn't know if Jana would ask Johnnie to replace him as a driver. Maybe she could no longer stand the sight nor sound of him.

Anyway, how could he even imagine it working between them? They had worse chances than a rebound couple. They'd be a couple by emotional and psychological default. It could never be.

And for Christ's sake, she might very well have been and may still be *with* Johnnie, he didn't know. And even though it killed him, knowing Jana was too good for a saint, let alone that prick, it was, again, none of his damn business. And never had been.

So, in the end, it was better for him to get good and used to not being near her, not talking to her, not thinking about her.

But, not thinking about her? Was it even possible?

Thinking about her made him happy. Being near her made him happy. Made him better. A better man. She made his days worthwhile, vibrant even. And as sad as it was, she'd undoubtedly been the impetus for letting Michelle go, throwing his ring into the Hudson and signing the papers. Jana had been his motivation for obtaining freedom.

And now, without her, what did he have?

Home, Antonio. You have home.

Home? And his fucking "number"? Without Jana and what she suddenly represented, none of the other things mattered a damn. Not a good god-damn and it was deadening to his heart.

CHAPTER 35

JOHNNIE CALLED HIM late Wednesday afternoon to make sure he'd be at the apartment at five to get them into Manhattan by seven-thirty. Antonio bowed out on his adult Tae Kwon Do students with apologies and rushed home to shower. He hadn't known of Johnnie's plans. The bastard probably assumed that since Antonio was on twenty-four-seven detail, he'd be at their disposal anyway. Which meant Johnnie didn't know Jana had dismissed him until Thursday morning. Why, though? Why was she waiting to ask for a replacement? God, he should take it upon himself to send someone else. It would be less torture on him. But for some reason, he couldn't. He had to take her Thursday. Something compelled him, and he couldn't answer for himself what. Or could he?

Antonio pulled up in front of the studio a few minutes before five, and Johnnie's seventy-five thousand dollar coupe was already there, double-parked as it were. A second later he watched Jana come out in a black satin dress, the continuation of her long midnight hair, with her slender neck holding up the fine black threads of the halter top of the gown. Johnnie Demonte was right behind her, ushering her to the car with his hand at the very base of her back.

Antonio shuddered as he came around quickly to get the door for her. His breath was caught due to Jana's exquisite beauty and the disgust lodged in his throat by Johnnie Demonte's proximity to her.

The drive seemed long, even though he drove faster and a bit more aggressively than usual, as to put an end to the torture. Faster the better. He focused hard on the road while absolutely refusing to look in the rearview. At all. Even though the backseat scene was like one of those illicit talk shows that you just can't *not* watch. Especially since this time he felt like he had a bit of a vested interest in one of the 'talk show guests.' And a deep disdain for the other.

Yeah, side mirrors Antonio. As if the center partition was up. But it wasn't. He kept it down for her, for her motion sickness. God, if he were in it for the long haul, he'd invest in rear bumper cameras. But thank God Johnnie and Jana were only talking shop. But still, he didn't dare imagine where the other man's hands were while they chatted. Or that man's eyes, those rat-like little orbs, grazing her body, tainting her soul.

He could kill or smash something right now, he swore, because worse still was Antonio's knowledge of the sickest part of the situation. Without even stealing a peek in his mirror, Antonio knew and read and abhorred Johnnie Demonte's un-fucking-acceptable thoughts, his revolting thoughts about the woman, the warrior princess in his back seat.

He drove on and got them to Lincoln Center in plenty of time. He told them he'd pull around to this same spot in three hours to wait for them there.

*

It wasn't hard ignoring Antonio's iciness, Johnnie being so monopolizing and all. She couldn't blame Antonio, but she also couldn't let her mind go there tonight. She had to focus on the task at hand, so she'd kept up the idle chit-chat in the back seat, with the carrot of getting paid at the forefront of her mind.

Yeah, that carrot was how she'd make it through this night. Only three hours. She could definitely do this. An evening taken up by a Lincoln Center performance? Hell, she might actually enjoy herself. She *should* enjoy herself.

She deserved to. And what sleazy-ass things could Johnnie possibly do in such a classy and totally public setting anyway?

*

Three hours of that piece of shit man-boy with Jana.

Until then, he'd try to read, take his mind off of the surreal situation.

He was reaching for his book in the glove compartment when he noticed his small black mp3 player on the seat, the earbuds wound tight and neat around it. She must've dropped it over the partition while he was holding their car door open, playing chauffeur for the lovely couple.

CHAPTER 36

S HE LOOKED MORE beautiful than he could have imagined, tastier than he knew she could. And he'd seen her everything, her velvety slit, her glistening tits sliding down cold metal poles, tassels on her red, delicious nipples, her smooth, tight ass cheeks divided splendidly by a barely-there thong. But tonight the difference was that she was his and his alone, and he'd be able to peel off the dress he'd gotten her as slowly and methodically as he wanted.

He even got her an open-back halter and pretended to have forgotten the correct bra so she'd have to go braless, her delectable nipples pebbling through the satin fabric, making his cock steel-hard. He wanted the god-damn show over before it had even started so he could get them heading to the real performance of the night.

But he knew he needed the time, the hours, the show's calming distraction, and the drinks. He went to get them both glasses of champagne the second they entered the hall.

And did she ever get looks; envious eyes from the women and hungry stares from the men. But again, she was his tonight. And tonight he'd have her. Yes, he'd thought that maybe he could wait weeks, but he'd been wrong. No chance, not with her so hot and so close.

He'd expedited his plans.

First he'd use the tip of his thirsting tongue to circle her sweet cherry nipples in the limo…if he could get enough champagne in her by then. If not, then at his place or at the studio. It hardly mattered as long as he got his piece.

But the limo, that image held a special something for him. And the sudden thought of that fucker, Tony, watching and wishing he were in Johnnie's shoes made him absolutely giddy. Yeah, that was the special something. He'd make sure the partition was down, cab lights on so Tony could see it all.

Except if she wanted a more intimate experience with him, in which case, he'd let the partition be up, but would make her come so damn hard and loud that Tony would feel the pleasure he was missing in his fucking ears. Her moans, "Oh, Johnnie, fuck me. Yes, Johnnie, yes," would echo in that smug bastard's head forever. That's what Tony would get for talking-up his conquest on Johnnie Demonte's dime.

"Thank you," she said, taking the tall stem between her slender little fingers.

"Cheers." He clinked his glass to hers. "To an amazing show we won't soon forget."

"Jana? Jana Park? Well, hello there!" A shorter man in a tux with a slightly crooked bowtie came over to them, Johnnie already pulling Jana in as a natural reflex.

"Doctor Brighton—"

"In *and* out of the hospital, please, do call me Andrew."

"So good to see you, *Andrew*."

A quick shot of unease ran up his spine with her use of the doctor's first name. It rang in his ears. Had she slept with him? *In and out of the hospital?* Had she called his name out over and over, the little-man doctor's tiny prick doing nothing for her tight silken cunt? He could take her blushing cheeks and the bashful upturn of her luscious lips as confirmation of his suspicion. But maybe not. Either way, *fuck those god-complex piece-of-shit doctors.* One-upping everyone else. Johnnie needed to move this reunion the-fuck-on. He didn't even want an intro.

"You too. Seems like we keep missing each other when I'm in to see your dad. You've been busy, yes?"

Johnnie watched Jana sigh and search for words, hopefully quick words so he could get her seated and comfortable with another glass of alcohol before the curtains lifted.

"Yeah, I have been. Just trying to, you know, make ends meet. Oh, I'm so sorry, this is my friend, Johnnie, Johnnie Demonte. Johnnie, this is my dad's cardiologist, Doctor Andrew Brighton. He saved my father's life."

Johnnie smiled politely and gave him his firmest handshake. Really fucking firm. "Thanks for taking such good care of my girl's father, doc. Really, thanks."

He ignored Jana's sidelong look and kept his wide phony smile spread across his face. It didn't matter that she wasn't his girl per se, even though she would be, because to this pompous asshole with a medical degree, she needed to be considered 'taken,' unequivocally 'off the market.' The good doctor needed to know her status and step off.

He felt her attention shift from him back to the good doctor. "Really good to see you again, Andrew, and enjoy your evening."

Good. She seemed as eager to move on as he was. She took a few steps in front of him, toward their seats, and then stopped short.

"Johnnie?" she asked, tilting her gorgeous head at him. "Why'd you refer to me as your girl? Not on a date, right? Just keeping each other company, yes? As friends." Brows lifted.

"Of course, but after going over last weekend's numbers in greater detail with my father today, you sure as hell are 'my girl.' Jana, Saturday night was double—double!—what Friday night was. And seventy percent better than the Saturday night over the year prior! You are pure magic, Jana, and I'd be proud to claim you to anyone who asked."

"That's amazing. Really…the numbers…" she said, taking a larger sip of champagne. "I'm happy that our business relationship is having such good results for the club."

She smiled and took another long drink from her glass as she walked toward their theater seats. He followed close behind her, but with just enough space to maintain his view of her glorious ass draped perfectly by the snug and glistening satin material of the dress he'd handpicked for her. It made him shake his head in disbelief. Where had this magnificent creature come from? And how did he get so damn lucky to have her re-enter his world?

*

She was mortified. And she felt horrible for Andrew. Had he even brought a date? She didn't notice any signs of one. Then to run into her! God, he must think her a total bitch, a horrid superficial bitch. "No distractions," she'd told him when he'd asked her out, and "I need to focus on my father," she'd explained. And here she is, out at a show. With a man who claims to be her significant other. Her polite letdown, spoken with true words and intentions, had been obliterated. She shouldn't have said yes to come tonight in the first place. Dammit! She should have said 'no' to the dress, 'no' to Johnnie-goddamn-Demonte, and maybe even 'no' to the entire deal in the first place.

But as she thought that thought, her eyes watched Johnnie take from his wallet a folded check. It read fifteen thousand dollars on the visible half. She felt her shoulders loosen but, God, the look of arrogance in his face made her stomach turn. She watched as he slid the check into the new Dorna Walter purse he'd gotten her, another little item she didn't want hanging over her head as she knew it probably cost him more than the theater tickets themselves. Always the money. The ball and chain, no, the prison. She couldn't goddamn wait for the end of her contract, God help her, when she'd leave the purse, the dress, and even the black shoes that she'd bought herself, at the apartment. With his key.

But this is three hours. How was she going to make it two-plus months?

He nodded at her and smiled with his eyes.

Fuck you, Johnnie. "Thank you, Johnnie."

"Oh, you're so welcome. You've earned it."

*

The lights dimmed, the show was starting. *Thank God.*

But his head didn't turn toward the stage. He kept his creepy gaze on her.

Please let the champagne kick in. At least, with a good buzz, she could ignore him and his ogling stare, his creepy vibe.

And while she watched the show and endured the awkwardness, she hoped Antonio was listening to the playlist she'd made him. Thanks to Laynie and her laptop, she synched all her favorites to the little music device Antonio had lent her. It was Jana's apology for the way she'd acted–like a damn child, a silly stupid little girl. The last person on Earth to deserve her wrath or her silent treatment was Antonio.

She could fix this. She'd been embarrassed and emotional, that was all. She'd had too much to drink the other night, two beers for her small build left her well-beyond buzzed, especially with how seldom she drank.

But Antonio had stopped her kiss. He hadn't taken advantage of her and he could have. And from the vibe he'd been putting out, it wasn't from of lack of interest. The looks they'd shared, the flirty-free conversations—the way deeper ones too—and the general unspoken connection between them while driving together in the front seat of his limousine. That was all real. He'd wanted to kiss her back, she knew it in her gut. He'd wanted to kiss her plenty of times before she made the upward leap.

An independent rush of icy warmth took her throat and face. Embarrassment with a spike of a chill at the finish from a solitary and suddenly disappointing thought. If she was wrong, if he had no interest in her in that way, well…still, he'd been a gentleman. A friend. A man, a fine, sweet man who'd only been good to her, really kind. Really *there*.

Damn him, though, with his understated virility and his 'tall, dark and sensual' mixed with sweetness and strength. He drove her wild and kept her grounded at the same time. Antonio made her realize, after so long, that she'd wasted precious time. She'd not allowed herself any pleasure or joy for herself. Finally, it took him, a limo driver slash martial arts master, to open her eyes. And her eyes were open to *him*.

But he'd pushed her away when she'd made her move, albeit rash and steeped in slightly-drunken desperation. But from him, no explanation. Not at the time or after the fact. No call, no text, no visit. Just nothing.

He had told her when she'd found Jocelyn Carlson's used souvenir that he'd since committed to putting his pride before all else. Second to nothing and no one. Jana had stomped on his pride for turning her down, treated him like an unruly chauffeur. Acted like…like…that rich bitch client Jocelyn Carlson. So what did she expect at this point? It made no difference if he had a spark for her like she now knew she had for him. It made no difference at all.

She shook her head and held back the threatening tears while a wisp of a laugh left her mouth. Really how little it mattered, because, in months from now, Antonio would finally be back in his precious seaside town in Mexico while she'd be back in her city, in her prestigious ER, in her rightful role as lead Trauma Team member. Nurse extraordinaire, and all alone.

Alone. She somehow dreaded the mental picture of her lonely future.

But as her boss leaned over the arm of the plush theater seat into her personal space and took a not-so-subtle sniff of her hair, she prayed to God for immediate solitude. She dug up a polite smile for Johnnie Demonte as the curtain drew open and the performance began.

*

Intermission. After downing another glass of champagne he'd handed her, awkward chatter spotted by Johnnie's own brand of sexual innuendo filled their airspace. She could hardly focus on Johnnie's swooning words, though. Was she on her fourth or fifth glass of champagne? She'd lost count. But as the second half of the performance began, she surrendered into her seat.

The theatrical performance on stage told a captivating story, really: Boy meets and gets girl, girl leaves, boy settles for another, then girl returns, and passion trumps all when they reunite. Jana's tears began to collect, but she held them back. *Not in front of Johnnie.* He was on his umpteenth glass of champagne as well, with assuredly looser hands now, and she just didn't want him attending to her…at all. If he saw her crying, she could picture him wiping her tears away from her face one by one, and the thought of his touch gave her the chills, and not in a good way.

He was young, that was all. Johnnie Demonte had an innocent crush on her—okay, an infatuation. All she had to do was limit one-on-one time like tonight's mistake-of-an outing, and keep reminding him of her lines. She'd manage his 'thing' for her with kid gloves. And she was okay doing that, as if she had a choice.

Because she still had to help her parents.

Yes, despite the heart-wrenching, blood-curdling knowledge that those bank statements had given her, she still had to help them. She still had to rake in this money, and she'd still have to manage her boss to do it for nine and a half more weeks.

CHAPTER 37

I N A BLINK, it was over. The curtains closed. She startled when his
hand brushed her arm to say it was time to leave. She could've lingered
there just to digest the ending of the performance, but he was already
standing, hand extended to help her up. Denying his hand, she stood, but a
wave of lightheadedness from the champagne made her stumble and blush.
Johnnie caught her elbow, though, and got her steady on her five-inch
spike heels.

"Oh God, thank you. How many glasses did I have, anyway?"

He locked her arm with his. "A few, beautiful, only a few."

Just a few? She felt sloshed, worse than two beers, four beers, six
beers even.

Through a blur of people and red-carpeted stairs, she leveraged Johnnie's
arm for balance and forward movement. God, she hated needing him or
anyone for that matter.

It felt like forever to get to the limo.

"Ahh, Antonio," she said looking up at her handsome guardian angel
holding the door for her. She started to say more, but Johnnie was already
pushing her head down so she wouldn't hit it as she entered the limo.

"Antonio, huh?" Johnnie asked her.

"Tony is short for Antonio," she explained, proud to know it. She
thought Johnnie really should call him by his real name too, out of respect.
Antonio deserved respect, the utmost. And happiness too. She wanted that

for him. So much. God, she hadn't realized how much she'd missed him over the last few days. She'd really, really missed him.

She leaned forward to the partition. She wanted to ask Antonio if he'd listened to the playlist she'd made him, but Johnnie held her shoulder. "Sit back, Jana. *Antonio* is pulling out now." He patted the spot next to him, and she slid back, more because of the satin material of her dress slipping over the smooth leather seat than her choosing to sit that close to Johnnie. And his arm around her shoulder, forcing her to lean against him, was far too much, but she had no energy or sense of equilibrium to move.

Then the privacy window started to lift as the limo pulled out into traffic. What was Antonio doing? He knew she needed it left down. Panic filled her chest, made worse by Johnnie, who squeezed her to him, more than skeeving her the hell out. And just as she opened her mouth to say something to someone to stop one or more of the completely unnerving happenings going on around her, the limo stopped short.

She moaned as a sudden wave of nausea tore over her. She clenched her teeth and forced her focus ahead of her, through to the disappearing view of the road ahead. She wouldn't get sick, not if she could keep her eyes on the road. But now she couldn't even open her mouth to tell Antonio to please, for the love of his interior upholstery, keep the partition window down. Her words and breath were caught in her throat.

*

He'd prepared himself, planned in his mind how he'd get into the driver's seat and drive. But the disgust and screaming injustice of Johnnie Demonte anywhere near Jana sent an earthquake through his bones. Her arm in his. Her sweet smile for him. Her light laugh for Johnnie-fucking-Demonte.

Antonio sent a mental apology through the ether to her as he brought the opaque divider up. He couldn't bear sight or sound of them. He just couldn't.

He buckled his seatbelt, intentionally keeping his eyes from the rearview while the partition lifted. He had started the car, doing everything not to break the starter with how hard he wanted to jam then turn the key.

She was drunk. Johnnie had probably pushed the wine or champagne. And he knew from the other day how her defenses fell with only two beers. She was strong but so small. That fucking cocksucker.

She's a grown woman. A strong, smart woman. And she's not your woman.

He didn't have to glance in his rearview to get out of the parking space. He really only needed his side mirror, but his eyes lifted anyway, betraying him. He had to check her state.

As expected, she looked a shade of green, panic in her hazy eyes, leaning on Johnnie Demonte's shoulder like a rag doll. Who the hell knew where the dickhead's right hand was? She was pulled so damn close to the fucker that it might have been wrapped around her, under her, goddamn in her for all he knew.

But what the fuck could he do? Again, she was a grown woman. On a date, albeit with this fucker. God, the prick in his backseat was a manipulative son of a bitch. He really pulled off an award-winning performance, getting one over on Jana, of all people.

Fuck! He was choking with rage and nausea. He should fucking do something. About what, though? Nothing had happened. She seemed somewhat content back there—not shouting or screaming or contesting.

Anyway, he wasn't her protector. He was a chauffeur, Johnnie Demonte's chauffeur. That was all Antonio was to her.

He continued pressing the auto-up button of the privacy window, which lifted at its terminally slow-ass pace. Once it was up, he'd be free from the back seat scene.

Hell, she'd be fine back there. *Her carsickness may not even be an issue.* Not with Johnnie…distracting her. *Oh God!*

He reached for the mp3 player she'd left him as a big "fuck you" and got ready to tune-out and drive. *Just fucking drive.*

He took a deep breath and pulled out of the parking space. Halfway into the lane, he spotted in his side view mirror a motorcycle shooting by and slammed hard on his brake. He heard a moan from the back seat and glanced up. Jana held a look of intense and desperate focus as she struggled to catch her breath. And incidentally, Johnnie's hand was up on her opposite shoulder, fingertips playing with the material of her dress, at her neckline.

He released the privacy window button, stopping its upward direction. Then he brought the partition back down for her. He didn't want her sick or scared, even if it meant torture for him.

He could tune them out. He could. He was trained to tune out, to center, to focus. He began breathing through his nose, deep centering breaths, as he focused his eyes on the road ahead like a sniper on his target. With his free hand, he adjusted the earbuds so they wouldn't slip out, then he fumbled with the device on his lap to get any music started, any distraction at all to replace his gut-wrenching thoughts.

It took a moment for something to cue up.

Then, *Jesus.*

He tore one earbud out and forced his fingers to the side of the device to take down the volume. His eardrums, his chest, his entire body felt the jolt, the hiked volume had hiked his pulse through the moon roof.

Not the distraction he meant.

He breathed deeply.

As the sound of his breath quieted in his skull, he could now make out what music remained piping in his one ear.

A Spanish salsa beat-based rhythm?

He got to the red light and looked down at the music player. The playlist was new and not his. 'Jana's I'm Sorry Songs' was the playlist's name.

Then he felt a kick to the back of his seat, a kick that sent rippling wrath shooting up his spine.

*

He yanked the earbuds out and shot around, glaring at Johnnie Demonte.

"I said it three times, man. Put the partition up!"

"Do not. Kick. My seat. And the divider stays down."

"Look, asshole, we want privacy, and I want it up. I pay you enough; do what I say. Your seat, your engine, your tires, they're all *ours*, and you still get paid a shitload extra. Put the fucking—"

"Johnnie!" Jana spat while holding her stomach as if she couldn't say much more without getting sick everywhere. "I get carsick. It has to stay down. Antonio knows that. Please."

Then she looked up at Antonio through the rearview. "Could you please...?" She paused with her hand over her mouth. Antonio had a bottle of water at her eye level the next instant. "Oh, thank you." She opened it and took a small sip as Antonio pulled over and put his hazards on. "Could you get me to the studio?"

"No, my place is only a few blocks away. You'll stay with me there."

"Johnnie, no. I want to stay at the...oh God...." She swallowed hard then took another sip of water. "I want to stay at the apartment, alone."

"Jana. Listen to me, you don't have to be in a car that long if you just stay with—"

"She said she doesn't want to stay with you." Antonio wouldn't hold back anymore. If Johnnie wanted to stop paying him, if his father wanted to call the loan on his vehicle and on his entire business, so be it. He wasn't going to let this shit go down, not to Jana. She *was* his business. He cared about her, and there were already too many vultures in her life preying on her. That hell was over.

"Mind your own fucking business, asshole."

"Get out of my limo. You live so close, go walk there—by yourself. I'm taking Jana to the apartment."

"It's my apartment, and you don't know who the fuck you're—"

Antonio was out of the car before Johnnie could finish his thought. He opened the back door, grabbed Johnnie Demonte's arm and yanked him out. "Jana is sick. You're drunk. Go walk it off." Antonio followed up by taking a step toward the other man, an up close and personal chest in the face. "Or I'll tell your father exactly what happened here, and he won't have a bit of trouble believing me. I can embellish a bit, too. Say the cops had to be called." Everyone knew Jake Demonte hated the cops. Johnnie's ass would be torn to next year for bringing heat to Jake's door.

Johnnie stood as tall as he could, chest out, but was still more than a head shorter than Antonio and obviously only half the muscle mass. Somehow the prick made the wise decision to step back.

"So what happened here?"

Johnnie said nothing, just fumed through his flared nostrils, death stare through half-lidded eyes.

"That's right...nothing. Absolutely nothing. Now go." Antonio turned back to the opened car door and looked inside. "Would you feel better sitting up front?"

She nodded and started to shimmy out of the car, her hand reaching for his.

"Listen, cocksucker, that's my date. My employee, my..." Johnnie was apparently still there.

Sitting at the edge of the seat, both heels now on the pavement, Jana looked up at Antonio, desperation in her eyes. She whispered, "I still need the money."

He gnashed his teeth and felt his left eye flicker as he turned to Johnnie. He hated to say the words, but for her, dammit, he would. "She's still your employee. She's just sick, dickhead. Go home. Tomorrow afternoon, after the hospital, I'll bring her to the club, like usual."

"Oh no, you won't. Send someone else. Anyone else but you, motherfucker. Trying to take my girl," Johnnie said, hailing a cab with one sloppy arm waving in the air.

Antonio ignored the rest of his ranting and helped Jana into the front seat. "Buckle up and hold the handle above you. It'll help with the queasiness." Then he drove off, Johnnie Demonte flipping him off in his rearview.

CHAPTER 38

"I'M SORRY. ABOUT the other night and tonight. God, what a—"

"Don't, Jana. Really, it's all okay. You're safe, that's what matters. God, I should have told you. I don't know when, but I should have said something…"

"About what?

"Johnnie. I wasn't sure about your relationship with him, and I didn't want to overstep. You're a strong woman, I just…"

"Spit it out, Antonio."

He grabbed a water from his console, opened it, and took a long swig. Offered it to her, but she waved it away. "No, thanks. I feel a lot better now. Just tell me."

"It's that I've taken countless women to Johnnie's apartment. Strippers, prostitutes. It's his pad, his bachelor pad. None since he's hired you, but two or three women a week before you. And I didn't want to put my nose in your business, but tonight might not have happened if I had."

She sat in silence for a time, staring ahead. Then took his bottle, and slammed half of it back. She swallowed and then burped. "Excuse me." Then she sighed in relief.

She looked at him. "Listen, Antonio. I was in the club scene for almost ten years. Johnnie Demonte is nothing. I knew about him, deep down I knew. Maybe I was in a bit of denial, sugarcoating his intentions because I needed—still need—the money. Convincing myself he was maybe safer than he is. But I definitely knew it was too good to be true. That's why I never let him touch me."

Oh God, thank you. A burst of levity starting in his throbbing heart circulated throughout his body. Johnnie Demonte hadn't hurt her or touched her. He looked upward. *Thank you.*

He could feel her eyes on him as she grabbed another sip of water. He knew she felt his relief. *Don't look away from the road. Don't even think about looking at her.* He couldn't. Not without losing it to the joy overtaking him. He'd kiss her, devour her whole for being so strong and smart. And sacred. Sacred and fucking stunning.

No. *Drive, man.* Nothing at all has changed.

Then a small snicker escaped her lips. "The issue is just, well, relativity. I've known so much worse than Johnnie Demonte. Johnnie is just…the watered-down vanilla brand of asshole compared to the sick fucks I've been in contact with."

"It's dangerous, Jana, playing with fire. At whatever level." It scared him shitless.

"Look, I'm no martial artist, true, but I'd know how to handle him if he got too aggressive."

He threw her a glass-shard glare.

"Fine. I wouldn't have," she admitted as he refocused on the road. "But you were here. I'm safe *and* not sick. I owe you so much."

"You owe me nothing." And he meant it.

"God, Antonio. You can't say that. You've been here for me not just tonight, but from the start of this fiasco. I mean, Jesus, somehow you were even able to salvage things for me with Johnnie, my job! Because you took the brunt!"

His lungs constricted. "Wait. Am I hearing you correctly? You're still going to do this thing, the club gig? Be in the same proximity as that asshole? Even after what I told you about his…his…fuck pad? And after what just happened?"

"I have no choice. My folks need the money. And I need to get it for them."

His blood boiled. But he closed his eyes to check his temper. *Breathe and think.*

Motivation, money. Always money, with everyone! Her loyalty to her selfish family. He could help her. But, her pride. *Fuck!* Her pride, like his pride.

He blew out a hard stream of hot air at his windshield. "Well, I don't want you staying in that apartment."

"I'm not trying to spend a hundred dollars a night on a hotel room, Antonio. He's not coming over, and he hasn't been over. I'm telling you, he's vanilla. Nothing to worry about."

She was not stupid, but was she blind? "Jana, tonight, if it had been any other driver...and that partition went up, he'd have—"

"Done nothing to me, because I would've vomited all over him." She stared out the window, seemingly done with the topic.

"Stay with me. At my place. I'll sleep on the couch. I'm done with taking Johnnie Demonte's orders. And I don't want his father's money either. But I'll still drive you, wherever you need to go. In fact, I insist."

Out of his peripheral vision, he saw her narrowed eyes focused on him. "You insist, huh?" She squirmed in her seat, obviously trying to keep her pride and temper in balance. "I don't know if you've gotten the rundown, but I don't do well with men insisting. I know you're trying to help, but—"

"I got your playlist. Thank you," he blurted out, completely out of context.

She swallowed, sighed, and then smiled at him. "You're welcome. But you can't go changing the subject on me, nice try, though." Her brows lifted for emphasis. "If you don't make money from driving me, you won't hit your goal."

"I don't need the money, Jana. I've been greedy, like all these money-driven assholes. I don't need any more. I just...I got hooked on a stupid 'magic number,' a kid's pipedream from nearly thirty damn years ago." He pulled over to the shoulder of the highway then, veering so hard that she bumped her head on the window. "God, sorry...are you all right?"

She nodded as she rubbed the side of her head, but confirmed with a slow blink and another nod, that yes, she was fine. "Is there a problem with the car?"

"No. No problem with the car." Just a problem with his thrashing heart warring with his goddamn brain. Because what the fuck was he doing?

*

Traffic zoomed past. The headlights of each passing car had a strobe effect inside the vehicle, making Jana's face come in and out of view, highlighting her features. He'd memorized her features. He could draw her face free-hand by now. Her high cheekbones and her cat-shaped eyes, currently underlined by a shadow of smudged makeup. Her delicate nose and her lush lips. God, those lips. Her mouth and her smile, presently taken over by a razor-straight and serious line, but that always came out when she sang, whether she knew it or not. And oh Jesus, when she sang. Or laughed, or spoke. With anything and everything she did, this woman twisted him tight and sent him reeling.

Calm yourself. He pulled a memory, the feel of her lips on his, that afternoon at the pub, and he closed his eyes to relish the thought.

A beat passed. He opened his eyes again. Her expression had morphed into a look of deeper confusion.

"That goddamn number of mine, Jana…it was an illusion. A decades-old illusion, an obsession. Me, never living, hooked on that damn number. But I'm hooked on something far more important now. More…rare, precious. I see…clearly now, Jana."

He swallowed and let his eyes meet hers.

She sighed, her eyes still questioning what the hell he was going on about.

The rhythmic and blinding headlights of each passing car slowed time.

"It's you. You're more important to me…than anything, Jana. And I—"

Before he could finish, her hands held his face, her lips softly at his lips. Then, tilting her head slightly, their mouths connected, fully interlocked in a long-awaited kiss of sweet and utter bliss.

Synergy.

Lips caressing, pulling, lingering, dragging. Synergetic sweeps of ecstasy.

There were only her lips, like heaven and clouds skidding over his mouth, and the resounding heat, burning heat filling his chest. All else melted away. But God, so much heat, fire. Like their spark had been given oxygen, life breathed into something that might very well be…love.

She pulled her lips away, pausing, panting, pensive. Her eyes soft, but searching. Had she heard his thoughts? Like he'd sensed hers ever since the first time he'd seen her in his rearview?

*

Their foreheads resting on one another, she dug into him with that look. No sunglasses. No shield.

"What is it?" he whispered.

A puff of laughter. "I'm hooked on you too, Antonio Ruiz. I am. Just completely, utterly hooked."

That internal heat raged hotter, higher, joy spreading throughout his being, healing his heart.

He slid his hand under her thick, lustrous hair, at the nape of her neck and pulled her into him, this time, he kissed her, devoured her.

His tongue swept in, tasting her, reveling in her, his fantasy meeting reality. He felt so alive, vibrant and alive.

Their breath fell into a rhythm as their passionate kiss waxed and waned, lips dragging and pulling, teeth nipping, tongues exploring and swimming.

She was hooked on him. Perfect and surreal.

Don't wake me, God. Don't you dare wake me from this dream!

The kiss continued, deepened, but he wanted every bit of her connected to him. He wanted it now. He wanted it always.

He pulled away, gasped for air. His eyes seared into hers. "Come home with me?"

"Yes. Let's go home," she said, a glint of fire in her eyes that he realized, then, had been there for him from the start; he'd just been too blind to see it.

CHAPTER 39

ANTONIO LED HER to his bedroom. It was pristine and tidy. The floor was spotless. There was a chest of drawers against one wall with only a lamp on its surface. An armchair sat by the window. The queen bed was centered on the wall opposite the dresser, and it was immaculate: hospital corners; crisp, tight sheets; and no blanket, only a throw, a weave of vibrant colors, assumedly from his Mexico.

She pictured him sleeping in that bed naked. And she couldn't wait to have him pressed up against her, his skin igniting hers on fire, his taut, muscular build wrapped around her. She looked up at him as he studied her, deliciously hungry for her. But it was a hunger so different than what she'd known before from the clubs, from Johnnie, and back to even her few boyfriends. This hunger wasn't to possess her, not to own or dominate her, and not even to pleasure her just to have been the one to do so. The starvation in Antonio's eyes was a selfless one. It was as if he was starving to give her immense joy just to make her happy.

And she wanted the same for him, to erase his wounds, his suffering, to give him release. She wanted to give him back what he'd given her already, that warm, glowing energy in her chest, pounding, exploding out of her, what she could only imagine was something like love.

And it started when he'd given her the music player. When he'd known what she needed when she'd needed it. And he'd gone without so she'd be happy.

"Hey." His voice sent vibrations through her.

She only smiled in reply as his hands reached for her.

His hands were stealthy and confident, unzipping her dress. He lifted the strings from either side of her neck, his fingers brushing her skin as he did. Electricity shot through her. God, it had been so long. Forever. Or ever? That such a sensation graced her body.

He gently pulled the straps wide, down over her shoulders, and down her arms. The brisk air of the room caught her off guard, and she felt her nipples harden while a chill sprinted up her spine. She had no bra, no barrier to his tender, sultry eyes. His fingertips tickled her skin as they slowly brought the satin straps down her forearms, the dress's halter now bunched at her bellybutton.

He smiled and shook his head. "You're...astonishing."

She watched his thick, muscular neck as he swallowed hard, and she quivered from her core.

He leaned in closer. At her ear. "You glow. You really do."

His breath in her ear drove her wild. Then, as if he knew she needed more, he pressed his lips to her neck, her collarbone, her shoulder while his fingers let go of the strings of her dress, and the black satin frock fell to the floor.

He tilted his head as if studying her bare body, then circled around her and placed his fingertips on her shoulders from behind, sending tingling ecstasy up her neck.

With his mouth at her ear, he kissed her lobe and moaned his apparent delight. "You are magnetic and mesmerizing Jana Park."

She was amazed and thankful and in heaven that he thought so.

He moved one hand from her shoulder across her collarbone, sending such intense shivers down her body that she couldn't help but giggle. His hand paused midway across the top of her heaving chest as his other hand dropped to her hip. He gave her a quick jerk back, and her ass was tight up against him and his solid manhood. A deep moan escaped her lips. He dragged the back of his hand now at her throat down her center and between her breasts, which were heavy with ache for him to hold her tight in his grasp.

But he didn't. He obviously wanted to take his time. And she'd be patient, trusting he knew exactly what she needed, what she wanted, what was best.

His hand reached her navel, palm flat against her stomach. Then he spun her around to face him. He pulled her tight to him and cradled her neck, gently forcing her head to look up. And in a swift motion, he kissed her mouth more deeply than she'd ever been kissed. His tongue and lips were masterful, teaching her mouth how to take such a sweet assault. The hand on her back swooped down her back, down to her thighs, and he hoisted her up, his mouth still taking hers, making her core tense with heightening arousal.

Three steps to the bed and he gently placed her down. He slowed his kiss to a halt and pulled back from her. His eyes absorbing her, she watched him examine her entire body. He stood back a pace, maybe better able to see her in full view? Of all the thousands of pairs of eyes on her in her lifetime, she'd never felt anything like his, like this. Antonio made her feel heavenly, priceless. Divine.

He blinked as if to take a mental snapshot of her, then he gave her a sultry smile as he moved his hand up to the top button of his shirt. "I want to dance for you, Jana Park. I want to strip for you."

*

He smiled, a troublemaking glint in his eyes. She shook her head as a light giggle fled from her lips.

He reached into his front pant pocket and pulled out his mp3 player. "Are you ready?" he asked with a painfully sinful quality in his voice.

Her core shuddered in response. God, she was so wet for him now. Anguishing.

He selected a playlist then moved to his side table to place the device on his speaker dock. He'd picked the second Latin track from her playlist. *Oh God, this was going to be good.*

He backed up a few paces and then anchored himself in a strong wide stance. As the punchy beat kicked in, he started the show with a slow and sexy hip roll. God, he was adorable and so scorching hot at the same time, it made her crazy with need.

He lifted one eyebrow as if he read her thoughts. "Do you like the show?" he teased as he took his top shirt button apart, then the next.

"I really, really do."

The music picked up then, and he really started to get into the role. A flare with his wrist here and a Latin hip snap there. He was making her laugh out loud, and at the same time, he drove her out-of-her-mind wild. She was already so primed for him, and she was only getting hotter as he teased on. His gentle gyrations made it impossible for her to ignore his bulging erection, held back by his snug black slacks. She'd leap off the bed and tear them off him if he didn't get closer to her soon.

His shirt finally fell to the floor. *Jesus*, his body was unbelievable, god-like. Then he started to work on undoing his pants. She licked her lips; she was so thirsty for him. With the way his body maneuvered, his rippling abs flexing with each body roll and hip thrust, she could only imagine his hardness over her and in her, rounding and seeking pleasure centers inside her she didn't know she had.

He was too damn delectable. Her mouth got drier as she watched him undo his belt, his clasp, his zipper. Oh God, she couldn't contain herself. She flipped over on her stomach and spun around on the bed for a better view. On her elbows, chin in hands, her nipples were satiated for the moment with the firm cool pressure of the comforter beneath her. That would have to do until Antonio was done teasing her. Then he'd begin pleasing her. Oh Lord, with his ever-loving mouth and hands and cock, would he ever satisfy all of her. Every bit of her ravenous body.

He grinned as if so pleased with himself, glad to make her insane with desire, and to make her wait for satiation. "Am I taking too long to undress for you, my beautiful princess warrior?"

She clenched her teeth and huffed. "You know you are."

He only smiled bigger, but instantly threw down his arms, and his pants and boxers were all at once crumpled at his feet.

He was so much man; she gulped down hard, imagining him forever inside her. "Antonio, I want you *now*. Please, just come here to me."

*

He leaped onto the bed, rolling her over with a light nudge of his knee. His enormous length hovered over her body, and she clenched hard at the sight of the glistening tip just above his silken smooth crown. God, she craved the taste of him like a parched lioness finally nearing the edge of a watering hole. The wait had been too long in so many ways.

"I want to make love to you, Jana. God, so badly."

"If you don't, I'll kill you." She smiled and pulled him to her, finally hot skin on skin, she dug her fingers into his back as she felt his glorious cock sliding in between her slit, but only hovering outside her sex, teasing there. He was so close it hurt.

He nibbled at her ear, his hot breath showing her how badly he wanted her, needed her, as badly as she needed him. Her lower lips held his beautiful cock, embracing him, keeping him while her sensory spots ignited with every rocking stroke. His hips moved expertly, and his hard ass cheeks tightened with every plunge forward, flexing with every retreat back. Her clit sparked to life, engorged and needy, getting more sensitive with every one of his thrusts forward. She hummed in response.

He continued to tease her there while he moved his mouth from her ear to her breasts. *Thank you, God!* Her heavy and incited breasts, her tight nipples, had been waiting for his attention.

His moist lips kissed one nipple while his hand gently pinched the other then cupped that breast firmly. It was like he'd goddamn read her mind–again. His kisses turned to wet trails with his tongue, the air in the room chilling her everywhere his tongue had been. Swirls around her nipple made her sex squeeze, his cock still just outside her need, waiting there, baiting her at the outside of her arousal. He moaned, and the pleasure in that sound made her demanding. "Be deep in me, Antonio. God, now, please." She was exhausted from waiting. For so long, she'd waited for him. The *him* she didn't know existed on Earth.

Finally, after such a life-crushing string of time, she'd been sent a gift from above. Antonio, her guardian angel, her rightful lover, her sweet and powerful friend.

CHAPTER 40

H E DID MAKE love to her, long sweet love. And he didn't ever want it to end. His fit with her was so perfect, too perfect. And their ability to read each other, find each other's every sensory spot, every pleasure point, was like nothing he'd ever experienced. Their lovemaking was a symbiotic joining of two souls. He was factually hooked.

He held her tight as she finally fell asleep. He was on the brink himself, but couldn't stop watching her and that glow of hers. He moved his hand to the space between her tender breasts to feel her chest rising with each breath. He didn't want to fall asleep and by mistake actually wake from the dream that he'd fallen into.

But sleep did take over. Not even a *Sahun* master can defeat the body's natural mechanisms, and when he woke with the sun, she was indeed gone from his side.

*

He stretched and reached for his boxers then left his bedroom to find his dream come true.

It didn't take him a minute to find her in his tiny apartment. Jana was leaning up against his kitchen counter, a coffee in one hand, his tri-folded morning paper in the other. A vision in white, she was wearing the shirt he'd worn the night before, and only that shirt. *Please, God, make this be every day.*

"Hey, you. How'd you sleep? You worked hard. I imagine you slept hard too."

"Sleep? Hah! Not with you tossing and turning," he teased. Actually, she hadn't moved a muscle. Her stunning body had fit perfectly along his, and she'd stayed tucked in his shape for the entire five hours. "Want some breakfast?" he asked, heading to the barely-filled fridge.

"No, thanks. I'm okay. Kinda want to get today started so it ends that much faster—the bank, the hospital and my mother, the club, Johnnie." Her smile wasn't convincing, but she tried all the same. "Coffee's here. Then maybe we can go through a donut drive-thru." She laughed. "I totally deserve deep fried sugar craziness after such a workout."

"You're so bad, and yes, we should. That is what we'll do. Deep fried sugar craziness." He winked in agreement, and then poured himself only half a cup of coffee. "Which bank do you need to stop at?"

"No bank with you in those boxer briefs," she said, eyeing him, her arm outstretched to pull him to her. "I'm bound to procrastinate our departure to anywhere with you in those. Or out of them."

Where had this woman come from? This could not be further from his reality, and in case it was a delusion or a waking dream, he moved toward her and kissed her mouth with all he had. He pulled away for air, then kissed her neck, pecking his way up her jaw line, her earlobe, and then drew back again, only his hand holding her hair back from her face. He stared, taking her in. In case it was a dream, he needed to memorize every minute detail. If it were a dream, he'd live it until the dream bubble burst. He placed his lips on hers again and lingered there until she slapped his ass.

"Let's go shower together," she said, hopping up excitedly. "The bank doesn't open until nine anyway."

*

His recurring shower fantasy had been nothing compared to the real thing.

Seeing her body glistening under the water's downpour, her curves highlighted, her soaking hair down the length of her back, it was enough to take him over the edge. And learning her body, exploring, discovering what made her writhe with pleasure, was his pleasure, and was pure and unadulter-ated magic.

Don't you dare wake up, Antonio. Because pure magic is what dreams are made of. *And they're as fleeting as this single moment.*

*

She was so used to taking care of people.

For the first time in her life, someone initiated genuine care of and for her. Antonio and his sweet attention toward her were too strange, too sur-real, almost uncomfortable, yet deliciously blissful at the same time.

But she couldn't hope to fight her nature, and really, she had no desire to, not with Antonio. She wanted to give him pleasure, happiness, and sweet ecstasy too, like he'd given her.

She made her way around his solid body and knelt down on the show-er's hard tile floor, the warm water pouring over her. She took his beautiful, shimmering steel into her mouth and worked to bring him to the ends of the earth. Every dip of her tongue, each deep insertion, and the energy she put into giving him release made her own sex clench and quiver. But her height-ening arousal wasn't nearly as important to her as him coming to his peak.

He came as the hot water ran out; the icy needles pelting down had no effect on the brute force of his orgasm, his cock's pulsating release rippling against her tongue. She held him in her mouth for the aftershocks, loving the power she'd pulled from him and the pleasure she'd given him.

He lifted her up from kneeling, hoisting her to his chest, cradling her bottom in his arms. Her breasts were flush with his chest's slick, muscu-lar planes.

He leaned her up against the shower wall, kissed her mouth gently, sweetly, and whispered through his kiss, "God what you do to me."

"Feeling's mutual." Her words couldn't do justice to what her body and heart felt while in his embrace.

"Now, it's my turn to get you, but we need to relocate, it's too damn cold in here." He laughed as he carried her back to the bed, laying her down drip-ping wet and shivering. He grabbed the throw from the bottom of the bed and covered her up. He bent her knees, holding her feet up at the edge of his bed, and ducked under the heavy throw.

When his soft lips grazed her clitoris, she bucked her hips up from the sensory overload. He pressed her hips back down with one firm hand while his tongue moved into place at her slit. Back and forth, back and forth, sweeping through her needy lips, hitting her most sensitive points all along the way. He took such delicate care of her, putting all his dedicated attention into every teasing twirl of his tongue. He sent a continual tingling wave up her spine, and she'd arch her back in response only to have him force her body back down so he could continue his onslaught.

Then he hit it, her point of no return. All the deepest and most closely guarded holdings within her were released in a torrent.

Oh God, this man. He was a cathartic potion that she'd never known before.

CHAPTER 41

AFTER THAT MORNING'S deluge of release, she thought she'd reached her maximum quota for the day. But when she left the dress, the purse, and shoes on the kitchen counter of Johnnie's apartment, another spark of relief warmed her insides.

But she'd have to see Johnnie tonight and the nights after that. Still, she wouldn't let anything get in the way of her current high.

She collected her clothes, threw them in her bag, and locked the studio apartment door behind her. It was a huge step away from being at Johnnie Demonte's mercy.

She buckled her seat belt as Antonio pulled away, heading toward the commercial district, for donuts and the bank before going north to Fort Lee. His hand slid over to her leg, and she took his hand and squeezed. She felt a constant rush of new life each time she thought of last night, of this morning, and of *them* now. She felt lighter than a damn cloud. Screw all else; she was happy.

"You good?"

"Really good. Yeah." She smiled at him.

"You nervous about seeing your folks? About the bank statements?"

"Nervous probably isn't the word. My fury from Sunday has just turned into exhaustion. And not the good kind of exhaustion, like this morning from last night. More like a deep and desperate weariness," she said, her shoulders falling that same instant. It was going to be such a long road. And her parents' insistence on continuing to support her brother was a losing battle. The whole situation was a lose-lose for Jana. But it was her obligation.

At least, Antonio was her glimmer of hope. He made her feel like it would all be okay. Like she'd find and fit all the floating puzzle pieces together over the next couple of months. Somehow. Somehow together, they'd make it work.

"You still sure you want to go in tonight, to the club?"

"I have no choice."

"You may have a choice."

"Winning the lottery?"

"That or I could loan you the money." His words lingered while his eyes stayed glued to the road.

Was he serious? She coughed, trying to clear the sudden knot of all-too-familiar warning from her throat. "I could never, would never!"

Like he even had enough. She didn't think he had a clue what kind of money was at hand here. "And you've been saving to go back to Mexico. I couldn't take that from you." Even though she didn't want him set on Mexico. She wanted him to be here, with her, near her work, her city.

Her heart sent a warning to her head in the form of a sudden headache, thick and furious. Morse code under her skull.

"I'm not leaving for Mexico without you, Jana. So if it makes things faster, takes care of your family situation, why not?"

Wait. Me in Mexico?

Her eyes must have spelled out her thoughts.

"We are too good together to be apart, Jana. Won't you come home with me? To Puerto Vallarta? You will love it. You won't believe how amazing it is. No cutthroat, superficial games, and bullshit like life is up here. Just you and me and my family in paradise. Our family…yours and mine, *princessa*. Our very own life, children, future."

*

A flood of confusion and wonderment swept through her.

A family? A real family? Their own family? With Antonio. *Paradise.*

Paradise? That's a state of mind, not a real place, right? A place of make-believe.

But being with Antonio definitely felt like heaven, like paradise. And it felt real.

Couldn't they be in paradise together wherever they were and stay here, in or near Manhattan? Because all she'd worked for, God, that was her paradise, too. Puerto Vallarta was a world away. Her lifelong purpose, since she could hold a toy stethoscope, was to be what she'd finally become.

A nurse?

A nurse, yes, but more. So much more! A member of one of the most skilled trauma teams in the biggest city in the world.

They have hospitals in Puerto Vallarta, Mexico, Jana. Come on!

Not the same. Not even close.

He said he wouldn't leave for Mexico without her. Could he, would he consider waiting? Years? Many years? Would he do that for her? Because even though she was falling for him hard, she didn't think she could ever opt to leave her position, not after all she'd done and been through to get it.

But that look in his eyes. If she cared about him, how could she ask him to give up his desire to return home? He craved home and detested the City, this entire area, in fact.

Damn it! All of this was too much to think or talk about right now, too damn much.

"Antonio, let's talk more about…all this…once I've gotten through this week. Okay?"

"Jana, I'm trying to get you through this week…by ending your family's financial problems, which would also cut your time out at the club altogether and—"

"Whoa. So that's what this loan is about? The club and Johnnie?"

She'd handled herself before Antonio and could damn well handle herself without him still. And even though his soft look of anticipation, a sweet hope in his face that she'd surrender touched her heart, she just couldn't fold.

No. He pushed her to the wall. "Listen. I have to continue this gig at the club, Antonio. I know that much. Aside from the money, which I need to *make on my own*, I made a commitment. I'm helping the girls, and I'm fulfilling the contract. I couldn't and wouldn't take your hard-earned money, anyway. I mean, I've known you for all of two weeks. Fourteen days!"

"But you and I both know it feels like a lifetime. Swallow your pride and open your eyes, Jana!"

Open her eyes? Swallow her pride? Thank God she had any pride left!

Yes, she couldn't deny that they'd had a mind-blowing connection that eluded her most of the time, but she wouldn't acknowledge it now. The bottom line was that she couldn't give in here. To be with a man that she *needed,* that she *owed,* that just went against her grain. Being indebted to him, under his control, owing him anything, it wouldn't work. It had to be symbiosis or nothing at all.

And her parents' burden was not his to take on, no matter how much he cared about her.

She faced the front and decided not to answer him. She'd have put the earbuds in right then, but the mp3 was probably still on his nightstand. It didn't matter. She had to focus. She couldn't be off in la-la land, escaping her problems like Antonio wanted to help her do. No, she had to figure shit out with her mother, discuss the release of her father with the doctor for tomorrow, arrange the homecare, pay the whopping hospital bill with the forty large she'd soon have in her damn purse, then deal with the club. Her two new dancers were coming in tonight.

But it was a lot, an overwhelming tidal wave.

Antonio had just tried to give her a life raft of a solution for it all.

What was she doing, tossing it back while the waves threatened to swallow her whole?

*

Shit, now she felt awful. She was giving him the silent treatment for Christ's sake, being defensive, stubborn and prideful. He was just trying to help her, which was more than the family she was born into had ever tried to do.

Why did Antonio even put up with her?

She gritted her teeth, stole a gulp of air, then turned to him. "Antonio, I'm sorry. Just, please, let me think. I need time to process all of this craziness."

She watched him nod with calm, objective understanding. No guilt, no hurt, even in their newer dynamic, his expression remained stoic, sweet. He continued down the thruway, but this time, he took her hand in his and wouldn't let go.

God, the strength and comfort and warmth of his touch. She did not deserve Antonio Ruiz. She definitely did not earn such a man.

CHAPTER 42

W HEN THEY GOT to the hospital, he parked and got out with her. She looked at him with an inquisitive eye.

"What?" He skewed his eyes. "I'm coming in with you, Jana. I'll wait in the waiting room, but I'm coming in."

She wasn't going to argue. His solid presence could only be a help to her. She smiled, reached her arms up, and clasped her hands around his neck. "I wouldn't have it any other way." She kissed him sweetly, and then he took her hand in his.

"Hey, before we do go in, I spoke to Jake Demonte while you were in the bank earlier. Needed to make sure things were all good. I let him know I had to diffuse a heightened situation last night, and, well, he knows his son and he knows me. Anyway, everything is fine. I'm still driving you, no matter what Johnnie says, and if you must continue this stint, I'll continue to drive you. End of story. The fleet is mine anyway, so I say who drives who."

She gave him a sideways look. "The fleet?"

"Yes. My company. I have a fleet. Of limos." He laughed as if she should know.

His company?

She remembered the business card he'd given her that she'd shoved somewhere in her purse. He continued talking about 'his depot' and 'the crew,' and how he'd started with only two cars and now had fifty-four? All the while, she rifled through her bag for that damn card. She needed to see that little piece of paper.

Her fingers got to the bottom of her purse and pulled from it a small, bent-up piece of card stock. "A.R. Limousine Service, Antonio José Ruiz, Owner."

Owner. *Owner?*

Like Ilana-fucking-Simon's father owned a large limo company? The association alone made her a little queasy.

And why was he driving a limo if he owned the damn company?

"Well, at least for now."

"What's that?" She tuned-in finally, settling her thoughts as best she could so she could hear him and understand this new aspect of him.

"I'm selling, liquidating. So I can get home. I've listed it for sale, for less than it's worth, but with you in my life, I know the money isn't important. Like I said, I have enough. I've got the universe now." He smiled at her and squeezed her hand. "So I'm just waiting on a bite."

Her perception of him had shifted upside down and irreversible, a one-eighty in a minute's time. Not like the day she'd watched this strong, virile, highly-skilled man in a *dobak* fly across a room in the library. No, not like that at all. The realization that this man was no struggling limo driver but a businessman with means and ambition, one who was accustomed to control, power—another man to be beholden to—made her breath halt.

The money's not important to him. You are.

Yes, he had said that. She felt that, too. And she'd heard his stories of struggle. He'd started over a few times over. He'd come from nothing.

But ambition's in the blood. And a metaphoric transfusion—giving it all up—would leave him lifeless. No ambition, no vitality, not for a man who needs that kind of power.

Confusion clobbered her. "Antonio, I should really get inside."

"Yes, right." But he held her arm before she took a step toward the entrance. "You look like you're going to pass out. White as a ghost…you okay?"

"Yeah. No, I'm fine. Maybe I should've eaten something more substantial than a chocolate glazed," she lied, and she headed into the hospital.

CHAPTER 43

"HEY, DAD. HOW are you feeling? Ready to get home tomorrow?"

He looked at her without answering, just a poker face and an eye roll. *That's fine.* She'd speak to the doctor, get real information that way anyhow.

"Mom...Mom." She gently nudged her mother awake in the chair. "Morning."

"Ja-Na. What are you doing here? Thought you stopped coming altogether?"

"Ma, I said Thursday. I needed the time to get the money, remember?"

Her mother sat up, rubbed her eyes and sighed. "The health inspector came to the restaurant, Ja-Na. Yesterday. I didn't call you, but they closed us down."

God is good! And, hell, why hadn't she thought to call the health department weeks ago? A service to the community and to her family. "I guess the universe *forced* you to take a break, huh?"

"That's all you have to say? It *was* probably you, like your father said. You probably called the inspector yourself!"

"No, I didn't, Mom." Fuming at their crudeness and their unwarranted disdain and their thanklessness. "But I wish I had thought of it. I really do." Spoken in her most even tone. "Anyway, I found these." She pulled out their bank statements. "A year or so ago you refinanced and sent eighty-five thousand dollars to Dane. After he gambled our lives away the first round, you did it again? Would you care to explain?"

"It was for his business…in LA, and it was going to 'go global' he said…"

"Jin!" her father piped. "It's none of her damn business. And she shouldn't speak so disrespectfully to her parents!" he yelled but was then overtaken by a coughing spell.

Jana moved to his bedside, adjusted his pillow, and handed him a cup of water which he slapped out of her hand onto the floor.

She stared at the puddle at her feet for a long moment while she willed herself not to cry. She couldn't let them see her tears.

"Dad…" She tried for a deep breath but only a shallow hiccup of air filled her chest. "Do you understand what I've been doing for you and for Mom?" *Do you understand that I've spent years dancing naked for hordes of filthy men?* No, of course, they didn't know what she'd done and sacrificed for them. A secret she'd held for all these years, and would hold forever to come. Because she just wasn't that brave, unwilling to sacrifice her image in their eyes, unwilling to face their loathing, disgusted looks, ones of hate and disdain *beyond* what she already felt from them as a lowly 'bed pan' bitch.

Instead, she said in a calm, clear, yet assertive tone, "I'm the slave, and you've made Dane the master. You continue to make decisions with *my* money, my blood, sweat, tears. And my education! The dynamic needs to stop. You take my loyalty for granted while Dane, who still hasn't even shown his face here, by the way, gets—" she stopped her rant, seeing her parents' glazed-over faces, knowing not a word had registered. They were deaf to a voice from 'a nobody.' She shook her head and asked, "How much more have you given him? Just tell me that."

"Ja-Na Sun Park, it is none of your damned business," her father stated through heavy, strained breath. Then that turned into wheezing, which became such a violent cough, the nurses rushed in since his heart rate had spiked, and the monitors were going crazy.

But all she could hear over and over in her mind was her name spat like poison from her father's lips. It was as if the Korean meaning of *Ja-Na Sun,* 'Good and Beautiful Child,' meant anything but. Why had the man lying before her given her such a name in the first place, then treated her with such disregard and downright scorn all her life?

"Ja-Na, you should be ashamed!" her mother said, pushing her away to get to her father, holding his hand while the two nurses tended to him.

Jana left the room without a word. They had basically confirmed to her that more, probably much more than the eighty-five grand was given to Dane. Probably from other accounts or credit cards. Who knew and, really, who cared?

Well, obviously, she cared…and too damn much.

Outside the room, she felt paralyzed. She leaned against the wall to steady herself. Her body was vibrating from the depths of her being. She looked at her hands. They'd aged. Her veins were more visible, similar to her mother's and to her grandmother's. And they shook uncontrollably right in front of her eyes.

Dutiful daughter? Accomplished nurse? Whatever the hell she was, she was loyal to the end.

So go now, speak to the doctor, gather the scripts, organize Dad's home transport, pay the bill.

Goddamn it, no!

She shoved her quivering hand into her purse and dug out her personal cell phone. Her finger selected her brother's number as she walked toward the waiting room where she knew Antonio was waiting. Whatever else she had learned he was today, he was there for her. Her solid, steady anchor. And she needed him right now.

As she pushed through the door, he was already out of his chair waiting for her as if he sensed her state of urgency, which finally did not surprise her. He followed her out of the building, into the parking lot, just when her brother picked up on the other end of the phone.

CHAPTER 44

ANTONIO TOOK HER by the shoulders and leaned her against the limo to give her balance and physical support. She was shaking. He stood next to her with enough space for her to breathe, but close enough to let her know he was right there for her. She had placed the call on speakerphone, letting him hear the insanity first-hand.

"How much, Dane?"

"How much what, Jana?"

"How much have they been sending you every month? How much of *my* hard-earned money?"

"Your *slut* money, you mean?" her brother said with venom in his voice.

"I put myself through school, earned myself a real job, a profession. I save real lives, Dane, while I managed to pay off our parents' home and business. I got their hole-in-the-wall restaurant back to even, damn it! I got them out of the six-foot grave you dug and shoved them—us!—into in the first place! All me."

"Poor you. Is that why you called me? To tell me your fucking sob story?"

Jana visibly bit down on her tongue. Antonio had never seen her so incensed, not even when he'd shown her the bank statements. He took a step away, allowing her a little more space, but she reached for him, grabbed his shirt and dragged him even closer to her, then grasped his hand and squeezed it for dear life.

I'm here, princess. I'm here.

He watched her eyes lift to the sky as if praying. Maybe hoping for lightning to strike her brother down wherever he stood? Antonio knew he sure as hell wanted that. Her evil tormenter done-in, ended.

"Dane, you will send the fucking money back; you will wire it. *Today.* Dad needs it and I'm tapped. I spent the last of my savings and maxed out all of my cards."

"Why the hell did you do that? God, Jana. Do you not get it? God, you're a whore and a moron!" The fucker started laughing on his end.

Whore? Moron? Antonio was ready to rip the fucker's throat out. He looked at Jana with his eyes no-doubt blazing, white-knuckling his free fist while crunching her hand in the other.

She placed one quivering finger on his mouth to stay quiet. To keep it together. Still her fight, remember. Then she pulled her hand free of his and shook out the obvious pain, glared at him, but then took his hand back in hers softly, easing his heightened rage.

"*Gentle,*" she mouthed, then gave him an understanding look and a nod. That it would be all right. She was fucking comforting him right now? *Jesus, this woman.* Even though her chest heaved rage and her hands still trembled, her eyes showed strength and patience, as if separate from her body's auto responses. Like she was so used to the torment. God, how had she done this alone up 'til this point? Heart convulsing, teeth gnashing, he quaked for her.

I'm here now, though. She's not alone now. And never would be again. He wouldn't let this pack of wolves at her. Not anymore.

He swallowed and parted his lips behind her finger, ready to kill with words.

But she stopped him with that finger, her soft and trembling digit still at his lips, pressing firmly as a second warning to keep his words in. A reminder—her fight still, not his.

Fuck, fine. *For now.* He'd stay quiet for now. Only for now. He tuned back in as the asshole's laughter finally waned, resuming his belligerent rant.

"They've never watched out for you, Jana. Hell, they've even known for all these years how you made all that money!"

What? What did the fucker say?

"Excuse me?" Jana asked in a long exhale. "What are you talking about?" Even though she'd heard her brother's words clear as crystal. Her own mother, her father? They knew she'd stripped to support them?

"Yeah. Mom and Dad, they've known all along, that you were slinging your sloppy cunt around."

Her eyes closed in slow motion like she'd been knifed in the throat while Antonio asked her if the bastard had said what he thought he'd said.

She could care less about the asshole's choice of words. Her parents knew, that was surreal and heart-stopping and devastating and disgusting. She had no words.

But Antonio obviously had words, so ready to erupt, she didn't know if she could stop him a third time. His fury emanated from every pore. She wouldn't dare touch him. Not a calming gaze or a word would snap him out of his depth of fury.

Antonio plucked the phone from her hand, squared his shoulders, feet anchored.

So no, there was no stopping him now. And she didn't want to stop him. Finally, someone was willing to fight for her, and with her, to defend against her tormentor who was supposed to want to protect her but instead wanted to bury her. Pride be damned, she was ready for someone else to take a stand.

Phone to his mouth, Antonio prepared. Readied.

She watched the volcano erupt, an explosion of spewing hot baritone.

"You motherfucking COWARD! You pathetic, balls-less nobody. Who the *fuck* do you think you are, treating Jana this way? Anyone this way? You hollow, sorry little prick!" An eight on the Volcanic Explosivity Index, all said in fast, furious…Spanish. Only Jana understood what her guardian angel had said because Dane spoke nothing but English.

"So you got yourself a spic pimp to pull your punches for you now, Jana?" Dane laughed.

Antonio blinked once. Then again. His jaw clenched in fury, Jana slid back, away from the danger zone that was Antonio. The radiating heat and hate from her lover was too much. Air and earth shattering. He heaved a breath, and she swore she felt a solar wind.

But with that breath, a sense of peace seemed to spread over Antonio's face. Suddenly and eerily calm, Antonio closed his eyes and said in podium-worthy English, "Jana obviously got all the strength and integrity in the family, while you, you spineless boy, got nothing. Have nothing. You will get yours. Karma alone will find you. But pray Karma delivers before I ever meet you. Be sure to pray very hard."

He handed Jana the phone and stepped away from her to pace out his rage and maybe to plot the day he'd ever meet her big brother Dane.

*

Mind whizzing, heart racing, her soul screamed thanks to Antonio and to the heavens for its slight taste of liberating justice.

Jana now held and stared at the phone. Silence lingered, until, for the first time in her life, she heard in her brother's voice a hesitance, the slightest hiccup of fear. She even heard the prick swallow before words came.

"Is he...fucking done?"

Done with you? Almost. But really, Dane wasn't worth an iota more of breath or energy. Of Antonio's or hers. But before ending the call, she needed answers. Closure. She inhaled slowly then eased out words. "Why Dane? Why did you tell them?"

"I didn't. It was Cousin Daniel. He went to some bachelor party at your club. He saw you and told Mom. Mom told Dad. Hey, that's probably why they continue to send me money when I ask for it. At least, they have one kid who does something reputable with life! You're so pathetic it's sad. And then, Jesus, you go from bedroom fantasy fodder to bedpan maid! Embarrassment to embarrassment!"

Antonio stopped pacing, looked up, and made his way back to her, next to her, took her hand and squeezed it, as if trying to infuse all of his strength into her.

Her profession was her identity, her life. The whore comments rolled right off, they meant nothing. But her struggle and strife for her esteemed nursing position, that hit her gut and raised further hell in her heart.

*

She couldn't hide her tears. And her breathing hitched. Antonio wished that arrogant bastard a slow, brutal death. Fuck her brother and her parents. Antonio was taking Jana far from her abusive, so-called family. Far from this psycho thinking and insanity.

He watched her collect a breath and wipe her tears. She seemed ready to say her piece, although he couldn't imagine any of it registering with the bastard. But he knew she needed to finish this once and for all.

"Who knows what you do day-to-day, Dane? You say you're in the entertainment business in LA, but more than likely, you're waiting tables. Or gambling it away again. Yes, I know shit about you too, big brother! Whatever you do, though, you aren't here right now for Dad. You aren't giving, but always taking. You are thirty-three years old, for Christ's sakes, and the money you get is the money I made! My 'dirty money,' as you call it, you self-righteous son of a bitch! At the end of the day, I sleep like a baby at night. How about you? How do you sleep knowing your little sister supports you? You tell your wife and kid the truth? You're a pathetic excuse for a man." But there was no response. Antonio watched her eyes zone out, just staring at the phone screen, where a flashing summary of minutes showed the call had ended who-knows-how-long before her rant had.

CHAPTER 45

DANE PARK HAD hung up on her. Like her parents, he was deaf to her words.

And just like her brother, her parents had known for all those years that she'd been stripping to support them all, filling their bottomless trough. She really had been a slave and still was a slave, a whore. And her parents and brother were her goddamn pimps.

A ding hit her ears. A text. It was probably her mother having just heard from her brother—a tattle tail into his thirties. Like any of it mattered. On autopilot, she opened her messages.

From Luly: *Dr. R. put Ilana on perm with T. Team. So sorry. Call me ASAP.*

Her heart rocketed into her throat then plummeted down to the pavement. She'd been gone not even three weeks!

"Fuuuuuuck!" She threw her phone clear across the parking lot. It shattered on the ground in a thousand pieces.

She looked over at Antonio and without need for a single word of explanation, he pulled her to him on cue, tight into his chest. She'd lost her position at her ER now because of her parents. They were the ruin of her. It wasn't supposed to be this way. It was never supposed to be this way. She screamed into his chest as he held her hard, held her together. She screamed her lungs out and her heart out. Her soul unleashed, unraveled. Antonio kept her upright while endless moments passed.

Chest heaving, she looked up into Antonio's loving eyes and knew he could read her intentions. She needed to do this, to go inside and buck up, rise up, stand up to the man who was supposed to protect her and love her unconditionally.

So she pushed back from Antonio, wiped her eyes, turned around, and marched back into the hospital, into her father's wing to tell the man who'd given her life that she knew. She knew the depths of his transgressions. And she didn't care about his state of health or mind. She didn't care about his wellbeing, just as he had never ever cared about hers.

But when she got to the door of his room, it was vacant.

*

She ran to the nurse's station. "Where is Chang Park? What happened? What's going on?"

"You are…the daughter?"

"Yes"—*also known as the goddamn pocketbook. And I've been here almost daily for Christ's sakes!*—"Yes, the daughter."

"They rushed him to surgery about five minutes ago. Cardiac arrest."

The nurse's words hung like lead in the air as Jana crumbled to the floor.

*

The next thing she knew, Antonio and a nurse were walking her to a chair. "He had another one…another attack." Jana's own whisper echoed in her ears.

"I heard. The nurse said it would be five or six hours until they know anything more. Only that he has to undergo another bypass procedure."

"Stress. *I* did this."

"Jana! Jesus, no! The nurses say your mother's been sneaking him food, maybe even cigarettes too."

Damn her mother!

But damn herself, too. Her anger for their treatment of her had made her care less for his wellbeing. How selfish of her. She may as well have wished him dead. Dear God, how cruel was she? Her dad on the brink again. Shame and a horrible torrent of guilt overwhelmed her.

"It wasn't you, Jana. Never you. You're only *good*. A *good* that they don't deserve."

Good? *No. Not good.* "He's my dad, Antonio. I don't want him to die. I never wanted that. What can I do? I have to do something. Something more!" Jana could only stare, tearless now, wrung out, but searching for relief from the dense severity yanking her heart out of her chest.

She looked up at Antonio.

His eyes were on her, willing her to be brave, his strong, firm hold of her shoulders keeping her upright. "Nothing more, Jana. There is nothing more you can do." He kissed her forehead, and she closed her eyes to absorb it.

CHAPTER 46

SHE STOOD UP.

A sudden feeling of raw strength swelled in her chest.

Nothing more. His words echoed loud and strong.

All at once she realized what she had to do. What she owed herself. She had to *live.*

She could no longer be beholden to her parents. They were lying in their own beds. She couldn't lie with them anymore. No more.

Antonio was standing, watching and nodding, waiting for her thoughts to become words. But the glimmer of pride in his eyes made her think he already knew her lines were being drawn, finally.

*

"Take me to Newark, to the club. I'm done there. If we go now, I can still be back before Dad wakes up."

Antonio took and squeezed her hand, then walked with her to the exit.

"Oh, I'll meet you at the limo. Need to take care of the payment really quick."

"You sure? Now? I mean, you did pass out...."

"I'm okay, really. It will put my mind at ease to get this taken care of," she said, her eyes wide referring to her purse's holdings.

He nodded, however reluctantly, and she veered to the business office window.

"My father's name is Chang Park. Here is forty thousand to put toward the balance."

"Let me look here, Ms....?"

"Park. Jana Park. I'm the primary contact on the account."

"Yes, yes, I see here. Well, Ms. Park, the file shows the balance is at zero. There is nothing due."

"That's impossible. That can't be right...is there an uninsured fund I don't know about? Because I already asked if—"

"No, no fund, but if you wait right here, I can get Ms. Buchard for you—"

"I actually don't have time to wait right now. Can you hold the file? I'll be back in about five hours."

"Yes, of course," the clerk answered while Jana was already running out the door.

What kind of tease was this? Close to two hundred grand, wiped? Just like that? Huge billing errors happened all the time in her hospital, but this, this amount was insane!

Also insane was the glorious sight of her guardian angel waiting for her at the limo. She walked toward Antonio as fast as she could, with an urgency pushing her through time and space. It was like the inertia that moved her during a code blue in her ER...

...which was no longer her ER.

No, not now, Jana. Don't let your mind go there now.

She shoved it down deep and resumed her quick steps forward. Because now, the difference; this energized speed walk took her not toward the possibilities of death and despair, but toward the promise of life. She'd been given a green light to live, to really live! And Antonio was that vibrant light that made her see it all so clearly now.

As soon as she reached him, her guardian angel, he kissed her, a deep, penetrating engagement of their mouths, one she wanted to last forever.

But he pulled away to catch his breath. "Mmm...my warrior princess." He beamed at her proudly, kissed her again lightly, then he ushered her into the passenger seat.

She watched him walk around the front of the car to get in, loving his man-jog, his energy, *him*. He fell into the driver's seat and started the car, smiling at her the entire time. God, she could melt from now 'til eternity in those morphing hazel eyes of his.

"Oh, here. You need to eat." He handed her a cold sandwich wrapped in plastic. "I got it from the shitty cafeteria, but it's something."

She thanked him by leaning over to kiss him sweetly as her hand went up to caress his face, loving the feel of his perfectly rough five o'clock shadow. Then she unlocked her lips without wanting to, pressed her forehead to his, and let her hand slide down his jaw line and back to her lap.

She smiled at the token of care that the crappy little sandwich represented, then unwrapped it. She took an enthusiastic bite silently as he backed out of the space. God, she hadn't realized how hungry she really was.

"It's not half bad when you're running on donuts, coffee, and acidic emotion," she said smiling through her very full mouth.

He smiled sweetly at her, then took his thumb to her chin to catch some dripping condiment, then quickly returned his eyes to the road. "So...I'm sorry to have to tell you this, *mi princessa*, but when your father comes out of that surgery doing just fine as I am sure he will be...I'll have to break both his goddamn legs." A slight smile lifted his face to note his mock seriousness, but his deadly tone resonated in the cab. Her heart pounded from the protective vibration.

And it triple-timed when he took her free hand and squeezed.

She squeezed his hand back. No words were needed for her guardian angel.

He remained quiet, giving her time to breathe, to settle.

But now, only minutes before getting to the club, he needed to know, after she'd decided to be done at the club, what her plan would be. Where were they headed? God willing, *they*. Yes, they could do anything now.

"Talk to me, princess. What are you thinking? What's going on in that gorgeous mind of yours?"

She took a deep breath and looked at him. "The text. It was from Luly. They gave my position away."

"The ER? They didn't hold your spot? Jesus!"

His heart pounded hard, forcing a flood of hopeful warmth through him. Yes, despite his awareness of her distress, he felt a wave of relief. And he didn't feel bad for it, either. Was he being selfish? Yes, a bit. But damn it, even her precious ER hadn't appreciated what they had in Jana! Giving her spot away? She didn't need another entity squeezing her. Taking and taking from her.

"No. Now I have to start over." She sighed while he let his mind relish the thought of them starting anew. Together.

"I'll have to track down Nora and get a solid recommendation to one of the other hospitals in the City. One of the other, God, fifteen near-worthy facilities have to have a spot for me," she said as if to herself more than to him.

He took his eyes off the road and glanced at her, eyes narrow. He didn't understand. He thought she'd finally gotten it. Turned the corner.

God, was it even worth his breath stating the obvious? If all of the shit— her family, Johnnie and the club, now the hospital—weren't enough to wake her up fully, what would his two cents do? It was so ingrained in her, being used and tossed out, then used some more.

A painful burn spread fast across his chest. The fact that now, with a clean slate in front of her, she didn't turn to him, see him, and choose a future with him, it fucking burned like acid. Mexico or Timbuktu, or hell, Manhattan, even! It didn't matter, if she'd just picked life with him, and they could go from there, have driven from there. If she'd said the words, "*We get to start over.*" Instead of, "*I have to start over.*"

But no. He hadn't been in her equation at all.

While, for him, like he'd told her in the parking lot earlier, the money, his built-up business, his 'number,' were of no importance to him now. All that mattered was Jana, his universe was Jana!

But the feeling, apparently, was not mutual. Not reciprocated. Not synergistic.

There was no *they*.

CHAPTER 47

JANA LEFT ANTONIO at the limo, saying she'd only be twenty minutes. She ran in past Erin at the bar. It was four o'clock and she hadn't even meant to be on time. She hadn't actually known the time since getting out of the shower with Antonio that morning when they'd rushed to get to the bank.

Careful going up the rickety back steps to the dressing room, she laughed out loud. With as much money as the Demontes made, they'd never thought to fix those damn steps. They'd been a hazard since she started at The Wet Spot more than nine years ago. All they needed was for one of the dancers in her five-inch platforms to bite it, break a bone, or worse. On the same lines as what Antonio had said, it's strange what rich people notice and care about, and what they overlook.

A few strides more and she was at the dressing room door.

But she didn't even need to open it to know what was behind it: the rhythmic noises, the laughter. Her prediction? It was a scene they'd definitely want her to overlook. If she was staying on, that is.

She opened the door despite herself. And the scene that was sprawled out in front of her eyes confirmed her prediction.

Sugar was on the loveseat, spread eagle, the DJ eating her out, making slurping sounds Jana could only try like hell to ignore. But her ears took them in, and her stomach turned.

Sugar's long red pinky nail was up her nose, having probably just inhaled all of her last night's earnings in the form of fine white snow.

Then there was Laynie and the back door bouncer, James. He had her bent over a stool, pounding her from behind while the girl nonchalantly snorted white powder up *her* nose with some rolled-up monetary denomination; her nails weren't as long as Sugar's because, as she had told Jana during the short time they'd known each other, her father and brother made her clip them for their own safety.

"For fuck's sake! Laynie, Sugar, Jesus! James and whatever the hell your name is, get the hell outta' here!"

"No, James. Keep fucking me. I'm definitely…not…done…ahhh… yet!" Laynie screamed.

"I'm going to get…"

"Security?" Sugar laughed.

"He's right here, *sweetheart*. Fucking the ever-loving hell out of me." Laynie laughed through her panting. "Could you maybe give us a few minutes?"

Sugar started laughing hysterically and pushed the DJ's face harder into her crotch. "Winter, I swear girl! All high and mighty because you're fucking our little boss man."

Jana's teeth ground out their fury as she walked out and directly up to Brandon, the bouncer at the front. But what the hell would he do? Probably take his own damn turn. So instead, she marched upstairs to Johnnie's office, even though he usually wasn't there this early—or at all, it being Thursday. He'd said he be back from Merrick on Friday.

And what was the point anyway? She was only there to be done, to say goodbye.

She stood there staring for a minute. How ludicrous, thinking she could change these girls' lives. She went to the empty bar, pulled a beverage napkin off the top of a pile, and started writing a note to Johnnie. She was done, she wrote. *Thanks for the opportunity. Goodbye.*

She'd leave it with the phone and the apartment key.

"Winter, this new girl is here to see you. Jasmine?" Brandon called from the far corner of the bar.

One of the girls she'd snagged from Piranha. *Shit*. Okay, well, she'd get her oriented for a minute then leave this shithole for good.

"Hey, come on over, Jasmine...and where's Courtney?"

"She changed her mind," the petite dark-haired beauty said.

"That's not good...is it, *Winter*?" came Johnnie's voice over her shoulder. He'd been hovering for who knows how long, and when she looked over at him, the tad of white dust above his upper lip made her know his state of mind. He was assuredly worse than last night. God, she needed to get out of there.

*

"Excuse me for a second, Jasmine. If you wanna go take a seat at a table?"

"Sure thing." She smiled and wiggled her way stage-side.

"I was going to tell you that Sugar and Laynie are done, but now we might need them. I caught them in the back—"

"In their fuck-party snorting my coke? Yeah, I know, and they're fine. More ready to dance than ever. Especially our little Laynie. But since you couldn't find sixteen replacements, let alone two, I'm gonna need you to dance tonight too. After I take you in the back, get you primed and fucked real good, you'll be star-level like the old days."

Jana's chest searched for oxygen as her mind raced. Which way around this asshole to get to the exit door?

This was retribution for last night. Of course it was. He'd invested in her dress and didn't get his return by helping her out of the thousand-plus dollar frock. Well, whatever the case, she stood up, slammed his phone on the bar along with his key, and without a word, skirted to his left toward the exit.

But his arm caught her elbow just as quickly.

"I know you were with Antonio at his place last night," he hissed. "GPS tracker and phone tap. Every moan, every conversation." He nodded at the phone in her hand. "You're a whore, but you're a whore who chose the wrong cock. I'm the one. Would've given you everything. But instead, you insult me."

"Let. Me. Go, Johnnie. I'm done here."

He reached his arm behind his back and pulled out a small pistol. "No, you're not." He slid the point of the gun up her side. Then he put his lips to her ear and hissed quietly, "You won't go. You need the money. And anyway, Ms. Winter Snow, your little Laynie needs you to dance." The gun tip pressed hard into her hip now. "No one will miss her if she disappears. And if she does disappear, it'll be because you left me stranded. I swear to God, you dance, or she's done."

He was high. Made no sense. Laynie bought her coke from him, pulled men in for his club. None of this was about any of that, though. It was about power. The power that he'd never had. Not over her, not at the club, not with his father, and hell, not even with his father's chauffeur.

Antonio. Outside. Right outside in the parking lot. Twenty minutes had come and gone, right? No clocks, she couldn't know. But she was certain Antonio would know she was in trouble and would come in. Any minute now.

But if Antonio did come through those doors, Johnnie'd have a field day.
Oh God help me, please.

Johnnie narrowed his eyes at her. "Oh, Jana…Jana, Jana, Jana. You looking to the door, huh? For your chauffeur savior? He won't be coming, my fuckable little Winter Snow." He nuzzled her ear with the gun's tip pressed harder into her hip now, then he whispered, "My guy's got your Mexi-Man by gunpoint right now. Yeah, he's done. That's gotta be. Disrespect comes with a cost, baby. Everything comes with a cost."

*

Her lungs deflated. Life-breath thrust out like she'd been kicked in the gut.

Johnnie was bluffing. He had to be. Jana had to believe that.

Antonio is too skilled, too smart, too strong.

And Johnnie was high, delusional. Sick in the fucking head! Playing a wise guy, like in a bad mob movie. Coked out and emasculated and pathetic and—*goddamn him!*—in complete control now. Because he had the gun.

Johnnie pulled Jana away from the door by her wrist to the tables by the stage. He threw her in a seat, commanded her to stay with a look.

A few of the girls came out on stage then, their soft, barefoot steps contrasting sharply with the bullet train of blood smashing through Jana's veins. They came out to practice pole moves before the rush. *Fucking great!* Of all times she wished they'd been late!

Run! Go! But mind readers they weren't, not like her Antonio.

Instead, just like Jana had taught them, all four girls got down on the stage floor to stretch out, freeing their hands of keys, water bottles, phones, and all tossing their stilettos on the floor with rapid-fire thuds. With each thud, Jana jumped, heart pounding triple-time, her eyes glued to Johnnie's gun.

None of them had a clue about the situation, none except for the new girl who was outside of Johnnie's peripheral vision.

His phone rang. He fumbled with it in his free hand with the pistol discreetly held by his side. He squinted at the phone screen as he tried like hell to silence the ringer and answer it. He turned toward the office stairs, his back was toward Jana, but he was still only feet from her. Too close for her to run.

Jana scanned the room. *Think, dammit. Breathe and think.*

Johnnie's voice rose to a shout into the cell, then lowered, apologizing to the caller. Pacing now, he seemed increasingly agitated. Back and forth, back and forth, huffing, sighing, and muttering as he shuffled. But even with his back still to her, she couldn't muster the nerve to run or even to get her cell phone from her purse. It was clear across the room. And she couldn't alert the girls on stage, as they were chattering, giggling, joyfully oblivious.

Antonio...*oh God.* She shuddered. *Hush, Jana. The little prick is bluffing. All talk. No proof. No chance Antonio's in danger. Keep focused until he comes.*

Across the room by her purse, Jasmine, the new girl, eyes wide with fear, caught Jana's attention. The other woman nodded at her. Jana swallowed hard. Then Jasmine stood up silently, slowly, her heels in hand. Jana watched Jasmine take a deep breath, clip behind Johnnie without looking back and sprint to the doors. The other woman slid out of the dark red-lit club to safety.

Oh God, thank you. Now please, get help!

*

Daylight let in by Jasmine's quiet exit caught Johnnie's attention. He let his phone fall to the floor and spun around, his arms extended and shaking, finger on the trigger of the pistol.

"Fuck! Fuck, fuck, fuck!" he called over his shoulder, "No one else move!"

He didn't turn back to the stage, to where Jana sat. "Jana!" he yelled in the direction of the entry doors. "I'll do what I told you! I swear it!"

Jana's heart rammed her ribs, waiting, preparing for him to spin back around. But it was as if he'd forgotten where she was; he just maintained his TV cop stance, gun still pointing, or rather waving, between the entry door and the bar. In his coked-out daze and fury, had he thought Jasmine the new girl, the escapee, was Jana?

*

Erin, the bartender, stood frozen, paralyzed in his wavering line of fire.

Johnnie swayed and muttered.

The girls on stage huddled, whimpering.

Jana could jump him from behind right then, but she knew she wouldn't be strong enough to make a next move.

But shit, Erin was a welcome and waiting target.

The door opened again—new light streamed in.

A series of shots rang out as the door hissed shut, bringing back the neon red illuminated darkness.

CHAPTER 48

N O SOUND, JUST sight. Tunnel vision in a deafening vacuum. Jana felt her heart slamming inside her, but she couldn't hear it in her ears. She blinked, swallowed, and gasped for air while her eyes caught a view of the sparks from the far wall spew then fizzle out as all the main and secondary lights shut down in sinking unison. The glow of one lone emergency light highlighted the soft smoke simmering from the shot-up metal panel. Then as the light yellow smoke rose to the ceiling, so did the brain-shock muffling all surrounding sound.

And the chaos broke through.

Screaming bounced off the walls and glass bottles crashed and shattered. She swung her head in the direction of the bar. Erin was no longer standing behind the bar, but the woman's wailing lifted above it, making Jana's instinctual alert system sound like a siren in her head.

She had to get to the injured woman.

But Johnnie was still too close, the gun hot in his hands.

Think of something, dammit! Do something!

As her hands went up to her ears to find quiet enough to think of a move, she heard a deep, low groaning coming from the entry doors, from the ground. Her line of sight was blocked by a large column, but she knew it was a man. From the sound of it, a dying man.

Oh dear God.

Johnnie *had* been bluffing. Antonio had come and was now gasping for air, for life.

He'd been shot. For her. She still couldn't see him to know how bad it was, but she needed to get to him. Her mind whirled, soul dove, eyes glazed, while her heart wrenched under the weight of planets and stars.

Don't you dare take him from me!

Antonio, hang on. Please....

CHAPTER 49

JOHNNIE SLOWLY TURNED back toward the stage.

Jana?

His eyes dry and wide, shocked to see her, he let his gun slide down to his side. "You didn't leave me?"

She glared back at him as if damning him to hell. Raw abhorrence.

His free hand raked through his hair over and over again, yanking as if clarity would come from pain. He was totally unsure of who was where, and who the hell was shot, but he knew one or two were down. Because of him.

He'd only meant to scare, not to kill. *Only to scare!* His father's phone call—*fuck!*—got him all messed up, distracted. But he swore Jana had snuck out, and a man had come in. He started shaking his head, trying to gain clarity and quiet in his cloudy, screaming brain. "Everyone shut the fuck up!"

*

She heard her pulse in her ears, blood threatening to boil over. The man at the door—her man!—now let out only short, hardly-audible wheezes from the floor. Erin's moaning behind the bar was becoming quieter, fainter.

"Let me go check on them? Please, Johnnie?"

"Don't you move," he snapped, the pistol being used as an extension of his pointer finger.

Pleading with him wouldn't work. He was beyond irrational. He was psychotic, and she didn't want anyone else hurt. She had to separate him from that damn gun, which he was practically juggling between his hands as he shook his head erratically and shuffled back and forth again.

Do something, Jana! Code fucking silver, for Christ's sakes!

All she saw around her were chairs, tables, napkins, water bottles, and shoes.

Shoes. Spiked high heel shoes. Right in that bastard's fucking heart!

She reached for one of the girl's spiked heels at the edge of the stage while his back was turned, then right as Johnnie pivoted toward her, Jana tilted her head, switching on an expression of sugar sweetness and light. "Johnnie, listen. I'll dance for you," she said swallowing back acidic bile and hate. "I'll dance on stage, or just for you. Whatever you want. I know I was wrong to not go with my feelings for you. Please, just put the gun away and we'll get everything—"

"Everything, what? Fixed?"

"Yes, fixed," she said as a sliver of light streamed through the entry doors and was gone the next instant.

Help is here? Oh God, please.

She kept her eyes on him and only on him. It seemed that Johnnie hadn't noticed and she had to keep it that way.

"Together, Johnnie, we *can* fix this. I'm a nurse, remember? And we work perfectly together, as a team, right?"

He rubbed the sweat from his brow and scrunched his eyes at her, a skeptical glare. Or was he just unsure if she was real or not? Either way, his gun remained in his trembling, deadly hand.

CHAPTER 50

S HE TRIED LIKE hell to ignore the dark silhouette that came around the wide column at the corner of the bar. A tall, broad-shouldered man in a cap, a police cap?

Oh, thank the Lord.

Jana felt air flood her lungs.

But Johnnie's glassy eyes shot her direction the next beat like he'd heard or sensed the saving presence.

Please no.

"You know, Jana," he said with a sharp focus on her. "My father can go fuck himself. Fuck his clubs, too. It's you, I want you. Only you. And I learned from him to take what I want. I'm taking you. Right now."

He went to grab her wrist, but she beat him to it, voluntarily extending her hand for him to take.

"Yes, Johnnie, I will...I will go with you, just put the gun down and let me take care of the two injured, okay?"

With his eyes still piercing hers, Johnnie's gun-hand lowered to his side, but he kept the piece in his grasp. She shut her eyes and took a deep breath for courage as she felt Johnnie's other hand connect with hers. His touch alone sent her stomach into a tumultuous fit, but she swallowed back her nausea with all she had.

"Come now," Johnnie said with victorious pleasure in his tone as he pulled her up from the chair.

She rose to her feet, and when she opened her eyes, the silhouette, the cop, was right behind Johnnie. A millisecond later, the other man grabbed Johnnie's wrist and squeezed some pressure point, making Johnnie drop the gun to the floor. In the next beat, Johnnie was face down on the ground with the other man's knee in his back, one arm pinned behind him, while she could only stare through the near-darkness as the cop struggled to get Johnnie's other flailing arm secured.

All the while, Johnnie screamed insanities and profanities that jostled her thoughts, her breaths, her nerves.

Block it out, Jana!

She could hardly see in the darkness or hear anything over Johnnie's yelling, but the cop was still struggling to keep the coked-out maniac down and away from the pistol.

Move, Jana! Go! Move the gun!

Jana shot forward and kicked the gun away from the scuffle. The man on top finally got Johnnie's other arm pinned. With Johnnie finally contained, Jana made a beeline for the door, to her Antonio. To her love.

*

As she made her way to the front doors like a blind bat in a dark cave, the strip club flooded with sunlight. More police officers, half a dozen, streamed in, thankfully, but their bum-rush kept her from her Antonio, who was assuredly bleeding out on the club's filthy floor. She had to get to him.

She pushed on, his body now in her sights, laid out flat on the floor to the right of the entrance doors. A paramedic entered then and knelt down. Then another. Thank God.

I'm coming too, Antonio. I'm coming for you.

*

She dreaded seeing his face, the pain, the brink, the end.

Her world without him, oh God, horror and despair flashed and burned through her.

She came up on the two medics, opened her mouth to announce herself, and forced herself to look at her Antonio's face.

It was Brandon, the bouncer.

Fluttering freedom one heartbeat, frozen fright the next.

Johnnie hadn't shot Antonio—*thank God!*—but Antonio wasn't here. And he sure as hell would have been after so much time had passed. So Johnnie wasn't bluffing about keeping Antonio somewhere else, with someone else, by gunpoint.

Flashing rings of light filled her vision and skewed the scenery. Then she was out.

*

He had her cradled in his arms now. "Jana," he whispered. "*Princessa*, come back to me."

Her lashes flickered and a large flood of air filled her chest. Then wide eyes as large as the universe looked up at him. "Antonio?" She blinked. "Am I dead? Are we dead?"

"No princess, we're okay. We're alive and well and together." *Alive, together.* Thank God, because he didn't know what he would have done. Forget driving home to Mexico, he'd imagined driving off a high cliff. If he'd lost Jana, ending it like his mother had didn't seem so far out there. Unfathomable…his life would've been unfathomable.

But with her alive and breathing, unharmed in his arms, he'd go or stay about anywhere as long as she was with him. Manhattan or Calgary. It didn't matter—however, with the insanity that had gone down tonight, he'd sure as hell make his case for them to go anywhere that was far away from there.

He looked down at her. Still so out of it, a soft smile reached her weary eyes as she reached up to his face. The gentle stroke of her finger down his cheek and along his jaw made him warm, made him whole.

She reached up for the cap on his head. "What's this?" she asked with a look of wonder and remembrance spreading across her stunning face.

"My chauffeur cap," he said smiling. The replacement for the one Jocelyn Carlson had taken. He'd had this one in his trunk since Monday. "When the one dancer came out of the club screaming about the gun-wielding maniac inside, I wasn't waiting for the cops, not a chance with you inside. So I grabbed the cap, figuring any head cover was better than nothing, and it resembled a police officer's cap at any rate. Stupid, I know, but hell, here we are, right?"

"You…you almost killed me," she mumbled.

"What's that?" he asked, not really expecting much of a coherent answer from her. She was in shock, confused, obviously and understandably out of it. Thank God he'd come up behind her to catch her when she passed out minutes ago.

"You were the Jersey limo driver. In SoHo. Chauffeur cap. Hunky. But dangerous," she murmured, smirking softly.

Holy shit! The night he fired Jocelyn Carlson. "Midnight sunglasses?"

"Midnight sunglasses? Yes, yes, sunglasses at night…to hide…" Her blanched cheeks were now gaining color back, rose color.

"Jesus, Jana!" *Unbelievable!* "I nearly killed you before I got the chance to fall for you!" He took her hand and pressed it to his lips. "*Mi amore,* lucky that I'm a damn good driver, able to avoid even the most exquisite of jaywalkers," he teased, then kissed her on the bridge of her nose.

She laughed lightly, sat up slowly, and slid her arms tight around his neck. Locked and holding him for dear life, he felt her tears on his neck.

Then in a deadly serious yet hushed tone, she said, "I thought…I thought you'd been shot and I couldn't get to you, and then that Johnnie's guy had you, to kill—"

"Shhh. I'm here. I'm here and everything is okay." He took her face in his hands and kissed her lips gently, a feather brush. "We're okay."

CHAPTER 51

AFTER THE POLICE had taken Antonio and Jana's statements, Johnnie had been taken in, the coke party in the back had been handled, and of course, Brandon and Erin had been loaded into ambulances. Antonio offered to take her back up to Fort Lee to wait out the surgery with her mother. Jana, shaking as if naked and stranded in the Arctic, insisted they go back to his place.

The image of Johnnie's crazed eyes wouldn't leave her. And the thought of life without Antonio had been more than she could bear. No, she couldn't be with anyone right now other than her guardian angel.

Antonio hadn't let go of her hand for even an instant. Again, he knew just what she needed, totally in tune, in sync. It was more confirmation to Jana that she'd never had it so right. They were so damn right it hurt.

But right now, his hand wasn't enough. Jana needed to be with Antonio in the deepest sense, as close as she could physically, emotionally, and spiritually be to her lover, and more officially now, her guardian angel. And if she had the choice, she wouldn't ever let him go.

*

She pushed him onto his couch, not waiting for them to reach the bedroom. "Do you think," she began through her kisses to his neck, chin, and cheek, "that I'm horrible for wanting you when I should be rushing up to Fort Lee?"

He slid his hands up to her hips, sat her on his lap, and kissed her mouth without yield until he apparently needed air.

"Was that your answer?"

He smiled. "Yes. But for translation's sake, since you did just go through a traumatic event, you, Jana Park, are the most wonderful woman—person—I've ever met. And if you didn't want to be with me right now after what just happened in that hellhole, and instead chose to be waiting at the hospital with your self-deluded mother for your self-absorbed father to come out of surgery, I'd be worried. Really worried…for me."

He smiled then kissed her again and pulled her core into his already bulging center.

"And, Jana, seriously, it's going to take time for you to learn to live… for yourself. Truly for yourself. You need to learn how to be selfish. And I won't rush you, I'll never rush you. But I'll sure as hell remind you"—he lifted her shirt up and over her head and then moved the cup of her black bra down to brush her breast with his sensual lips, kissing her all around her already-tensed nipple—"that you deserve every damn ounce of happiness. I won't ever let you forget that."

He then tipped her dark cherry nipple with his tongue and pulled away. "We have a lot of damn pleasure to catch up on in life, you and I," he said before opening his mouth again to encompass her entire breast, circling her nipple with his wet, tickling tongue, sending spikes of electricity down to her core.

He paused then. His eyes met hers and his head tilted slightly. "I need you to know, Jana, that I will never let anyone hurt you. Not ever."

"I know," she whispered.

"And so you also know then, that I'm insanely in love with you?"

Her eyelids fell as her chest filled.

In love.

She felt lost and found all at once.

Antonio's love.

Even as he held her there, letting his words resonate, she felt the truth of his words. She sensed a never-used chamber of her heart fly open as if she never needed to take another breath, not a single next breath ever again. Hearing and feeling his declaration, his infinite adoration, was like nothing she'd dared to dream of before.

"Look at me, *princessa.*"

No, she didn't want to, but she wanted nothing more. She yearned for the sight of him, for eternity, this man. But her emotion, her weakness, her fear…

"Look at me, Jana, *mi amor.*"

Her heart cried as she willed her lids to open to his adoring eyes. And God, his gaze was so intense, so raw, it made her quake then melt inside, molten lava reaching every part of her being. She couldn't escape, and she didn't want to escape. His eyes were absorbing her whole, his look pouring over her, a look as close to idolizing love as she could ever hope to imagine. Could ever hope to hold.

*

No more words were spoken. Antonio made love to her, such slow, deep love. All the pain and heartache that she'd been bombarded with over the last days and weeks and years was being lanced away, driven away with each and every powerful, electrically charged thrust.

"That's it, princess," he whispered as she spasmed through a climax of life-changing proportions.

"Antonio," she murmured, panting from the tidal wave she'd somehow managed to live through. "Feel my heart. Can you feel it?" She'd never felt such jackhammering joy pulsing through her before.

He placed his palm flat on her chest. "Jesus, Jana." He looked proud, concerned, and glad all in a single look.

She threw the blanket from her seething body, sat up to take his face in her hands, and kissed him desperately, longing for their connection to be always tangible, palpable, constant.

He took her hands from his cheeks and brought them to his chest, to *his* heart. "I want *this* with you always, Jana. You and me, always." He kissed her cheek and pulled her into him, holding her close and tight, his firm embrace making her know safety, security, and yes, his love. *Love.* That she'd definitely never known before Antonio.

*

When they were done and spent, he carried her to the shower and washed her down, soaping her from head to toe, shampooing her hair, loving her clean.

"What's this, princess?" he asked, eyeing something on her upper arm. "Did he fucking hurt you, touch you? You said he didn't."

She saw the tiny dark blue mark he'd noticed and shook her head. She knew Johnnie'd grabbed her by the wrist and left no mark, but this type of bruise was different anyway. It was a pinching bruise, one she recognized from her many others, those that had appeared on her hands and arms without her remembering when. "I did this, babe. When I get anxious, nervous, scared. I haven't done it in so long. Not since…not since…meeting you, getting to know you," she said, loving the realization. "It's a trick, pain for pain."

"No more pain," he said, kissing her bruise better. Then kissing her elbow, her wrist, her palm, and each finger.

"I could get used to this kind of medical attention, Mr. Ruiz."

"You better get used to this my warrior princess. You'd better."

She smiled at him as she grabbed the body bar from his hand. "Turn around."

He lifted his brows but did as he was told.

She lathered her hands up and loved him clean right back. Soaping his wide, strong shoulders, his iron-hard back, his tight muscular behind and down his legs. It made her swim inside to take care of him like he did her.

Yeah, she could see a future with him. She definitely could. Her dreamed-for symbiosis.

"What you said before. Me too." She turned him around to face her and kissed his mouth sweetly. "I want *us*, always, Antonio. There's nothing in the world I want more."

CHAPTER 52

WHEN SHE GOT to the hospital, her mother came running at her. She'd never seen the woman move that quickly in her life.

In frantic Korean, "Ja-Na, you didn't answer. Again, you didn't answer your phone!"

She remembered her phone was in shards outside in the parking lot. "What, Ma? What happened?"

Antonio's hand was at the cusp of her back. She inhaled, so conscious of her lungs filling that she got caught there, unable to let go of the breath.

"He's in a coma. He's on life support, Ja-Na," her mother sobbed. Jana's shoulders dropped drastically as her breath finally found its way out.

"Jana, what's going on?" Antonio whispered at her shoulder.

She shook her head slowly and whispered to Antonio her father's status.

They walked her distraught mother to the row of faded pastel chairs to wait. It would be another hour at least before the doctor would be out to speak to them. And Jana didn't push like she might have before. Now she just wanted to let things move by their natural course. She didn't have to be the safety net anymore. That wasn't her place, shouldn't ever have been, and she'd be sure it never would be again.

After some minutes, exhaustion hit her, and Jana dozed off on Antonio's shoulder.

But rest was not in the cards it seemed, as her mother's phone buzzed her awake. Her mother was asleep on her shoulder, so Jana grabbed the damn thing to stop the awful noise. She glanced at the screen. Her brother. She silenced it and let her head fall back onto Antonio's shoulder.

"The longest day of my entire life," she said in disbelief.

"Yeah. Mine too." Antonio placed his hand on top of hers. "Rest as best you can. I'll wake you when there's news."

"Thanks, babe. I'll try."

*

A whole hour had passed when a nurse finally came out to tell them it would be an extra thirty minutes or so before Dr. Brighton would be out.

"More waiting?" her mother whined in her half-sleep.

Jana could handle the waiting. But being able to take her mother was another story. "I'm going to the office to finalize the billing situation. Be right back." She got up from the horrendous chair and stretched out the immense kink in her lower back.

"You sure? It's so late. Why not do that in the morning?" Antonio asked.

"I told them I'd be back to clear things up, some crazy error on the account, and really, it's a good distraction for me right now." She threw her chin toward her mother, who'd begun to fall onto Antonio's shoulder now.

"It's okay," he whispered. "She can lean on me." He smiled while Jin continued her snooze. Jana took a mental picture before leaving the waiting room.

God, he really was amazing.

*

"Hi again. Back to see if my dad's account had been figured out? The whole zero balance thing?" Jana said with a tight-lipped smile. If only she was the type of person to accept such an error, a boon as some would consider it, however immoral. She wouldn't stoop to the low level that so many people in her life had found.

"I do have the file here…but it looks like Ms. Buchard wasn't able to address your question before leaving this evening. Heck, you can take a look at it yourself, though. If you'd like." The young desk clerk handed Jana the folder with a sympathetic glint in her eyes.

"You are tremendous, thanks so much." She took the file to a chair against the wall and let it fall open on her lap. Staring up at her was the billing statement dated that day with a hand written check paper-clipped to the sheet. On the top left of the check showed its maker: A.R. Limousine Service. Just like the business card. The check was for a hundred and ninety thousand dollars and change.

She shut her eyes tight. A kick to the head might have felt better.

Damn it, Antonio. *What had he done?*

He'd ruined everything is what. Because whatever direction her life and her relationship with Antonio was taking, it wasn't going to be without trust between them, nor was she going to let her pride, what little of it she had left, go to the wayside.

*

"Ma…hey, Mom! Sorry, wake up…I need Antonio for a second."

"Who?"

"Mom, the man you are leaning on, my…Antonio. Just stay here; I'll be right back." She motioned for Antonio to follow her. To speak in private. To ask him what the fuck he was thinking, paying down the bill after she'd already flat-out refused the offer.

But her mother's purse rang again, and at the same time, the unit's doors burst open. Dr. Andrew Brighton was standing at the entrance with news.

"It's Dae Han," her mother said looking at the cell, the haze of sleep still apparent.

"Ignore it, Ma. Doctor…Andrew, what's my dad's status?"

"You both can come see him. It's important to see him now, though. Jana, he may not make it through the night."

Her mother burst out crying, gripping Jana's arm for dear life. "It's best to stay as calm and as unemotional as you can, or, I'm afraid, we can't let you go in, Mrs. Park." But her sobbing only worsened.

"I'll stay with her, Jana. You go," Antonio offered.

She was ready to tear his head off for what he'd done, going behind her back and against her wishes, dipping into his savings! An inner growl built in her chest, but she had no other choice at the moment but to keep quiet and accept his offer to stay with her mother.

Because she needed to see her father or it would haunt her, maybe forever.

She nodded to Antonio with a pencil line smile and followed the doctor to her father.

*

A frail remnant of her father, of Chang Park, lay in front of her eyes.

"Daddy."

She sat next to him. She didn't take his hand because she thought the deep-seated hate within her would overwhelm her still deeper, undeniable love for the man, and it might stop his heart before the self-inflicted heart disease did. Death by hate, by daughter. *Oh God.*

His eyelids fluttered lightly, as if in a dream. Maybe he *was* in a dream. And maybe he wasn't frowning or disappointed or struggling in that dream. Maybe he had everything he really wanted there in dreamland.

But damn it, what he was supposed to have wanted was happiness and goodness and safety for his little girl. Every father was supposed to want that!

"How could you have known, Daddy, and let me dance? And for so long! All the while, bleeding me, berating me, hating me! Daddy, how could you love me so little?"

And then she wept soundless tears. It was the best chance she had to unload her sorrow, with her father in a deep dream state, a coma.

Through her tears, she saw his hand move, only a fraction, though. It could have been her imagination. But she ventured a look at his face, and his eyes were wide open with fear. He tried to make a sound, but the intubation tube wouldn't let him. The pools of glistening tears in his life-weary eyes were unmistakable. Then a softening, an almost apologetic and pained expression wiped over Chang Park's face. His hand twitched. Did he want her to hold it?

She softly covered his hand with her own, no longer scared that her rage-fueled hatred would stop her father's heart from beating in his chest.

Because obvious regret oozed from the man's eyes. He'd missed out, messed up, let her down—and he knew it. He'd ignored the love of a daughter, his daughter, and now knowing that was enough justice, enough payback for Jana. And whatever the night held for her father, she felt peace. Having seen the man's iron heart pierced with emotion, that maybe somewhere in there he'd loved her and knew his failings, she found closure.

CHAPTER 53

THE LOOK JANA gave him had slashed his heart, slashed his damn heart to shreds.

Antonio knew she must have found out about the money. Damn it! She was worse than Celeste, with her damn pride.

Whether Jana hated that he'd dipped into his savings or she was worried that he'd hold it over her head as she'd been taught to watch for, he'd stand by his act. He knew why he'd done it. And he'd damn well do it again and again. He loved her. And he hated her to be in pain.

He couldn't see Jana and him as anything but a unit, one heart, the way he and Michelle were supposed to have been.

But Jana was his true match, his only match. He knew. He also knew he could make her happy. He'd take her home with him to Vallarta if she could just get over the bounds he'd overstepped. He prayed she would see the intentions behind him signing that check. She had to see that his intentions were pure.

His phone buzzed again. It was the fourth call from Jake, but he looked at Jana's mother on his shoulder and hit ignore again. He'd left a message for Jake at the crime scene earlier, and that would have to be enough for now. He was taking care of his family, and nothing else mattered. Even if Jana hated him right now, he would be here for her.

Back in the waiting room, Jana helped her mother up so she could walk her down to her father's room.

She smiled politely at Antonio. "Thanks for staying with her. I'll be fine here…why don't you go? Get some sleep—"

"No, I'm staying here with—"

"No, Antonio. Really, you should leave." Voiced with a very deliberate harshness. "Oh, and here." She gave him ten jagged-edged pieces of his check and pressed the small pile hard into his hand, like a stamp of shame. "Thanks anyway."

And she sensed his dismay as she put her back toward him and continued walking her mother into the unit. But she couldn't care. Or at least, she shouldn't care, not for another man trying to put her under his thumb. Like Johnnie had tried, and Dane and her damn father had done to her mother and to her. And like she'd seen so many men do to so many women in her life. Char, Amber, Laynie, and on and on. She just couldn't go there. She had to close this chapter and get back to her life, her work, her calling. As a medical professional. Saving lives.

Saving lives where? Her ER had closed its doors on her. She'd been replaced. Just like that.

Her beloved and esteemed ER wasn't what she thought it was, Antonio wasn't who she thought he was. Everything and everyone, all just illusory.

So then, who and what the hell was real and good and true? If anything at all?

CHAPTER 54

THE UNIT DOOR slammed shut, jolting her out of her thoughts.

A new stoic emptiness had infiltrated her every cell with every next heartbeat. She willed a deep breath as if she were outside herself, like it was a mechanical function she had to consciously instruct her lungs to perform. And in the same robotic mode, she shifted her body, her head, and her tired, tainted eyes to focus on her wilted mother beside her.

"Remember, Mom, you can't stay in there long. And please, keep calm. He needs peace."

She felt sad for her mom as the woman shuffled her way toward her dad's room. Yes, even through Jana's curtain of detachment, or maybe because of that screen, Jana found pity for the woman. And now knowing that her father had a deeply buried spark of feeling in the center of his severely damaged heart, she also understood that her mother was just a scared little girl, completely reliant on the man. Jin Park must have been terrified, because if Chang, the woman's husband of thirty-something years, didn't make it through the night, the only people Jin could look to for support were a deadbeat son or a daughter who Jin full-well knew she didn't deserve.

What *would* Jin Park do?

And what would I do?

"Ma…wait." Jana stopped Jin from going too far down the hallway. An answer had come to Jana, a solution for whatever occurrence, one that would keep Jana within her own boundaries, her newly-drawn lines. Jana dug into her purse and withdrew from it a glossy, sharp-edged business card. "Take this. Call the number," she explained, handing the card to Jin. "Ask for Joe P. Tell him you're Winter's mother and that you need to discuss a personal bankruptcy having to do with uninsured medical. Did you hear me, Ma? 'Joe P., Winter's mother, bankruptcy.' Understand?"

Her mom looked ill, bottom lip quivering. "Jana, I don't know how—"

"Yes, Mom, you do. You can. I know you can, and…you don't really have a choice at this point, because I'm done. I can't give anymore, Ma. I know you love me, so you will call."

Her mother stared at the card, fresh teardrops forming in the woman's eyes. Jana hugged her mother then, and held her tight. "Be strong, Ma. Be strong."

Jin only whimpered and sniffled in response.

Jana loosened her grasp. "Go now. Be with dad."

Jin nodded and turned with a reluctance Jana had never seen in her mother. As her mother took one heavy step forward, Jin's phone rang. Her mother was so out of it, the woman didn't even register where it was coming from.

That goddamn phone. Fourth time tonight while it should've been muted or powered-off in the first place, per all the posted hospital signs. Jana shook her head, wanting nothing more than to send the stupid device flying to its death in the hospital parking lot like she'd done to her own phone.

Especially knowing who was calling.

Especially knowing *he* was calling.

She tried hard to bury the growl forming in her chest. "I got it, Ma." Jana pulled the phone from Jin's purse. "You go to Dad." With the gentlest nudge, she pushed her mother in the direction of her father's room, then looked down at her hand. Down at the ringing, vibrating phone.

And instead of silencing it, Jana accepted the call.

*

"What the fuck do you want, Dane? Because if you really wanted to know how he was doing, if you gave a damn about anyone but yourself, you'd be here," she said in a way-too-loud voice for a hospital unit or a prison wing for that matter.

The desk nurse, who'd already been glaring at her because of the phone's disruptive presence in the first place, now rushed over and ushered Jana back out to the waiting area.

"Jana? Is that you? It's me, Alexa."

"Oh, God. Alexa...." And through the heavy unit door that was closing behind her, she watched her mother disappear into her dad's room.

"How are things?"

How the hell do you think they are? "They are what they are, Alexa. I don't really know what to say. He's on the brink...but the real question is, why isn't Dane calling himself? Why isn't he here, Alexa?"

"He's meeting some big clients tonight from out of town, so he has me on duty to follow what's happening."

"On duty, huh? To see what's happening?" He went to a business meeting with their father on his deathbed? *Jesus Christ.* Because big clients were of course more important.

Wait.

"Sorry, did you say clients?"

"Yeah, between the boom of the new business and the twins on the way in a few months, things have been crazy. And your parents made him promise to stay put and said that you'd handle things. You're a real trooper, Jana, honestly."

She felt her heart in her chest squeeze then release, squeeze then release, high-speed and slow-motion at the same time. *It keeps getting better.* She could feel the hot anger broil within her. Blinding, deafening anger.

"Jana?"

"Yeah, sorry. I'm here. So"—she swallowed back the new knot of disgust—"things are good with you guys?"

"Well, other than the distress surrounding your father's hospitalization, yes, you could say that. The business has been growing by leaps and bounds, and we're moving next week into a new house that's closer to the downtown office. We needed a larger place for when the twins come anyway, so it all worked out."

Jana saw it all then.

That greedy bastard.

And her *parents? Jana will handle it?* Of course. *Stay put?* But why? Wouldn't her father want to see his beloved son before the lights went out? Or did Chang and Jin really think this wasn't the 'real deal,' the possible, even probable end-of-the-line for her father?

Jana wanted to vomit.

Insane. All of it.

"Alexa…I'm not sure you understand. I mean, I don't know how much Dane or my folks have told you, you know, about…how bad things are and how much I've had to—" Then she paused.

She took a long full breath.

What did any of it matter? She'd already made her decision to be done.

In fact, this knowledge made it that much easier to wash her hands of them. Besides the pro bono legal route Jana had handed her mother, she now knew that Jin, and her father if he survived, had another avenue to take. For funds, they *could* go to her brother. He was not *broke*. He was filthy, stinking rich.

"Never mind, Alexa. Congrats on everything, the twins, your new home. I wish you the best. I'll have my mom call you in the morning to update you, okay?"

"Thanks, Jana. Please give your parents our love. And take care of yourself. Bye now." And the eye-opening call ended with Alexa's words echoing in her awe-struck brain. *Take care of yourself.*

She sank into a hard plastic chair in the barren waiting room.

God, she wished Antonio was with her.

Antonio.

Jesus, what had she done?

So her brother was no longer a poor, money-grubbing prick, but rather a well-off penny-pinching prick. It didn't matter what Dane's financial statement said, he was still a heartless devil while Antonio, no longer the lowly chauffeur, but the well-off entrepreneur, had bled his bank account for her and for her crazy family. His noble, selfless and insane act wasn't to control her, it was a genuine gesture. It was love-in-action, love incarnate, and it melted her heart, her heart that beat for him. Only for him.

She had to go to him. She hoped to God he hadn't written her off for being so prideful, so hurtful, so damn blind!

*

She got reception to call her a cab and then grabbed a pad from the clerk to write her mother a note: *Had to run. Will be back asap.*

She was bringing the man she loved back with her.

Then she asked for a paperclip and pulled out from her purse the photo of her as a small girl sitting on the lap of her mother's strong and adoring father, Jana's *abuelo*. She put the note with the photo and inserted both into her mother's flip phone.

"Please do make sure Jin Park gets her cell phone. She's with Chang Park in the ICU."

CHAPTER 55

A NTONIO WASN'T AT his house. She had knocked twenty times in case he was asleep. Where the hell was he then?

She hopped back into the cab just before it left and pulled out Antonio's business card. Pointing to it, she said, "Please, take me here instead?"

Only a few minutes down was the depot for A.R. Limousine Service.

"Thanks and keep the change," she said, handing the cabbie more than a twenty percent tip from the way-too-huge amount of cash she still had in her purse, which she hugged tightly to her chest.

She approached the tens of limo drivers all gathered around, smoking and shooting the shit in front of one of the many large bays of the enormous garage.

"Excuse me? Can you tell me where to find Antonio Ruiz?"

One of the men pointed to a row of offices on the far side of the massive depot. Only one of the offices was lit. "Boss Man's that way."

She thanked him and walked straight back past the fleet of about thirty-five black stretch limos and two stretch SUVs. More were probably out and about she guessed. She couldn't believe he handled this level of operation and drove full-time himself. But, actually, yes she could.

Jana was only fifty feet from Antonio's office when his office door flew open. And a scantily dressed woman came out, pulled her little dress down at her thighs, screamed, "Fuck you!" then slammed the door behind her.

Jocelyn Carlson, no doubt. The woman's face had been sprawled all over the tabloids for months.

The woman stormed past Jana, pausing for a split second to look her up and down, and oh God, the woman's assuredly expensive scent made Jana nauseated. Then the great Ms. Carlson huffed out of the garage to the driver's side of a bright yellow coupe.

Oh, poor thing. The woman had to drive herself? Jana laughed. Apparently *no* limo service would drive the wretched woman.

Just before vanishing into her vehicle, the other woman gave Jana the middle finger, *so classy*, and Jana, on instinct, smiled wide then blew the other woman a big fat kiss.

*

Already supremely emotional, her day having been made up of one hell after the next, it felt good, in contrast, to laugh. And God, that woman was laughable. Whatever Antonio said to Ms. Carlson to bring her to the next level of fury, it made Jana feel even better.

But what would bring Jana to the brink of ultimate satisfaction was to have Antonio's arms wrapped tight around her.

She watched him through his office window. His head in his hands, elbows on his immaculate desk. She knocked on the glass window of the door.

"I already told you, Ms. Carlson, to get off my premises, or I'll—"

"You'll what?" Jana said in her most seductive voice as she opened the door a crack.

Antonio lifted his eyes, then his head, which tilted just slightly while the right side of his mouth curled. And his eyes softened to match a sigh that she took to be relief. He waved her in and stood up.

"God, I'm glad you're here. Your dad?" he asked, moving toward her, arms extended, obviously ready to pull her into him.

But Jana slammed into his arms before any answer came. She hugged him hard and tight, like a reunion from being forever apart.

"I know why you did it, even though I hate that you did it when I asked you not to. Thank you, Antonio. For loving me."

*

He pulled her onto his lap and held her. After the day from hell, this was sheer heaven, his princess in his tight embrace, her breath in synch with his own. He knew though they should get out of there, to a less peopled place. Neither of them needed any more visitors, not Jocelyn Carlson, not anyone.

But he let a few more minutes drift by, as she seemed to need the tranquil stillness for a little longer.

"So my father, we're not sure what will be..." she whispered, answering his question from minutes ago. "But he and I made our peace."

"I'm so relieved you got to talk to him," he said stroking her thick silken hair down her back. "It still haunts me, not having told my mother all I'd wanted to before she...passed."

Jana looked up at him and into him, injecting him with her empathy, her compassion.

"She took her own life." His words left him on an out-breath, his heart rattling his rib cage. "I was, *am still* so...angry with her. She left us, just gave up. Robbed us of the most wonderful person." He choked back emotion and grabbed a deep, clearing breath. "I wish you could've met her, Jana. And, oh God, how she would have adored you."

"I'd love to hear all about her, Antonio. I'm sure she was amazing."

"She was. But Jana, you...you blow my mind. Just when I thought there was no more *goodness* in the world, you appear."

He kissed her lips lightly, then pulled away, hearing his drivers laughing and hollering, causing a ruckus. Probably carrying on about the most recent Jocelyn Carlson episode.

He shook his head. "Hey, let's get outta here. I think we both need some air, some peace, and maybe even some goddamn levity for Christ's sakes!"

"Yes, sir," she agreed with a sharp nod. "Maybe we can go for a drive?"

They got up and moved out of his office. "Sure, we can drive anywhere you'd like, *mi amore*."

*

A few steps outside his office, she felt a rush of excitement and heat. *We can drive anywhere.* His words hit her. *Freedom.* She'd finally pulled open the dark curtain she'd been living behind, unveiling a sweet and bright future. A life with Antonio. It seemed like a dream.

From an uncontrollable urge to share this weightlessness with him, she looked up at Antonio and threw her arms up to his neck. Antonio took her hips in his grasp and lifted her high above his head. Then, bringing her down to his face, he kissed her madly.

Whooping cheers, whistles, and applause broke their kiss, and Jana felt her cheeks turn bright red. Antonio laughed out loud.

He nodded to his crew. "Show's over. Get going, boys. Go home!"

The drivers dispersed and he returned his attention to Jana, holding her close, her feet still dangling as he swung her from side to side, her cheek pressed to his.

She whispered, "I drew my line with my folks, I'm done with the club, and now I'm done with them. I'm free! I'm free to be happy, and I'm happiest with you, Antonio."

He slowly let her down, her body sliding down his strong, protective torso, and when her feet touched the ground, he held her face in his hands. "Without being condescending, princess, I'm so damn proud of you."

She smiled as he moved to kiss her again. His lips pressed against hers, then he took her hand and started leading her across to the next bay where she saw his limo parked.

"You know," he said, "my family's going to eat you up alive. They're going to love you, and you'll know what real family is, maybe too much real family!" He laughed.

Pausing his stride, he turned to her. "You deserve the world, Jana Park, and if you come back with me...to meet them and to live...God, you will, *we* will have such a wonderful life. Will you? Will you come with me, officially? I know the prestigious hospitals and doctors aren't there, but—"

She stopped his words with two fingers to his lips. "Yes, Antonio. I'll go with you. Wherever you go, I'll go."

She replaced her fingers with her lips. An all-confirming kiss which told him yes, what she wanted first, foremost and always was a life with this man.

He pulled away from her reluctantly. "Wait, are you sure? Your ER, your friends here, your city-life…."

"I am sure. My friend, singular, Luly…she'll visit us, or I will visit her. And the ER, Manhattan…screw the prestige, the superficial facade!" God that felt really liberating. "I can make a difference in Mexico, the same as I could here. Maybe even more so, right? Bringing my level of training and experience to people who really need it. Yes, I want that life. I want that life with you, Antonio. I do. I know for certain, I do."

She laughed. She had no idea what this feeling was, this lightness. She'd never dared to imagine it for herself, not before Antonio.

He squeezed her hand in his. There was a glow in his eyes that matched the grace that had devoured her heart. No question, wherever she was, if it was with him, she was home, and she was loved.

*

He loved her radiating glow, her excitement. But the next instant, her expression flickered then morphed to a soft surrendered lull. "So, where to? You choose."

He didn't blame her for not wanting to pick their destination. God, she'd had more critical decisions to make in this one day—hell, in one lifetime—than was even fair for someone so young, and so damn good. A lifetime of insane obligations and expectations and burdens.

But all that was over now. He was with her. Always with her.

"Well, I thought we'd head up toward Fort Lee."

Disappointment wiped over her face in a flash.

He lifted her chin with a soft touch. "Not to the hospital, at least not first thing." He smiled at her with an absolutely intentional glint of something naughty in his eyes. "But then I kinda think we should head to the hospital. Shouldn't put it off. You can officially introduce me to your folks and then say your goodbyes?"

"Goodbyes?" she said as if thinking out loud, a happy wonder floating in her voice.

He smiled and nodded, waggling his eyebrows, brimming with his news. "Listen, I got a bid on the business today, it's as good as sold. We might be able to leave in a matter of days, Jana. I even get to keep my vehicle as part of the deal. We can take turns driving down. We'd make it to Vallarta by the end of the month unless we stop along the way…and we can if you want to. Whatever you've been hoping to see. New Orleans, maybe?"

She cocked her head, excitement and a dash of worry in her eyes. "Antonio…there's something you need to know about me."

"You were a stripper, princess. Do I need to sit down for this?"

She punched his shoulder lightly and issued a playful warning look. "It's just…I don't drive," she said, her brows lifted as if expecting his tremendous disappointment.

"What do you mean you don't drive? You let your license expire?" he asked, chin notched to the side, waiting to hear the catch.

"I never learned…to drive. I never needed to. I've never even been behind the wheel of a car, well, except for the bumper cars at a carnival when I was ten."

He broke out laughing and took her right hand. He turned her palm up, slapped the keys in it, and ushered her to the driver's seat of his vehicle. "Any woman of mine had better know how to drive a damn car." He smirked playfully. "Lessons start now."

"It's pitch black outside!"

"And there are hardly any cars on the road. It's perfect."

"No license!"

"Quit with the excuses and get in," he ordered, slapping her sweet ass to move her along.

*

Antonio laughed at Jana's wide-eyed look as she sat in his driver's seat. And she was so tiny, only her chin was above the steering wheel. He'd have to get her a pillow for the long haul.

The first part of her first driving lesson would be backing out of the massive garage, so as long as he had her in reverse, there was absolutely nothing to worry about. But her expression of eager nervousness was completely adorable and insanely fucking hot.

He went around the back of his limo, kicking his back tire on the way to surface check its pressure. Then he opened the passenger side door to get in, which was totally bizarre for him, bizarre but unbelievably freeing.

And that's when he noticed the tall shadows on his depot's cold gray floor.

CHAPTER 56

"TONE, YOU DIDN'T answer my calls," came the deep Jersey accent from the front of the garage bay.

Antonio stopped, stood up straighter, took a full breath, and turned. Jake Demonte and a tall gorilla of a bodyguard had come for a visit. And he was unsure how long they'd been standing there.

Jana. She was so small that she couldn't even be seen inside the vehicle. *Have a reason for being on this side, damn it. Pull something out of the vehicle. Now!*

"Jake, gimme justa second." He leaned inside the passenger side, pulled the car manual from the glove box, and whispered, "Jana, stay there, head down." Then he stepped back out of the passenger's seat holding the thick book in one hand while shutting the car door with the other.

The sound echoed throughout the garage.

He made his way up to his lender, his longtime friend, hand outstretched for a handshake. It was reciprocated with Jake's usual gusto. "Jake, I know I missed your calls. Sorry, man. A family member's in the hospital, and there's no cell service at the ICU, but you got my voice message?"

"I got your message, Tone, yeah."

"Again, sorry you had to come all the way down here."

"Well, Tone, it had to be face-to-face, this level thing, you know? Where can we talk, son?"

Antonio led Jake to his office with Jake's personal ape following right behind them.

Completely hyperconscious of the men's eyes scanning the garage, his limo—with Jana hidden in the driver's seat. It was parked far enough away from the row of offices, and its windows were tinted, but he didn't want to take any chances. Antonio maintained an easy, relaxed stride. Jake couldn't know she was there, and he couldn't know her importance to him. Just in case.

He opened his office door and motioned with a welcoming sweep of his hand for Jake to enter, but the man paused first. "What's the next office down?"

"My salesgirl's."

"Eddie…" Jake said, motioning with a sideward nod for his bodyguard to check it out. "Can't be too careful," he whispered by Antonio's ear. Once Eddie came out of the sales office nodding his 'all clear,' Jake brought up his volume. "Looks more comfortable in there." Jake Demonte took the lead to the next office over.

"Thanks, Eddie. Go on and wait in the car. Tony and I are gonna talk business for a few." Jake made himself comfortable behind the desk. Antonio took the other chair by default, laughing in his head at the movie-esque feel of the entire situation. Hell, laughter was better than panic, right?

"Jake, a bottled water?" Antonio asked, up again at the mini-fridge against the wall.

"Yeah, sure," Jake said, swiveling the chair back and forth across from him.

Antonio handed Jake a water and then opened one for himself, slammed a gulp, and then slowed to a single sip. *Keep calm.* Because on the inside, he was already going over that same years-old-response he'd rehearsed in his head: "Sorry, Jake, there's no extra room in my trunk."

Seriously God, please let this be a benign visit.

*

They sat in silence for a minute, what seemed to Antonio to be a quiet, passive-aggressive game of 'who speaks first.' But Jake was visiting his place of business, so...was this it? Was this the time Jake would call in that favor Antonio had expected for so long? God, had he been stupid enough to think that *The* Jake Demonte had cut him a break? Letting the whole 'son I wished I had' spiel really brainwash him. Antonio was smarter than that, but maybe hope had trumped intellect this time.

"Tone, my kid fucked me. Big time. He deserves what he gets."

Okay, this was, at least, a good start. The other man knew that the whole club fiasco was all Johnnie. The little prick had tweaked the hell out and, beyond nearly killing two innocents, he'd threatened Jana. Scared her senseless. The bastard could've really hurt her. *Killed her.* A surge of rage shot up his throat for the umpteenth time that day, but he swallowed it back. *Keep it together, Antonio.* In front of Jake, for Jana, he had to stay calm and controlled. His fists tightened at his sides while he worked to keep the anger from showing itself in his face.

Antonio unclenched his jaws, took a subtle breath and said, "Man, Jake, I don't know what to say. Glad no one else got hurt. It could've been a real bloodbath."

"Exactly." The other man cleared his throat, his eyes on Antonio. "The club, though...the authorities shut it down. Indefinitely, they say. It was my only open shop up here, you know, since Manhattan's still bein' renovated and Merrick...well, it was delayed even before Johnnie landed himself in a cell last night. Goddamn 'im." Jake looked down at his hands, interlaced and white knuckled. "Tone, my guy on the Newark force, he needs a month or two to let this die down. That much coke running through...goddamn that sloppy little fucker spawn o' mine! Lost the Vallarta club because of the white stuff, now this? And the shootings?" Jake's fist slammed down on the desk hard, then the guy shook his head with his eyelids closed, inhaling deep.

"Jake, have a drink of water," Antonio said, a little worried that the out of shape sixty-something-year-old man would work himself up into a heart attack or a stroke. That's what Antonio needed, Jake Demonte keeling over in his goddamn office. Jake slowly opened the water bottle and sipped it, nostrils flaring and forehead lines deep.

"I need a favor, Tone. And I need it now."

*

Antonio's chest froze, stale air stuck in his chest. But he forced his brain to re-engage the next second, unlocking his lungs to gain a shallow breath. Of course, he knew it was coming. From the first sight of the tall, warped shadows on his depot floor. But again, a skeptic can turn optimist, especially having met Jana.

Jana. Oh, God…Jana. Jana was only one degree apart from a sleazy thug like Jake Demonte. If he put her at risk, if a favor for a damn wannabe mobster ever touched her, and, after all she'd been through with her own screwed-up family, he couldn't live with himself.

But that fact didn't matter a damn. There was absolutely only one thing he could say to the man sitting in front of him. And Antonio knew it. "Jake, what can I do?"

*

"Son, I need my money cleaned. I'm gonna need your shop."

Jake wanted his shop? His business?

He'd seen enough movies to get the concept of laundering money through a legitimate outfit. But, damn it, wasn't that only in the movies? But then Jake's furrowed brow; squinting, targeted eyes; and razor-straight lips, all said no, it wasn't just in the movies.

"How can I help with that, Jake? I'll do what I can, of course."

"I have to take the keys, call the note of the half mill loan. It's not what I want to do, Tone, but I got too many people depending on me. I'll hook you up later, I know you got your 'magic number' to reach, but I can't let my kid's screw up derail everything."

For fuck's sake! Call the loan?

Sure, fine. He had a buyer at the ready; the proceeds of that deal would clear Jake's loan. But that's not all Jake wanted. The man with the upper hand wanted the fucking *operating* business as a front. And he wanted it for free! And even though Antonio had paid each month's P&I a day early with extra to principal, it didn't matter a damn. Fair, legal or legitimate, none of those were Jake's priorities. Not even the history or supposed bond between he and Jake mattered. It mattered not at all.

And to Antonio, nothing mattered but Jana. And, goddamn it, his financial goal was not an issue minutes ago. He'd been happy to take a hit, come out of the legitimate deal he'd procured that day with way less than his goal number, but with more than enough to take care of Jana and their future life together. Now this man wanted to snap his fingers and take his business? Jake would catch him up later? What, and more favors in the meantime?

What the fuck had he gotten himself into? Jesus Christ, what had he done?

*

You see the problem, now focus on the solution. Focus, fast.

Jake needed a business front while Antonio needed his safe, secure dream with Jana to become a reality before he lost way more than money. He didn't need the million dollar mark. At this point, the money was a blur, a second thought. All he could see was Jana in his head. In his heart.

A business front. To wash a lot of money. The more money, the better.

"Jake, how about a cleaner, far more productive way to get your storefront? You buy this place from me at market value. I had it appraised a few months back in preparation, you know? If you call my note, you only have daily operating expenses to wash your money with. But if you buy me out, on paper…here, let me show you the report—"

"No, Tone. I trust you. And I'm listening…."

"Two million was the certified appraisal amount. We make a purchase contract for that. But under the table, you give me something…whatever you think is fair. Oh, and my limo, I keep my car. But I transfer the business, the licenses, the leases for the rest of the fleet, the land and building, of course, which you're in first position for anyway. On books, you have every dollar over five hundred grand up to two mil to use for your…*cleaning* needs. And hell, the business isn't a strip club, but it nets a good twenty-five percent. Completely under the radar, as you know."

"I'm listening, Tone, and I'm thinking," he said, moving the bottle of water to his mouth, but then he paused and put it down before pulling a sip. "What's that 'fair off-the-books' amount you're thinking? 'Cause you never did tell me your magic number." Jake lifted his brows.

Antonio blew the air out from his body. "Jake, I want my car and"—he took a long pull from his water bottle. Yes, a stall tactic. Antonio knew damn well that naming his number named him the loser, but he already was the loser here. But as long as he kept Jana safe, and with him, he was the richest man in the universe. "A million. At age six, a million dollars was the shiny magic number."

"Let's do this. A million it is. I wipe the loan of five-hundred grand and bring the other half-a-mill to the closing table. But, you gotta stay on, run the show. Make extra salary, and you'll reach ten million by the time you're forty-five." He held out his hand to clinch the deal. "This'll work out fine."

But Antonio could only stare at the man's outstretched hand.

*

It was getting really hot, so stuffy that she could hardly stay awake anymore. If only she could see him, make sure he was okay. He'd gotten a personal visit from Jake Demonte? The strip club mogul was no joke. The things she'd heard about him while working at his clubs, not a guy to mess around with. Rumors or fact, he scared the hell out of her.

And even though she knew Antonio's history with Jake was a long and professional one, this was one long talk. And again, it was Jake Demonte.

God she prayed Jake wasn't blaming Antonio for the mess at the club, especially since she had single-handedly created that nightmare. Why the hell did she have to go back to the club in the first place? For her damn ego was why; to check on the girls, who, as it so happened, couldn't give a shit less; and for her contractual commitment to Johnnie? God, how moronic of her. How fucking stupid.

Then the office door opened and she ducked an inch further down in the seat.

"A week, Jake. Two tops. I'll have someone more than ready. I've already got a few guys groomed at this point. Not an issue at all." Antonio's hand connected firmly with Jake Demonte's, and Jake added a back-slap slash man-hug to end.

"I'll send my attorney with a purchase contract and the check in the morning. Get some sleep, Tone. And hey, thanks for keeping the drama down as much as you did at the club. If it weren't for you, more people woulda been hurt, or worse."

Peeking over the dashboard, she watched Jake take a few steps to leave, but then he paused and turned. "And, Tone…that Winter Snow, one gorgeous girl, right? But she's gonna melt into a pool of sweet nectar in that car if you don't get her out soon. Gorgeous piece o' tail, that one. My Eddie wanted that ass like no other! My piece-o'-shit kid, too, from what I hear."

Jana's heart rate spiked, and embarrassment and fear boiled up to her cheeks. She watched Antonio turn toward her with clenched jaws, and he gave her a hardly noticeable nod, but she caught it. His wordless message told her that she was still fine and to just stay in the car, hidden.

Then he turned back to Jake, and with all the nonchalance in the world, he said, "You gonna head back to Jersey City tonight? Or crash at the studio apartment?" Completely ignoring Jake's comment altogether. Okay, that's one way to handle it. *Men.* Whatever, *please just get the guy gone*, because, God, her hands were shaking like she was buried in snow while it *was* hotter than hell in that limo.

The club king seemed to go along with Antonio's redirect. "The studio? Jesus, I wouldn't stay in that fuck-fest hole-in-the-wall if my life depended on it." The man's laugh faded as Antonio ushered Jake out of her line of sight, out to the parking lot, out of the depot altogether.

*

She scrambled out of the car and jumped into his arms, desperately and repeatedly kissing him on the mouth, not able to get enough, never wanting to let him go. He slowed her down, though, with his magic touch, his calming way. His hand moved smoothly over her back, and then using the tip of his tongue to delicately line her lips before dipping back into her mouth, she began to breathe, loosening her grip on him, relaxing into his embrace. Then he pulled away slowly, his hands now softly cradling her face.

"I'm fine, Jana. And more importantly, you're fine."

"But he knows I was in the car. How'd he—"

"He was probably lingering a few minutes before he came up. But, yeah, he was bustin' my balls that whole time. Doesn't matter, Jana. We're not in danger. It's all okay. It turns out to be really damn good actually." He picked her up, swung her around and around.

"What are you talking about?" Her arms held on for dear life to his neck, not seeing how any handshake with Jake Demonte could be anything close to good.

He let her feet touch the ground. "Nothing…just trust me." Then he stopped, pulled her over to the limo, and opened the door to the driver's seat for her to get in again.

"Are you serious? I can't stop shaking let alone drive…not for my first time!"

Handing her the car keys, he whispered, "Jana, listen, after tomorrow, we're done and set." He squeezed her elbow. "A million. My number. It wipes my debt, leaves us with five-hundred grand in cash, not including what I've got in my operating account! All I've worked for…I'm finally done. No strings, Jana. You and me, and, you know…our future, it's ready for us."

She looked at him sweetly, but couldn't hide the worry from her eyes. "Antonio, it sounds…perfect. But, sometimes perfect is anything but."

He waved off her comment and kissed her cheek, then her nose, her chin, her lips. "Come on, let's get going. You gotta get your first driving lesson under your belt. Two weeks from now, we'll be heading home to Mexico."

CHAPTER 57

A HALF HOUR LATER they got to the Palisades Park exit, which was only a few minutes south of Fort Lee. It was sweet, her excitement, driving up the thruway for the first time.

"Pull off here, princess."

"Oh no! You're queasy from my driving. I told you I'd be bad—"

"No, not at all. I showed you this place in the daytime, now I want you to see it at night." He smiled but held his stomach to mess with her. "And I'd like to throw up in a scenic environment." He laughed and she punched his arm. She hadn't looked at him since getting on the road, and now she couldn't seem to take her eyes off him.

"Left! Left here!" he shouted, helping her with the wheel.

He was glad when she looked back at the road and coasted smoothly, proudly into the park.

*

God, it felt like ages ago, their moment by the river. But it had only been a matter of days. A high-speed, time-surpassing love, that's what they had.

As she followed his finger to where she should park, she realized something: a stark, solid feeling throughout her entire being. She was in the driver's seat and in complete and utter control, control that Antonio had given her. And she didn't feel the least bit carsick, not the slightest bit nauseated, better even than when she sat shotgun.

She felt absolutely, definitively grounded in herself, but at the same time, flying higher than high. The feeling was similar to a recent dream she half remembered.

"Come on. I want to show you the riv—"

"Wait." She grabbed his hand. "Wait a minute. You gave me my first driving lesson. But I want another first." Pure seduction and desire laced her words. "I want to make love to you, Antonio Ruiz. In the backseat of this limo. Right now."

*

She watched him beam.

"And here I was trying to be a gentleman, biding my time, but yes, let's stay right here," he said, his words and tone sweet and so goddamn sexy. "Because I didn't know how I was going to make it all the way to the river without attacking you on the way. Plus the mosquitoes, poison ivy," he rambled and snickered as he unbuckled her seatbelt and hoisted her over the divider without hesitation.

*

Before he joined her in the backseat, she watched him reach forward for a button, and the moon roof opened, letting the star-filled sky show through. Then he connected his mp3 player, and the fourth track to the hot Latin beats playlist she'd made for him filled the car, and flowed through her body.

A moment later, he tumbled over the partition and landed gently on top of her, and proceeded to slowly and sensually peel off her clothes. "I'll gladly make love to you, Jana Park. It will be my honor, always."

He kissed her then, and she kissed him back harder.

But he broke away the next beat.

"What is it?"

"I mean it, Jana. I want 'always' with you. Marry me? Be my wife."

She tilted her head at him, studied his deep, sweet eyes.

"Of course. Yes. I'll marry you, Antonio José Ruiz. I'll be your wife. It will be *my* honor."

CHAPTER 58

I T WAS A crazy, pivotal, life-changing kind of day.

By the time they got to the hospital, her father was out of critical condition, and Dr. B's prognosis was positive. *If. If* her father changed his habits, like maybe his earlier tears indicated he would.

And when Jana approached her father's bedside, Antonio's hand gripped tightly in hers, the smile her father gave made Jana think that somehow he'd remembered their last minutes together.

"Daddy, this is Antonio. Antonio José Ruiz, my future husband." A flood of warm excitement rushed through her veins as she'd said it.

Her father's hand moved slowly toward the edge of the bed. The man was actually extending his hand to Antonio, and Antonio took it.

"Sir." He bowed like he had that day in his Tae Kwon Do class, stepping off the mat to come and see her. "Your daughter is everything to me. I'm honored and blessed that she's accepted my proposal. And she'll never want for anything, sir, especially"—he looked into Jana's eyes—"not for love."

Her father's eyes were damp, but they shed no tears. He only pointed and made writing motions with his hand. She handed her dad a pen from her purse and held a pad out for him. He wheezed and groaned a bit as he wrote, then he nodded his head slightly toward Antonio when he was done.

Antonio took the note and tried with squinted eyes to make out the message. Jana smiled, came around to his side to help decipher the scribble.

She cleared her throat, inhaled deeply, then spoke in a light hush. "It reads, 'Ja-Na Sun, my good, beautiful child. Make her happy.'"

*

She buried her face in Antonio's chest, gasping out tears from the deepest springs of her soul. If it weren't for Antonio, she felt like she'd float off like ashes on the wind, her father's wistful words struck her so deep.

And as Antonio held her tight, anchoring her to him, he responded to her father's note. "I will, sir. I promise you I will make her the happiest woman in the world."

And of that, she knew. Without a shadow of a doubt.

*

The bitter sweetness of the landmark in time would be branded in her memory always. And this, she knew, would be the last time she'd ever see her father. She was going to start her new life with Antonio. This was a perfect end, now on to her new and wondrous beginning.

CHAPTER 59

HE CAUGHT HER smile as she pulled onto the highway. Then she reached for his hand.

"You're good, princess, but you're not one-hand-on-the-wheel-good just yet." He laughed, returning her hand at the proper two o'clock position, then sliding his hand onto her thigh to fulfill the connection he knew they both craved.

He loved her driving him to his, or rather, their place. At least, it was their place for another two weeks. Then their home would be a spot he'd picked before he'd left Vallarta three years ago...right on the beach.

"Oh, I gave your mother my cell number. You know, since yours is in pieces in the hospital parking lot."

"God, yes. Thank you for thinking of that. Wow...doesn't that seem like a year ago, but it was less than twenty-four hours ago? Jesus. In a day...all that's happened...."

No dwelling in his car, not on this high they were riding. "Your mom cracked me up when you told her we were getting married. I thought she was gonna jump into my arms!"

"I know, right? From my birth, she'd been waiting for me to get engaged."

"But no ring. You know she looked for it on your hand. Like it wasn't all real without a ring."

"Please. Like I give a shit about what she thinks?" Jana smiled and looked in his direction. The car floated left, and she jerked the wheel to correct, but with no traffic on the road that late at night—or early in the morning—he just winked at her. He watched her relax back into control of the wheel. "She doesn't know how big a diamond you *could* buy me if I wanted it. In just a few hours from now... But seriously babe, I don't want a diamond. I don't need one. You know I just want—"

"You will have a ring on that finger so everyone knows you're taken," he said with mock firmness. Because he knew a ring meant nothing, at least, it hadn't with Michelle.

But for the symbolism of the love he and Jana shared, he had the perfect token, one worthy of his love, his warrior princess. It was ready and waiting in Vallarta. His mother's band. Yesinia Ruiz had left it for him. She'd said it was a representation of all the strength and love from above that could be bestowed on two united souls. A perfect description of him and Jana. Such soul-lifting, stupid-love perfection.

"I've got you covered, though. A simple band. Because you won't want to get the soft white beach sand into a diamond setting."

"Sounds like heaven, living on the beach."

"And anyway, a big honking diamond gets in the way all the time, and it could scratch the babies. *Our* babies." He smiled at her with raised eyebrows, squeezing her leg, unable to get enough of her heat, her glow.

"God, Antonio. *Babies*," she said and sighed with obvious delight, not despair this time. No more despair for his Jana. "The beach and *our* babies..."

She started crying then, almost uncontrollably.

"No, no, no. You can't cry and drive, princess. You're fine. Just...you wanna pull over?"

"I'm fine," she gasped, wiping her eyes with the back of her hand. "No, I'm okay, really." Her sobbing turned into laughter from the depths of her soul. It was an all-freeing kind of laughter.

He shook his head and started to laugh too, but he kept his eye on the road for her, and the hand he'd had on her leg was now on the wheel, just in case.

CHAPTER 60

THE NEXT MORNING Antonio had to leave Jana in bed, though he hated to do it. God, he could've watched her sleep forever.

But he had to get ready to meet the attorney. The text message from Jake had said ten sharp.

He read the paper over coffee. When he turned the page, a large image of Johnnie Demonte being shoved into a squad car took up half of page two. The Wet Spot sign could be seen in the background. The headline read: TWO INJURED IN SHOOTING, CLUB CLOSED INDEFINITELY. Then a sub-article below it showed an image of stacks of clear plastic pouches of cocaine in what seemed to be a basement. It was a real win for the mayor's war on drugs. Johnnie Demonte was being held for drug trafficking, not to mention two counts of criminal assault charges for Brandon and Erin, who were both so far still alive. But the article stated that things would go downhill fast if either of them died.

Antonio had no trouble picturing that asshole rotting in prison. But what mattered most was that Jana was safe, the prick's bail had been set at close to five hundred thousand dollars, cash or bond—Jake wouldn't drop a dime for his disappointing offspring, Antonio was sure.

Antonio looked down to finish the article as he took another sip of his coffee. Then he nearly spat it out. A dancer who'd been taken into custody, only eighteen years old, had told the police that the accused had forced her to use narcotics even though she'd told him she was pregnant. If that was the case, fines doubled. Charges worsened. Antonio shook his head while chills crawled up his arms. This shit was too much.

His eyes shot to the top half of the page, the second column. Defense attorney, Brian Hart, stated on behalf of his client that regarding the shooting, his client was acting in self-defense. A perpetrator had entered the club, and his client had missed his target and accidentally hit the young female bartender and the male bouncer. And as for the loads of cocaine or the use on premises, Johnnie Demonte apparently "knew nothing of it."

Jesus Christ. This was too intense for comfort.

"Morning." Jana's melodious voice took his head out of the paper. She was showered and ready, glowing and smelling like his shampoo and some floral scent that reminded him of his family's vibrant rose garden back home. "When do we leave for your meeting?"

They were engaged now, and of course, she'd want to be a part of this huge happening. She leaned over to kiss him, her soft slender fingers on his neck, sending new chills of her excitement down his back.

"Princess, I think I better go on my own. A lot of boring papers to sign then running to the bank…"

"Babe, those are the best parts, the boring paperwork. And I wanna see your face when you get the check in your hand. All your hard work is culminating today. I want to witness your smile."

God, he loved her.

But after reading the article, which he hid now by folding the paper back up, he couldn't risk her being there. It would make him too nervous, and today of all days, he needed to retain his placid-like calm.

*

He set her up at his laptop.

"My screen password is '1m-i-l-l-i-0-n.'" He winked. "Surf, email, do whatever. I'll be back before you know it." He kissed her forehead and walked out. She was irritated, but she wouldn't argue. She trusted his instinct, she trusted him.

She watched out the window as he got into the car. He was wearing a crisp white shirt and slacks and looking so sleek, and God, so *hers*. She couldn't wait until he got back home to her.

Then a movement on his computer screen brought her eyes back to present. It had switched to screensaver mode. *$1,000,000.00* floated across the monitor followed by another and another, each figure a different vibrant color. She laughed out loud and shook her head. His childhood dream was becoming a reality today. She pushed down the disappointment rising in her throat that she wouldn't get to see it in person, but they'd celebrate later, no doubt.

Then she let her mind drift into a daydream. The freedom they'd have in the paradise he'd drawn for her of Puerto Vallarta! She'd be starting a family there…with him. She felt tears coming again but held them back, not wanting to damage the laptop. She decided to wiggle the mouse at her fingertips, getting busy on her Internet search.

She needed a new phone provided by a US company that was on the same cell network as that of Puerto Vallarta because she was moving there. Holy shit! She was actually moving there. She felt as light as a cloud.

The new phone search led her to beachfront properties in Vallarta, and then hospitals she might apply to, and then schools for her future kids. She was still in a dream state and didn't want to wake from it. Vallarta was stunning. Antonio was stunning. Life would be stunning.

*

He looked at the number on the screen: Jake Demonte.

"Give me a second, boys," he said to his dispatch operator and two senior drivers.

Antonio walked away as he hit 'accept.' "Hey there, Jake."

"Tone, listen…Got another small matter. It's nothing big. You see the paper today?"

"No, Jake," he lied. "Got in late from the hospital. Just got to the garage so I wouldn't be late for your lawyer."

"My lawyer, yeah…we should talk. Now. I'll come there. See you in five." And he hung up.

God, please. Don't let there be anything more. Not another favor. Not a tag-on. Nothing to do with Johnnie, for Christ's sakes. No. Just...god-damn no.

*

"Tone, it's my damn ex-wife," Jake Demonte said as his wannabe goon checked a different office for bugs. The six-foot-something man came out with his thumbs up, and so they went inside to Antonio's bookkeeper's office since she was out sick. "She's freaking out at me about Johnnie. Even though the little prick deserves the drug sentence, he ain't no premeditated nothin', even if one or both of 'em die. You and I both know he ain't even that smart. So, I may need ya to stick around for a few months or so for the kid's trial. As a witness. Since you was there."

Since I was there...Jesus. Sweat trickled down his back. He sat forward, unstuck his shirt from his skin, and threw back his bottle of water. Since he was there? *Fuck!*

Jake took a legal pad from the corner of the desk and grabbed a pencil. "You told me you saw a strange erratic guy goin' into the club before you heard the shots, right?" He then scribbled something on the top sheet of the pad and slid it across to Antonio. *Say "right." Or I find sweet Jana and I blow her away. Say "right" and you still get the sale and the kickback. Your number, remember?*

Heart plummeting, blood draining, Antonio coughed in shock, then swallowed, but his mouth was too dry. Dry as dusty desert bones.

Not in a million years would he have thought Jake would go there. A favor is one thing, but a threat against Jana? Another fucking threat against *his* Jana.

"Right, Jake. Yeah. The guy had his hands in his jacket pockets when he went in, and being summer, I couldn't help but notice. Too suspicious, you know? But by the time I got out of the car, shots were fired. And with the shock of it all, when the police came, I'd forgotten about the guy. I only cared about getting in and making sure everyone was all right."

"Did you make out his face? Could you sketch it for the cops?"

"Yeah, sure, Jake."

"Great. I've arranged for a good friend of mine on the force to come by now and do just that. Should be here any minute."

Antonio nodded. He wanted to write a note back to Jake Demonte on the pad before they got up. Something like, shove your filthy fucking money up your fat ass, along with your insane son's pistol, and be sure to fire. That would've felt so goddamn good, so goddamn right.

But he didn't. It wasn't the time. As he put it out of his mind, Jake ripped the page out and took it upon himself to insert it into the shredder under the desk.

"Oh and, Tone, I'm gonna need your girlfriend, Jana, to repeat what she saw in the dressing room. Pregnant and forced to snort that shit, my ass! That needs to be cleared up fast or I'll lose another half a mil into this bullshit. So bring her down here so my friend can take both your revised statements."

Antonio clenched his teeth and hid a sigh. "Yeah, okay."

Jake stood there staring. Waiting. "Now, son. Call her *now*."

Antonio bit down hard on his bottom lip. This fucker.

He took out his cell, and remembering Jana had no phone of her own, he'd have to call his house line and hope she'd pick up.

Six rings with Jake glaring at him made sweat trickle from his brow.

"Hello?"

"Hey, it's me. The police need to hear what you saw in the dressing room the other night. The girls and the drugs…I'm going to send a limo for you now."

"Babe, what's going on?"

Then Jake grabbed the phone from Antonio's hand, which was within millimeters of jabbing the man in the jugular. *Control yourself.*

"Hey, doll, it's Uncle Jake. You gotta give your revised statement down here at the depot. We'll see ya here in a few." He handed Antonio back his phone.

"Hey. Be calm. I'm sending—"

"Be calm!" Jana shouted, totally panicked. "What the fuck is going on right now? Be goddamn calm? Is this for real?"

"Yes, it's real. But I'm okay. And you're okay. Just be calm. I'm sending Chris Jones to get you now. Check his business card before you get in." And he hung up the call and radioed Chris, his most trusted driver.

Fuck he hated how scared she sounded. So close, they were so goddamn close to being free.

*

Jake's dirty cops hadn't shown yet, but the limo pulled up with Jana in the front seat. She got out in a huff and stormed up to Antonio. She stared at him, completely ignoring Jake Demonte, and pursed her lips, obviously waiting for an explanation.

"Terrific then," Jake said, ignoring her right back. "Tone, my attorney got held up anyway, so it'll be perfect timing. The detectives will do their thing once they damn get here, then once they leave, my attorney will come and close the deal," he summarized so damn succinctly. "Okay, so…I'll keep you posted on the trial date. You'll both be called to testify. I got the top defense attorney in the whole Tri-state, so Johnnie's gotta good shot."

Then Jake held out his hand. Hiding his disgust, Antonio gripped it firmly, as firmly as the fury in his chest gripped his goddamn heart.

*

Jana looked at Antonio's face in utter disbelief. What the hell had he done?

She'd seen the news online. Eighteen-year-old dancer, in custody? Laynie was the only eighteen-year-old dancer the club had right now. Pregnant?

And had Antonio just agreed to help Jake Demonte? Had she been strong-armed into throwing Laynie under the bus? An eighteen-year-old girl? An abused child?

And did her fiancé, her future husband agree to help get that crazy asshole off? Johnnie Demonte might go free? For all that he pulled?

Didn't that mean that the crazy son of a bitch would probably go after her and after Antonio, in retribution? A pretty boy like Johnnie in jail for a day let alone a week would give the guy plenty to be angry about beyond the current state of things…wouldn't he try to kill them?

"Antonio…please, God. What is happening?"

He shook his head at her but kept silent. He nodded toward the parking lot, at the Town Car that Jake was in, waiting there.

"Antonio." She said his name as a quiet directive.

"Jana," he whispered, "do you trust me?"

Did she? Her life, now their lives, were being derailed because he got into bed with a dirty thug for goddamn money. So did she trust him?

She looked up at him, shaming and damning him with a slow shake of her head. They'd been so close to freedom. She inhaled hard and fast, lifted her hand, and slapped him hard across the face. "I'm not doin' this. Keep your fucking sewer money. I will not—"

"You will. There is no choice here, Jana."

How dare he? She glared, nostrils flaring, then she lifted her other hand to slap him again, but he caught it midair. Then he gently released her wrist as his eyes dug deep into hers, a dark gravity in them. "I. Need you. To trust me," he said in a dead calm tone.

But she didn't trust him or need to do a damn thing he said. She turned and walked to hail a cab from the busy avenue. One stopped in a matter of moments. She got in and shut the door.

In a flash, she saw Antonio, one hand on the car hood the other motioning to the driver to stay put.

He said nothing as he opened the back door to usher her out, then bent down and whispered in the sweet and calm tenor she was used to, "Princess, five minutes more." Then he stood up and raged at her. "Get the hell out of the car! Now!"

Confused, she slid out, fuming, degraded, terrified. Shattered.

She wasn't sure what was happening, but she was certain of one thing: There was no need to replace one unbearable burden for another. When Jake's dirty cops came, she would not be cooperating. And after the phony police leave, she'd be gone too, because Antonio Ruiz wasn't the goddamn man she thought he was.

Jake was still in his lot, watching, making certain they'd cooperate.

Jana was too, but she looked awfully sick.

God, where were they?

And as Jana vomited on the pavement, he saw the flashing lights of not one of Jake's friendly in-his-pocket cops, but twenty-five US Marshals led by Antonio's student, fifth degree black-belt Detective Sean Alexander.

Antonio came behind Jana, grabbed her shoulders, and quickly pulled her into the garage, and proceeded to shut all the bay doors with a push of a button on the wall. Jake Demonte was surrounded, and the evidence had all been picked up by the hidden cameras in Antonio's offices.

Antonio was sure that Jake Demonte was no longer a threat to Jana, to him, or to anyone else for that matter. The man would be in prison for no less than money laundering, witness tampering, and threatening bodily harm or intent to commit murder, having threatened Jana in writing, all picked up on video. Johnnie was also clinched now. And he and Jana would be in Mexico—where Jake Demonte wouldn't dare go—way before any high-powered defense attorney could even hope to get either Demonte out.

CHAPTER 61

S HE GOT OFF the phone with Luly, wiped her tears away, and took Antonio's non-driving hand. "I *am* going to miss her."

He kissed her hand. "You'll talk and video-chat plenty, and hell, we'll fly her down. Her and her little crew. And by the way, I'm *really* liking my chauffeur cap on you," he said, with his searing eyes that just wouldn't quit.

She smiled, enjoying the thought of her dearest friend merging with her new life. Luly's kids and her future children playing together on the beach; dear God, it was a dream.

Antonio's phone buzzed her back to present. He took his hand back from her and struggled to pull the cell out from his back pocket. By the time he got it and handed the cell to Jana, the buzzing stopped.

"Isabel."

"Oh, call her back for me, princess?"

Jana hit 'call back' and handed him back the phone.

When her future sister-in-law answered, Jana got to hear Antonio's beautiful Spanish, which always melted her from the inside out.

"*Estamos llegando hogar, m'iha.* We are coming home."

Then he pressed speakerphone so Jana could hear.

If Antonio hadn't told her that Isabel was his favorite, she would've known by the tone in his voice as he spoke to her. And she couldn't wait to meet her. She couldn't wait for real siblings, a loving, caring family...

how alien and unfamiliar, but so damn wonderful her heart beat harder in her chest.

"Antonio, are you really? Don't mess with me…I'm in no shape."

"We are. We're halfway already."

"How are the girls? And Celeste? The car must be packed to the brim!"

"No, Isa. They're in Jersey. They're staying. For a while more, at least."

"Then who's 'we,' Antonio?"

He smiled and leaned over and kissed Jana sweetly, his eyes still on the road. "My soon-to-be wife is with me, Isa. Her name is Jana Park. I found her, Isa, I found my love, but lost everything else." He laughed out loud.

He hadn't really. They'd been lucky that the original buyer of Antonio's limo company didn't spook after all the police chaos. It was a quick, albeit deeply discounted, cash out sale, and Jana and Antonio, as well as their future family, would be more than comfortable for many years to come. Four hundred and fifty thousand dollars was a true blessing.

Isabel's shriek of joy completely overpowered Antonio's laughter. And it made Jana tear up, laughing and crying. Antonio smiled, practically speechless.

"Isa, you will love her. And she'll love you too. To death. You're on speaker, say 'hi!'"

"Jana? Hello. I can't wait to meet you," Isa said, now sobbing as well. "My brother has waited too long for the perfect one. I am so happy for you both."

But Jana couldn't call up words to answer. She just couldn't do it through her own tears. She only nodded because she, too, had waited way too long for Antonio, for her *one*.

"Jana's nodding," he said, then he laughed. "It's all pretty sudden, and crazy-emotional, you know?"

"Of course, I do definitely know."

"Yes, you of all people. And speaking of sudden, listen, Isa, I am sorry I gave you no notice, but can we crash in your guest room for a few weeks when we get there? So I can finalize things with the beach house? We're gonna be there, what, in another week?" he asked Jana.

She nodded. They were going to stop in Nashville, New Orleans, and then Austin along the way.

"Of course, yes, you guys will absolutely stay with us, but I'm afraid you can't stay in the guest room. The pullout's the only option. Unless you can both fit in a crib…."

"A crib, you said?"

"Yes. I said a crib."

"No!"

"Yes."

"Are you kidding me? Isa's pregnant," he told Jana as if she wasn't next to him, hearing the same conversation.

Jana smiled at him and then watched his face change.

He stayed quiet, but the raw emotion in his eyes, his welling tears made her heart turn to liquid love.

"My baby sister…is having a baby," he said to Jana, now putting on his turn signal and pulling over to the side of the eight-lane highway. Jana had heard only briefly about Isabel and the tremendous tragedies in her life. Far worse than the traumas in Jana's. Antonio didn't think a relationship or children would ever be part of Isabel's future, not after her first several marriage attempts had ended fatally. But now, finally, Isabel was getting the happiness she deserved. Antonio squeezed Jana's hand tight. She watched him swallow back the tears she knew were threatening him. "I'm speechless and thrilled for you, Isa. And for Zack."

"Thank you, brother. *Tio*. And we're going to name her after Mommy."

He broke down then, handed Jana the phone, and just looked out his side window, hand covering his eyes.

"Oh Isabel, that's wonderful news! How are you feeling?" Jana took the baton, giving Antonio a chance to check his emotion and his breath, letting him just *be* like he'd let her a billion times before.

"Oh, Jana, I feel perfectly, amazingly sick to my stomach. But perfect!" She laughed. "I feel perfect."

"I'm so happy for you," Jana said as she reached over to kiss Antonio on the cheek. "And I think your brother has to call you back to talk more, Isa. He's just…collecting himself." She laughed.

"I'm sure you know by now, Jana, that my brother is steel on the outside, but a pure, squishy ball of fluff on the inside."

"I do know. And I love it. More than life itself."

*

He had to let her drive then, too emotional to focus. He reclined his seat and found himself completely content in the passenger seat. Isa was pregnant, and he and Jana were heading back to Puerto Vallarta. It was all so very right.

Jana had gotten them off at the scenic highway toward the Blue Ridge Mountains and was cruising along smoothly, confidently. He felt safe with her at the wheel, and he hardly felt safe being driven by anyone.

He watched her facial features change with the moving sun. He loved how enthralled she was with the views, the curves in the road, the foliage. She opened the windows to feel the mountain air. Then she'd look at him to be sure he was seeing what she was seeing. He loved that she wanted to share it all with him.

"Princess, a reminder from your driving instructor, here. Keep the pointing to a minimum and your eyes on the road," he teased, his hand reaching for hers.

"Oh God, babe…I totally had déjà vu!"

"Oh, yeah?"

"Yeah, wait, no."

"What?"

"A dream. This is all from a dream I had. That first night at that asshole's apartment I fell asleep…lights on, clothes on. The last thing on my mind that night before I drifted off was…was *you*."

He felt his face flush. Had she felt the connection that early on like he had?

"Don't go getting a big head about it or anything," she said with a wink. "Anyway, I was driving, clutching the steering wheel with the windows open, down a winding, scenic road like this one. I mean strangely *exactly* like this one. I felt like I was in heaven. And you…it was you"—she took the chauffeur cap off her head and placed it on his and let her eyes linger on him for a moment—"Now I know it was you who was with me. In this exact scene, babe. It was you and me."

He smiled at her, in awe of her excitement, in awe of her glow.

She looked down at the mp3. "This calls for road trip music. Like in the movies!" She smiled at him. "You control the music in your limo, right?" She laughed.

He leaned forward, kissed her neck as his hand reached for the device. "Especially now that I'm sitting shotgun. It's officially my job."

He hit play and hiked up the volume. The voice of an angry angel filled the vehicle, and it competed with the torrent of wind rushing in from the open windows.

"Oh my God, Antonio. It's the song…I'm not kidding," she said. Then she leaned over, pulled him to her by the nape of his neck, and kissed him. Then pulled away to return her attention to the road. "It was this song playing in my dream, babe. I swear to God!"

She started to sing, no wail, the words, *"Never doubt you are the one. The phoenix…"* while he took a long deep breath in, leaned his head back, and let the sounds of perfection take him and his princess warrior south… to paradise.

THE END

AUTHOR'S NOTE

So that's Antonio and Jana's story, from my soul to yours—I hope you loved it as much as I loved writing it for you!

Now, do you want more good stuff featuring all the sizzling hot couples in the Paradise South series—*for free*? Just go to [www.RissaBrahm.com/Join] and you'll get a deleted scene from each of the Paradise South books as they come out:

Tempting Isabel — (Isabel & Zack)
Taking Jana — (Jana & Antonio)
Catching Preeya — (Preeya & Ben)
Satisfying Ali — (Ali & Dev)
Freeing Kyla — (Kyla & Liam)

And…

You'll receive 1 Free Novelette called *P.S. in Paradise* — (Full Epilogues for all 5 Books, which will only be sold as part of the Paradise South series Box Set) — for FREE! So, head to [www.RissaBrahm.com/Join] and get your free stuff on!

Also reserved for my newsletter subscribers: first-to-know news on release dates, fabulous giveaways and other cool bonus material like character sketches and interviews, failed flings, and more! So, go check it out! xo~Rissa

P.S. Your candid and detailed review of *Taking Jana* posted on Amazon helps other romance readers know if my stuff is *for* them. Your opinion really matters and is so appreciated! [www.RissaBrahm.com/Taking-Jana]

P.P.S. I always love hearing from you directly! Reach out anytime…

    e: me@RissaBrahm.com

    p: www.RissaBrahm.com/pinterest

    f: www.RissaBrahm.com/facebook

    g: www.RissaBrahm.com/goodreads

    t: www.RissaBrahm.com/twitter

OTHER BOOKS BY RISSA BRAHM

PARADISE SOUTH SERIES:

Tempting Isabel, Book 1

Taking Jana, Book 2

Catching Preeya, Book 3

Satisfying Ali, Book 4 (2016)

Freeing Kyla, Book 5 (2016)

P.S. in Paradise (The series' Epilogue Collection Novelette, 11.2016)

From unsought soul mates to second chances, the couples of Paradise South will spike your temperature, your heartbeat, and your need to read more of my soul-deep & sensual romances. So enjoy them all: www.RissaBrahm.com/Books

ACKNOWLEDGEMENTS

Infinite thanks:

To my content editor, Tessa Shapcott; and copy editor, Kristie Stramaski, and proofreaders Michelle Josette, J.F. and Markham Correct.

To my beta readers Phyllis B., Penny L., Gretchen H., Kerrie K., Penny L., Saleena C., Kirsty F., Tammy R., Rachel N., Liz W., Amy P., for your feedback and love of the story.

To my Launch Team: Lauren S., June M., Saleena C., and everyone else who shared, tweeted and cheered!

To my soul sister in Vegas, a truer friend could not be had.

To my mother, for her first and twentieth impressions!

To my dark hero for his constant motivation, inspiration, and collaboration.

To my girl, for whom I want to write strong, smart, self-secure heroines.

To VK and GRP, for your ever-loving push on the path.

ABOUT THE AUTHOR

American contemporary romance author Rissa Brahm writes full time while roving the world with her husband and their young daughter. The gorgeous paradise of Puerto Vallarta, Mexico, the core setting of her soul-deep & sensual debut series, Paradise South, is Rissa's most recent and beloved home.

When not chained-by-choice to her MacBook, she loves laughing to tears with a good rom com; reading scintillating scorchers and mind-bending philosophy; biking, taking long walks, and yoga; zoning out to killer music from across the decades and the globe; and getting lost just to discover a new and exciting route home again—wherever home may be at the time. You can connect with Rissa on Facebook, Twitter or by email anytime by heading to www.RissaBrahm.com.